Praise for
Beyond the Blue

"*Beyond the Blue* is a story of war and loss and adoption and hope, but mostly it is a journey of letting go, of allowing the past to transform us rather than define us. We all know a Gen and Jeff who suffer hardships that, while agonizing, are seen in a new perspective when compared to the trials of another family far across the sea. *Beyond the Blue* is a great love story of mothers and daughters, of fathers and sons and husbands and wives, even aunts and uncles, and how two families separated by oceans of pain and disappointment are brought together. I agonized over every obstacle these characters faced, fearing the outcome, feeling their tension, staying up late to read every last word, wondering if this fine author could bring about a hopeful ending birthed in life's uncertainties thrashed by the tumult of war. I am pleased to say she does!"

—JANE KIRKPATRICK, award-winning author of *A Land of Sheltered Promise*

"We don't always see how one life impacts another…especially when they are complete worlds apart. From the war-torn aftermath of Vietnam to the challenges of international adoption, *Beyond the Blue* reveals an authentic and gripping tale you won't soon forget. Way to go, Leslie!"

—MELODY CARLSON, author of *Finding Alice* and *Crystal Lies*

"In *Beyond the Blue,* Leslie captures the sights and sounds of Vietnam so vividly, you feel like you are right there walking the streets of Vung Tau and Ho Chi Minh City. Her insight into the birth mother's feelings is amazing, and she captures all sides of the adoption triangle: the adoptive parents' perspective, the adoptive child's, as well as the birth mother's. This is a must-read for all adoptive parents."

—NICKY LOSSE, Vietnam Program Director, Children's Hope International

Beyond the Blue

BY LESLIE GOULD

Garden of Dreams

Beyond the Blue

the

Blue

a novel

LESLIE GOULD

WATERBROOK
PRESS

BEYOND THE BLUE
PUBLISHED BY WATERBROOK PRESS
2375 Telstar Drive, Suite 160
Colorado Springs, Colorado 80920
A division of Random House, Inc.

The characters and events in this book are fictional, and any resemblance to actual persons or events is coincidental.

ISBN 1-57856-822-6   JUN 1 7 2005

Copyright © 2005 by Leslie Gould

Published in association with the literary agency of Alive Communications, Inc.; 7680 Goddard Street, Suite 200; Colorado Springs, CO 80920.

Library of Congress Cataloging-in-Publication Data
Gould, Leslie, 1962-
  Beyond the blue / Leslie Gould.— 1st ed.
    p. cm.
  ISBN 1-57856-822-6
  1. Mother and child—Fiction. 2. Birthmothers—Fiction. 3. Adoption—Fiction.
4. Vietnam—Fiction. I. Title.
  PS3607.O89B495 2005
  813'.6—dc22

                             2004024714

Printed in Canada
2005—First Edition

10 9 8 7 6 5 4 3 2 1

Dedicated to my four children,
to birth mothers and adoptive mothers throughout the world,
and to my own mother, Leora Egger.

Part 1

March 1975–November 1999

Out of the mouth of babes and nursing infants
You have ordained strength,
Because of Your enemies,
That You may silence the enemy and the avenger.

PSALM 8:2

Gen sat cross-legged on her bed, clenching her fist around the figurine of the Vietnamese girl, digging her fingernails into her palm. Tomorrow her mother would leave for Vietnam. Gen closed her eyes.

Bombs exploded. Jungles burned. The Viet Cong marched toward Saigon. Nhat cried—all alone—in the orphanage.

Her eyes flew open.

She hadn't been afraid when her mother traveled to the country a year ago. But now Gen was older; now she was nine; now she knew to be frightened.

Where *was* Mom? Her mother tucked her into bed every night. What was taking her so long?

Gen opened her hand. The figurine's dark eyes shone above her tiny nose and lifelike smile; carved braids framed her face. She wore a red tunic and pants and held a miniature wooden doll.

"Time for bed!" Mom hurried into the room.

Mama. Gen squeezed her hand shut again, completely covering the carving.

Her mother sat next to Gen and pulled her close. "You're going to be the best big sister ever."

The red fluid in Gen's lava lamp bubbled and cast a glow over her mom's face. She was going to Vietnam to bring Nhat home; Gen would finally be a sister.

Her mom smoothed Gen's dark hair back from her forehead. Her touch was gentle. "Are you worried about anything?"

Gen bit her lower lip and reached for her mother's hand, holding it tight.

"About my leaving? About Nhat coming home to live with us?" Her mom leaned her cheek against the top of Gen's head.

Gen snuggled closer. They had been waiting all year for the paperwork to be approved so they could adopt Nhat. She pictured her new little brother holding a bowl of rice, his only meal for the day.

"Mom?"

"What, sweetheart?"

"Does Nhat use chopsticks?"

Her mom smiled. "I don't think so. He's only two."

Photos of Nhat hung on the refrigerator. He was only a year old when the pictures were taken; he was Amerasian with light skin and wavy hair, and he peered at Mom with adoring eyes and a big smile. In one picture, his hands were entwined in her long, dark hair.

"Will you teach him to use chopsticks?"

Her mother's cheek still rested on Gen's head. "Yes."

"And me?"

"And you, Genni." Genevieve was her given name. Mama was the only one who called her Genni.

Gen slowly opened her hand. The carving was part of a family of place-card holders that her mother bought last year in the open-air market in Saigon. "When will we use these?" Gen ran her finger along the slit that would hold a card in the girl's back.

"When we have special dinners. Birthdays and holidays." Her mom laughed a little. "You'll see. I'll cook more than Hamburger Helper when I get home. Things will calm down. I'll spend all my time taking care of you and Nhat."

"Tell me about Vietnam." Gen settled her head onto her pillow and stretched out her legs, holding the girl in her open palm. Her mother had lived in Vietnam in 1961, when she was twenty-one, after graduating from nurses' training. Gen never tired of hearing about her adventures.

"It was the most amazing year of my life." Her mother stroked Gen's hair as she spoke. "I lived in a hut with a thatched roof on a mission compound. I picked mangoes, coconuts, and bananas off the trees outside my door. I ate *pho,* noodle soup, for breakfast. Geckos scampered up the walls of my room and kept me company through the muggy nights. I made friends with a Vietnamese nurse named Kim, whom I love like a sister. I took care of people with leprosy who were missing fingers and toes, noses and ears."

"Why didn't you stay in Vietnam?"

"A doctor, a missionary, and a nurse were captured by the Viet Cong when I was home on furlough. My mission organization didn't think I should return. Then I married your father. Then we had you." Her mother smiled. Gen's dad was eleven years older than her mom, but his age didn't make him seem old, it made her mother seem young. They had met when her mom spoke at his church. Gen closed her hand over the figurine.

Mom put her hand over Gen's and squeezed. "But I could never stop thinking about Vietnam; it was in my blood. That's why I raised money and collected supplies for the orphans and hospitals. That's why I went to Vietnam last year to work in the orphanage and help other people adopt. That's why we're adopting Nhat."

"I want to go with you." Gen reached for her mother's hand. She wanted to go even though she would be afraid. She didn't want her mother to go alone.

"I know." Gen's mom squeezed her fingers. "It's too dangerous right now. Maybe we can go together someday." She let go of Gen's hand. "Try to keep your room clean while I'm gone. You know how much it bothers Daddy when it's messy."

Gen nodded.

"And be nice to Aunt Marie. She loves you. I know she can be harsh, but remember she's hurting. She means well."

Gen nodded again. Aunt Marie was her father's sister; she would stay with Gen after school while Mom was gone. Her husband had died six months before, and sometimes it seemed that Aunt Marie was angry at everybody because of it. She criticized Gen's mother's housekeeping and cooking, Gen's schoolwork and hair. Nothing felt right when Aunt Marie was around.

"Sally," Gen's father called to her mother from the hallway, "you still have to finish packing, and we have to get up early to take you to the airport."

"G'night, sweetheart." Gen's mom leaned toward her. "Always remember how much I love you. Remember to trust God; that's how you can show your faith. Remember that all things work together for good." Her mother unclasped the gold chain of the jade cross that she wore and fastened it around Gen's neck, kissing her forehead.

"I want you to wear this until I get back." It was the only jewelry her mother ever wore besides her plain gold wedding band. Gen set aside the figurine and fingered the smooth, cool cross.

Her mom pulled her close and kissed her forehead. Gen breathed in her mother's lilac scent. She touched the green stone again as her mother hugged her tight.

Before she fell asleep, Gen padded down the hall to the bathroom. As she passed her parents' bedroom, she overheard them talking. Her father's voice was deep and serious. "Sally, it's a war zone over there."

"We've waited long enough. If I don't go now, we may never get Nhat out. What will happen to him?"

"Then I should go." Her dad sounded worried.

Gen took a step closer to the door. *Daddy wants to go to Vietnam?* A suitcase lay open on the bed. A stack of disposable diapers leaned against it.

"No, Marshall, it will be much easier for me."

Her father sat down on the edge of the bed. "I want this to be over. I want you to stop caring so much. We can continue to support the missionaries there, but I want you here with us. I don't want you going back."

"I doubt that there will be missionaries to support in Vietnam after this, not with the Viet Cong marching toward Saigon." Gen's mother picked up the diapers and wedged them into the suitcase. "The Communists will kick them out. There won't be much I can do after this either. It's my last chance."

Her father put his head in his hands. Her mother turned toward the door. Gen ducked around the corner and into the bathroom.

"Genni, go to bed," Mama called after her with a tired voice. "I'll check on you in a minute."

⁂

On her mother's sixth day in Vietnam, Gen sat beside her father on the mauve couch in the den and watched the *CBS Evening News*. A man wearing a khaki vest reported that the first planeload of babies had taken off from the Saigon airport. President Ford had given his blessing. Operation Babylift was under way.

"They're on that plane! Your mama and Nathaniel are coming home!" Her father called the boy Nathaniel; her mother called him Nhat.

Gen shook the Etch A Sketch she held on her lap, halfway erasing the staircase she had created. Mama and Nhat were coming home!

"That's the way it is, Thursday, April 3, 1975," Walter Cronkite said.

That's the way it is. The words comforted her. Life couldn't be helped; it happened. There was no way to change it; that's just the way it was. But this was good news, not the bad news of the war with pictures showing naked children running from bombs, soldiers with cigarettes dangling out of their mouths and sadness in their eyes, and protesters screaming into the camera. No, this was good news. These babies had families waiting for them, and Mom and Nhat were on the plane!

"You need a haircut." Her father peered down as if he hadn't really seen Gen for six days. But she didn't want a haircut. She wanted to grow it long, like her mom's. Gen's dark brown hair was tangled at the nape of her neck. Her mother usually braided it every morning before school. Gen had tried to keep it brushed, but still the tangles grew. Her father smiled at her affectionately, his gray eyes twinkling under his bushy eyebrows and full head of graying hair. Long sideburns framed his face.

He gazed around the dark, paneled den and then back to Gen. "Things will get back to normal now. We'll be a family again. You'll see." Piles of papers leaned against each other on the coffee table, and clean clothes covered the vinyl hassock. Her father liked order. He said it was in his blood, from his German father. He stood and turned the knob on the Zenith television; the screen faded to a dark olive green.

"I'm hungry," Gen said.

"Then I'll make some eggs." Daddy headed toward the kitchen. He hummed softly, which made Gen happy. They were going to be a family again; Mama was on the way home.

Gen stabbed at her egg and watched the yolk run onto the white Corelle plate. Her father always cooked the eggs just right. Nhat's highchair with the red and blue plaid vinyl seat waited for him in the corner, and Gen imagined lifting him up to the chair and fitting the metal tray into the slots.

The phone rang. Her father jumped from the table, bumping his knee against the corner, and dashed to pick up the receiver.

"Hello," he said. "Sally, is it you? Where are you? The line is bad. Can you hear me?"

How can Mom be calling if she's on the plane?

Daddy cradled the receiver of the pink princess phone between his chin and shoulder and grabbed a pen and notepad off the desk. He leaned against the counter, the pen poised on the paper.

"You didn't get on the plane? You're still in Saigon?" He stood straight and took two steps to the center of the kitchen.

Gen took a deep breath and held it.

"You think you can get her out too?" He frowned as he talked, and his voice was stern. "You went to get Nathaniel out, not someone you worked with over a decade ago."

Gen chewed on her bottom lip, trying not to cry. She wanted her mama to come home.

"Sally, I'm telling you. Get on that plane tomorrow with Nathaniel," he pleaded. "For the love of God, for the love of us, get out of there."

Daddy's salt-and-pepper eyebrows rose in question marks. He was quiet for a minute. "No, no, I admire you for wanting to help her. But think of Nathaniel. Don't risk him. Don't risk everything we have."

He was silent for another minute, and then his questions riddled the room. "What? Nathaniel is on the plane? The plane with all of the orphans? The one that flew out today? You put Nathaniel on the plane alone?" Her father turned and flung the pen onto the counter. "Promise me, Sally. Promise me you'll get out on the next flight." He stepped away from Gen and pulled the cord tight.

He fell silent as Mama spoke on the other end, nodding as if she could see him. As if she stood in the room with them. "Okay, okay," he finally said. "We love you. We need you. Remember that. Just come home."

Gen reached for the phone. She wanted to hear her mother's voice; she wanted to tell Mama that she loved her too. But her father slammed down the receiver with a clatter as Gen's hand hung in midair.

"Nathaniel's on the plane coming out. Your mother stayed another day. She's trying to help her friend Kim. They worked together at the mission. Your mom found her in Saigon."

"When will we get Nathaniel?" Gen asked.

Her father shook his head. "I don't know. The plane will land in San Francisco. Maybe he'll stay in the Bay Area until Mama gets there. Maybe someone will escort him to Seattle or here to Portland." He shrugged. "We'll have to see how it all works out."

Gen hurried down the stairs the next morning, dressed in her new bell-bottoms and her paisley blouse, ready for school. It was Friday. Perhaps on Saturday they would drive to Seattle and pick up Nhat. Maybe Mom would be there by then too. Her heart raced at the thought.

Her father sat frozen on a chair in the middle of the kitchen, the pink phone balanced on his knee, the receiver pressed against his ear. He wore his gray-striped flannel pajamas, and he hadn't shaved. Why wasn't he ready for work?

Gen walked into the den and turned on the morning news. She watched a Tide commercial and then heard the words "Tragedy in Vietnam." She moved closer to the TV. A plane, loaded with babies, had crashed at Saigon's Tan Son Nhut Airport; the first plane had landed in San Francisco. The newscaster said that the South Vietnamese officials couldn't confirm why the plane had crashed, but authorities were investigating the possibility of a missile attack by the Viet Cong.

She sat down on the shag carpet and stared at the dark paneling that covered the walls until her father came into the den and turned off the TV.

"You saw?" His face appeared almost gray, the craggy lines around his eyes deeper than usual.

She nodded, biting her lip.

He folded his body down to the floor and sat beside her. "The call was from the U.S. Embassy. Mama died in the crash." He put one arm around her and squeezed her tightly. Gen fell against him. *Mom dead? Not her mama.* Daddy began to pat her back, softly at first, then harder, jarring the sob that lodged between her heart and throat. Still the tears didn't come.

Her father didn't cry when he talked about her mother, but he did cry when he talked about Nhat. "Sally would want me to take him, I know. But I can't. A child needs a mother. Nhat needs a mom."

Why did he call her little brother Nhat now instead of Nathaniel? It scared her to watch her father cry. Why couldn't Nhat come live with them anyway? Her chin started to tremble, but she ducked her head to hide her tears.

The day of the funeral Aunt Marie worked hard to brush the tangles out of Gen's hair. Finally she smoothed the top layers over the knot at the base of Gen's neck. Neither Daddy nor Gen cried during the church service; they sat in the front pew, hanging on to each other's hands. Aunt Marie sat beside Gen and dabbed her eyes with a tissue. At the burial they huddled on metal chairs under a canopy, the black coffin in front of them, the open grave on the other side.

"Of course it won't be an open casket," Aunt Marie told a friend the day before the funeral. Overhearing the words gave Gen nightmares. What did her mother's body look like? What was left? How badly had she been burned? Panic surged through her now as she stared at the casket.

"Dust to dust," the pastor said. Gen shivered, holding tight to her father's hand. The spring mist turned to rain. The group of mourners, hunched under umbrellas beside her mama's grave, stared at Gen and her daddy.

Afterward, people filled the house. Aunt Marie pushed Gen's bangs out of her eyes and then headed to the kitchen with the other women from their church. They seemed to multiply.

"Sally was so headstrong, so impulsive, so unsatisfied. It's a good thing Genevieve is such an easy, practical child." Aunt Marie's words floated around Gen's head as she stood in the kitchen doorway, feeling lost.

"It's a pity that she looks so much like her mother though, small with that dark hair and those dark eyes—it will haunt Marshall," said one of the church ladies. The women spoke in quiet voices but not low enough that Gen couldn't hear.

"How could she have thought it was safe? Sally's the only person I know who would do something like that. Shame on her for going to Vietnam in the first place." Aunt Marie's voice grew louder with each word.

No, Mama did the right thing. She and Daddy wanted Nhat. We all did. Gen had prayed for a baby brother for years. If only the plane hadn't crashed. If only Mama and Nhat were here with her now. She walked into the living room and stood in front of the mantel, staring up at a picture of her parents. Her mother wore her hair in a french roll; her father's eyes smiled. They stood side by side in front of their Dutch colonial house that overlooked the Rose City Golf Course.

Gen felt empty inside. Her throat thickened.

Her father knelt beside her. "How are you doing?"

Her lips began to tremble. He took her hand and led her out the front door to the porch steps. She tried not to cry for Mom. Tried not to cry for Nhat. If she couldn't have her mother, why couldn't she at least have her brother?

Her father patted her back.

"There, there," he singsonged. Gen buried her face against his shoulder and began to sob.

The day after the funeral, Aunt Marie took Gen to the old-lady hair salon and told the beautician to cut Gen's hair short, to get rid of all the tangles. Gen left with a pixie, a haircut that not even a six-year-old would wear. When they returned home, Aunt Marie cleared the stacks of papers out of the den. When he arrived home, Daddy scanned the den and nodded.

Then he noticed Gen and smiled faintly, without the twinkle that she loved. "Your hair looks good short. I like it."

Gen ran to the mirror. She hated it. But it made her look less like her mother; maybe that's why her father liked it.

Later that night he boxed up her mother's things, including everything from Vietnam, even the family of place-card holders, except for the figurine of the girl that was propped against Gen's lava lamp.

A week later her father pulled her mother's dresses and her silk *ao dai,* the long Vietnamese tunic and trousers, out of her closet. Gen sat on her parents' bed and held the garment in her arms. She breathed in her mother's lilac scent. "She thought there could be peace, now, on this earth," her father said. "She thought she could save the world."

Gen nodded, pretending to agree to please her father, to ease his grief. She fingered the cross at her neck. She would wear it forever.

"She named you Genevieve because she thought it meant peace. It's a lovely name, but it means white wave." He sounded angry. "It was one of her many illogical decisions."

Gen let go of the cross.

The correspondent on the CBS news reported the plane hadn't been shot down; something had been wrong with the door. More than half of the three hundred passengers had been killed. Gen overheard her father tell Aunt Marie that Mom had been in the nose of the plane taking care of the babies, and that Nhat had gone to a family in Michigan.

The last Babylift took off on Saturday, April 26, 1975. Altogether, twenty-seven hundred children were evacuated.

The next day during Sunday school Aunt Marie, who taught the class, said, "All things work together for good to those who love God, to *those* who are the called according to his purpose." She said it was a promise in the Bible.

Aunt Marie didn't think that Gen's mother had been called according to God's purpose, so she probably meant that Gen had better be, otherwise things would never work out. When her mother quoted Bible verses, it sounded like poetry, like hope, like something good. When Aunt Marie quoted verses, it sounded like something bad was going to happen, something worse, something evil.

After Sunday school ended, Gen clicked her heels on the brown linoleum outside her classroom and thought about Aunt Marie's words. She clicked her shoes again, this time harder. Gen liked the sound of her shoes in the hall. Aunt Marie walked toward her, wagging her finger. Her father said his sister was a pillar of the church, which made Gen imagine a statue of Aunt Marie holding up the sanctuary ceiling. The image made her smile and almost forget the scowl on Aunt Marie's face.

That evening Gen watched the news again with her dad. The Viet Cong were launching rockets on Saigon. Gen watched the people on the roof of the

U.S. Embassy trying to cross the barbed wire, trying to reach the helicopters, trying to get out. Her father shook his head. "Why couldn't your mother have been content?" His voice was soft.

Gen nodded out of habit. She hoped that her mother's friend Kim had made it out, hoped that she was safe.

Three days later she watched the news alone. Walter Cronkite's face filled the screen. "That's the way it is, Wednesday, April 30, 1975." She turned and saw her father standing in the doorway.

"It's all over." Gen stood and picked up her spelling list off the vinyl hassock. The war was over, but she felt no peace.

That night she frantically shook her Etch A Sketch. She couldn't stop. She had to make the whole staircase go away. The faded lines that she had drawn weeks before, the night the first Operation Babylift flight took off, had set in the sand. She hit herself in the forehead with the toy, and the red plastic split her skin.

Gen's father reached for her, pulled her into his arms, and held her tight while blood dripped onto the wide collar of his dress shirt. She cried against his shoulder. The war was over, but there was no peace. No peace. No Mama. No Nhat. Her father washed her forehead, pressed a butterfly bandage over the wound, and then wrapped his arm around her as they sat silently on the couch in the den.

That night she dreamed about babies crying. Vietnamese babies who couldn't stop crying. And blood dripping. She woke startled. The bandage on her forehead pulled the skin tight. If her mom were alive, Gen would tiptoe to her side of the bed, and her mama would reach out and pull her under the covers beside her. She might sing "Do Lord" softly. "I've got a home in glory land that outshines the sun...," she would sing, and Gen would breathe in her lilac scent and feel Mama's warm arms around her.

Gen closed her eyes and saw the dripping blood again. Her eyes flew open once more. "I'm the luckiest mother in the world," her mother told her nearly every day. Gen would laugh and say, "No, you're not." Mama would answer, "Who? Who is luckier than I am?" And then Gen would relent and say she didn't know, and her mom would laugh and say, "See? I am. I'm the luckiest mother in the world."

Gen stared at her bedroom ceiling, at the outline of the crown molding in the dark. She reached for the figurine of the Vietnamese girl on the bedside table. "Mama, why wasn't I enough?" She wrapped her fingers around the carving. "Why did you have to go to Vietnam? Why did you want another child?"

Chapter 2

*E*ight-year-old Lan sat on the frayed blue divan and glanced from Mother to Older Sister. Mother squatted on the floor and listened to the battery-operated radio. No trucks sped by on the highway. No planes flew overhead. No bombs exploded. Lan had never known such eerie silence. Older Sister, whose name was Cam My, stood staring out the doorway of their house toward the grove of rubber trees, her back to Lan and Mother.

The radio crackled, and Mother turned it off. "The war is over," she called to Cam My. Lan smiled and clapped her hands. Father would return, and Older Brother, whose name was Quan, would come home. There would be no more fighting, no more land mines, no more soldiers on the road, no more night visitors stealing food.

"Stop clapping." Older Sister turned abruptly toward Lan. "We lost." Tears streamed down Cam My's face, smearing the mascara under her eyes onto her high cheekbones. She wore a fitted orange dress and high heels; she smelled of French perfume and cigarettes.

She took a step toward Lan. "I'm leaving."

Lan sat up straight. *Leaving?*

"No." Mother pushed the radio under the low table. "You must stay here with us."

"We won't be allowed to stay here," Cam My said. "The Viet Cong will take the land and the house." She flipped her auburn-streaked hair behind her shoulder. "Cam" meant orange sunset. "My" meant pretty. Older Sister was beautiful.

"It's our home," Mother said, standing. She wore her long black hair twisted into a bun at the nape of her neck.

Cam My shook her head. "Mother, don't be a fool. I'm leaving before they make me leave or, worse, take me." She headed to the back room.

Lan glanced down at the pleated skirt of the uniform that she wore. Her school had closed nearly a year ago when the nuns returned to France. Now Older Sister wanted to leave too. Mother sat on the divan beside Lan and put her head in her hands.

Cam My returned to the room, carrying a market basket and an armload of her belongings. She dropped everything onto the tile floor.

"What are you doing?" Lan bit her lip, watching her sister.

"Packing." Cam My stuffed fancy dresses and high-heeled shoes into the bag. "The Viet Cong will be harder on us because of Father. Mother, you and Lan should come with me."

Mother shook her head.

"Father will come for us. Older Brother will return," Lan said. Leave the house? The family altar? The groves of trees? The ancestors and Second Brother buried by the river? Never.

Older Sister twisted her jade and gold bracelets from her wrists and buried them deep in the basket. "Father can do nothing to help us now." She wedged her makeup and perfume among the clothes.

Mother took a deep breath, started to speak, and then stopped. Cam My pulled her dress and slip from her thin body and wadded them on top of the basket. She took a plain tunic and pants from the floor and pulled them over her lace bra and panties.

"Cam My, where do you plan to go?" Mother whispered.

"Saigon. Then to America."

Mother shook her head "What will you do?"

"I'll figure out something." Cam My cinched the drawstring of the pants around her thin waist.

"I'm going to make tea." Mother headed down the hall. Cam My followed her to the kitchen. Lan sat back on the divan. Everything had changed after the Americans left. Father stayed in Saigon, but his army checks stopped. Mother sold the furniture, except for the divan and table. Father sent bags of rice and sugar with the words "U.S. ARMY" across the front. Mother sold what they didn't need, causing Older Brother to protest and say,

"Why should we have food and money when others are starving?" He left the house more and more during the night to meet the Viet Cong. One morning, before Cam My took her daughter, Chi, to the orphanage, he did not return. The Viet Cong had lured him away.

Older Sister had been moody since she gave away baby Chi, with the round eyes and light skin of her American father, two years before. "I sent her to America where she'll have a future," Cam My had said back then. Chi had just learned to walk; Lan had held her dimpled fists.

Lan loved baby Chi. All she wanted was for all of them to be together, but Chi brought shame. Lan heard it in the clucking of the neighbor women, saw it in the furtive glances at the market, felt it one day when the boys from the village hurled rocks at them and called Older Sister names.

Older Brother loved Chi too, but he was ashamed of Cam My, ashamed that she had a baby when she wasn't married, and doubly ashamed that the father was an American.

"Lan!" Cam My called out. "Have you seen my carton of cigarettes?"

"They're behind the fan, beside your sleeping mat." Lan missed the way Older Sister was three years before, when she was quick to laugh and smile. Back then her dark eyes danced, and her steps were light as she raced across the courtyard.

Mother carried the steaming teapot and three cups into the room, followed by Cam My, who clutched her cigarettes. Mother poured the tea. "Wait a few weeks," she said, handing Older Sister a cup.

Cam My took a sip of hot liquid and then shook her head. "The sooner I leave, the better."

"We need to take care of each other," Mother said. "That's what families do."

"Then come with me." Cam My held her teacup close to her face like a shield.

"What would we do in the city?" Mother's eyes drooped at the corners.

"Father," Lan said. "We can find Father."

Older Sister gave her a sad look. Lan sank into the divan.

Father had come for short visits over the years. He would often beat Older Brother and Second Brother when he came home. Handsome Older Brother with his thick, jet black hair and square chin had played the role of protector to Lan. He carried her on his shoulders, shared his food with her, and played with her in the grove of trees. Older Sister's American boyfriend, the man with hair the color of sand and eyes as blue as the sky, cared for Lan too. He taught her English words and brought her gum and candy.

Cam My's teacup clattered across the low table. Mother's hand came down on top of it and stopped its spin before it fell to the tile floor. Older Sister pulled her basket of belongings to her side, pulled out a cigarette, and lit it with an American lighter.

"I'm not going to miss another opportunity." Cam My waved the smoke away. "I'm not going to wait and let the Viet Cong decide what to do with me."

Mother filled Cam My's cup again.

"No." Cam My held up a hand, palm out. "No more tea."

The sun set. Older Sister promised to wait until morning to leave. As Lan drifted off to sleep, she heard Mother's voice rise and fall and then Cam My's sharp retorts until finally they were quiet.

Lan sat up and straightened her skirt in the dim morning light.

"The Viet Cong are here," Mother said.

"Where is Cam My?" Lan's eyes darted around the room, searching for Older Sister's basket.

"Gone," Mother said.

"Come out!" A man's voice called out from the courtyard. The engine of a truck sputtered and then stopped.

Lan stood.

"No," Mother said. "Sit down. Don't move."

Mother slipped through the front door. Lan stared at the white paint that peeled in chunks around the doorframe. Mother's voice floated through the window followed by a man's deep voice. Lan's stomach growled. She pulled a strand of dark hair between her fingers and toward her mouth, pulling it in with her tongue. Mother hadn't braided her hair in weeks. The shutters stood open to the morning, and a slight breeze tiptoed into the house and then left, as if it were afraid to stay.

She dropped the wet hair from her mouth and peered through the window out into the grove. She remembered her family's laughter from four years before as if it still hung in the branches of the trees. She and Older Sister and Older Brother and Second Brother had chased each other through the grove of trees, up and down the tunnel-like rows. Her sister and brothers hid from Lan, but she always found them because of their laughter. That was before Second Brother stepped on the land mine. Older Brother had staggered through the rubber trees carrying him to the house. Mother draped her body over the bloody corpse of her younger son. Older Brother finally had pulled her away.

Now Mother's rising voice interrupted Lan's memories. "You are no son to me, Quan," she shouted.

Lan hurried to the doorway. Older Brother stood straight and tall, his thick, black hair like a crown on his head, his square jaw more pronounced than before. An older man nodded at Quan. Behind them, an open truckload of Viet Cong soldiers held rifles across their chests.

Older Brother extended one hand to Mother. She spit in his face. He wiped it away and grabbed her arm.

"Mother!" Lan screamed and then clamped her hand over her mouth. *Why did Mother spit on Older Brother?*

He looked toward the doorway and then said to Mother with disgust, "Everything has changed. The land belongs to the people; we have a country to rebuild. And Father is not coming back; he's dead. I saw him die yesterday when Saigon fell." He pulled a wad of papers from his shirt pocket. "Here are his documents." He threw them in the dirt.

Lan kept her hand clamped over her mouth. *Father? Dead?*

Mother bent and slowly picked up the papers. She stood and glared into her son's face, as if she might spit again. "Where is he buried?"

"I don't know." He straightened his shoulders and stood with his hands clasped behind his back. "Now go pack what you need, but leave the valuables. Those belong to the people."

Quan nodded toward the soldiers in the truck. Mother glanced at the papers in her hand. "There are no valuables, Quan," she said, squinting at her son. The man standing beside Older Brother smiled, and the soldiers jumped over the truck railing and fanned out around the house.

Older Brother took long, quick steps toward Lan. He'd grown taller and thinner since he had left. He was eighteen now, a year younger than Older Sister. "Where is Cam My?" he demanded.

"Saigon."

"Where is her baby?"

"America." Lan whispered the word through the cracks between her fingers.

"When?" Quan demanded.

"Two years ago." Lan bowed her head.

"Right after I left. Chi is in America then. The pigs. She'll be ruined. Blood should stay with blood." He glowered at Mother and then peered beyond her to the older man standing by the truck. Lan thought of Older Brother holding his niece, cradling Chi in his arms. Lan held the memory close because it had surprised her, and now his talk of blood surprised her too. So many felt that American soldiers' babies didn't belong in Vietnam, felt that their blood was bad.

Quan hit the doorframe. His anger had not lessened with the end of the war, even though his side had won.

Mother stood in the middle of the room shifting onto her tiptoes and then back down to her heels. She looked like a stork, perched on the branch of a mangrove tree above a raging river, not knowing whether to dive for food or fly away to safety.

Lan heard Older Brother's voice in the courtyard. "The trees are healthier. Much stronger than two years ago. The workers can stay in the house. Another grove should be planted behind this one."

Mother planted her feet firmly on the tile floor. "Get two rice baskets. Put your sleeping mat, mosquito net, and a pair of clothes in one. Get a bag of rice and the packet of dried pork from the cupboard," she ordered.

Lan quickly did as Mother instructed and then sat back down on the divan, the basket between her feet. She watched Mother take the photographs of Lan's four grandparents and the photo of Second Brother off the family altar. One by one Mother wrapped each in a swatch of silk. She turned toward the bookcase and took down a photo of Father in his uniform and wrapped it in silk too. Then she pulled a slender stack of snapshots from between two of Father's books and added it to her collection.

"Get two sets of chopsticks, two spoons, the rice pot, the teapot, two bowls, and two cups." Mother placed the photos in the second rice basket. "Wrap the breakable things in your clothes."

Lan nearly tripped as she hurried back and forth to the kitchen. "Slow down!" Mother's tone was stern. She kept her eyes on the basket as she worked.

Lan saw her mother's beaded jewelry bag wedged between the wrapped photos. "How long will we be gone?" Mother didn't respond. "When are we coming back?" Lan turned her head to the side and peered up into her mother's face.

Mother bowed her head. "We're never coming back."

Never? Lan swallowed a sob. "Where are we going?"

"I don't know."

"Is Quan coming?" Lan pulled a strand of hair toward her mouth. "Will he take care of us?"

"Of course not."

"I don't want to go." Lan dropped the strand of hair. Mother shook her head. It was tradition—Older Brother should care for Mother.

Lan buried her face in the rough fabric of the divan. It smelled of dust and sweat, of rain and time. *Leave this house? Their land? The ancestors and Second Brother?* Cam My had been right.

"Come, be brave. Get up. We must go." Mother picked up both baskets and handed one to Lan.

Mother glanced to the left, then to the right, squinting beneath the brim of her hat. Lan knew that Saigon was west, to the left, and the South China Sea to the right. They had gone to the ocean once when Father came home for a week, before Second Brother had died. Her throat tightened.

Mother looked to the left again. Then she took Lan's hand and turned to the right, toward the sea. The two started walking, away from the house, away from the grove of trees, away from dead Father, away from Second Brother, who was buried under the slab of concrete with the red and gold Buddha sitting on his chest, away from the ancestors, away from Cam My and Older Brother and baby Chi, far away in America.

Mother didn't look back, didn't look at the house she'd swept three times a day for twenty years, didn't look at the trees. Lan looked back over her shoulder quickly. The breeze moved the branches of the trees. *Caoutchouc,* the French word for rubber tree, meant "wood that weeps." The nuns had taught her that. A single, jagged sob stumbled from Lan's mouth.

"Walk, don't cry. You're all that I have left," Mother said.

That night they slept on the edge of a rice paddy with the mosquito net wound around them. Before dawn, half-asleep, Lan drew near to her mother. Tears from Mother's face fell against Lan's cheek. She could feel Mother's chest heave. Mother needed her. *I will take care of you,* Lan vowed. *The way Older Brother should.*

The nuns had taught her a prayer, a French prayer. *Notre Père qui es aux cieux, que ton nom soit sanctifié. Our Father, who art in heaven, hallowed be thy name. Father. God. Ancestors. Someone. Help us.*

*G*en gazed out the backseat window as her father turned into the Rose City Cemetery. It had been over a year since Mom had died, and he had come home early from work to take them to the cemetery.

Aunt Marie sat up front on the passenger side. "Are you feeling up to this, Marshall?" she asked.

Aunt Marie still stayed with Gen every day after school. Gen hoped that next year her father would let her go to a friend's house or stay alone.

"We're having an end-of-the-school-year party tomorrow." Gen hooked her hands over the back of the front seat.

Aunt Marie turned toward her slightly. "Genevieve, it's inappropriate to talk about school right now. Sit back against the seat. Use good posture." Dad inched his way around a curve in the road.

Why had it taken over a year for Mom's gravestone to be made? Gen wanted to ask the question out loud, but she was certain Aunt Marie would scold her for that, too. Her father parked the car next to the mausoleum near the back of the cemetery.

"Don't walk on the graves," Aunt Marie chided, her sweater buttoned tightly across her front, her sheer burgundy scarf tied under her neck. Gen studied the ground, not sure where the graves were. She fell in step behind her father. He stopped and stared straight ahead. Gen read the marker slowly. *Sally Jane Hauer. Beloved Mother. September 14, 1940 to April 4, 1975.*

"Good grief, Marshall!"

Gen glanced at Aunt Marie.

"Why did you put your name on it too? What if you remarry?"

Gen read the marker: *Marshall Frederick Hauer. Beloved Father. February 26, 1929 to*—and there was a blank space. She began to cry. Her father patted her shoulder, but she cried harder.

"That's enough, Genevieve," Aunt Marie said, clutching her purse.

Gen stared at the ground, at Aunt Marie's practical beige shoes, and tried to stop.

"It's all right." Her dad patted her shoulder again, then took her hand and led her toward the car. She hid her face against his sports jacket.

A month later he sat in a lawn chair in the middle of the backyard, facing the ridge with the golf course below. The green and white weave of the plastic stretched across his back.

"Dad?" Gen called from the patio. He didn't respond. It was July third, a Saturday, the day before America's bicentennial. He was in charge of the picnic at church the next day. Gen walked across the lawn and tapped her father on the shoulder. As usual, he didn't answer. When Mom was alive, she would say, "Marshall. Gen's talking to you." Now it was up to Gen to get his attention, but sometimes it wasn't worth the effort, and she pretended she hadn't spoken at all.

Worried he'd forgotten to buy the supplies for the picnic, she tapped him again. Was he asleep? It was so unlike him to sit down; he kept busy with housework, yard work, and "work work," as Gen called the briefcase full of papers he brought home from his job at the downtown insurance company.

Gen stepped in front of him. He wasn't asleep. She peered into his gray eyes, shaded by his bushy eyebrows. "Daddy?" Again he didn't respond. He was going for the record, the longest delayed response ever. She was sure he would mumble "Yes?" in another minute. It was always a question, that "Yes?" with his voice rising in a hint of surprise, as if uncertain she had spoken.

She sat cross-legged on the grass and stared at him for a moment, but then her throat tightened, and she looked away. She glanced down at her denim cutoffs. The ends were beginning to fray. She wore her Lassie League baseball shirt with the words *Rose City* across the front. She played second base. The red sleeves were splashed with pink because her father had washed the shirt with a load of whites and lots of bleach.

Gen held her head up again. "Dad, are you okay?" She reached out and gently shook his pant leg. The fabric felt cool, the midmorning sun heated her face, and the thick grass tickled her bare legs. The warm scent of the freshly cut grass filled her nose. She could hardly breathe. She pulled on her father's other pant leg. Again, he didn't respond. He looked eerie. "Dad," she said. "We have the church picnic tomorrow. Is everything taken care of? Do we need to buy paper plates or anything?" Gen had been excited about the bicentennial all year.

Tomorrow, after the church picnic, they would watch the fireworks over the Columbia River. She swallowed again; her mouth felt dry. *What is wrong with him? Why is he acting this way?* She sat and stared, and every few minutes she checked her new Timex watch that he had given her for her birthday. She should call Aunt Marie. That's what her father would want her to do. She squinted against the bright sun and then glanced over her shoulder, wishing someone would appear to help her, to tell her what to do.

At 11:15 she walked into the house and phoned her aunt. "I think something's wrong with Daddy."

Ten minutes later Aunt Marie stormed through the house to the backyard. Her gray hair bounced as she walked. She halted in front of her brother. "Marshall, what is going on?" He kept staring. "Snap out of it!"

Minutes passed. Gen felt her heartbeat keeping time. Still her father sat, staring.

"He's had a nervous breakdown," Aunt Marie finally said, standing with her hands on her hips.

A nervous breakdown? Why? Have I been bad?

"That Sally," Marie muttered. "I know she was your mother, and I shouldn't talk this way, but I'll never forgive her for what she's done to him."

Aunt Marie called the doctor. Gen sat in a white metal lawn chair on the patio and listened to her aunt in the kitchen. "No," Aunt Marie said. "I will not call for an ambulance. We'll get him there if we have to drag him."

The breeze pulled the scent of honeysuckle across the patio. A bee landed on the arm of the chair. Gen jerked her hand away. Aunt Marie hung up the phone and hurried through the open door. "Come on," she said. "I need your help."

They each took one of Dad's arms, hoisted him from his chair, and propelled him around the side of the house in a lopsided fashion to Aunt Marie's Chevy parked in the driveway. Aunt Marie forced his head down and his body into the backseat. Gen climbed in beside her father.

"Psychiatric ward," Aunt Marie said to the man dressed in a white coat at the emergency entrance.

Gen started to climb out of the backseat. "No," Aunt Marie commanded. "Stay there."

The man rolled a wheelchair up to the car. Only really crazy people ended up on psychiatric wards. *Did they ever leave? Did they ever get better?*

She watched her father disappear behind the glass-and-metal hospital doors. Would he ever come home?

Late that afternoon Gen and Aunt Marie shopped for the picnic. "We'll go to church, then to the picnic, and then to see your father," Aunt Marie said as she pushed the shopping cart across the parking lot. "I hope we bought enough paper plates. I hope your father recruited people to set up and clean up." She unlocked the trunk of her car.

"Dad and I planned to go watch the fireworks tomorrow night." Gen lifted a bag of paper plates from the cart.

"Oh, no," Aunt Marie said. "We won't have time for that."

The heat from the asphalt swirled around Gen's legs. "What did the doctor say?"

"That your father will be fine." Aunt Marie unlocked Gen's door and hurried around to the driver's side. Gen climbed in, rolled down the window, and sank against the burning vinyl, relieved.

Aunt Marie continued to talk as she started the car and gripped the steering wheel. "The doctor said that the breakdown was caused by stress and grief. Your mother should have thought of this before she flew off to Vietnam, shouldn't she?"

Gen trailed her hand out the window, staring at her wristwatch. Her sweaty legs stuck to the seat.

During the picnic when people asked where Gen's father was, Aunt Marie answered that he'd been hospitalized the day before for tests. "It could be his heart," she said. "Maybe his stomach."

Afterward, Aunt Marie drove to the hospital. Gen started to follow her through the double doors into the psychiatric ward, but Aunt Marie turned sharply with her hands on her hips. "Children are not allowed."

Gen stayed in the waiting room. It didn't feel like her father was going to get better. She sat down on a green vinyl chair and smeared her index finger on the metal arm. Her heart pounded. *Why, Mom? Why did you have to go to Vietnam?* She stood and turned the chair so that it faced the wall. She kicked with her right foot, hitting the white wall with the toe of her dress shoe. *If Mom were here, Dad wouldn't be sick. If Mom were here, we'd go to the bicentennial fireworks.* She wanted to stop missing Mom. She wished she'd never heard of Vietnam. She wished the country didn't exist.

She thought about how she had burned her thumb last winter when she was heating water for hot chocolate. She had put a large bandage on the burn, but a few days later it became infected. She took the bandage off, examined the yellow pus oozing from the base of her thumb, and then put a bigger bandage over it. A week later her teacher asked to see her hand. The teacher called Gen's father, and he took her to the doctor. "Don't ever put a bandage on a burn. It needs air to heal," the doctor said and then wrote a pre-scription for an antibiotic.

"Didn't your mother ever tell you that? Not to put a bandage on a burn? She was a nurse." Her father scowled as he talked, as he drove up Sandy Boulevard toward their house. Gen stared out the car window. *So somehow this is Mom's fault too?* It was as if they were all covered with yellow pus. No one wanted to talk about how they felt. No one wanted to *feel*.

She shouldn't have cried at the cemetery, even though it was about Dad's name on the marker, not about Mom's. Maybe he knew she still hurt though, still had a bandage over an icky, oozing wound. She kicked at the waiting room wall again.

"Genevieve." Aunt Marie stood in the doorway with her hands on her hips. "You're marking the wall with black streaks."

Gen turned toward her aunt.

"And wipe that pout off your face."

Gen didn't go back to day camp that summer. Aunt Marie said with all the trips to the hospital it was easier not to worry about it. Her father stayed in the hospital for two weeks. After he came home, Aunt Marie brought a meal, along with Gen, and then lectured her on keeping her room clean. She showed Gen how to scrub the toilet and scour the kitchen sink with Ajax. "I know I shouldn't say this, but I have to be honest. Your mother wasn't known for her housekeeping." Her aunt rinsed the sponge under the faucet. "You need to learn to do better."

Her father seemed more relaxed. He said he finally felt rested. He had two new bottles of pills in the medicine cabinet, and Gen kept track of his moods. On sad days she would be especially quiet, she wouldn't disturb him while he read the paper, and she would set the table without being asked. He sat and watched more television. Sometimes he didn't mow the lawn until Gen commented on how tall the grass had grown. When her father went out of town on business later in the summer, Gen stayed with Aunt Marie. She left determined to keep him well.

She cried sometimes at night, relieved that her father had come home, that he hadn't had to stay forever in the psychiatric ward. "God, please don't let anything happen to him," she begged. Sometimes it made her nervous to pray. God hadn't kept Mom safe. Could she trust God with Dad?

Still she prayed, for her father and for her mother's friend Kim. Often she held the figurine of the Vietnamese girl while she prayed. It wasn't true, not entirely, that she wished she had never heard of Vietnam.

*P*atriotic music blared over the loudspeaker nailed to the dead tree outside the shack. Lan rolled away from the static racket. After the first song, a metallic voice shouted, "Exercise! Four, three, two, one." Mother curled on the mat beside Lan and slept through the commotion. It had been three years since Mother and Lan had left the rubber tree plantation, since they had walked six days until they reached the city of Vung Tau on the South China Sea.

When the light filled the shack and music replaced the exercise program, Lan gently shook Mother. "Time to wake," she said softly. Three mornings a week Mother reported to a reeducation program led by their cell leader, the man in their neighborhood who reported to the Communists. It meant Mother had two fewer hours on those days to sell fruit in the market. This was one of those days.

Mother had hocked her jade bracelets and pearl earrings for rent money and bought a large bag of rice with the change when they first arrived in Vung Tau. She sold the rice, even though it was illegal, and then bought more rice. Now she bought fruit, drinks, and snacks from the vendors and loaded them in the baskets attached to her yoke to sell away from the market at a higher price.

Lan went to school during the day. She longed to quit. She was eleven—she should help Mother, not waste her time in school.

"Go start the rice." Mother sat up, stretching her arms. The dirt floor felt cool beneath Lan's sleeping mat. Rain pelted the tin roof, pounding out a vicious rhythm. Three feet away, her father's eyes stared at her from his photograph atop the wooden fruit box turned on its side and used as the family altar. He wore a serious and proud expression beneath his captain's hat. Lan thought it brave of Mother to display the photo. Second Brother, eternally young, smiled in his photo. Lan smiled back. "No one knows what each day brings," Mother often said.

Lan stopped smiling.

Lan listened to the teacher lecture the children. "The state is most important." She walked to the other side of the classroom and rapped her ruler on the knuckles of the boy sitting by the door. He'd been biting his fingernails. "The state is more important than family, play, religion, and traditions. The state is even more important than work and school." She walked back to the front of the class and pointed at the only picture in the room, a photo of Ho Chi Minh. "Uncle Ho loved the people of Vietnam. The people of the North went hungry to free the corrupt South from America and the puppet regime."

Lan stifled a yawn. The cement-block building trapped the heat. Three shifts of students took turns throughout the day; her class met in the afternoon. They all sat on wooden benches with no backs. Lan glanced down at her thin white shirt that, years ago, Mother would have used as a rag. She tugged at the hem of her blue skirt; it was too short, and teacher would surely notice.

"Sing with me." Teacher clapped her hands. The song was "Who Loves Children More Than Uncle Ho?"

"Last night I dreamed of Uncle Ho…" Lan sang, and then she yawned again.

Teacher abruptly stopped singing. "Are you bored, Comrade Lan?" The rest of the class stared at the floor.

"No, Teacher." She bowed her head.

"Then sing."

"His beard was long, his hair was gray. I kissed him tenderly on both cheeks…" Lan mouthed the words. *Who loves children more than Uncle Ho?* she asked herself. *Well, he's dead. And Mother loves me most anyway. And*

Father loved me more too. But did he? He went off and fought for the South and got himself killed. Did Older Brother love her more? Last they heard he was the leader of a collective farm not far from their grove of rubber trees, but he hadn't tried to find them. If he did come to see them, Mother would probably spit in his face again anyway.

Lan swallowed her next yawn. "Character!" The teacher glared at Lan. "Character is what makes a person strong; moral integrity is what you must learn." *I've learned nothing in the time I've been in this school. I should be helping Mother.* The boy sitting next to the door bit his fingernails.

After class Lan and the neighbor girl, Thi, rushed out of school. Lan's feet spread over the edges of her flip-flops and slapped against the dirt road. Calluses covered her heels. Thi was also a refugee. Her father had been sent to a reeducation camp two years before. Her mother, with three of her eight children, had made her way to Vung Tau from the highlands. Most of their other classmates were from the North and had been resettled in Vung Tau by the government. Their fathers fought for the Viet Cong and now worked on the oil rigs out in the South China Sea. "We had no electricity in the North," one girl had bragged. "Now we have a television." Lan often thought of the girl's TV. Sometimes she and the other market kids stared through the window of the electronics shop downtown until the owner shooed them away, saying they were bad for business.

"Wouldn't it be fun to hike up to the Giant Jesus?" Thi smiled at Lan.

Lan shook her head. "Too far." The nuns back home had told her about the Giant Jesus on the south end of Vung Tau. It had been built two years before the end of the war. It was a giant statue with arms spread wide that looked over the sea. The nuns had told her that Jesus would protect her. Mother had no interest in ever seeing the Giant Jesus. Lan was too tired to think of walking that far.

"Doesn't a bowl of beef noodle soup sound good?" Thi asked as she skipped two steps and then swatted at a mosquito on her arm. She crouched on the road to pick up a rock that suddenly caught her attention.

Lan's stomach growled. This was a better idea than hiking to see Jesus in the heat. "With sweetened mung beans for dessert?" she said.

Thi fell several steps behind Lan. "Look at the butterfly!" she called out. Thi annoyed Lan as she jumped from subject to subject. Thi turned off the dirt road into an overgrown garden.

"Come back!" Lan called out. Mother had told Lan never to leave the road. "Get out of the garden!" Lan shouted. The girl turned toward the road. The explosion knocked Lan to the ground. She felt the shrapnel sear her back; she heard her own faraway scream and felt the warmth of the blood against her skin.

Thi was silent.

Lan slipped into darkness, her face pressed into the powdery dirt of the roadway.

&

"My son is a collective leader," Mother said. "Find him. Tell him his sister must go to the hospital."

"You are the wife of an enemy of the state," the cell leader answered. "Besides, there is no room in the hospital."

"What did you fight for if there is no room in the hospital? Isn't that the least the state can offer us?" Mother hissed. "Find my son. I will not lose another child."

Mother wrapped her arms around Lan, pulling her head and torso upward off the roadway. It started to rain; the afternoon deluge broke from the sky in sheets of water. The water mixed with the dirt and blood. Lan struggled to pull air into her lungs.

&

"Mother," she whispered. "Where are you?" No one answered. People stood in line in a dark corridor. Where was Mother? *Que ton règne vienne. Thy kingdom come.* She thought of the nuns, of her father, of Second Brother, of the ancestors. *Does Mother have a photo of me to put on the altar?*

The next time she awoke she was in a room. Mud caked her arms, a skinny tube ran into a vein, and a towel was draped over her chest. She heard Older Brother's voice. "Her lung was punctured; she'll need to stay for a few days. Do what the doctor says."

"I have no money for medicine." Mother's voice was low.

"I'll settle that tonight, but I'm leaving for Hanoi tomorrow." So Mother had begged Older Brother to help them. She hadn't spit in his face.

"What about medicine? For after she's out of the hospital?"

"I cannot give you what I do not have," Quan said.

Lan turned her head toward her handsome brother. He wore a faded green camouflage uniform and stood straight and tall with his hands behind his back. His jet black hair framed his square face.

"We need your help." Mother squinted at him. Long, loose strands of hair hung from the bun at the nape of her neck. "We are all alone with no protection, no opportunities, no choices."

"You already made your choice," Quan said. "You chose to support the United States and the South Vietnamese Army. Now you pay for that choice."

"I chose to support your father."

Quan glanced away from Mother with a cold, distant expression. "You were foolish to do so." He squared his shoulders.

She shook her head. "I didn't care about the North or the South, the Americans or the Viet Cong. I only wanted your father to come home. I only wanted to have my family together, to live on the land. I just wanted the war to be over."

"Foolishness," Older Brother said.

"No, not foolishness. Wisdom. The wisdom of a mother, of a wife. The rest of you were fools." Mother stepped backward. "What about the

Socialist Republic of Vietnam?" Her voice held a hint of sarcasm. "Why can't it help us?"

"Because it doesn't have the means right now either. Haven't you heard? We're at war with Cambodia. Are you still so foolish? Only thinking about your child, your family, instead of the country?"

"You may think me foolish, but I'm still the woman who bore you."

"Mother," Lan whispered. *Please stop.* Mother must not insult Older Brother, must not show her anger at him, must not cause him to lose face. They needed his help.

Mother raised her chin.

"Take us with you." Lan coughed as she spoke. She tried to raise her head, but it fell back on the cot.

Quan drew a blank face and glanced away. Older Brother used to share his food and carry her on his back. "Help us," she said.

"I will try."

Lan knew he couldn't say no; he would lose face. But she was sure that was what he meant. He turned to go and then looked back. *Take us with you. Don't leave us again.*

"You were lucky," he said. "Your friend is dead. Now, be more careful."

I have to go home and fix dinner." Gen hugged her social studies book to her chest. In just over two months she would be done with eighth grade.

Angie cocked her head. "So you can't ride the bus downtown with us?"

Her father would never allow her to ride the bus downtown.

"You have to go cook dinner? My mom does that," Stacy said and then giggled. Angie elbowed her. Gen shrugged and peered beyond the playground and over the roof of the red brick school. Dark rain clouds filled the March sky.

Two fifth-grade boys and a fourth grader played monkey-in-the-middle on the playground. The younger boy laughed as he ran from side to side, chasing the football.

"See you tomorrow." Gen walked away.

"No fair!" the boy in the middle yelled. The older boys laughed. The younger one kept running from side to side, frantically waving his arms. Gen left the playground and walked the six blocks home. She washed the breakfast dishes and put away the box of Cheerios that she had left on the counter. The phone rang.

"Genevieve," Aunt Marie said, "Easter is coming up."

"I know."

Aunt Marie paused. "Of course you know. Did you know that I need your help with the Sunday school Easter egg hunt on that Saturday?"

"I assumed so." Gen wiped the dishcloth over the counter as she talked.

"Getting awfully smart, aren't you?" Aunt Marie asked.

Gen stayed silent.

"I'll pick you up at nine that Saturday. And I'll expect you and your father for dinner on Easter Sunday."

"Thank you, Aunt Marie." They went to Aunt Marie's for every holiday dinner.

"How is your father?"

"Fine." Gen rinsed the cloth under the faucet.

"Well, we're coming up on the anniversary," Aunt Marie said.

"I know." *The anniversary of Mom's death.*

Aunt Marie changed the subject back to Easter and the supplies that she needed to buy for the egg hunt. Gen pulled a can of spaghetti sauce from the cupboard. After a few minutes she said, as politely as possible, "I need to go, Aunt Marie. I want to have dinner ready by the time Dad gets home."

Gen hung up the phone and walked upstairs to her room where she pulled a newspaper out from under her bed. The headline read FORMER MISSIONARY TO VIETNAM TO SPEAK. She scanned the article again. Paul Wilcox, who worked in a mission in Vietnam from 1959 to 1975, was speaking at the Missionary Alliance Church in Northeast Portland that evening. She wanted to go, but she couldn't decide if she should.

If she went and her father found out, he would be hurt. Gen didn't want that. Her aunt would be furious. Gen didn't care as much about that.

What would her mother want her to do? *Mom.* Aunt Marie made it sound like Mom had gotten herself killed on purpose. People at church acted that way too.

"Should I go?" Gen whispered the words. What held her back? Aunt Marie's criticism? Her father's pain? The memory of her mom? How many almost fourteen-year-olds had mothers who had died in Vietnam? It was absurd. One boy at school had a father who had died during the war. Gen overheard two teachers talking about it, but they both stopped and then blushed when they realized she was close enough to hear.

Her father's car pulled into the driveway. Gen glanced at the newspaper. The service started at 7:00 p.m. She pushed the newspaper back under the bed and hurried down the staircase as her father opened the front door.

"Hi, Dad. Dinner will be ready in twenty minutes." He smiled a faraway smile. *Another week until the anniversary.* She would go hear Paul Wilcox. It would make no difference to her father—as long as he never knew.

❧

"Dinner's good." Her father spoke as he cut his spaghetti with his knife. He hadn't taken a bite yet. He usually complimented Gen on dinner before he started eating. Gen wondered if he was afraid he would get distracted by chewing and forget his manners.

"Thank you," Gen said.

"How was school?" It was nearly the same script every night.

"I have a report to do on the Incas."

Her father smiled. His thick hair was entirely gray, and his sideburns were white.

"I need to go to the library this evening."

"I have an elders' meeting tonight." He concentrated on buttering a slice of white bread. Gen had counted on the meeting.

"Could you drop me off on your way?"

Her father smiled. "You'll be okay? For those two hours at the library?"

She wound the spaghetti around her fork. "Sure." She swallowed the lie with her food. It was easier this way; the library was right next to the church.

"How was school?" He blushed as he realized that he'd already asked that question. "I mean, what did you do today?" She knew he was proud of how well she did in her studies.

"I got an A on my English test." She passed her father the green beans. She didn't tell him about the new student in art, a Vietnamese girl, a boat person who didn't speak English. Gen guessed that she lived in Halsey Square, the apartment complex down the hill on the other side of the golf course, where most of the other Vietnamese kids who went to her school lived. The girl wore her long hair in a single braid. Her name was Hoa. The other kids laughed when she was introduced.

৵

Gen sat in the back of the church auditorium. Paul Wilcox wore a traditional Vietnamese outfit, a man's ao dai made from emerald green silk with a gold dragon embroidered on it. He played music on a single-stringed instrument, haunting music that made tears well in Gen's eyes. She pulled her puffy ski jacket tight and crossed her arms.

Mr. Wilcox stepped to the podium and leaned forward, his expression filled with passion. He spoke of the last days before South Vietnam fell to the Communists. He told of his escape from Saigon and how the Christians he left behind feared for their lives. Since the end of the war, he had worked in a refugee camp in Thailand, helping to care for boat people who escaped Vietnam and were picked up by ships or were fortunate enough to make it to Thailand.

"Many have been lost at sea," he said, "or killed by pirates. Those who made it lost everything—their homes, their extended families, sometimes their children, sometimes their parents. Many are sick. There is never enough food or medicine. Most of the refugees stay at least two years before being placed, but some have been in the refugee camp nearly five years, and there are no schools for the children.

"Many who escaped tell of church buildings in South Vietnam that have been turned into government buildings and even discos. Others say the church has gone underground and is gaining strength."

Mr. Wilcox continued, saying that he was traveling around the U.S. to seek help for the refugees, searching for people who could give financially, people who could sponsor a family, and people who would be willing to travel to Thailand and help in the camps.

Tears pooled in Gen's eyes. She wanted to go. Would they still need help after she graduated from high school? She felt God's touch. Was this what people meant when they said they felt God's calling?

Mr. Wilcox talked about how people could help. The sleeves of his ao dai moved with the motions of his arm. His voice filled with emotion. "Pray. Pray for a particular person." Gen thought of her mother's friend Kim. "Let God lead you to pray for a person, maybe around your age, close to your station in life." *A thirteen-year-old Vietnamese girl.* What would her life be like? Tears filled Gen's eyes again, and a startling wave of fear swept over her. Why did she feel afraid?

Was it because she thought God might call her to follow in her mother's footsteps? Was she afraid of finally understanding her mother?

Maybe it didn't matter. She would never go anyway. When the offering plate came around, she dropped in her allowance money and then glanced at her watch. It was 8:45. She wiped her eyes on the shiny fabric of her jacket, eased out of the pew, slipped through the front door of the church, and hurried next door to the library. She pulled a book on the Incas from the stack and sat at a table, leafing through it mindlessly.

Her father found her there, staring at a photo of a clay vessel painted with flowers and parrots. Guilt gripped her. She had never lied to him before, not like this.

"You seem tired," he said.

"Not really."

Neither spoke as they drove home, but when her father pulled the car into the driveway he asked, "What's wrong, sweetheart?"

She drew in a breath. "I wasn't at the library, not the whole time. I was at the church next door. A missionary who used to be in Vietnam spoke there tonight."

He reached out and touched her shoulder. She turned toward him. "I'm sorry I lied."

"I'm sorry you lied too." They sat in silence for a moment. "How was the meeting?" he said.

"Really sad." Without explaining, she headed to the dark house.

❧

That night after her father had shut his bedroom door, Gen dug in the bottom of her sock drawer and found the figurine of the Vietnamese girl holding the wooden doll. Gen held the carving under the light of her lava lamp. The tip of the nose had chipped off. The figurine smiled back at Gen, and she clutched it close, thinking of that last night with her mom.

She would pray for Kim and for the nameless Vietnamese girl. She would pray about what God might want from her someday, trust that it would be something she could do, something that wouldn't bring her father more stress and grief. She gripped the carving tightly as she prayed.

Chapter 6

Twelve-year-old Lan pulled her torn plastic poncho closer as she huddled beneath the makeshift tarp that stretched over the shack's outdoor cooking area. A curtain of rain fell, dripping through holes in the tarp.

It had been nearly a year since the shrapnel from the land mine pierced her lung, but she still struggled for breath when smoke from the factories and oil refineries hung in the air. She hoped Mother brought more food, maybe some fish for the soup, or vegetables, or bean curd.

Lan struggled to her feet to heat the broth from last night over the charcoal stove. Saliva filled her mouth. She swallowed hard. She added dark green morning glory leaves that she had pulled from beside the road and a handful of cooked rice from breakfast. She watched intently until the tiny jumps of liquid grew into exploding bubbles, spurting broth toward the top of the soup pot. She turned down the heat. Mother was late.

The relentless rain continued. Not the hot, sun-heated rain of the afternoon, but a constant cool rain that left her chilled.

She hadn't been back to school since the accident. It had taken months for her to heal. An infection had kept her in bed and sent Mother off to borrow money to buy the medicine. Now Mother owed money and needed her help.

"Hello, Lan." A shy neighbor stood at the edge of the yard in the last light of the day. He was young, just twenty. His wife, Nhu, was expecting their first baby.

Lan stood. The young man hung his head. "I need a shovel. Do you have one?"

Why would they have a shovel? Lan stifled a giggle as she imagined grabbing one four years before when they left the rubber tree grove and then carrying it all the way to Vung Tau. Did he want to dig a latrine? Perhaps his was full.

She smiled. Nhu had sat with Lan after the land mine accident. Nhu reminded Lan of Older Sister—pretty, talkative, outgoing, cheerful, ready to help. The way Older Sister acted before her American boyfriend left. The young wife had talked constantly of her baby even though she was just a couple of months pregnant then. How smart he would be. How tall. What a good job he would have someday. Remembering Older Sister and home had made Lan want to cry. They would all be there if it hadn't been for the war. But she had been thankful for the company of the neighbor woman, thankful for the chatter, thankful to be included in Nhu's hopes for her child.

Lan shook her head. "No. No shovel here." She wished Nhu had come instead of the man. He was hard to talk to. She squatted to stir the soup. She thought of the husband she hoped to have someday; he would know how to carry on a conversation.

"Is your mother home?" he asked.

Lan shook her head again. The light was too dim to see the neighbor's eyes. She held the wooden spoon over the pot as she turned her head toward a rustling at the edge of the yard. She expected Nhu, but it was Mother. Her yoke hung across her shoulders, and her two baskets swung as though empty.

"What is it?" Mother's conical hat bobbed as she spoke. "Is it time for the baby?"

The neighbor shook his head. "The baby came already. A boy. But he's dead. I must bury him."

Lan's hand flew to her mouth.

"Lan, go ask old Mr. Nguyen for a shovel. Bring it to us as quickly as you can." Mother put her arm around the neighbor and led him toward the street. His shoulders shook.

A sob escaped from Lan. *Why? Why did Nhu's baby die?*

It took half an hour to find Mr. Nguyen drinking rice wine in the soup shop down the street. Timidly she asked to borrow the shovel. "Speak up," he shouted. He stood when he found out that Nhu's baby had died. He bumped the table and then knocked over the red plastic chair behind him.

He shuffled back to the shack he shared with his four grown daughters and pulled the shovel out from the dark corner behind his hammock.

A sliver from the decaying handle pierced the pad of Lan's hand as she carried it through the rain. The metal blade of the shovel dripped orange rust into the mud. She stood in the doorway of the neighbors' shack. Rain ran down her face and matted her hair where she had tried to brush it away from her eyes. Under her useless poncho, the rain had plastered her thin shirt and pants to her skin. Finally Mother turned and saw her. Lan jerked her eyes away from the sleeping mat where the man crouched beside his wife and dead baby.

As she handed Mother the shovel, Lan opened her mouth to speak and then shut it again quickly.

"What?" Mother asked. "What is it?"

Lan shook her head.

"Go ahead," Mother said. "Ask me."

Lan opened her mouth again, paused, and then carefully formed her words. "Did you bring any food? I'm hungry." She longed for something more than thin broth and rice.

Without answering, Mother turned away from Lan and walked back toward the grieving couple.

Lan slowly opened her eyes. The shack was dark except for the ribbon of moonlight that trespassed through the crack in the wall. In her dream she'd been running through the grove of rubber trees.

The rain had stopped; the silence must have awakened her.

She reached over for Mother under the mosquito net. She wasn't there. Lan regretted asking Mother if she had brought food. It was obvious she hadn't, and Mother had taught her better than that. She had taught her to honor others, to show compassion to those who hurt. Lan sat up on her mat and hugged her skinny knees to her chest, squeezing away the panic. She wrapped her arms around her thin body and felt the scars on her back. The threads of her still-damp cotton top separated between her fingertips as she touched the scar tissue. It wouldn't be long until her only shirt was full of holes.

Lan's stomach growled. Soon the loudspeaker would crackle with the five-thirty morning reveille. When Mother came back, she would yank the comb through Lan's hair to pull out the lice, and then they would go to the market to sell fruit.

Where was Mother? What if something happened to her? She heard a rustling in the corner. Rats. Why did they come every night? There was no food. Lan thought of Nhu's dead baby. She struggled to breathe in the humid night. *Que ta volonté soit faite,* she silently recited, remembering the prayer the nuns had taught her. *Thy will be done.*

Footsteps fell in the doorway. Lan stiffened. Quietly Mother slipped through the door, carrying a bag in one hand and a bundle under her other arm.

"Lan, you should be asleep." Mother stepped out of her flip-flops.

"Where were you?"

"Getting food." Mother put the bag that she carried next to Lan's sleeping mat.

"I'm sorry I asked about something to eat when I brought the shovel. I shouldn't have." Lan peeked up at her mother.

Mother squatted beside Lan and put an arm around her. "Hush, hush," she said. "You were hungry."

Lan pulled in a deep breath.

Mother still held the bundle in her other hand.

"Where did you go? What's in the package?"

"I went to Mr. Vuong's. He had rice for us—and some vegetables, even some bean curd. I went to pick it up after I finished helping the neighbors."

Lan thought of Mr. Vuong, the clothes merchant in the square. His shop stood next to the new mural of Ho Chi Minh. She'd seen the way Mr. Vuong leered at Mother. He was old with greasy hair. She imagined her mother breaking the curfew, sneaking to the shop, and then hurrying back, walking in the shadows, perhaps barefoot so no one, especially their Communist cell leader, would hear the slap of her flip-flops against her feet.

"Here." Mother handed Lan the bundle of silk. "He sent pants and a top for you."

Lan unwound the clothes. This wasn't the first time Mother had come home in the middle of the night with food. It was the first time she had brought clothes. Lan had heard Mother talking with the other women who worked in the market about men, about how few there were after the war, about how none of the women would find a husband.

"We'll do the best we can," said the woman who sold hats. Sometimes she spoke French to Lan, and Lan would repeat what she said, thinking of the nuns, remembering what they had taught her.

Mr. Vuong had stared at Lan last week with the same hungry expression she'd seen him give Mother. She had blushed and darted around the corner. "Your daughter's growing up," Mr. Vuong had said to Mother.

"No, no. She's only ten," Mother had lied.

"She's pretty, like you." The tone of his voice frightened Lan. She wondered what expression passed across his face.

"No, no." Mother's voice had sounded strained. "She's just a child."

"Why do you go to his store in the middle of the night?" Lan asked as Mother stretched down on the mat beside her.

"Hush. Let me sleep. I'm sick from exhaustion, and it's almost time to get up."

"Why do you go?" Lan asked again, her voice louder.

Mother rolled away from her daughter and toward the wall. "I am the widow of a captain of the South Vietnamese Army. We have no future. I go to Mr. Vuong because I love you. You'll understand someday. Now go to sleep."

❧

In the morning Lan cooked the rice but refused to eat it. Mother, her eyes red and heavy, scowled at her, squinting against the bright sun as Lan squatted by the stove, but said nothing. Lan worked Mrs. Le's fruit stall in the market while Mother sold lychee nuts on the beach. At noon Mother took the money Lan had earned to help pay their debts and sent her home to rest.

It was after sundown when Mother returned. Lan hadn't started dinner. Mother sighed and squatted to start the stove. She bent over to light the charcoal, but it was gone, and the bag was empty. She dug in her money pouch and counted the nearly worthless bills in her hand. She went into the shack, curled up on the mat, and fell asleep. The next day she brought a bag of charcoal. Lan refused the rice again.

Mother ignored Lan and ate her dinner in silence.

The next morning Lan rose too quickly and, feeling faint, bent down. When Lan could finally stand upright, Mother shook her head. "Stay home and rest. Eat the rice while I'm gone," she muttered. "All I need is for you to get sick again."

That evening Mother brought half of a smelly fish to cook with the rice. Lan wondered if Mother had been able to pay any money on their debt. Lan intended to refuse the rice again, but Mother grabbed her tightly by the arm while dinner cooked. "Don't insult me with your principles. Don't be a stubborn idealist like your brother. If you don't eat, I'll lose you, too. You're all I have."

"You have Mr. Vuong."

Mother spit in the dirt.

Lan ate the fish and rice.

unt Marie, I'm going for a run." Gen opened the front door and welcomed the cool upturn of autumn air. "I'll be back in an hour!" The
district meet for cross-country was next week; she was on the varsity team.

"Genevieve!"

She sprinted down the walkway to the street, not wanting her aunt to
comment on her running shorts.

"Genevieve! You didn't comb your hair," Aunt Marie shouted.

Gen forced a smile and ran her hand through her short hair. "It's fine,"
she called back.

"How long will you be gone?" Aunt Marie stood on the porch with her
hands planted on her hips.

"An hour." Gen headed down the middle of the street and flinched as
she heard the front door slam. Thank goodness her father would return in a
few hours from his conference in Washington, D.C. She couldn't stand
another night at Aunt Marie's. She turned onto the sidewalk on Fremont
Street and headed east.

The crisp air filled Gen's lungs. The branches of the maple trees that
lined the street lurched in the wind, and soggy leaves littered the sidewalk.
Where was she headed? *Home.* It was two miles from Aunt Marie's. Last night
when Gen had asked if Aunt Marie would take her home this morning just
a few hours before her dad returned, her aunt had answered firmly, "No. I
am responsible for you. I'll take you home, with your father, after we pick
him up at the airport."

The chain-link fence across the street caught Gen's attention. It had been
six years since she'd gone inside the gate. She sped across the street and ran
through the entrance of the cemetery and then turned onto a pathway lined
with holly trees, their scraggly, haunting branches pointed toward the ground.

She passed the Gypsy graves and estimated twenty-five with the same last name, all crowded together. Many of the markers were large crypts made of concrete and marble. She imagined the extended families, all of them related somehow, and then thought of the generations, both dead and alive, and the ones to come.

The wind lifted the tiny twigs of a nearby birch tree as loneliness swept over her. She ran faster, away from the crypts, away from the endless family, away from the loneliness that raced beside her, toward the mausoleum. She slowed. There it was. Sally Jane Hauer. She stopped. *Mama.* The wind of loneliness stirred again; it seeped through her skin, wrapped around her bones, crawled along the base of her spine.

A green plastic pot of soggy chrysanthemums sat on the concrete pad against the sandy-colored marble stone. Had Dad brought them? All these years she assumed he didn't stop at the cemetery. Had she been wrong?

"I graduate next year." She said it out loud. She hadn't meant to. "I'm sixteen, a junior. I'm getting an A in chemistry. I'm thinking about becoming a nurse like you, or maybe a teacher. I'll probably go to OSU, down in Corvallis; it's only a couple of hours away." After a short pause she said, "I just got my driver's license. I'm running cross-country—it drives Aunt Marie nuts." Gen laughed just a little. "She says it's crazy for a girl to run. Everyone says I look like you, except for my short hair."

Beloved Mother. It sounded so old-fashioned. She couldn't keep her eyes away from the other half of the marker. *Beloved Father.* Why *had* her father put his name on the marker? "Dad's coming home from Washington, D.C., today. He didn't say whether he was going to see the Vietnam Memorial or not. We watched the dedication on TV—I think you would like it." Gen raised her arms over her head, took a deep breath, and then dangled her hands at her side. The loneliness eased. "I can't figure out the Vietnam thing," she said. "How I feel about it. The war. You going there. You dying there. Sometimes I think I understand why you went. Other times I don't.

"Dad says that the U.S. never should have pulled out of Vietnam when they did, that we should have seen it through, made sure the South stayed democratic. He said that you didn't think the U.S. should have ever gotten involved, that Ho Chi Minh won the election and should have been the leader after defeating the French. He said that you thought that Ho Chi Minh cared about the people of Vietnam.

"I did a report on Vietnam last spring. Dad told me to include that Kennedy got us into Vietnam with good reason. He said that Vietnam was one more domino to the Russians and if it wasn't for the U.S. the whole world would be Communist."

Gen paused for a second. "It was the most he'd said at once for a long time. He's a good dad. He loves me. He loves you, too. He still misses you." She paused again, glanced back at the Gypsy crypts, and then continued. "I miss you too. We're doing okay, but it still feels like everything fell apart after you died. I try to be nice to Aunt Marie, really I do." She crossed her fingers behind her back.

Gen didn't feel foolish talking to the slab of marble. Mom couldn't hear her; at least that's what Aunt Marie would say. Still, it felt good to speak out loud.

What would Mom want to know? "There are kids at my school from Vietnam. Lots of them. Some fled at the end of the war, but most escaped by boat with their families. Things are really bad in Vietnam right now. Not enough food or medicine. The people who fought for the South are in re-education camps, and they can't work. It would make you sad."

The loneliness washed over her again. What did Mom look like now? All bones and dust? "Okay," she said, swinging her arms back and forth, growing more self-conscious. "I guess that's all I can say for now. Bye." She turned and ran quickly back to the gate. She crossed the street and headed toward home. *Home.*

Hoa, the Vietnamese girl from school, stood on the sidewalk at the bus stop. Gen smiled as she ran by, and Hoa waved, a tiny wave. Two Vietnamese guys in their twenties driving a white Trans-Am pulled up to talk to Hoa. The Asian kids were in English as a Second Language classes at school. She only saw them outside in the park, in the halls, and in the cafeteria. They mostly kept to themselves, and the boys refused to respond, even if other kids tried to pick fights.

Hoa flipped her hair over her shoulder and laughed as the car sped away. Gen knew that some of the Vietnamese girls married early; several of the ones at school had married by the time they were sixteen. Would Hoa marry soon? For years Gen had wanted to get to know her but hadn't. What would Mom be doing now if she had lived? Would she help the Vietnamese students at the high school? Would she help Hoa apply to colleges next year?

Gen ran down the middle of Sacramento Street, her street. In another year she would apply to colleges. In another two years she would be away at college, only to come home on some weekends, maybe during the summer. She would be out from under her aunt's rules and her father's sadness and her mother's tragedy that shadowed everything she did. She turned down her own walkway and approached the house. Two pumpkins stood sentry on the porch. It wouldn't hurt to go in for just a few minutes. Gen jogged around to the backyard and pulled the key from under the mat. She opened the door, let herself into the dark kitchen, and walked into the den, turned on the light, and sank into the old mauve couch. She picked up a copy of *Parents* magazine and leafed through it. Her father didn't read it, but he'd never cancelled her mother's subscription. She wanted to curl up and take a nap, but Aunt Marie would start worrying soon. They would need to leave for the airport in an hour.

A loud knock at the front door woke her. *Dad!* He must have gotten an earlier flight. She rushed down the hall. The front door flew open. Aunt Marie filled the entryway. "I thought you'd be here. Your dad's in the hospital. He took an earlier flight—and then had a heart attack."

Wires ran from her father's chest to the machine above the bed. Gen stepped closer; Aunt Marie stood behind her. A white thermal blanket covered him from the waist down. His pale lips moved when he saw her. "Hi," he mouthed. His white hair stood up in bunches against the pillow.

"You okay?" she asked. *Please be okay.*

He nodded. The word *orphan* and the image of Aunt Marie's guest room rushed through her head. The monitor beeped. Gen jumped. "It's all right," her father said. "It keeps doing that. I don't think it means anything."

Gen tried to smile. She would go to college and become a teacher. Nursing was definitely out. This hospital thing, this ICU scene, gave her the creeps. The nurse walked up to the bed.

"How was your trip?" Aunt Marie asked. Gen had forgotten for just a moment that her aunt was in the room.

"Fine." Her father extended his arm to the nurse. She wrapped the blood pressure cuff around his biceps.

"Did you see the Vietnam Veterans Memorial?" Gen regretted the question as soon as the words flew out of her mouth.

Her dad nodded his head.

"How was it?" the nurse asked.

"Horrible," he answered. "Absolutely horrible."

A week later Gen closed the low-fat cookbook and placed it on her father's dinner-tray table. Aunt Marie had brought the book the day before, glowered at Gen, and said, "You two are going to have to change your diet. Your father isn't a young man anymore."

Her dad had been moved to the recovery floor three days before. The nurse was down the hall filling out his discharge papers. He looked odd in slacks and a dress shirt after wearing a hospital gown all week. He glanced at the cookbook and then up at Gen. "Your mother always said that the Asian diet was the best way to eat." He hardly ever spoke of Mom anymore. "She loved the food in Vietnam."

Gen nodded. *Vi-et-nam*. He had said it slowly, enunciating each syllable. Gen began filling a brown paper bag with her father's things, the cookbook, his bathroom bag, the three new prescription bottles, the packet of instructions about diet and exercise.

"It wasn't the memorial," he said. For a second Gen didn't know what he meant. "The monument is well designed—all black and smooth, as if it forced itself out of the sloping hill. It was the people. Grief rushed along the granite like a raging river. I felt as if I were drowning."

He stood. "Where is that nurse?" His white hair stuck up in the back. He put on his jacket and sat back down. His eyebrows needed to be trimmed. He seemed older than fifty-three. "I thought I was dying as the plane landed. And then I thought about you. I begged God to let me live, literally begged him out loud as the other passengers stared at me. I couldn't bear for you to go through what we went through after your mother died…not you alone." Tears welled in his pale gray eyes.

Gen sat down beside him on the bed.

"None of this turned out for you the way I thought it would. The way your mother and I wanted it to."

Gen took his hand.

"I'm sorry you're stuck with just one parent. With me." He tried to laugh.

"Don't say that, Daddy."

"I'm going to take better care of myself. I'm going to stick around for you."

Why was he talking this way? She put her forehead against his shoulder. He let go of her hand and pulled her close.

L an followed two white men on Front Beach, sure they were Americans. They stopped ahead of her and stared out across the South China Sea. She hurried her steps. "Hello," she called out in English. They turned their grim, unshaven faces toward her. Their tall bodies cast long shadows across the hot sand. They wore shorts and white T-shirts. "Hello," she said again. That was what Older Sister's boyfriend had taught her to say all those years before. The bigger man shook his head. Lan felt confused. Then he shook his finger at her and began to laugh. Lan stepped back. It was rude of him to shake his finger.

"Russian." He pointed to himself and then out to the South China Sea. "Oil." *They must work on oil derricks beyond the horizon.* She offered to sell him a cup of coconut juice from her basket, but he shook his head again and then reached out to touch her hair. She ducked her head. The friend laughed. Lan turned quickly and hurried toward the street, away from the ocean. She loved the beach, the salty smell of the water, the activity of the fishermen, the breeze sailing in off the water, but today she wouldn't stay.

Lan glanced back toward the sea. The Russians stood leering at her, still laughing. She scrambled up the bank of sand to the hot sidewalk, turned, and stumbled into a young man on a bicycle. "So sorry," she mumbled.

"Lan?" She glanced up. It was Chinh, Mr. Vuong's son. He was twenty-two, four years older than she was. He'd come from Saigon two months before. *Ho Chi Minh City,* Lan reminded herself. Others chided her when she called the city by its old name. Chinh had been staying with relatives. His father said that he came back to Vung Tau to help with the family's dress shop.

"Are you all right?" Chinh asked.

"Yes. Fine."

"Do you want a ride?"

"No. I'm just going to rest for a moment." She sat down on the curb on one side of the tree-lined boulevard.

"Are you sure?" he asked.

Lan nodded, peeking up at him from under her hat. He had lively eyes, big ears, and hair that looked as if he cut it himself. Did he know about what had gone on between her mother and his father? Mother no longer visited Mr. Vuong in the middle of the night, but sometimes they chatted as if they were old friends. Chinh's father seemed to have his eye on a younger woman who sold jewelry on the square.

The next week Lan stood under the mural of Ho Chi Minh next to Mr. Vuong's shop. According to the market gossip, the government had charged him a tax that almost put him out of business, because the Communists saw a dress shop as an extravagance. It was rumored that Mrs. Vuong had family in the party and the tax had now been lifted.

Chinh stepped out of the store and smiled at Lan. "Hello." He bowed slightly. He was nothing like Mr. Vuong. "Let me take your yoke and baskets." He reached toward her. She ducked her head under the pole as she handed it to him. Ripe mangoes rolled in the baskets, and their sweet scent filled the air.

As they walked along, Lan hurried ahead to the side of the road to pick morning glory leaves to go with rice for dinner. Chinh caught up with her. "In Saigon there is nothing to forage."

"But your family is wealthy. You didn't need to forage for food." Lan tucked the leaves into one of the baskets.

"Not so wealthy. My uncle works for the government. He helped the Viet Cong during the war. Still they live off little, and their apartment is very small. It was too crowded to have me there once their baby was born."

"Is that why you left?"

Chinh hesitated. "Partly. I was going to a church, a home church. I wanted to learn about Christianity. The authorities infiltrated our group. In a sweep, they closed down ten home churches. They claim Christians use the mask of religion to preach against the state. They sent my pastor to prison."

"Did they want to send you to prison?"

Chinh shrugged his shoulders. "My uncle rescued me and sent me here. Now my family wants me to go to America. Then I can send them money."

America. Lan wanted Chinh to take her to America. She slipped off her hat and fanned it in front of her face. In that moment the sky opened, and the afternoon rain flooded over them. They laughed and ran for cover under the awning of a noodle soup shop. Three barefooted neighborhood children joined them, two little boys and a girl. Chinh handed the yoke back to Lan and then lifted the little girl onto his shoulders. She swung her hand against the awning, causing the water to cascade to the dirt below. Chinh held on to the little girl's ankles, steadying her as she reached.

"Did you convert?" Lan asked as the rain slowed.

Chinh nodded. "Yes." His ears wiggled a little as he talked. He smiled again at Lan but not in the hungry way of his father. Still, she bowed her head and blushed. Chinh swung the little girl back to the ground, and the children raced through the muddy street.

"I've heard you speaking French with a woman in the market." Chinh took her yoke again.

"I really can't speak it." Lan blushed.

"But you were reciting the prayer, the Lord's Prayer. I recognized it."

Lan nodded. "The nuns taught it to me years ago. Before the war ended."

"What else did they teach you?" He turned to her, his dark eyes intent.

What else? It had been so long ago. She took a deep breath. "I can't remember the exact French for this, but this is the translation. You shall love the Lord your God with all your heart, mind, and soul and love your neighbor as yourself."

Chinh remained silent for a moment. "That's good," he finally said. "Do you believe it?"

"Some. Mother says to take a little from all of the religions, to take what works, to use whatever brings good luck."

Lan woke to the crackling sound of the loudspeaker. It was like another being, an annoying neighbor who wouldn't shut up or a tropical bird that cackled and cawed, permanently chained to the palm tree outside the shack. Except Lan seldom heard birds anymore. The devastation to the jungles during the war had caused the birds to flee or die.

Would Chinh flee? Would he take her with him?

Mother rolled from her hammock. Her bare feet slapped against the hard dirt floor. "Get up, lazy girl." She stood over Lan and smiled, showing the two gaps in her mouth where teeth had broken.

"Why are you up so early?" Lan sat up and ran her fingers through her hair.

"I feel better. Our luck is changing. I saw the way Chinh stared at you when he walked you home yesterday. You have done well to wait for a boy like Chinh." Mother coughed, a deep hacking cough that had hung on for a couple of months. She took a deep breath and continued, "Your brother should care for us, but a nice young man like Chinh will do."

"Mother, don't talk that way. He only walked me home."

"I see how the two of you exchange glances in the market. And I watch him. He searches for you with his eyes every day, every hour." Mother coughed again and took a drink of water from the green plastic cup that sat on the floor beside her hammock.

If it hadn't been for the war, Lan would have a dowry. Her parents would negotiate to find a suitable match. Her future mother-in-law would have to approve of her. Could she cook? Care for a husband? Take on the responsibility of caring for her in-laws in their old age? Run a business? Would she honor her husband's ancestors as her own? Now, in their poverty, there would be none of those traditions.

What would Chinh's mother think of her? Did she know what used to go on between Mother and her husband? Lan knew Mother wasn't the only woman Mr. Vuong had sought comfort with, not the only woman he'd given food and clothes to. Why couldn't Chinh just be a young man she happened to meet in the market? Lan rose from her mat and went to the spigot outside to wash her face.

Mother took the comb from the shelf and handed it to Lan. "You two must live here."

Lan shook her head and said, "Mother, you must not talk about what we do not know."

"It wouldn't do for you to live with Mr. Vuong and his wife, although she may be leaving for Ho Chi Minh City soon."

"Why?" Lan ran the comb through her hair.

"She's going to take care of her brother's new baby so the mother can go back to work."

"But Chinh said the apartment was too crowded." Lan worked her hair into a single braid.

"Too crowded for Chinh's religious beliefs is what Mr. Vuong said. They could have had their electricity cut off because of his ties to Christianity. They could have all been imprisoned. It was foolish of the boy to become involved in that."

Lan looked through the door of the shack to the family altar.

"At least Chinh has an education. He might actually have a sense for business, unlike his father." Mother coughed again.

Maybe he'll have a better sense of loyalty. Lan handed the comb back to Mother, then stood and stretched her back. She wouldn't admit it to Mother, but heaven, *ciel,* as the nuns had taught her, was smiling. *Sur la terre comme au ciel. On earth as it is in heaven.* Finally their luck was changing. Except for Mother's cough. It seemed to be getting worse, not better.

*M*r. Curls hurried into the student center at Oregon State University with a guitar case slung over his shoulder. Gen had seen him on campus many times and was drawn to his quick, dazzling smile. She admired the way he moved with confidence and grace. Months ago she had nicknamed him Mr. Curls.

The rain started just as she ducked through the door. It was Gen's first Campus Crusade for Christ meeting even though she had been at OSU for nearly two years. She took a seat with the group of girls from her dorm who had invited her to attend. Mr. Curls was up front, but now he was Mr. Electric Guitar.

Gen turned to the girl next to her. "Who's that guy?"

"Jeff Taylor. He's a nice guy."

"What year?" Gen worked her hands into the pocket of her sweatshirt.

"Junior, I think. At least he should be."

After the meeting Gen overheard the man who led the singing tell Jeff happy birthday.

"The Ides of March." Gen smiled as she took a step toward Jeff.

"Pardon?" He was polite. She liked that.

"March 15. Today is the Ides of March."

He smiled at her—an open, spectacular grin. "Like in *Julius Caesar*," he said. "Beware the Ides of March."

She nodded. He knew. She liked it that he knew Shakespeare. He was handsome, really handsome, with brown eyes and dark, long eyelashes. But he didn't seem to know that he was good looking, or maybe he didn't care.

"I've seen you around campus," he said.

"I've seen you, too." *Mr. Curls.*

"You're a good student. I see you in the library a lot." He stood tall, well over six feet.

She laughed. "I don't sound like much fun."

He shook his head. "I didn't mean that. I'm impressed by people who are good students."

"You're good on the guitar," she said.

"Thanks, but I'm not that good. I just play for fun." He gave her his full attention, didn't glance around at anyone else.

"What do you have planned for your birthday?"

"I'm going home tomorrow, to my family's cherry orchard outside The Dalles. My mom will cook dinner and bake a cake. The works."

She could tell that Jeff liked his family by the way he spoke, that he liked to go home. No pessimistic, college angst from him.

One of the girls from Gen's dorm tugged on her sweatshirt sleeve. "Want to walk with us?"

"Okay." *Not really.* She would rather talk with Jeff. Instead she said, "See you around."

Jeff smiled. "I hope so."

❧

The next week Gen walked with the group of girls from her dorm to the Campus Crusade meeting. Gen heard steps and turned; Jeff ran to catch up with them.

She smiled. "Where's your guitar?"

"I'm not playing tonight." The two slowed their pace, falling behind the group. "I wanted to sit by you."

He walked her back to her dorm after the meeting and talked about Campus Crusade. He had been involved in the group since his freshman year. "I went to Sunday school and all that," he said. "But I didn't really understand until my first year here that God has a plan for my life."

They walked without speaking for a moment. Even in their silence, Gen felt at ease. She stretched her arms behind her back. "What plans do you think God has for you?"

"I hope this doesn't sound boring"—Jeff smiled at her—"but I think he wants me to go back to The Dalles. Work with Dad in the orchard. Learn everything I can. I'll get involved with my church there. Maybe work with kids." He liked kids. She only liked guys who liked kids.

"I hope he has plans for me to have a family someday, a wife, kids." He stopped.

She expected him to blush, but he didn't, or perhaps it was too dark to tell.

He peered at her intently. "What do you think God has planned for you?"

She had the urge to tell him about the Vietnamese refugee camps in Thailand, about her mom's friend Kim, about the nameless girl in Vietnam that she sometimes still prayed for. No, she wouldn't tell him about all that. It wasn't what God had planned for her. "I want to become a teacher," she said. "After that I don't know." She often imagined herself teaching and living in Portland, available to her father when he needed her.

As Jeff told her good-bye in the lobby of her dorm, she stepped back, surprised by the affection she felt for him.

"Want to study together tomorrow?" He raised an eyebrow. "In the library?"

"Sure," she answered.

"I'll come by at six thirty." He reached for her hand and gently squeezed it.

The next evening Jeff studied his horticulture class notes. "You should know that I'm not a good student. Not like you."

Gen tilted her head. *What does he mean?*

"I'd rather be at home working now," he said. "But my parents thought I should go to college." He paused and then smiled. "And they were right. I'm glad I'm here."

Gen took her developmental psych book out of her backpack. "Tell me about the orchard." She gazed into his eyes.

As he spoke, she imagined the cherry orchards east of Portland that she and her father drove by one spring. The acres and acres of flowering trees had enchanted her. Jeff told her about his family, his great-grandparents who had homesteaded the land, his grandparents, and his father, Don. His mother, Sharon, loved being a mom. His brother, Jake, was graduating high school in June and going to Willamette University in the fall. "He's really smart," Jeff said. Their little sister, Janet, ran sprints and hurdles in track and played varsity volleyball as a sophomore.

When Jeff asked about Gen's family, she glanced at her watch and said she needed to get back to her dorm. That night, sitting on her bed, she wrote in her journal that she thought she could marry a man like Jeff someday. He was kind, and he had a plan and an optimism that calmed her. He knew what he wanted, yet he desired what God wanted. The Dalles was only ninety minutes from Portland, from her dad. Jeff wanted a family; she wanted a family.

A week later in the library Jeff asked if Gen's mother planned to come for the special Mother's Day tea. Gen thought of Mothers' Weekend the year before and how unprepared she was to see her dorm mates walking through the halls with their moms.

"Earth to Gen." Jeff smiled at her from across the table. "Mothers' Weekend. Is your mom coming down?"

Gen shook her head. "No. I'm going home that weekend." He looked disappointed. "Look, Jeff"—she drew in a deep breath—"I lost my mother." She hated the euphemism, as if Mom had simply been misplaced, as if one day they'd stumble across her in a box in the basement or in the neighbor's garage or hidden in a junk drawer in the kitchen. Why was it so hard to say, "My mother died"?

"When?" He seemed shocked, as if he thought it might have just happened.

"It was a long time ago. I was nine." Gen tried to smile a little. She didn't want him to feel uncomfortable.

Jeff leaned toward her, his hands folded on the table. "How?"

"An airplane crash." She picked up her pen and clinched it tightly.

"Where?"

She took a deep breath. "Asia."

"Asia?"

Gen nodded. Why had she said Asia? She could have at least said Southeast Asia instead of just Asia, just the largest land mass in the world, just the largest, vaguest geographic answer possible.

"Where in Asia?" His voice was soft.

"Vietnam." It was so hard to say the word.

"Really? Why was she there?" Jeff placed his strong hands flat on the table.

"She was taking care of orphans." Soon she would tell him about Nhat, about the little boy who almost became her brother. And about Kim and about her father's broken heart. But not now. She would save that for later.

"I'm sorry, really sorry, that she died." He didn't say it the way most people did. Gen opened her French notebook. Jeff retrieved an orange highlighter from his backpack. He glanced up at her and smiled, holding the pen like a cigar. "Want to hang out with me and my mom that weekend?"

"No, thanks, I really did promise Dad I would go home." But even as she spoke the words, she wanted to change her mind.

After Mother's Day, Jeff went to The Dalles every weekend to help his father get ready for harvest. Then, as soon as his last final was over, he headed home, stopping to tell Gen good-bye. He kissed her and said, "I'll call."

He did call, not as much as Gen would have liked, but at least a couple of times a week. After harvest ended, he drove to Portland, and they played miniature golf, and then her father took them out for Chinese food. Gen poured tea for the three of them from the blue ceramic pot as her dad ordered, first asking the waiter about the seafood, how fresh it was and where it came from. Gen played with her chopsticks. What if Dad and Jeff didn't like each other? What if Dad didn't approve? What if Dad had the idea that she would come home after college, teach in Portland, and take care of him? He'd been sick again; just last month he'd had a blood clot in his leg. Fortunately he'd gone to the doctor in time and gotten on medication that dissolved the clot. Still, he was pale and tired.

The waiter announced each dish as he brought it to the table, delighting in the interest Gen's father showed. Jeff seemed at ease as he enjoyed the dinner—won tons, orange chicken, salt-and-pepper squid, tempura shrimp, pork fried rice. Her dad seemed relaxed as he asked Jeff about living in The Dalles, about the orchard business, his church, and college. Gen picked at the food with her fork.

After dinner Jeff headed back to The Dalles, and Gen and her father sat on the patio, their chairs turned toward the setting sun.

"I like him," her dad said. "I like him a lot."

"Do you think we're too young?"

"Too young for what?" he swatted at a mosquito.

Gen pulled her legs up to her chest and wrapped her arms around her knees. "Too young to get serious."

"Are you getting serious?"

Orange and pink streaked the sky, broken by the silhouettes of the towering Douglas fir trees on the golf course below. She shook her head. "Not yet."

"But you think you might?" Her father swatted at another mosquito.

"Maybe. I don't know yet." The night was unusually humid; sweat trickled down the back of her leg.

"Let me know when you do know." He stood and took a step, limping slightly. "I'm going inside before I'm eaten alive."

"Will you be okay if we do get serious?"

He glanced down at her and chuckled. "Oh, Genni. Don't think your getting married someday will change how I am. I'm fine." He turned, opened the screen door, and then muttered as he stepped inside the house, "Mostly."

After school started in September, Gen and Jeff drove to Portland in his old Chevy pickup and went to Saturday Market. It was a warm, Indian summer day, and after lunch Jeff suggested they go for a hike. They drove east along the wide Columbia River. The leaves of the deciduous trees were yellow and orange against the dark evergreens. Ahead, the hills rose up from the river in shades of blue and gray, fading from dark to light against the hazy sky.

"Do you know much about the Columbia Gorge?" Jeff turned on the pickup's headlights as they sped into a tunnel chiseled through the rocky hillside.

Gen shook her head. How many times had she been up the Gorge? Just the one time to the orchards of the Hood River Valley and a few other times with her father to Multnomah Falls where they stopped to have hot chocolate in the lodge.

Jeff turned and smiled at her. "Three catastrophic events created the gorge." *Catastrophic events.* Gen hated the sound of the two words. "Volcanic eruptions, the flooding of ancient Lake Missoula, and then landslides that blocked the river channel and changed its course."

Gen studied the rock formations along the wide, wide river. Life was like that: one or two catastrophic events could totally change its course.

Jeff exited the freeway and turned onto the Scenic Highway, stopping at the Horsetail Falls trailhead. They climbed out of the pickup and gazed up at the falls, just a few yards from the road. "Let's keep going. Ponytail Falls is just up the trail." He talked about his family while they hiked through the dense forest filled with Douglas fir, mossy rocks, and lush ferns. The falls were less than an hour from his home.

Down the tree-lined trail they took a turn farther into the forest and came to a creek where the bridge had washed out. Maidenhair ferns grew along the banks. Moss covered the rocks along the creek. Gen breathed in the cool, sweet air.

"Climb onto my back." Jeff grinned as he gave her a little bow. A laugh bubbled up from deep within her as he carried her piggyback across the water, jumping from boulder to boulder. She wrapped her arms around his neck, felt the warmth of his back, and leaned against him, unafraid.

She trusted Jeff intrinsically, as much as she trusted that the water flowing beneath them would find its way to the Columbia River and then on to the Pacific. She felt, perched on Jeff's back, as if the scale of her life had finally balanced. She knew as she slid to the ground on the other side of the creek that she would marry him.

L an sat inside the hut with Mother and waited for Mr. Vuong and Chinh. She fingered the snag in the ao dai, her wedding garment that she held in her lap.

"The silk is cheap," Mother said, nodding at the outfit. "It's so like Mr. Vuong to give you the worst that he has." Mother picked through a basket of rice, sorting it with her fingers.

"It's fine." *It's the best I've ever had.* She would change into the silk tunic and pants after she and Mother prepared the wedding meal.

"Chinh's mother decided not to come for the wedding." Mother spread out her fingers and watched the rice flow back into the basket.

Lan nodded. Chinh had told her last night.

The People's Committee had granted Mrs. Vuong permission to move to Ho Chi Minh City. If Chinh weren't marrying Lan, Mrs. Vuong would attend her son's wedding.

His family didn't approve of Lan. Although Chinh wouldn't say that, he implied that they had wanted him to wait to marry until he saved some money. It wasn't just Mother who made them think she wasn't good enough for their son; it was Lan's lack of education, her poverty, her life with no future.

"Mr. Vuong still plans to send Chinh to America." Mother leaned closer toward Lan, whispering. She smiled, showing her blackened and missing teeth. "As his wife, his family will send you, too. Tell Chinh that I must go with you. You and I cannot be separated."

Lan stood, hung her ao dai back on the peg, took the comb from the shelf, and quickly pulled it through her hair as she turned toward the door. She couldn't imagine Mr. Vuong's paying her way to America, let alone Mother's. But maybe his heart would soften if Chinh insisted. Then she and her husband would work hard and send for Mother as soon as possible.

She knew several people who once worked in businesses around the market who had disappeared; it was rumored that they had escaped with their families to America. Their cell leader reported that Thai pirates raped the women and then murdered those who attempted to escape. The few who made it to land were kept in filthy camps and were never allowed to emigrate. Lan didn't believe the cell leader; she knew of those who received money from their extended families in America.

"Mr. Vuong and Chinh should be here by now." Mother dragged the basket over to the rice pot. "They'd better bring a pig to roast. The fire is ready."

Lan picked up the bag of ingredients to make salad rolls and took them to the low table in the yard. The coals in the open pit burned hot; Lan had started the fire in the middle of the night. Mother would cook the meat, and then the women from the market would come to celebrate.

Mother followed Lan into the yard and turned on the spigot to fill the pot. "Our luck has changed," she said as she turned off the water. "Associating with Mr. Vuong all those years has finally paid off. Chinh will take care of us." She walked to the edge of the yard and peered down the street. Mother was thin, and the outline of her shoulder blades showed beneath her blouse. She coughed as she squinted down the dirt road. Mother had been thirty-six when the war ended; now she was forty-eight. She needed someone to take care of her.

"Here they come!" Mother's face brightened.

"Don't be a fool," Mr. Vuong shouted above the roar of a motorbike on the road as they came into the yard. "Of course you must go alone—"

"Lan!" Chinh called out over his father's voice. They carried a pig on a pole between them.

Lan bowed her head. *Go alone.*

"Put it on the spit." Mother motioned toward the fire.

Lan glanced up and smiled at Chinh. Would he stand up to his father?

She turned her head away from her groom. It was no use. She and Mother didn't have the money to pay their way. Chinh didn't have the resources either. Mr. Vuong would pay for his son only; he had nothing to gain by sponsoring her and Mother. Their only hope was that Chinh would make it to America and then send for them.

Six hours later Chinh and Lan shared tiny cups of tea during the traditional ceremony while Mother and Mr. Vuong watched and the market women gossiped in the yard. The silk of the ao dai felt cool against Lan's skin. Her hair fell halfway down her back. Chinh's eyes searched her face. Lan glanced out the door to the women gossiping and then back at Chinh, and they smiled at each other. Lan saw the future in his eyes. *America. A home. Children. A strong man to help with Mother. Maybe even a garden someday.* She would enjoy every minute with her husband until he left and then hope that she, along with Mother, would soon have a future in America.

Three months later Mr. Vuong asked Chinh, Lan, and Mother to gather in his shop after closing. Mother was suspicious and clucked her tongue at Mr. Vuong.

"What is it?" Chinh asked.

"Come into the back room." Mr. Vuong spoke softly. "I have something to tell you."

They gathered around in a circle, squatting low to the ground. "I have good news," he said. "I've been given permission to live in Ho Chi Minh City." Lan concentrated on not smiling. She and Chinh could manage the shop together. A woman's touch would bring in more customers. They would be out from under Mr. Vuong.

Her father-in-law ran his hand through his greasy hair. "And that's not all!" He clapped his hands together. "Chinh is to emigrate. I've arranged for a boat. When he gets to the U.S., he will send for my wife and me."

Lan turned her head toward Chinh. He whispered, "I'll send for you, too." His eyes were earnest.

"I've been a fool," Mother said.

"Chinh will send for both of us," Lan said softly, taking her mother's hands. She searched Chinh's face; he nodded. Behind him Mr. Vuong shook his head.

The next day Mr. Vuong hired a van and loaded half of the merchandise from his shop, leaving the rest to give the appearance that the store would stay in business. He left for Ho Chi Minh City by late afternoon.

That night Lan and Chinh took their sleeping mats from Mother's shack to the back room of the shop. Lan bought the last catfish from the fish vendor and cooked dinner in the alley on Mr. Vuong's charcoal stove. After they ate, Chinh wrapped his arms around her and kissed her. Happiness filled her, for a moment.

"I want to go with you," she said. "I don't want to live without you."

He took Lan's hand. "I wish more than anything that I could take you with me, but I can't. I will send for you as soon as possible. I'm sorry I don't have the money to take you now, and I'm sorry I can't tell you more about when I'm leaving or where I'm going, but I don't want to bring trouble to you. We will stay here until I leave. One night when you come home from work, I won't be here. Take our things and go back to your mother."

Lan nodded.

"Take this too," Chinh said, pulling his small Bible from his bag of clothes. "I want you to have it."

Lan took the book from her husband and opened it. How long had it been since she had read? The ink seemed to swim on the pages. She closed the Bible.

"Lan, my wish for you is that you would learn to love Christ most in life, more than yourself, more than me, more than our future children. He is the One who will never leave you."

Chinh had told her stories from the Bible, stories about Moses and Jonah, about Jesus feeding the hungry, being nailed to the cross, and rising from the dead. Some of the stories she remembered from the nuns. Could she love God with all of her heart, mind, and soul? Could she love God more than she loved her husband? She wasn't sure what it meant to love that way. Maybe God would show her.

"Christ forgives our sins and shame," Chinh said.

Lan nodded. She understood. Notre Père. God, our Father, from the prayer she had recited for as long as she could remember. He forgave.

She prayed with Chinh. Peace moved in alongside her happiness, alongside the wedge of fear she had for a future without her husband, alongside her hope for a better life. They talked late into the night. Chinh said that he would pray for her every day. A cricket began to chirp in the alley, then a second one joined, and soon a choir serenaded them.

Two months later Lan came home to a locked store. Her husband was gone. She entered through the back room and gathered their things, pushing Chinh's Bible to the bottom of her bag. Night fell as she walked to Mother's. Clouds covered the full moon. Was Chinh crouched on the beach waiting for enough moonlight to run to a boat? Lightning flashed across the sky, followed by thunder. The rain fell in sheets, soaking her clothes. The wind wrestled the sleeping mats that she carried over her shoulder. She quickened her steps. Tears began to stream down her face. Happiness flew from her, through the dark sky, toward the sea. *Notre Père,* she prayed, *you've taken my happiness. Please leave my peace. Please take care of my husband.*

The next full moon was clear. The sky darkened, and the moon rose as Lan hurried home from selling fruit on the beach. She rushed into the yard and made it to the charcoal pit before she vomited. Mother came out of the shack and held Lan's hair back from her face. Lan had eaten nothing since the little bit of rice porridge that she'd had for breakfast.

"Hello!" It was Mr. Vuong's voice. Why wasn't he in the city?

Lan quickly wiped her mouth on the tail of her shirt.

"Are you sick?" He looked at the vomit and then at Lan. "Perhaps a baby is on the way."

"No, no," Mother said. "She must have eaten something bad." Loose strands of black hair fell around Mother's face.

Mr. Vuong's eyes narrowed. Lan moved by the door of the shack, away from him. What did he want?

"I came for the rest of my merchandise," he said. "My brother-in-law has found me a job in the garment district and an apartment for my wife and me." He turned to Lan. "If Chinh contacts you, tell him I am established in the city and then let me know. It may be a few months until he reaches America. I expect that he'll contact his uncle's house first, but he may try to reach you." Lan nodded. The nausea swept through her again. *Chinh is nothing like his father. He will send for me and Mother.* Mr. Vuong turned to leave.

"That's it?" Mother stared at him.

Mr. Vuong ran his hand through his hair.

"She's your daughter-in-law. You can't just walk away." Mother squinted in the darkness at Mr. Vuong. Her thin body shook.

He stretched out his arms and held his palms upward. "I have nothing to give her. I already gave her my son."

Mother raised her chin at him. "And then took him back."

Mr. Vuong chuckled and sneered at Lan. "That was his choice." He turned and walked into the darkness of the street.

Lan rose and vomited in the charcoal again. "There, there." Mother patted her back.

"It *is* a baby." Lan wiped her mouth again. She ached for her husband. She would work harder than she ever had to save money for the baby's birth and the months after. She would take care of Chinh's child, of her child.

"I know," Mother said.

"Should I have told Mr. Vuong?"

Mother shook her head. "He doesn't deserve to know. He wouldn't help us anyway."

Later that evening Mother sat on the sleeping mat and cried for the first time in thirteen years. Frightened, Lan sat down beside her.

"You're all I have," Mother said, her head in her hands. "All I have for my old age." Lan took her mother's hand and patted it. "Promise you'll take care of me."

"I will," Lan said.

"Even if Chinh sends for you?"

"I promise." *Chinh will send for me. He will let me take Mother, too.* She could never leave Mother behind.

Six months later Lan stood beside the boarded window of Mr. Vuong's shop. The hat woman's five-year-old daughter and a group of other little ones ran through the fruit stalls. They were the market kids, the poorest children in town, dressed in rags with dirty faces and protruding stomachs. They begged and stole what they could while their mothers sold their wares, snacks, and fruit. In the afternoons the younger children curled up close to where their mothers worked and slept. Lan shifted the weight of the pole over her shoulders. She'd only sold two bags of lychee nuts. Mother had stayed home, sick again.

The baby kicked inside her. She prayed that Chinh would send for her soon or her child would be of the market too. She had nothing more to offer him. *Him.* She could only hope. A son to take care of her in her old age, to take care of Chinh, too.

What if Older Brother hadn't joined the Viet Cong? What if he were here to take care of them now? Her face reddened. Would he believe that she was married? That her baby was legitimate? She shook her head. If he hadn't joined the Viet Cong, Older Brother would probably be dead now. Like Father.

Sometimes Mother would cry out Brother's name in the night. "Quan, help us."

Lan would reach and touch her mother. "Shh," she'd say. "It's all right."

She both wanted Older Brother to come and feared his coming. He might hear Mother's nighttime cries and search them out, only to judge. Or perhaps he'd hear her cries and come and save them.

"Be a boy," Lan whispered to the baby inside her belly. *Be a boy.*

In the night Lan woke to her first pain. Exhausted, she fell back asleep after it ended. Later she woke to another pain and to Mother's coughing. She rolled to her knees and waited until the pain stopped.

"Lan, what is it?" Mother sounded worried.

"I don't know." Were these the pains of childbirth?

She waited until dawn to tell Mother to ask the neighbor for a ride to the hospital on his scooter. "No, no," Mother said. "It's too early to go to the hospital."

Mother ran water into a pan and started the stove outside the hut. "I'm making tea and soup." She pulled the plastic poncho over her head against the morning rain. The day became a blur of pain. Just after the sun had set, Lan heard the neighbor's scooter return as she paced inside the shack. "Ask him to take me to the hospital."

"No," Mother said. "It will hurt just as badly in the hospital. And you never know how much they'll charge."

Did Mother think that they didn't have the money to pay a hospital bill? "I saved enough money for the birth," Lan said, her voice rising. She had worked hard to save the money stashed inside the tea tin behind the altar.

Mother folded her hands together.

"I owed money for medicine. The doctor wouldn't see me again unless I paid," she finally said. "Did you want me to die before I saw my first grandchild?"

Lan turned her back to Mother and buried her face in her hands. An hour later Mother hurried to the neighbor's to borrow a big plastic bowl to use as a basin. Lan curled up on the floor on her sleeping mat and thought about Chinh. Had he died in the South China Sea? Or had he made it to America? Would he send for her soon? And his child? And Mother? *Que ta volonté soit faite. Sur la terre comme au ciel.* She thought of the nuns. *Thy will be done; on earth as it is in heaven.* She thought of Older Sister when her baby girl was born. Lan had waited outside and listened to the screams.

"Notre Père," she cried in desperation. "Please help me."

The night hung heavy. Lan could see the full moon through the open boards of the shack until the clouds swallowed the heavenly body and the rain began to fall.

"It hurts!" Lan cried. Nothing felt right in the world.

"It's supposed to hurt," Mother said.

Too tired to move, Lan stayed on her side and pushed. She didn't care anymore if the baby was a boy or a girl. She just wanted it out of her. She thought of Older Brother. There were no guarantees that a son would take care of her. If it were a girl, Lan would never let her quit school.

The urge to push overwhelmed her again. "You're close," Mother said. "The baby's head is coming."

Lan rose and squatted on the mat. "It's midnight," Mother said, squinting at the wind-up clock.

"Can you see the moon?" Lan gasped.

Mother stood and peered out the window. "Yes."

The baby tore through Lan. She grabbed the child and pulled her close. God was with her. She had never known such power, such holiness, such peace, all twisted into her longing for Chinh.

"A girl," Mother said, not masking the disappointment in her voice. She lit more candles. Lan shivered violently as her daughter lay on her chest and peered at her with old, wise eyes. Mother covered them with two thin blankets, then spread trousers and shirts, and then the wedding ao dai over Lan and the baby.

"What will you name her?" Mother asked.

"Hang."

" 'Angel in the full moon'? Too fancy."

"No," Lan answered. "That's her name."

Mother wrapped her skinny arms around Lan and the baby, and all three slept until morning.

Merci, Notre Père, Lan prayed as the dawn crept into the shack. *Thank you, our Father, thank you for the baby.* She smelled the little one's head, ran her hand over her daughter's body, and cried for her husband.

*G*en stood on the brick walk leading to the white farmhouse and held Jeff's hand. She had met his parents and his little sister, Janet, briefly at the homecoming football game last fall, but this was the first time she had been to his house. Daffodils bloomed in the front flower beds, the porch circled three sides of the house, and two gables topped the second story.

They had come for Jeff's birthday dinner. Afterward Jeff would drive Gen back to Portland and then return to work in the orchard all weekend. His dad had injured his knee and needed more help.

The screen door slammed. "There you are!" Sharon Taylor, a thin middle-aged woman with short blond hair, wiped her hands on her apron. "I heard your car but didn't see you in the drive." She wore gray slacks and a red cardigan sweater under the apron. Gen glanced down quickly at her own Levi's and running shoes.

"Hi, Mom. I wanted to walk Genni up the front steps." Jeff led her up to the porch.

Jeff's mother took Gen's hand, squeezing it quickly. "I'm so pleased to see you again. I'm happy you could come for Jeff's birthday dinner." She turned to Jeff and hugged him hard. "We're happy to have you here too, stranger. It's been so long since you've been home."

They followed Sharon across the porch and into the living room. A stenciled border of birds stretched around the top of the room just under the crown molding. A plush blue couch, an oak coffee table, and a cranberry leather wing-backed chair created a sitting area in front of the brick fireplace. "I just need to check on the roast," Sharon said. "Dad will be in soon."

The glint of late afternoon light on the dining room window caught Gen's eye. She turned. An oak table in front of the window filled the room. She stepped closer with a startled gasp. The orchard, the foothills sloping upward toward the mountain, and Mount Hood in the background were spectacular, even more enchanting than the house.

"What's wrong?" Jeff came up to stand behind her, then he grinned, following her gaze.

"It caught me off guard." She laughed, glancing up at him. "I've never seen anything like it."

"Let's go up to the top of the knoll," Jeff said. "You can see both Mount Hood and Mount Adams from there."

Jeff held Gen's hand as they walked down the road lined by cherry trees. His dad drove by in a new Chevy pickup; Jeff waved. His dad stared off to the side at the trees. "He's like that." Jeff chuckled. "Focused."

He darted into the orchard. "Look at the buds." He gently pressed a twig between his thumb and forefinger and held it out for her to see. Delicate leaves unfolded. "Want to come back next month when the trees are in bloom?"

"That would be great." She felt another smile begin.

Jeff grabbed her hand and started to jog up the hill. Gen let go and passed him. He laughed and picked up his pace. They stopped at the top of the knoll; Mount Hood loomed ahead. Jeff placed his hands on Gen's shoulders and turned her around to look at Mount Adams. The two majestic white caps stood like guardian angels. She scanned the orchard below them and spotted a small cottage among the trees. "What's that?" she asked.

"The original house. It's still in good shape." He took her hand again and led her to a big oak tree. "My great-grandpa couldn't bear to cut this tree down, so he left it. I used to climb it as a kid." He paused. "Actually, I still do." He laughed.

Gen assessed the height of the bare-branched tree and grinned at him. "Show me."

Jeff grabbed the lowest branch and swung himself up. He deftly propelled his lean body from branch to branch. Perched on a thick limb, he wedged his back against the trunk and waved at her.

She laughed. "I'm coming up." She jumped to grab the lowest branch. On the third try she caught it and climbed onto the limb. Jeff met her lower in the tree, and they sat, straddling a branch. Jeff swung his legs back and forth. Gen hung on with both hands. "This is the first time I've ever climbed a tree." She looked out into the orchard instead of at the ground.

"You're doing great," Jeff said. He touched her hand. "I wanted to talk with you about something."

Up here?

"I had lunch with your dad." Jeff met her gaze, his expression intent. Gen's stomach felt queasy. She had never been afraid of heights...until now. She concentrated on Jeff's eyes even as his hand moved toward the pocket of his jeans jacket.

He pulled out a small velvet box.

Her stomach lurched, and her balance wobbled. She glanced at the ground and started to slide. "I have to get down from here."

Jeff slipped the box back into his pocket and swung to the ground first and then helped her down. "Are you okay?"

She leaned against the tree trunk, waiting for her knees to stop shaking. "Did Dad give his blessing?"

Jeff smiled. "He said he would be honored to have me for a son-in-law if you would be honored to have me as your husband." He reached into his pocket again.

Her heart was pounding, and she bit her bottom lip. "Could I talk to Dad first? When you take me back tonight?" She leaned toward him.

Jeff stopped smiling and returned the box to his pocket. The disappointment in his eyes stabbed her heart.

"Have I ruined everything? Your birthday? Being here with your mom and dad?" She felt sick to her stomach. She leaned back against the tree. She'd known for months that she would marry Jeff someday. Why couldn't she just say yes?

"No. It's okay," he said. "You should talk with your dad first." He took her hand. "Let's go see if dinner is done. Then I'll take you back to Portland."

Sharon shot Jeff a questioning glance during dinner. He lifted his eyebrows and smiled, tipping his head toward Gen. Jeff's father, Don, caught the exchange and winked at Gen. He was tall and lean like Jeff but nearly bald.

Janet hurried in from track practice halfway through dinner. Jeff stood and hugged her. Sharon talked about Jeff's brother, Jake, saying that he was studying Japanese and definitely planned to go on to law school.

Gen watched Jeff's family laugh and joke and exchange winks and smiles. They enjoyed simply being together. It was the kind of family that Gen had always wanted, the kind she had dreamed of for years, the kind her mother had tried to create by adopting Nhat.

Family. That was what life was all about: following God and family. She swallowed the sting in her throat, wondering why it was so hard to say yes to Jeff's proposal. Was she afraid to love? Afraid the love might disappear?

After cake, Jeff thanked his mother for the birthday dinner. "I'll be back late," he said. "Don't worry."

His dad handed him the keys to his new pickup. "We want Gen to be safe." He patted Jeff on the back. "We want her to come back, as part of our family."

❦

They listened to Dire Straits during the ninety-minute drive. Jeff hummed along to "Money for Nothing." When they reached her house, Gen asked Jeff to wait. "I just need to talk to Dad alone."

Her father wore his pajamas and navy robe and sat in the den watching the news. "Daddy, can we talk?" He patted the couch beside him. Gen, with her sweatshirt still on, sat down. "Jeff's out in his dad's pickup."

He frowned. "Well, ask him in."

"I want to talk with you first. He said that you two went out to lunch."

Her dad smiled and reached for Gen's left hand and then met her eyes with a puzzled expression.

"I haven't given him my answer," she said.

He stood and turned off the television. "I didn't think you would hesitate."

Gen sat crosswise, facing her father when he sat down again. "I wanted to talk with you first." The mantel clock ticked in rhythm with her heart. "Do you think I should get married?" She studied his lined face. Ill health and worries about her had aged him in the last few years. A wave of affection swept over her. He had gone to the doctor the week before because his blood pressure was high. She hoped the new medication would bring it down.

"If you think he's the right one, of course you should marry him." He paused. "But there's more to your question than just that, isn't there? You're not really asking my permission, are you?"

Gen reached out and touched her father's shoulder. "Will you be okay if I get married?"

He peered into her eyes. "You're worried about me?"

She let her gaze drift away from him. "Partly." But that wasn't all she was worried about. Had God really wanted her to go to Southeast Asia all those years ago? Is that what she should be preparing for now? She had said no because of her father. If she married Jeff, was she saying no to it forever?

"Genevieve," he said, "I want more than anything for you to be happy. That's what makes me happy. If you love Jeff, marry him." He gave her a gentle smile, reached for her hand, and patted it. "Stop worrying about me."

Maybe he didn't need her the way she had always thought, the way Aunt Marie insisted.

She had one more question. "What do you think Mom would say about Jeff?"

"I think your mother would adore him."

She couldn't stop smiling. "I think Jeff will make a good husband and a good father." She paused, watching his face. "That's what Mom used to say about you. That you were a good husband and father."

He stood. "I think she was talking about money. That I could provide for a family."

"I don't think so." Gen stood with him, took his hand, and squeezed it.

Gen opened the passenger door of the pickup, sat down on the bench seat, and looked at Jeff. "He wants me to be happy. He doesn't expect me to take care of him."

Jeff nodded. He knew that. "Are you okay then?" His smile was as wide as hers.

She nodded.

He took a deep breath. "Will you marry me?"

"Yes." He was what she wanted. She thought of the little house in the orchard, of Jeff caring for the trees, of Sharon and Don as grandparents. She wanted it all.

That night Gen sat on her bed, stretched out her fingers, and turned her diamond in the light. Jeff would graduate in three months and move back to the orchard. They would plan to marry in a year in her church in Portland with Janet and Jake as attendants. They would live in the little house in the orchard, and she would do her student teaching in The Dalles.

She took a deep breath and let it out slowly, saying a final good-bye to the refugee camp, to the motherless babies, to the hungry children, to her mom's friend Kim, to the girl she prayed for. Life was full of choices, of losses and gains. Gen held her hand open, palm up. She could make out the tiny reflection of her face in the shiny gold metal of her ring.

Where was the carving of the Vietnamese girl holding the doll? How long had it been since she had seen it? She searched her bedside table, then her dresser, then her closet. She couldn't find the carving anywhere. Why hadn't she taken better care of it? She put her hand up to her neck and fingered the jade cross. At least she still had her mother's necklace, but where was the little girl?

ou need to find another man." Mother sat hunched in front of the altar, her long hair, streaked with gray, falling out of the bun that she hadn't bothered to undo the night before.

Lan ran the comb through six-year-old Hang's hair, pulling out the nits and lice. Mother's argument was at least five years old. Hang held Chinh's Bible in her lap. She liked to look at the words even though she couldn't read.

"I'll pray about it," Lan said. Usually she said nothing to Mother's suggestions. Her stomach sank. Why had she said she would pray? It had been months since she had even recited the Lord's Prayer. For years she had believed that Chinh would send for her. She prayed every day. Over and over she imagined his joy when he found out about Hang. At first she thought of Chinh in a refugee camp—perhaps he was forced to stay for a year or two or even three. Then she imagined him immigrating to America. He would have to learn the language and get a job. As the years went by, it became harder to pray, and the peace that had sustained her slowly left. If this God cared about her, if he would never leave her, then why hadn't she heard from Chinh? Was he alive and in America? Or dead, drowned that first night at sea, or, worse, killed by pirates?

Lan tugged on the comb. "Ouch," her daughter squealed. Lan held her hand against Hang's head to ease the pull. She needed to hurry; she needed to sell as much fruit as possible today. Her frustration grew as she looked up at Mother.

The old woman coughed and then shook her head. "Don't bother to pray for a man. Do you think your God cares about such a little thing? It's not up to him; it's up to you. You're the one who must take care of your child. A mother does what a mother has to do."

Lan quickly divided Hang's hair and braided each half. "Put the book away," Lan said to Hang. "We need to get to work." She rose to her feet and pulled the comb through her own hair. In the years since Chinh left, several men had shown interest in her. The last one laughed when she told him she was married. "Ha," he had said. "Your man has a new woman in America. A new family. Why would he waste his money on a poor Vietnamese wife when he can have a rich American woman?"

Had she been a fool to dream that Chinh would send for her, that her life would get better?

"What's for breakfast?" Mother turned from the altar.

"Rice," Lan said. "It's in your dish on the table."

"Bring it to me," Mother said to Hang. The girl quickly obeyed.

Lan worked her own hair into a single braid. "I'll bring your medicine, Mother. Make sure to get some fresh air."

◈

Hang stood at the entrance to the market and rubbed her stomach with one hand; the other she extended with the palm turned upward. After all these years more tourists were coming back to Vung Tau. The Japanese woman turned to her husband. He shook his head.

"Little one," Lan called to Hang from the fruit stall. Sheepishly she walked away from the couple. If she held out her hand and the person put money in it, Lan did not call her back. Hang knew then to bow and smile. If the person seemed irritated, Lan quickly summoned Hang to her.

It had been a slow day. Lan still needed more money for Mother's medicine and for their dinner.

"When will I go to school?" Hang squatted beside Lan. The sun was straight overhead. Lan swatted at a mosquito on Hang's arm and then pushed her daughter's hair away from her face. *When would she go to school?*

"Maybe next year." Lan didn't have money for the uniform and books, for the paper and the pencils. Most of her money went to caring for Mother.

A horn honked. Mr. Doan smiled as he zipped around the corner on his scooter. He often bought fruit at the market. During the day he delivered goods on his motorbike—pineapples, chickens, eggs, kegs of beer, tools, bicycle parts, whatever needed to be moved from one place to another. He was lucky to have the scooter. Lan had seen him with a woman, she presumed his wife, in the market. Still he smiled at Lan every day, but she cast her eyes down and did not respond.

Some in Vietnam were doing better. The fall of the Soviet Union had caused the Vietnamese government to open up trade with other countries. More goods were being imported, including black market items from Cambodia and Thailand. More Vietnamese had been allowed to immigrate to the United States, which meant more people were sending money back to their relatives. It seemed everyone was better off than they had been five years ago—except for Lan, Mother, and Hang.

"I'm tired." Hang glanced up at her mother.

"There, there." Lan clucked her tongue as Hang curled up at Lan's feet and closed her eyes. Lan sold fruit from street to street during the morning and late afternoon, but during the early afternoon she watched the stand in the market for Mrs. Le. She pulled her hat over her eyes and relaxed against the plastic chair. It was her favorite time of the day. Her eyes grew heavy, and flies buzzed around her face. She heard a motorbike come around the corner and stop. She halfway wished the driver would visit another stall—the basket seller or the vegetable vendor or the noodle soup lady. Lan pushed her hat from her forehead and sat up straight, ready to smile. It was Mr. Doan.

"How are the grapes?"

"Try one." Lan reached forward, twisted a large purple grape off a stem, and handed it to him.

"Good," he said, after he'd swallowed it and spit out the seeds. "I need a big bunch for my children."

"How many do you have?" Lan pulled a plastic bag from the cardboard box beneath the table, stepping around Hang to reach it.

"Four that I know of." He smiled. She half expected him to wink.

He peered over the table at Hang. "Is she yours?"

Lan nodded.

"Who else is in your family?"

"Just the two of us and my mother."

"I thought so." He paid her for the grapes, smiled again, and then climbed onto his motorbike and sped away.

Lan settled back against the hot plastic as she watched Mr. Doan drive around the corner. She repositioned her hat over her brow. What did Mr. Doan want from her?

Lan heard the motorbike again. She peeked out from under the brim of her hat at Mr. Doan grinning as he sped by, headed in the opposite direction.

"He's trouble."

Lan turned to see Mrs. Le. "Do you know him?"

"He's married to my cousin's girl." Mrs. Le pulled out the cashbox from under the table and then counted the boxes of fruit on the table. "Tsk, tsk. You'd better get out there. You'd better find some buyers on the street. If they won't come to us, you'd better go to them, or the fruit will rot, and you'll go hungry tonight."

Lan stood to fill her baskets.

Mrs. Le stepped over Hang and sat in the chair. "Take the girl. I can't have her underfoot."

Lan walked down the dirt street to the shack, pulling Hang with one hand and supporting her yoke and baskets with the other. She walked slowly. Hang was too heavy for her to carry. It had been easier when Hang was a baby, safe in the sling against Lan's breast.

"Faster." Lan tugged on her daughter's hand. "Stay with Grandmother. Play with the neighbor children. I'll get money for dinner."

They entered the shack. Lan stood for a moment as her eyes adjusted. Mother crouched in front of the altar holding a joss stick. Smoke and incense filled the shack.

"It that you, Lan? Did you bring medicine?"

"I brought Hang. I'm going out to sell more. I hope to have money before the day is done."

"My cough is bad today, and my back and hands hurt."

"I'm doing the best I can."

"Ask the pharmacist for something stronger." Mother put the joss stick on the altar.

Annoyed, Lan took a step toward the door. "Get up and get some fresh air. Move around. That will make you feel better." *Older Brother should care for Mother. I shouldn't have to do it all alone. I should be able to use my money for Hang's school, for food, and for clothes.*

Lan walked out of the pharmacy. She had sold enough to buy medicine for Mother but not enough to buy food for dinner. She tucked the small bottles of medicine into her pouch and turned to walk home. Behind her a horn honked. She moved to the right. It honked again. She turned her head. Mr. Doan rode his motorbike on the sidewalk. He grinned. "Want a ride?"

She shook her head, remembering what Mrs. Le had said.

He reached into the plastic crate strapped to the back of his scooter. "I have some rice for you," he said, holding up a brown parcel. "And fish and vegetables."

Lan bowed her head.

"Come on," Mr. Doan beckoned.

She smelled the rain a split second before it started. The sky opened, and the torrent began. Mr. Doan pulled two clear plastic ponchos from his crate and flicked them open, one after the other. "Come on." He tossed the smaller one to Lan. "I'll get you home."

She hesitated. He smiled. *A rain slicker. Food for Mother and Hang. A ride home.* Was that what she was worth? Exhaustion and hunger welled up inside of her, spilled over into her muscles, flooded her stomach, seeped into her shaky bones. The rain cascaded over her hat and onto her shirt and pants, pressing them against her skin. Already she stood in a puddle of water.

She slid her yoke over her shoulders and lowered her baskets to the ground. She held out her hand for the poncho, pulled it over her head, and climbed onto the back of Mr. Doan's motorbike. As he drove through the streets of Vung Tau, she balanced her baskets across her shoulders.

$\mathcal{G}$en stirred as Jeff rolled away from her and then sat on the edge of the bed. The air conditioner in the window whirled in the hot night but brought little relief. "What is it?" Gen asked, stretching her arm to touch his back.

"Someone's at the door."

Gen squinted at the clock—2:30 a.m. Harvest had started two days before. Exhausted, she fell back on the pillow. She patted her stomach. It was still flat. She was only nine weeks along. For five years they had tried to start a family. Finally she was pregnant.

"Genni." Jeff's voice tugged at her, pulled her out of sleep again. "José's here. Marta is in labor, and they're worried because the baby is coming fast. I'm going to drive them to the hospital. Could you follow me? Do you feel up to that?"

She kicked a bare leg out from under the sheet. "Marta's going to have her baby?" Plump Marta with her round belly and gaggle of four daughters, who followed her everywhere. "She's early."

"At least two months early. That's why José wants me to go along."

She planted her feet on the worn, cool boards of the floor. *A baby.* She patted her own flat stomach again. They were waiting to share their good news, waiting until harvest was over, until she had reached the second trimester. All these years of trying had made them hesitant to share their news too soon. *Trying.* It felt like playing the lottery. She'd gone through tests, endometriosis, and surgery; she had found out that one tube was permanently blocked. She'd taken rounds of fertility drugs. Now, finally, a baby grew inside her.

Gen pulled on shorts, slipped on her bra, and wrestled a T-shirt over her head. She sat on the side of the bed and worked her feet into her sandals.

The gears of the old pickup ground as she shifted and turned onto the highway. At the hospital, after Jeff talked with the emergency-room doctor, Gen sat beside him in the waiting room. "I just want to make sure everything is okay before we leave," he said. Gen curled up in the chair. José and his crew had helped with harvest for over a decade, and she knew Jeff would do anything he could for José and his family. She shivered in the air-conditioned room and reached for Jeff's arm, hoping to draw some warmth from it.

When she awoke, a flannel sheet covered her, and José stood in front of them talking. "It's another girl." He grinned. "They say the baby is fine. Even her lungs are healthy. But she's small. Only four pounds." Jeff stood and shook José's hand.

Gen sat up straight. Jeff handed José the key to the old pickup. "Stay here as long as you need to."

"I'll be out this morning."

"No, no," Jeff said. "Take today off. We don't need you today."

"I'll be there." José tossed the key to his other hand. "And, boss, thank you."

Jeff smiled and nodded.

Gen slept during the drive back to the orchard. "You okay?" Jeff asked as he parked the pickup.

"Just tired." The first light of morning tiptoed over the knoll. Pickers holding plastic buckets crowded around the yard and waited for their assignments.

"Go back to bed. Sleep for a few more hours. I'll let you know when the truck is ready to drive to the plant." Gen nodded and squeezed his hand, too tired to talk.

She drove the truck for the next two weeks and napped in the cab with the air conditioning on whenever she could.

Late one afternoon she stretched out under the willow tree on Sharon and Don's lawn. The heat of the day had forced the pickers out of the orchard. The fruit was too delicate to risk bruising in the one-hundred-degree weather.

Sharon came out the back door and sat beside her. Marta started toward them and called out, *"Buenos días."*

"She says hello," her six-year-old daughter translated. Gen nodded with a smile. Marta held the baby out to Gen. She stood and took the little one in her arms, noted the flutter of her eyelids and the slightly pursed lips. She held the tiny, tiny baby against her breast, squeezing slightly. Tears filled her eyes.

Sharon stood. "Are you okay?"

Gen smiled and blinked quickly. Jake had a girlfriend but no plans to marry. Janet had married three months before and was getting her master's in education in Texas. She had said adamantly that it would be years before they started a family. Gen knew she and Jeff were Sharon's only hope for a grandbaby anytime soon. Her mother-in-law patted her back in sympathy. Gen nearly told her the good news. This time her tears were not from sadness.

The bleeding started that evening. A month before, Gen had had some spotting but not enough to be abnormal, according to the doctor. But this was bleeding. "Put your feet up, and call us if you start to cramp," was the answer from the gynecologist on call. At 4:00 a.m. she gasped at the sharp pain in her side. She woke Jeff, and he called the doctor.

At 10:00 a.m. the ultrasound technician ran a wand over Gen's lower abdomen, sliding it through the sticky jelly. Jeff stood beside Gen and held her hand. They both stared at the screen as the faint image of the fetus appeared through a fuzzy forest of gray shapes.

"Is that our baby?" Gen whispered, overcome with relief. An hour earlier the doctor explained that the baby might have implanted in a "horn" of the uterus, a sectioned off area, or it could be an ectopic pregnancy or severe pain due to Gen's endometriosis.

"My guess is that you're further along than nine weeks," the technician said. "More like fourteen weeks." Jeff squeezed Gen's hand. The technician repositioned the wand, and the image grew clearer. The baby began to move, pushing out with arms and legs.

"We need to do a laparoscopy," the doctor said that afternoon, "and possible surgery."

The tears started. Gen had been determined not to cry, not to jump to the worst-case scenario. "Surgery? But the baby seemed so active during the ultrasound."

"We won't know for sure until we send in a camera. I'm scheduling the procedure for seven o'clock tomorrow morning."

"What do you think is going on?" Jeff scooted his chair closer to Gen's and reached for her hand.

"There's no way to know until we take a look."

"Will it hurt the baby?" Gen swiped tears from under her eyes with her free hand.

"If the fetus is in a horn of the uterus, everything should be fine. You may need a C-section when the time comes. If it's an ectopic pregnancy, we'll try to save the fallopian tube, but there are no guarantees. There's no way to save the fetus if it's in the tube." The doctor paused and glanced from Gen to Jeff. "We'll know by tomorrow morning."

That evening Gen put the ultrasound photo on the refrigerator while Jeff talked with José in the yard. Jeff would miss another day of harvest. *We'd better tell Dad. And Jeff's parents.* She was well into the second trimester after all. Better to let them know why she was going into the hospital tomorrow than try to explain it later.

Gen opened her eyes; a mauve blanket covered her. She turned her head. Jeff sat with his head bowed. Was he praying?

"Hi," Gen whispered. He looked at her with red eyes. "Tell me," she said.

"We lost the baby—and the tube."

Lost the baby. She closed her eyes. She wanted to float, to float away to somewhere safe, with her baby, with that little baby who would never race to the top of the knoll, never climb the oak tree, never learn to read.

"Genni, it was a boy," Jeff said. "I asked the doctor."

Hot tears rolled from her eyes. Jeff put his head against hers. The little boy baby floated on without her, away from the river, over the town, toward their little house, above the knoll, beyond the orchard, toward Mount Hood. *I couldn't keep you safe. I couldn't keep you with me. Know that I love you,* she silently called after him. Would her baby, her little boy baby, be with her mother? Was she waiting for him? Waiting for Gen to let go?

She reached and touched Jeff's curls, wound her fingers through them, held on. In her mind, clouds floated by, turned dark, began to rain. She didn't ever want to let go, but he was already gone. A naked boy baby floating in the clouds, floating away to be with God. She sobbed and sobbed, and Jeff, with his face pressed against hers, mixed his tears with hers, and together they soaked the pillow.

"All I wanted was to be a mother and for you to be a father."

"I know, Genni," he said. "I know."

A week later Gen watched the doctor leaf through her chart. "You can try in vitro." He glanced at Gen and then at Jeff.

"We'll have to think about it." Gen took a deep breath after she said the words. She'd eyed a credit card application that came in the mail just yesterday with a ten-thousand-dollar limit. She had thrown it in the garbage.

The doctor stood. "Think about it. I can refer you to a specialist in Portland."

"What do you want to do?" Jeff asked as he pulled his pickup out of the doctor's parking lot.

"Let's talk about it later, okay?"

They rode in silence for several minutes. The late morning sun bounced off the hood of the truck.

"I talked to your dad last night after you were asleep. He wants to come out soon. He's worried about you. Aunt Marie sends her love too." Jeff accelerated up the hill, leaving the city limits behind. Soon dust rose from the gravel road as they drove up the lane. He slowed as they approached his parents' house. A new white BMW sat in the driveway.

"Looks like your brother's here," Gen said. Jake would stay a few days. Janet and her husband were flying in tomorrow and staying a week.

Jeff stared at the Beemer. "Must be nice for Jake to have all that extra cash, huh?" Jake had graduated from law school two years earlier and worked for an international firm in Portland.

"We should go in and say hello," Gen said, though it was the last thing she wanted to do.

"You don't need to, not if you don't want to." Jeff stopped the pickup in front of his parents' house.

She closed her eyes against her pain. "Thanks," she said. "I'll come back this evening. Maybe I'll feel better then."

"I need to get back to work."

"I know." She wanted to be alone. She would ask her dad to wait a few more days until he came out—and not to bring Aunt Marie. Her aunt had called two days ago to say she had heard about Gen's "little problem." Gen couldn't handle the thought of a face-to-face conversation with Aunt Marie right now.

"I'll take you home first." Jeff smiled at her.

Gen shook her head. "I'll walk. I need the fresh air." She climbed out of the pickup and started toward their house, slowing after the first few steps. She'd had a migraine the day before. Hormones and stress, the doctor had said.

Another few steps and Gen saw Marta standing in the yard with her girls. *"Señora,"* she called. Gen waved. She didn't want to talk to anyone. She didn't want to hold Marta's baby. A week ago it had been heavenly. Today it would be unbearable. For years infants had disarmed her. By the time the baby was six months, it was its own person, who it was meant to be, and it wasn't meant to be Gen's. But as an infant, it felt like any baby could be Gen's baby. She felt a twinge of guilt for her desire as Marta and her girls stopped in front of her.

Marta chatted away. "She says she's sorry," the oldest girl translated. "About your baby. She'll light a candle in church and pray that you will be the mother of many." Then Marta handed the baby to her daughter and hugged Gen tightly. Gen breathed in the sourness of the baby's spitup on Marta's shoulder mixed with the sweet smell of sweat and love and grief, and she began to cry.

*H*ang quickly loaded bananas into the two baskets. Pain shot through Lan's lower back as she stood. She straightened the rest of the way slowly and then adjusted her hat. Dust covered her shirt and pants.

"Go to school now," she said to Hang. "Study hard." *Study hard.* She said it every morning. *Study hard so you won't have to sell fruit on the street. Study hard so you can take care of me when I'm old like Mother.*

Lan hoisted the yoke that held the two baskets onto her shoulders. Her belly pushed against the elastic of her pants. Pain shot up her back again, this time from the weight of her load. She wondered how this baby grew on such a little bit of rice. Hang stood on her tiptoes and kissed Lan's cheek, brushing against her belly. She was eight now. She didn't seem to know there would soon be a baby. Of course, Mother knew, but she hadn't said a thing. Lan had her answer rehearsed. She would say, *I understand now what a mother does for her child.*

Hang started off to school. *Study hard.* For what? What kind of job would she get someday? No matter how hard she studied, she would never go to university. No matter how hard she studied, she'd never get a government job. Or a job with an oil company. Or a job as a businesswoman. Maybe she could work cutting hair or in a factory. Lan could only hope.

She headed toward the beach to sell the bananas. Her back and feet hurt. One of her molars ached; in another decade she would have a grin like Mother's. It was Friday, and tourists from the city should be arriving. The baby kicked inside her. One of the young women in the market had taken her little girl to the orphanage the year before, and a family in America had adopted the baby. Lan thought of her own niece, of Chi, who would be a woman now. Perhaps she'd graduated from university in the United States.

Would Older Brother give Hang a job someday? Lan shook her head—

it was pointless to think about Older Brother. They hadn't heard from Quan since all those years ago when she had been in the hospital. In the two decades since the war, they had never heard from Older Sister. Did she make it to Saigon? to America?

Lan barely made enough money to feed Hang and Mother. What would she do with this baby? The money from Mr. Doan sent Hang to school, but she had no romantic ideas about Mr. Doan acting as a father to Hang or this baby. He had a wife and children of his own.

Lan thought ahead to dinner. They had enough charcoal for the stove and a handful of rice; perhaps she could get a fish at a good price at the end of the day. She never enjoyed a meal. If they had enough to eat, she worried about how she would pay for the next meal. If they didn't have enough to eat, she gave her portion to Hang and Mother. She stumbled going down the sand embankment to the beach, catching herself before she fell forward, the baskets swinging against her hips. *Girl or boy?* It was a wild one, that was certain. If the baby was a girl, she'd take her to the orphanage. If it was a boy? She would wait and see.

Lan pulled the money from her pouch and counted out seventy-five percent from the sale of the bananas to Mrs. Le. "I need to talk to you, Lan," the old woman said, tucking the money into her shirt. She nodded at Lan's belly. "My niece is humiliated. She says everyone knows your baby belongs to her husband." Lan bowed her head. "My business is owned by my entire family. I can't have you work for me anymore."

Lan glanced up into Mrs. Le's face.

"I know, I know," Mrs. Le said. "You've worked for me since you were a child, but I must do what's best for my family. I have a friend in the fishing village, Mrs. Hien. She needs another girl. Go talk to her."

Lan's stomach roiled at the smell of rotting fish. She sat under the blue tarp that trapped the afternoon heat; rows and rows of screens layered with fish covered the sidewalks for blocks. A dog urinated a few feet away from Lan. Mrs. Hien said that the fish would be turned into pet food, but Lan wondered.

She needed to find a different job. The walk was long and exhausting and too far to check on Hang and Mother during the day. Lan missed the women in the market. Working in a rice field or tending a shrimp pond would be better than turning smelly fish. She thought of Hang and then thought of the baby. She didn't want a daughter to have to scramble this way to feed a family. She imagined a daughter growing up in America, going to school, well dressed and well fed.

The early light of day crept into the yard. Lan dried her face on the tails of her shirt, lifting it over her belly.

"When will the baby come?" Mother stood in the doorway.

"A month…or so."

"What do you plan to do with it? Take it to the orphanage?" Mother walked slowly to the stove and then bent to light the charcoal.

"I'll wait and see if it's a boy or a girl," Lan said.

"So you would take a daughter to the orphanage but not a son?" Mother scowled at Lan, squinting against the rising sun.

"This sort of life with no future for one daughter is enough. I couldn't bear it for two."

Lan woke Hang and braided her hair. "Be a good girl," she said. "Study hard." *Study hard because I don't know if next year I'll have enough money to send you to school.* She hadn't seen Mr. Doan in two weeks, not since she'd left the market. She made less money drying fish than she had selling fruit.

The pains started as she walked from the fishing village toward home. She had to stop every few minutes in the fading light. She began to fear that she would deliver the baby alongside the road. "Please help me," she called out to a woman, a stranger, on a scooter. "I'm to have my baby very soon."

The woman stopped, and Lan climbed on the scooter and shifted her weight backward on the seat, aware of the strong smell of fish on her clothes. She directed the woman to the shack. "Thank you, thank you," she panted as she climbed from the scooter. Hang played in the dirt with a neighbor girl. "Don't come into the shack," Lan called out, trying to relax her face. "I need to talk to Mother."

She stopped in the middle of the yard to let a pain pass. The baby pushed against her, determined to escape. "Mother!" she called out. "Help me."

Mother stood in the doorway. "So soon? Isn't it early?"

Lan nodded. "I think so. But it's coming. Now."

"Take this one to the orphanage, Lan." Mother took her arm and led her to the sleeping mat. "You can't support another child. Promise me you'll take it to the orphanage."

"Mother, hush. The baby is coming."

"Mama?" Hang stood at the door.

"Go away," Mother called out.

"Mama, are you okay?" Hang asked.

"Go play," Lan said. "Come back in an hour."

Hang turned and left the doorway. Lan staggered out of her trousers and felt for the baby. "The head is coming."

The baby flew into Lan's hands in a flood of water before Mother could help. Lan knelt and took in her son, gazed into his dark, frightened eyes, ran her hands over his tiny, skinny body. He began to cry. She held him to her chest and felt the wet fluid and blood soak through her shirt to her skin.

Hang curled up beside Lan and patted the baby's head. "A brother," she said. "I've always wanted a brother."

"He's going to the orphanage," Mother said.

"Why?" Hang frowned at her grandmother.

"We can't afford to keep him."

"Shh," Lan said to Mother and patted Hang's head. "Don't talk about that now." The baby slept. Lan held him against her breast. She would work hard; she would wait and see; she would do everything in her power to keep him, to keep her son, Binh, as long as she could.

*A*re you against adopting?" Gen rose from the table, leaving half a muffin on her plate. Were they at an impasse? They planned to attend an information meeting on domestic adoption that evening even though they hadn't decided for sure what to do.

"No, I'm for adoption." Jeff folded the sports page.

"What is it then exactly?" Gen wore running pants and a windbreaker. She planned to go for a quick run before getting ready for school.

"I want to be sure of what God wants us to do, without a doubt." They'd had this conversation several times. *Without a doubt.* It was so unlike Jeff. He usually made decisions quickly. She was the one to hold back, to want to wait. This time she just wanted to do something.

"Is it the biological thing?" She took a glass from the cupboard and filled it with water.

"Wouldn't you like to have our own baby?" Jeff brushed crumbs from the tabletop into his hand and then onto his empty plate.

She nodded. "But adoption seems like a surer option. It's our only chance to be parents for sure."

"We should keep praying about it," Jeff said.

Gen took a drink of water and dumped the rest into the sink.

"I'd better get going. We're pruning today." He stood and gave her a quick kiss. "I'll pick you up after school."

"See you then." She headed down the hall to their room and tore the last page out of her journal, folding it into fourths and then shoving it into her pocket. She still had time for a quick run through the orchard before heading into town to prepare for a day of teaching twenty-nine third graders, all antsy for Halloween.

When Gen and Jeff first married, she loved the symmetry of the trees—

the rows, the life, the yearly cycle. After they lost the baby, she hated the orchard. For months she didn't run through it, didn't marvel at the spring blossoms and summer fruit. Now, over a year later, she had come to peace with the life-bearing trees. She breathed in the cold, cold air, held it tight, then blew it out, and watched the vapor disappear into the darkness. The acrid hint of wood smoke from Don and Sharon's chimney spiced the air. Her favorite time in the orchard was fall. Orange and red leaves crowned the trees, filled the crisp autumn days with color. She knew the beauty was fleeting, that it would soon give way to the damp, dull fog of winter.

After the tubal pregnancy, they decided to wait a year until they made a decision. Should they try in vitro? Should they adopt? They'd gone to the specialist in Portland, then to a support group for infertile couples. "I don't ever want us to be like that," Jeff had said when they drove away from the meeting. Gen agreed. Some of the couples, at least the women, seemed overly obsessed with getting pregnant. And it had taken a toll on some of the marriages. One couple confessed they were near divorce. "I'll keep trying to get pregnant even if our marriage fails," the wife had said. After the meeting, Gen and Jeff began talking about adoption.

She struggled to pull out the piece of paper from the pocket of her jacket. She had jotted down two lists in her journal last night. Clumsily she shook open the paper.

She'd scrawled "reasons to adopt" and "reasons not to adopt" across the top. Under "reasons to adopt" she had written:

> 1. *We've always wanted to be parents.*
> 2. *There's a child out there who needs a home, who needs us.*

Under "reasons not to adopt" she had written:

> 1. *Money.*
> 2. *Small house—would social worker approve us?*
> 3. *Risks—drug affected? Birth mom might change mind.*

Having enough love for an adopted child had never been a concern for Gen. She knew from loving her students that she could love a child who hadn't been born to her.

The biggest drawback to in vitro was the money, the physical and emotional pain, and the low rate of success. The benefit was that the child would be their own biological baby. She hadn't written the in vitro pros and cons down. They were cemented in her head. She knew Jeff wanted a biological child for them. So did his mother.

When they had brought up the idea of adopting, Sharon said, "But what if the baby doesn't look like either of you?"

"Oh well," Gen had responded flippantly.

"It wouldn't matter," Jeff had said respectfully.

Immediately Sharon had added, "Don't get me wrong! I think adopting is a wonderful idea." Gen knew having a baby that resembled them did matter to Jeff and to his mother. She also knew that Sharon was growing more desperate for a grandbaby. Jake had broken up with his latest girlfriend, and Janet had declared last Christmas that she wouldn't think of becoming a mother for at least another decade.

She folded the paper, put it back into her pocket, and began to run. Light shimmered down through the nearly bare branches of the trees. She jogged up the knoll and stopped to stare at the sheets of granite exposed on Mount Hood; only the glacier showed white against the baby blue sky. She turned toward Mount Adams. *God,* she prayed, *show us what to do.* She took a deep breath of frosty air and exhaled slowly. She wondered how important it was to her father to have a grandchild who favored Jeff or her.

She'd forgotten a hat. Her ears burned from the cold. "That's not fair," was the cry she despised the most at school. She explained over and over to her students that life wasn't fair, that making the best of what one had was most important. But, in truth, she felt the words "that's not fair" deeply. The death of her mother. The infertility. Their baby who died.

Gen headed back to their little house. When they moved into the cottage, Gen had imagined the bassinet beside their bed. They could easily convert the mud porch into a bedroom for the baby later. She was sure Jeff's parents would have moved into their rental house in The Dalles by now and turned over the larger house to Jeff and Gen if they'd had a baby.

Conflict with Jeff made her anxious. He was the one person she depended on, counted on. She was used to him agreeing to do what she wanted. Until now. Why was he holding back? *Does he really want to try in vitro? At what cost?* She jogged out to the road and back toward their house and then across the corner of her garden where pumpkins still clung to the vines. A row of dried corn stalks stood guard over the squash. *All I want is a baby, God. All these years that's what I've wanted.*

Jeff had been playing his guitar again, and last night, while she read in the bedroom, she heard the chords to "You Can't Always Get What You Want." The last song he played before coming to bed was "I Want to Hold Your Hand."

We'll go to the meeting. See what the adoption people have to say. Maybe it's not as risky as Jeff fears. She headed into the house to shower before leaving for work.

Jeff picked her up at school. She dozed on the way into Portland, and when she woke, gray clouds filled the sky as the day turned to dusk. They stopped in Troutdale for dinner and then drove the rest of the way into inner Northeast to the Boys and Girls Club of Portland. Gen hurried down the hall, Jeff a step behind her. She glanced at her watch as they entered the room. They were nearly ten minutes early, but the room was full. All the other wannabe parents at the adoption meeting appeared to be professionals, city professionals, and older than Gen and Jeff. A few wore suits—accountants, engineers, and lawyers, she was sure—and had obviously just rushed in from work.

They presented themselves as sophisticated and prepared, as if their four-bedroom, three-bath, two-car-garage homes on the west side of town were more than ready for a baby. Gen pictured them as just the kind of couples young women would choose to adopt their newborns. Jeff and Gen found two vacant seats at the front of the room.

The social worker started the meeting right on time. After outlining the adoption process, she asked if anyone had any questions. One of the men wearing a suit asked how often the birth moms changed their minds.

"It does happen," the social worker said. "I don't have any statistics on how often, but I've been involved in cases where the adoption isn't completed."

A woman asked how many of the babies tested positive for drugs.

"That happens too," the social worker answered. "Again I don't have statistics."

Jeff asked about the cost.

"It varies widely, depending on the birth mother's physical, emotional, and medical needs, plus loss of income, the lawyer's fees, the baby's needs, and travel expenses."

"What if the birth mother changes her mind?" Jeff clasped his hands as he spoke. "Is the money refundable?"

"That would be a question for your lawyer." The social worker took a stack of papers from her briefcase and passed out sheets listing attorneys who specialized in adoption and organizations that facilitated adoptions. She suggested those interested in adopting domestically put advertisements in newspapers to catch the attention of women looking to place their children. Finally she scanned the room. "Any more questions?"

Gen glanced at Jeff; he studied the piece of paper.

As they drove along the Columbia River on the way home, a torrential rain kept Jeff focused on the freeway. Gen thought of the mud forming in the orchard, of the snow falling on Mount Hood.

She balanced the packet of adoption papers on her knees. Out the window Multnomah Falls, lit up in the darkness by spotlights, crashed through the rocks. The ribbon of white water sped down the cliff. She caught a glimpse of the bridge across the waterfall. It was gone in an instant.

She turned to Jeff. "What do you think?"

"I don't know if we could handle a drug baby, not for our first."

Gen shifted her weight on the seat. Could she handle a birth mom changing her mind? *No, that would be worse than the infertility, as bad as the tubal pregnancy, probably worse.*

"I want a baby. Believe me, Genni, I do," Jeff said. "But I still don't know what we should do." He gazed intently into the rainy night. "What about in vitro?"

Gen thought about frozen embryos being stored in Portland for years and years. "I feel more certain about adoption." She stared through the window into the dark forest. She would pour herself into teaching. Maybe they could go to Hawaii for a vacation. There had to be more to life than desperately wanting a baby.

"What about international adoption?" Jeff kept his eyes on the road. "It seems less risky than domestic adoption."

"There are lots of children *here* who need a home." She concentrated on the silhouettes of the trees. Why not international adoption? *Mom... Nhat...Mom's friend Kim...the Vietnamese girl I used to pray for.* Maybe Vietnam was what was wrong with international adoption.

Jeff wanted to try in vitro. She wanted to adopt domestically. The adoption packet fell from her knees to the floor of the pickup.

Jeff glanced over at her. The rain eased. "Let's pray about it," he said. "Is that okay?"

She nodded and put her left hand on his shoulder.

"Lord," he prayed softly, simply, "please show us what to do."

Chapter 16

*H*ang stopped in front of the church. "We must hurry," Lan said. "Let me peek inside." Hang ran up the stairs, and Lan followed. A group of boys dressed in white robes held candles and followed a priest down the aisle. Lan and Hang stepped inside. The church was nearly full, with men on one side and women on the other. The smell of incense thickened the already humid air. A statue of an Asian Mary, unlike the French Madonnas Lan remembered from her childhood, stood beside the altar.

The priest began to pray in Vietnamese: "Our Father who art in heaven, hallowed be thy name."

"Mama, it's your prayer," Hang whispered over the priest's words.

"Give us this day our daily bread. Forgive us our trespasses—"

"We must go," Lan said. "Cuong will give us a ride if we hurry."

They ran down the stairs. "Did my father go to a church like this?" Hang asked.

"No," Lan answered. "He went to an underground church. The government approves this big church. His wasn't approved."

"Why not?" Hang asked.

"I don't know." Lan felt impatient. "Some are, some aren't."

Cuong sped around the corner on his new motorcycle. Sunlight sparkled on the red tank. He slowed to a stop and pulled a cigarette from his pocket as Lan and Hang climbed on behind him. As they accelerated, the smell of smoke, the odor of sewage, and the exhaust from the traffic fell away, coming only in quick whiffs instead of oppressive layers.

Lan had met Cuong in the fishing village when Binh was an infant. The baby was a month old and hungry all the time, and she had decided to take him to the orphanage, but Cuong talked her out of it. "Things are getting better in Vietnam," he had said. "Don't send the little one away. He'll help

Hang take care of you when you are old." He gave her formula for Binh and took her to the pagoda to beg for money.

Cuong traded on the black market—cigarettes, beer, whiskey, and Cuban cigars. After Lan had known him a few months, he gave her merchandise to sell, and soon she left the fishing village. Some days she sold hats and T-shirts for one dollar American and sets of fake jade Buddhas for three dollars American.

Hang and Binh called Cuong "Uncle," and he was nice to them, although he had little patience with Binh's busyness. Lan wondered if, in time, he might beat the boy. She often saw him with other women, all younger. Still he gave her extra money, and the work he provided earned far more than turning fish.

Cuong wove through the traffic toward the Giant Jesus statue on the hill. The tourists were mostly weekenders from Ho Chi Minh City and other parts of the country, but travelers from China, Japan, Australia, New Zealand, France, and even America came too. She'd seen middle-aged American men, probably soldiers from the war. Some had built an orphanage on the outskirts of the town. She'd also seen American couples with Vietnamese babies. "Baby so lucky," she would say in English and think of Binh, who was now three. He would be better off if she had taken him to the orphanage; he would be in America now with plenty of food. Mother insisted over and over that Lan was stubborn and selfish to keep Binh. Lan laughed when Mother called her selfish; stubborn she could accept, but not selfish.

Binh was a wild one, just as he had been while he was inside her. She worried about his being home with Mother during the day. Would Mother doze? Would Binh run off?

Cuong leaned his bike around a corner, and Hang tightened her grip around Lan's waist. Lan patted her daughter's hand. Hang could hardly control Binh either. She was back in school now, one year behind the other children her age. She needed a new uniform shirt, and Lan hoped to have the money by next week. Every day she worked hard; from sunup to sundown she scurried to earn a living, to buy food, to buy medicine for Mother. Every night she collapsed, exhausted, her children curled against her on the sleeping mat.

"Some friends and I are getting together tonight. We're going to have a few beers. Want to join us?" Cuong glanced over his shoulder at Lan.

"Maybe." Lan looked ahead at the water buffalo in the road. Cuong swerved around it at the last minute.

"I'll be back in two hours." Cuong pulled into the parking lot and idled the bike. Lan and Hang climbed off and stared across the street at the Giant Jesus looming above them. Lan spotted a group of Americans, she assumed, starting up the steps. It was a long hike to the top.

"They've come to adopt babies," a T-shirt vendor said. "That's their van." He nodded at a blue vehicle with curtains on the windows.

"Where are the babies?" Lan reached for Hang's hand.

"At the orphanage. They'll get them tomorrow. They don't want to bring the babies here. It's too hot. They'll buy from you when they come back," the vendor said. "Relax. You'll have a good sale." He climbed onto his scooter and pulled out onto the road. Lan sat on the curb and watched the people grow smaller and smaller as they climbed closer to Jesus. They returned an hour later, red faced and sweaty, even the women. None of them bought from Lan when they came back to the van. Instead, they climbed in and pulled the curtains across the windows so Lan and Hang couldn't peek inside.

Cuong idled his motorbike in the yard while Lan and Hang entered the shack. Binh sat on the sleeping mat, and Mother squatted beside him with a bowl of rice. "Binh was naughty again today. He walked to the market while I napped." Mother shoved the spoon into Binh's mouth and then looked up at Lan. "And that's not all. An official from the department of industry came by today. He said a manufacturing plant is going to be built…here."

Lan glanced from Mother to Binh and then around the shack to the altar with Father's proud military face and Second Brother's smile, the same smile that now lit up Binh's face. Older Brother helped the people of Vietnam but not her and Mother. Dead or alive, Chinh was gone from her forever.

"I forgot something," she said to Mother. Her legs carried her toward the door. It was as if she couldn't stop herself, as if her body belonged to someone else. She couldn't stay in the shack another minute. "I'll be back after a while."

Binh cried out, "Mama!"

Hang reached out her hand. "Don't go."

Lan hurried toward the sound of the motorbike, toward Cuong. She would not think about Binh running off, about the coming factory, about the need for a new home. It had been so long since she'd had any fun.

Part 2

December 1999–May 2001

There are three things that are never satisfied,
Four never say, "Enough!":
The grave,
The barren womb,
The earth that is not satisfied with water;
And the fire never says, "Enough!"

PROVERBS 30:15–16

A child's voice drifted from the balcony of the condo next to theirs. Gen shook her head. "What's up?" Jeff asked.

She smiled, just a little. "It's nothing." She had hoped that six days on Maui would be a distraction from the baby aisle at the grocery store, invitations to baby showers, and seeing babies everywhere she turned. She and Jeff could be a couple and think about each other, not about their baby impasse. But in a second, the sweet voice of a child brought it all back, and Gen stepped onto their balcony to see if she could spot the little one. A tiny Asian girl pointed out to the ocean. "Swim, Mommy?"

"In a little bit, sweetie," her mother said.

Later that day Jeff and Gen saw the little girl on the beach and struck up a conversation with her parents. The little girl's name was Joy, and she had been adopted from China. She was two years old. Gen made a sandcastle with her on the beach. It helped that Joy wasn't an infant. Still the overwhelming desire for a child filled her.

They saw Joy with her parents several more times during their vacation. One time Jeff and Gen watched the family on the edge of the beach under a palm tree, from a distance. Jeff finally took Gen's hand and led her in the opposite direction for a walk beside the waves.

Jeff turned to her as they flew home from Hawaii. "Would you reconsider international adoption?" He took her hand and stroked the scar at the base of her thumb. Gen sensed the caution in his voice. The timing was right, he explained. They had money in the bank, and his parents were moving into town the first week of January. They would finally have the big house. International adoption would mean less chance of getting a drug baby and no last-minute decision by the birth mom to keep the baby.

When Gen didn't answer, he continued, "We wouldn't adopt from

Vietnam or even Asia if that is what's bugging you." Still she didn't answer. "Genni, this is about us, about our family, not about your father or your mother or Nhat."

"I know." She met his gaze. "I know that it's about us. It's just so hard to keep it separate."

The word *Vietnam* stayed in her head. At first it was just a whisper in the clouds high above the Pacific, but it grew louder through the January fog and the early February rain. Vietnam took her mother and broke her father's heart, yet it was more than that to her. It was the geckos Mom talked about, the lepers, the open-air markets, the family of place-card figurines, the mangoes, Mom's friend Kim, the nameless girl Gen had prayed for all those years ago, the orphans. Somehow, although she wasn't sure exactly how, God was a part of Vietnam. Maybe it was Mom's faith. Maybe it was God's plan. Gen wasn't sure. What she knew for certain was that the word *Vietnam* stirred both awe and fear deep inside her.

Gen pulled two lamps, a coffee table, and two end tables into the middle of the dimly lit storage room in her father's basement. She and Jeff needed more furniture for the farmhouse, and her dad had invited her to take what she wanted from his collection of outcasts. It was Presidents' Day, and Gen had decided to drive into Portland and get serious about furnishing their big house.

She found a flashlight by the door and ran the beam along the boxes on the shelves. Each box was neatly labeled: "Kitchen," "Garden tools," "Past taxes," "Christmas." The musty smell reminded Gen of how frightened she had been as a child to go into the basement alone. She needed Mom by her side. She swung the flashlight up to the top shelf. Tucked in the corner were two boxes labeled "Sally." Gen put the flashlight down and stood on her tiptoes, pulling the first box toward her. She balanced it carefully as she eased it to the floor and then opened it. On the top was the mahogany box of place-card holders. Gen lifted the box out, sat on the floor, opened it, and carefully examined each one—the boy riding the water buffalo, the father holding a scythe, the mother with a baby strapped to her back, the grandmother squatting in front of a basket of mangoes, the grandfather with the white beard holding a perfectly carved cane. The little girl she had played with and loved was missing.

"Gen." Her father stood in the doorway. He flipped a switch and a fluorescent bulb bathed the room in light. "Do you need some help?"

Gen quickly turned off the flashlight.

"What did you find?" he asked.

"Mom's stuff."

He scowled at the Vietnamese figurines and then winced just a little as if suddenly the light was too bright. "I should have given those to you years ago. Take what you want."

"I've thought about these place-card holders recently," Gen said. "Actually, I never stopped thinking about them."

"Just do me a favor," he said. "Don't put them in your house where I can see them." That was exactly what she wanted to do—put Mom's things where everyone could see them. They had been boxed up for too many years.

"I'm a silly old man," he said. "But seeing them still makes me as sad as if it were twenty-five years ago."

Gen had planned to talk to her dad about Jeff wanting to adopt internationally but decided not to. The timing was wrong. She didn't want to bring up more sad memories. She carried the two boxes of her mother's belongings to Jeff's pickup. Her father helped her with the tables and lamps.

Almost a month later Gen put the ginger chicken in the oven for Jeff's birthday dinner. Sharon and Don were coming for dinner. She had invited her father and aunt, but her dad had a meeting at his church about the youth group's upcoming trip to Kazakhstan, and Aunt Marie didn't want to drive to The Dalles alone. Her father planned to chaperon the youth group's trip; he had called last week to explain his decision. It was so unlike him. Here he was seventy-one years old, and he hardly ever left Portland except to drive to The Dalles. At first his decision troubled Gen, but then it made her feel lighter, ready to make a decision of her own.

She closed the oven and climbed the stepstool, opened the cupboard above the sink, and pulled out the box of place-card holders. Since her dad wasn't coming, she would use the Vietnamese figurines.

Jeff's mother would find the carvings quaint. His father wouldn't notice. Jeff would.

The tires of Jeff's pickup rolled across the gravel driveway. He had been spraying the upper orchard. She hurried into the kitchen and then out to the mud room. He climbed the steps as she opened the back door. "Happy birthday!" His hair curled around his baseball cap. He bent down to kiss her as he stood on the door stoop.

"Go get your shower," she said. "Be quick, okay?" Sharon and Don would arrive soon. Gen felt her before-company anxiety rise.

Jeff sauntered through the kitchen door into the back hall singing, "Splish splash, I was taking a bath" as Gen headed the opposite direction through the swinging door into the dining room. Sharon and Don had left the oak table and eight chairs because they couldn't fit the antiques into their house in town. Gen counted out four goblets and four plates from the china hutch. She quickly set the table and then took the dad, mom, grandma, and grandpa place-card holders out of the box and put them around the settings. Everything was in position. She glanced from figurine to figurine, one by one, on the table. That was what she wanted. A family. She wrote their names on index cards and slipped them into the holders.

She turned her attention to the jar filled with daffodils, cut the stems, and placed the flowers in a crystal vase. Jeff's great-grandmother had planted the original bulbs eighty years before. The daffodils almost always bloomed for Jeff's birthday.

Gen heard the bathroom door open and checked her watch. Jeff's parents were scheduled to arrive in five minutes. They were notorious for being early. She hoped Jeff was almost ready.

The front doorbell rang. His parents never rang the bell.

Gen peeked out the living room window, across the porch and through the white railing. There was a silver Buick in the driveway. *Just like Dad's car.* She stopped with her hand an inch from the knob. It was Dad's car.

She opened the door, thinking of the figurines on the table.

"Dad! You came!" She looked behind him. "And brought Aunt Marie."

"Didn't you get my message?" He raised a bushy brow. Aunt Marie bustled through the door. Before Gen could answer that she hadn't checked her voice mail, he said, "The meeting was canceled. So I came and brought Marie." Her father gave her a quick hug, and Aunt Marie kissed her cheek.

"Marshall, you made it!" Jeff said, swinging through the kitchen door. His long legs quickly covered the room. He stretched out his hand to his father-in-law. "And Aunt Marie." He turned toward her with a hug. "How nice of you to come for my birthday dinner."

Aunt Marie smiled and blushed slightly. Jeff made her happy.

Gen opened her eyes wide and leaned her head toward the dining room table, willing Jeff to gather up the figurines, to make them disappear. She had told him when she brought them home that her father didn't want to see Mom's things. Jeff should know she wouldn't have put them out if she had known Dad and Aunt Marie were coming. Jeff smiled back at her with his light-up-the-room smile. His wet curls framed his face.

Jeff's parents started up the porch steps. "Oh, look at the daffodils!" Sharon said as they came through the door.

Gen's dad shook Don's hand. Both were tall and thin, but Jeff's father was now completely bald in contrast to Gen's father's full head of white hair.

"And these figurines!" Sharon exclaimed, walking toward the table. "Gen, where in the world did you get these?" Jeff turned toward the table. Sharon picked up the mother carrying the baby. The place card that read "Gen" fell to the floor. Aunt Marie stared at the table. Dad let go of Don's hand.

"Is this your way of saying yes?" Jeff's eyes met hers. "On my birthday!"

Gen glanced from her husband to her dad and pressed her lips together.

"It's obvious that you didn't get my message," her father said.

"Gen!" Sharon took a step toward her daughter-in-law, her arms stretched wide. "Have you two decided to adopt?"

Gen wondered if Jeff had told Sharon they were considering international adoption. Did Sharon realize that the child wouldn't look like any of them? *Oh, stop.* "We're thinking about it. Tell you more later, okay?" She kept her voice low, hoping her father really was growing as hard of hearing as he claimed.

Aunt Marie crossed her arms.

Gen's father quickly regained his composure. Jeff took two more china plates and goblets from the hutch while Gen hurried to collect napkins and more silver. She reached for the place-card holders.

"Gen," her dad said, his hand on hers, "leave them. It's okay."

When she called everyone to the table, her father sat at the place with the carving of the old man with the white hair and beard. He took the card with Don's name on it and put it in the middle of the table. After grace he chatted with Don about the cherry crop, complimented Gen on the ginger chicken, and asked Sharon how Jake and Janet were doing. Sharon explained with a sad face that Jeff's sister was now in Arizona getting a doctorate in education while her husband stayed in Texas. Gen ate silently, thinking about Janet and Sharon, about mothers and daughters, and trying not to think about her father. Aunt Marie stared at her off and on throughout the meal.

❧

Jeff put the figurines in the mahogany box while Gen finished loading the dishwasher. "What country do you think we should adopt from?" Jeff turned toward Gen.

She knew the answer. She felt the door to a far-off room in her heart ease open. "Vietnam."

"Are you sure?"

Gen nodded and then opened the box to look at the figurines before she put them away. The grandfather was missing.

A thin woman moved to the lectern and turned to the five couples and three single women sitting with Gen and Jeff around the long metal tables. "Hi, I'm Maggie. Welcome to Mercy for Children's spring preadopt class." She wore a denim jumper, a red blouse, and navy clogs. Her gray hair hung loose around her shoulders, framing her pale face and confident smile.

The adoption agency was located in an old Victorian house in northwest Portland.

"I'm the director of Mercy for Children," Maggie said. "I'm also the Vietnam program coordinator and the mother of four children. Two were adopted from Vietnam."

Jeff caught Gen's eye and winked. "Just you wait," he had said as they drove into Portland that morning. "I have a good feeling about this. It's going to go our way. It's going to be a snap."

"We also have programs in South Korea, China, Russia, and Guatemala," Maggie continued. "Families from all over the United States adopt through our programs."

Maggie passed out a binder to each family unit. Gen glanced at the tabs along the side: DECIDING. PARENTHOOD. FAMILY. ISSUES. BONDING. MEDICAL QUESTIONS. POST ADOPTION. RESOURCES.

Maggie outlined the process on a whiteboard affixed to the wall: three Saturday morning preadopt classes, paperwork, a home study, and a background check. They needed to be fingerprinted and go to INS in downtown Portland. A dossier would be compiled, the papers would be sent to Vietnam, and a referral would be made.

"Referral?" A single woman at the end of the table leaned forward. "What does that mean?"

Maggie smiled. "A referral of a child. You'll get a photo and all the information we have about that particular boy or girl. Then you make the decision to accept the referral." *Accept the referral. It sounds so cold.*

"What about gender requests?" the same woman said. "Are we allowed to choose?"

"We want you to request what works best for your family. But keep in mind, most adoptive families want girls, which means there are more boys available. China is the exception. Because of their one-child policy, far more girls are available for adoption. Even in Vietnam, more girls are given up for adoption, but because the majority of American couples request girls, more boys are available."

Gen and Jeff had already talked about the gender issue. "I want a baby," Gen had said. "I don't care if it's a boy or a girl. I want God to decide that." Their decision not to request a girl would most likely mean adopting a boy.

A man in his forties across the table from Gen tapped his mechanical pencil on the binder. "How about the birth moms? Do they ever change their minds?" His wife ran her hand through her long blond hair and bit her lip as they waited for Maggie to answer.

"Very seldom," Maggie said. "In fact, I've never had it happen in the Vietnam program." *Birth mom.* Gen hadn't thought about a birth mom. She had imagined a baby whose mother had died or a baby who had been abandoned and left on the steps of the orphanage. "In fact," Maggie continued, "in Vietnam the adoptive parents often meet the birth mothers. That's really a wonderful thing."

Wonderful? It sounded unbearable.

During the break the blond-haired woman introduced herself to Gen. "I'm Robyn." She extended her hand across the table. "This is my husband, Sean." Jeff shook Sean's hand.

What was their story? Had they tried in vitro? Considered domestic adoption? Robyn seemed to be Gen and Jeff's age. All the other prospective parents, including Sean, appeared to be older.

"What program are you interested in?" Sean studied their faces.

"Vietnam," Jeff said.

Sean met his wife's eyes before turning back to Gen and Jeff. "Really?" he said. "I think we're leaning toward that one too." Robyn nodded.

❦

Jeff drove over the Broadway Bridge above the Willamette River. The docks and railroad yards spread out along the banks. Gen held the adoption packet. The blue sky covered the city like a promise as they sped along. Hope grew inside her.

She saw the flash of a freight train pick up speed as it headed south in the railroad yard below. Nine months, Maggie had said. Nine months and they would have their baby—if all went well. Gen realized she was holding her breath and let it out.

"I really like Maggie." Jeff downshifted and slowed for the stoplight by Memorial Coliseum.

Gen wanted to like Maggie, wanted to trust her. Would Mom be like Maggie now if she had lived? Mom had been idealistic. Maggie seemed pragmatic. Maybe idealism grew into pragmatism.

"I hope she'll travel to Vietnam with us," Jeff added. "Wouldn't it be great if Sean and Robyn went with us too?"

Gen nodded. She didn't want to talk about traveling to Vietnam yet. She wanted to fill out the paperwork, have the home study completed, buy furniture for the baby's room, and try not to think about the Vietnamese woman who would give up her child.

"What do you want to eat?" Jeff said.

"How about Vietnamese food? Yen Ha is on Sandy, not far from Dad's."

Jeff glanced at Gen and grinned. "Let's call your dad and see if he'll go with us."

"We can call, but he won't want Vietnamese food. We'll have to go somewhere else." He'd say it was too spicy. But he ate Mexican and Chinese food all the time.

Gen dug in her backpack for the cell phone.

"Hi, Dad. We're in town. How about lunch? We were thinking about the Vietnamese place on Sandy." She winked at Jeff as she listened to her father. "Sure, sure, Chinese is fine. Zien Hong would be great." She winked at Jeff again. "We'll meet you there in ten minutes."

"You were right," Jeff said, turning right. "When do you want to buy a station wagon?"

Gen couldn't think about buying a station wagon. First they had to tell her father they were going to adopt from Vietnam.

"What are you in town for?" Her dad glanced at Gen over the top of his menu, peering above his wire-framed reading glasses, a shock of white hair hanging over his forehead.

Gen exchanged a look with Jeff.

Jeff cleared his throat. "A preadopt class."

"Really? It sounded as if you were headed that way at the birthday dinner."

Jeff nodded.

"What agency?" Her father set down his menu and focused on Gen.

"Mercy for Children," she said.

"Domestic?"

"International," Jeff said, pouring tea for the three of them.

"What country?"

"They offer programs through Russia, South Korea, China, Vietnam, and Guatemala." Gen rushed her answer, aware of how she'd buried the word *Vietnam* in the list.

Her father raised his eyebrows.

Outside the window, up and down Sandy Boulevard, the yellow and red striped flag of South Vietnam fluttered. It was mid-April, halfway between the twenty-fifth anniversary of her mother's death on April 4 and the fall of

Saigon on April 30. The flags, hung by expatriates whose businesses lined the street, commemorated the fall of their country.

"We plan to adopt from Vietnam," Jeff said to his father-in-law.

Gen pushed her chopsticks away from her place mat. *What am I afraid of? Dad's pain...his disapproval? After all these years?*

Her father took off his glasses. "I'm just going to say this once," he said. "This is your life and your decision. Choose China. Choose South Korea. Choose Guatemala. Choose the United States. Or how about Kazakhstan? I'll find out about adopting from there. Don't choose Vietnam. Only heartbreak comes from Vietnam."

*L*an stood in the middle of the one-room apartment. She feared the concrete in the Russian-made building would crumble in the heat and humidity. Outside the open window a dirt yard ran the length of the building, and a single rusty slide offered amusement for the children. This morning a dozen little ones crowded around it. Binh would soon join them, swinging from its ladder.

Cuong carried a box of belongings into the room, and Mother followed him with a basket. Lan placed the fruit box used for the family altar in the corner of the room.

"One more trip and you will be moved," Cuong said. Lan nodded. It had taken only three trips on a motorbike. She heard Hang and Binh racing up the stairs.

"This is so far from our grove," Mother said. "From our land." Lan clucked her tongue and touched Mother's shoulder. She talked more and more about the past, about Father, about the land, about Older Brother and Second Brother, even Older Sister. It made Lan sad. What would their life be like if there had been no war? If they hadn't been forced to leave their home?

Hang rushed through the door and lifted Binh into her arms. Her eleven-year-old body was still a child's but strong enough to carry her brother.

"Come over tonight," Cuong whispered to Lan.

She thought of the cost of the apartment. It was twice as much as she had paid for the shack. Lan hoped the tourists would want to buy more cigarettes and souvenirs or that Cuong would give her more money.

Lan walked to Cuong's house after fixing rice and fish for Mother and the children. Cuong and several of his friends drank and gambled, barely touching their dinner from a nearby restaurant. After his friends left, Lan cleared away the beer bottles and joined Cuong in his bed.

Long after midnight she said it was time for her to go. "Spend the night," he said, stroking her hair, working it out of the braid. She shook her head. Matter-of-factly Cuong said that he might have to be gone on business for a month or two. Lan kept silent. "Someone from the commerce ministry has been snooping around," he said, "asking about smuggled goods. I'm going to go to the city to see if I can work for a cousin who manages a sugar refinery."

Who will I work for? Who will help me? "When will you come back?" she asked.

"I don't know." He rolled away from her. "You should hook up with Truc." He spoke slowly, as if he were almost asleep. "She said she needed someone to help her sell." Truc was a businesswoman that Cuong traded with sometimes.

Lan sat up against the wall and did not move until she heard Cuong's breathing quiet. She slid off the low bed, dressed, rebraided her hair, and then tiptoed around the one-room apartment, collecting food into a plastic bag—half a plate of salad rolls, a bowl of orange rice, leftover chicken with lemongrass, and three steamed mooncakes. The food would be her family's celebration for tomorrow's midautumn festival. She slipped out the door and hurried down the open stairs into the night. Staying in the shadows, she walked quickly back to the apartment.

They wouldn't be able to stay. Cuong had given her money off and on for the last two years—money for medicine, for Hang's school, sometimes for food. Her heart raced as she hurried up the three flights of stairs to the apartment. She opened the door and peered down at her sleeping children.

She knelt beside them and recited the prayer, the French prayer—it had been so long since she had said it. She lingered on the words *Donne-nous aujourd'hui notre pain de ce jour. Give us this day our daily bread.*

"Lan." Mother swung her feet out of the hammock. "Lan," she said again. "We can't stay here. I'd rather live under a tarp. The air is thick; I can't hold a breath. The building steals oxygen from me."

"Shh. Go to sleep." Mother was worse than a sick child waking in the night.

"Promise me, Lan; promise me that we'll find another place."

"Yes, Mother. I promise. We *can't* stay here." Lan opened the shutters wide. She would talk to Truc tomorrow about work and somewhere else to live. Lan had seen Truc's home once when Cuong had dropped off a case of whiskey for Truc to sell. Her dilapidated shack seemed like something Lan could afford.

Mother took Lan's hand. "When will Quan come to help us? When will your brother take care of his old mother?"

"Shh," she said. "Go back to sleep."

"Maybe Cuong will marry you. It's been three years since you've known him."

Lan shook her head. "No. He's going to the city. I may never see him again."

"Who will take care of us?" Mother pulled Lan's hand to her old, wrinkled face.

"I will. I will take care of you, of all of us."

$\mathcal{G}$en stood by the loading dock as Jeff moved the crates of cherries onto the truck with the forklift. Marta's youngest daughter, four-year-old Melissa, held her hand. Jeff smiled at Gen as he turned off the motor. "It's all yours." He walked toward her and kissed her on the lips. The little girl climbed into the truck. "I think ice cream is in order," Jeff said in a stage whisper. Melissa giggled.

Gen pumped the brakes slightly going down the drive to the main road. After all these years the heavy loads still made her nervous. As she turned toward town, her cell phone rang. She fumbled it from her belt, thinking it would be Jeff with an errand he needed her to run in town. It was Aunt Marie. "Genevieve, your father's in the hospital."

"He's on his way to Kazakhstan," Gen said, glancing at Melissa in the booster seat beside her.

"He had an attack last night," Aunt Marie said.

"A heart attack?" Gen tried to keep her voice steady. Her father's health had seemed so much better in the last few years.

"No. Some other kind of attack. You need to get to the hospital."

"Is it serious?" Gen needed to get the cherries to the plant. They had their home study for the adoption tonight.

"Why would he be in the hospital if it wasn't serious?"

Gen turned the pickup around and headed back to the orchard.

Aunt Marie met Gen in the lobby of the hospital. "Panic attack," she said. "That's what the doctor called it."

"A panic attack?"

"Good thing he had travel insurance. He'll get a full refund." Gen checked her watch—one thirty. She could still make it back in time for the home study. She hadn't called the social worker yet to cancel. "Genevieve, I want to talk to you before you go to see him." Aunt Marie stepped toward two chairs grouped around a small table. They both sat. "It's probably none of my business, but what's this nonsense about you adopting from Vietnam?"

Gen lifted her eyebrows.

"Your father is distraught. Really, Genevieve. What are you thinking, going to Vietnam?"

Gen crossed her arms over her chest, realized she appeared defensive, and then clasped her hands over one knee. She examined her dusty khaki shorts. "I should go see Dad." She started to stand.

"I have more to say." Aunt Marie locked eyes with Gen. Gen sank back into the chair. "You may not realize this, but your mother and I were friends. Despite the age difference, she reached out to me in her endearing way. I couldn't, as you've probably guessed, have children. In some ways your mother was like a daughter to me. And then when you were born, I finally had a baby in my life." Aunt Marie looked tense, the cords in her neck bulged. "When your mother couldn't get pregnant again, she became obsessed with having another child. She spent your father's money on specialists, to no avail. Then she decided to adopt. I warned her not to. Warned her of the heartache. Told her to accept God's will. She had one beautiful child already. Why would she risk so much for another?"

Gen crossed her arms again and left them that way.

"Before she flew over there to pick up that little boy, I called, begged her one more time." Aunt Marie scowled. Gen shivered as her aunt continued. "Now I'm begging you, because I love you, to learn to be satisfied with what God has given you. I learned to be content with not having children. Your mother should have learned to be satisfied with one." Aunt Marie gazed at Gen intently. "You can learn to be content. Don't go tramping off across the world. You're father's terrified of losing you."

"And that's why he had a panic attack on the night before he was supposed to fly to Kazakhstan?"

"He never should have planned to go on that trip. His intentions were good, but it was foolishness. But to have you planning to go to Vietnam is too much. He's an old man now." Aunt Marie shook her head. "There's a reason, one you may never know, why God has closed your womb. You should accept it."

"I have accepted it." Gen rose. "I'm not going to birth children of my own. That doesn't mean God doesn't have children for us to raise. I've wanted to be a mother for as long as I've understood what a mother was." She paused and then added, "I think I'm beginning to understand why Mom went back to Vietnam for Nhat."

Aunt Marie started to speak and then stopped.

Gen continued, "I think it's great you accepted what God had for you. That's exactly what I'm doing too." Gen peered intently at her aunt. "If God doesn't make a way for us to adopt, I know we will eventually come to peace about not having children. Right now, though, that doesn't seem to be where God is leading."

Gen waited for her aunt to answer. Aunt Marie opened her mouth and then closed it.

"I'd better go see Dad," Gen finally said.

"He's in 412." Aunt Marie looked away from Gen and crossed her arms.

Gen's father wore slacks and a short-sleeved cotton shirt and sat on the edge of the hospital bed. He turned as she came through the door. "What are you doing here?"

"Aunt Marie called me."

"I asked her not to, not with you in the middle of harvest."

"I'm glad she did. Are you okay?" She sat beside Dad and took his hand.

He laughed a little. "I'm a little embarrassed. I was sure it was another heart attack. I must have been more stressed about the trip than I realized. I guess I'm older than I thought."

"Oh, Daddy." Gen kissed his cheek.

"I'm ready to go home," he said. "Will you take me?"

"Why don't you come home with me? You can ride with me in the truck while I haul cherries to the plant."

He shook his head. "I'd just be in the way."

What was I thinking to schedule the home study during harvest? Gen pulled the brush through her short wet hair with one hand and ran a washcloth over the bathroom counter with the other. The social worker would arrive in fifteen minutes. Jeff still needed a shower. Gen rushed into the bedroom and slipped her feet into her sandals. She had planned to move her school boxes from the baby's room, cut stargazer lilies for the table, and bake chocolate chip cookies to make the house smell good. Instead, she hurried around the living room and dining room collecting junk mail and shoes.

Jeff came through the kitchen door. "Ten minutes," she barked, dumping the shoes onto the floor of the mud porch. Surely the social worker wouldn't look in there. Jeff took off his baseball cap and ran his hand through his curls. "Yes ma'am!"

"Hurry." She heard a car in the driveway. *Oh, no. She can't be early.* She glanced out the window. It was her father. "Dad?" she called from the porch.

"I decided to take you up on your offer." A white sedan turned toward the house. "Who is that?" he said.

"Probably our caseworker." She *was* early. Was Jeff even in the shower?

"Caseworker?"

Gen chuckled. "For our home study, for the adoption. No, we haven't done anything bad."

"Then I'm intruding."

"No, you're—" Gen stopped in midsentence as José, driving the old pickup, tore up the drive.

He shouted out the window. "Where's the boss?"

"Inside."

"Tell him Matthias fell from a ladder. He's unconscious."

Gen caught sight of a middle-aged woman climbing from the white sedan and then turned and hurried into the house, calling for Jeff as she ran.

Gen looked at her watch and then at the caseworker. They'd just finished a tour of the house. "Would you like to see the yard?"

The woman shook her head, sat down, and straightened the papers on the table in front of her. "I really just need to chat with your husband for a few minutes."

"I'll call him. I hope he won't be much longer." At least she'd had the foresight to toss the cell phone at him as he rushed through the door, his hair dripping wet. They'd heard the siren of the ambulance. Gen was sure Jeff had followed it into town.

He didn't answer the phone. She left a message and hurried back into the dining room.

"What do you think of your daughter and son-in-law adopting from Vietnam?" the social worker asked Gen's father. *Oh, no.*

"I think they'll make wonderful parents."

"What do you think it will be like to have a Vietnamese grandchild instead of a biological one?"

He nodded in a noncommittal way and coughed a bit. "Excuse me," he said, standing. "I need to get a drink of water."

Tires rolled over the gravel drive. It had to be Jeff. Gen rushed to the window and watched him pull his weary body from the rig.

"Matthias is going to be okay," he said, walking into the house. He stopped when he saw the caseworker. "The home study. I'm sorry. I forgot all about it once Matthias got hurt." He strode over to the table and extended his hand. "I'm Jeff. Jeff Taylor. I'm so sorry to keep you waiting."

Relieved, Gen sat back down in her chair.

The next day Gen drove over the bridge across the Columbia River to the cherry plant. The wind whipped at the truck. She felt it sway back and forth, under the weight of the crates. "Dad," she said.

He didn't answer.

"Dad," she said again, "did you want to adopt Nhat, or was it all Mom's idea?"

Her father glanced quickly toward her and then back at the bridge. "It was your mother's idea, and, yes, I wanted to adopt him. I wouldn't have gone along with something like that if I didn't want to, no matter how much I loved your mother."

Gen held the steering wheel tightly. She didn't entirely believe her father, but it was clear he didn't resent her mother for wanting another child. At the end of the bridge, just as the back wheels rolled over the end of the metal grating, she asked, "Were Mom and Aunt Marie friends?"

"Your aunt was very fond of your mother, but I don't think your mother trusted Marie. She was hurt by Marie's criticism more than once."

"What kind of criticism?"

"Oh, everything. Housekeeping, parenting—all that."

"Aunt Marie told me she accepted not being able to have children, that if God wanted her to have kids she would have gotten pregnant." Her father didn't respond. They started up the hill toward the plant on the highway that ran above the river.

"I'm trying to remember exactly what your Uncle Bert told me all those years ago when we decided to adopt Nhat," he finally said. "It was right before Bert died." Her father stared out over the river. A train, tiny in the distance, sped by on the other side. "I think he said that he was surprised I was willing to take in someone else's child, to raise a child that wasn't my own." He paused. "As it turned out, I guess he was right. I wasn't willing to raise someone else's child, not on my own." Gen stole a look at her father. He stared straight ahead now. "It's one of my biggest regrets," he added softly.

"What is?"

"Letting Nhat go."

*M*other lit the three sticks of incense and then knelt and whispered the grandparents' names, Father's name, and Second Brother's name. She folded her hands in front of her chest and invited the ancestors to eat with them, commune with them.

Then she said the Tet blessing. "Happiness as vast as the southern sea, longevity as lasting as the southern mountains." Lan tried to smile. It was the New Year, time to be positive, to believe the coming year would be better than the last. If only she could feel even a glimmer of happiness, a wave of peace. She had cleaned the shack. She had bought a new shirt for Hang and sugared fruits and New Year's rice cakes wrapped in banana leaves as treats. Mother had steamed crabs and prepared fried rice and spring rolls.

They sat to eat around the low table in the shack below Truc's home. Lan had moved the family seven months before. Truc supplied Lan with cigarettes and souvenirs to sell. Cuong hadn't returned to see Lan's belly grow bigger and bigger with his baby.

"I hope the little one is a girl," Hang said.

"Hush," Mother said. "It's Tet. Talk about good things."

Binh held his chopsticks over his bowl, waiting for his food.

"It doesn't matter if it's a girl or a boy." Lan handed her daughter the plate of spring rolls. "This baby will have to go to the orphanage."

Hang slept on the grass mat with one arm draped over Binh. The younger child had rolled onto the dirt floor, pulling the mosquito net off his sister. During the day Binh tormented Hang with his constant motion, but at night he wanted nothing more than to cuddle with her. Lan squatted by the open fire and watched her two older children through the open doorway.

The nine-day-old baby girl lay on the mat beside Lan. The water for Mother's tea began to boil. The baby, Mai, began to fuss. Lan tried not to call the little one by her name. Hang called her Thi, "little girl." Altogether the name was Tran Thi Mai. Lan opened her blouse to nurse the infant. Today she would take the baby girl to the orphanage.

They had no more rice, Mother claimed to be sick nearly every day, and Hang needed new schoolbooks. Lan had taken a few days off work when the baby was born, and now they were down to nothing.

She would take Binh to the orphanage too. He was skinny, too skinny, and sick nearly every day. She had been stubborn long enough. His ear infections lasted through the rainy season; he wheezed and coughed at night and sometimes when he played too hard.

The baby began to cry. Lan's milk wasn't enough to feed her. She put Mai back on the mat, stood slowly, and wearily slipped into her flip-flops. Because she was taking Binh, too, she would go up to the door of the orphanage, introduce herself to the director, give her the names of the children. If she were only taking the baby, she would simply leave her inside the gate.

The infant pushed her tiny hand into her mouth and sucked, her eyes shut against the rising sun. Hang and Binh came out of the hut. "Wash up," Lan said. "Get ready for school, Hang." The baby began to cry again. Lan motioned to Binh. "Come here, little one."

She sat again, pulled her only son onto her lap, and ignored the cries of his baby sister. "Would you like to have enough to eat?" she said. Binh nodded. "Today I will take you to a place where you will have plenty of food. I will take Baby Sister, too."

Lan brushed her hand across her eyes, pushed Binh off her lap, and stood. She felt lightheaded and waited, standing perfectly still, for it to pass. "Hang, go ask Truc if we can borrow her basin." She would bathe the children before taking them to the orphanage. When Hang returned, Lan filled the container with cold water from the spigot in the yard as Binh pulled off his clothes. He climbed into the basin, splashing water onto his mother. For months he'd bathed himself under the spigot, but this last time Lan would wash him.

Lan said the prayer out loud, saying the last line slowly. *"Car c'est à toi qu'appartiennent le règne, la puissance et la gloire, pour les siècles des siècles."* She repeated it. "For thine is the kingdom, the power and the glory for ever and ever."

Hang glanced up from her bowl of rice. "Mama, don't. It doesn't make any sense."

Lan rubbed the soap in Binh's hair and shivered. It had made sense all those years ago, but maybe Hang was right. Maybe it didn't make sense anymore.

The orphanage director turned her back to them as Lan said good-bye to Binh.

"I will come visit you," Lan said, kneeling down on the concrete floor.

"Mama, what are you doing?" He clung to her neck.

"Shh. You be a brave boy. Do you hear? You must stay here and take care of Little Sister."

"I want to go home with you."

She pulled away from him and hurried down the stairs.

"Mama!" His cries followed her and rang for hours in her ears.

"What will happen to the baby?" Hang said that evening. Lan bowed her head. She couldn't speak, couldn't tell her oldest that the baby would be adopted. Hang went on to her next question. "When is Binh coming back?"

"I don't know," Lan said, feeling Hang standing over her. She had her father's good heart. Lan could not bear to tell her that she planned to give Binh up for adoption, that a better life awaited him.

"I can take care of him." Hang crouched on the floor. "Let me take care of him. I can take care of the baby, too."

"No, you must finish school." Lan observed it again and again, the oldest girl raising the younger children, having no opportunities of her own.

Hang shook her head. "Mama, how can you do this? How can you do this to our family?"

Lan stood and walked into the yard without looking back at Hang. She didn't expect her daughter to understand, not now.

That night Lan reached for the baby in her sleep, then woke. The baby was gone. Moonlight filled the space between the frame and the door. She crossed her arms over her tender breasts as tears slid from her eyes. *Stop,* she chided herself. *It's for the best. It's what's best for them. A mother has to put her children before herself.* That was what Mother had told her all those years ago. *All I've wanted, really, is to take care of my children.*

She ordered the grief from her body, but it refused to leave. Life was full of losses. At least she still had Hang and Mother. Even though Mother made life harder, she loved her. She rolled to her side and then sat up for a moment before standing. She wanted more for Hang. She slipped on her rubber flip-flops and straightened her shirt. Her belly was still soft from the baby.

She shuffled out to the yard and turned on the spigot, letting the cool water flow over her hands before she splashed it onto her face. The sun would soon rise. She wouldn't have to worry about Binh brushing against the hot stove or hiding from her in the market or running out into a busy street or too far into the waves.

She would sell souvenirs today if Truc had extras. It was Saturday. She hoped tourists from Saigon would fill the beach.

"Where is your baby?" Truc said to Lan as she handed her eight cartons of cigarettes and three boxes of jade Buddhas.

"I took her to the orphanage."

Truc nodded. "I thought you might." Lan couldn't say she'd taken Binh too. She swallowed hard.

"I have lychee nuts today too. Mrs. Le in the market had extra. Do you want some?"

Five old men sat together and passed around a clear plastic bottle filled with amber liquid. "I'll take a pack of cigarettes," one called out. The group was from Saigon, she was sure. Ahead, young men played soccer, and children ran into the waves. In a few hours, by noon, in the heat of the day, the beach would be nearly deserted. By evening it would be busy again.

Lan saw a white woman out of the corner of her eye. The woman wore her hair short. Ahead a man walked with a baby strapped to his chest. If Lan felt better, she would have laughed at the sight.

A boy just younger than Hang shouted in English at the American man. "Vietnam baby?" A crowd of children gathered around the man and the baby. The American woman headed toward Lan.

"Hello," she said.

"Hello," Lan said.

The woman pointed at the lychee nuts. Lan held up one hand and opened and closed her fingers two times. She wanted to communicate ten thousand dong. The woman handed her an American five-dollar bill. *Now what?* Lan didn't have change for that much money; she quickly bagged more lychee nuts, hoping the woman wouldn't protest.

The woman shook her head. She pointed at the money in Lan's hand and then at Lan, and then she smiled. It was six times more than what the woman owed. Lan could buy fish and vegetables for dinner and medicine for Mother.

*T*his is Maggie," came the message over the answering machine. "Call me as soon as you can."

"Jeff!" Gen called as she reached for the phone on the kitchen counter. "We have a message from Maggie. I'm calling her back." *Please be there.* Gen looked at her watch after she dialed the number. It was 5:10. *Please, please be there.*

Jeff swung through the kitchen door.

"Hello, Mercy for Children," Maggie answered.

"It's Gen."

Maggie's voice danced. "Gen, would you and Jeff be willing to take two children?"

"We said we'd take twins," Gen said.

Jeff's eyes widened.

"How about a sibling set?"

"Siblings? How old?" Gen's brain slowed. The word *siblings* reverberated through her head. She turned toward the kitchen window. A light dusting of late-winter snow covered the orchard and coated the branches of the trees.

"A baby. A little girl," Maggie said. *A little girl. I was so sure our child would be a boy.* "She's a newborn named Mai; she's just over two weeks old. She was born February 10." *A new baby. A little tiny baby!* "And her brother, Binh, who was born September 26, 1996." *A four-year-old? That old? What kind of problems would he have? Attachment disorders? Bonding problems? Abandonment issues?* The questions jostled inside Gen. Jeff stared at her.

"The birth mother is destitute. She's in the process of relinquishing them." Maggie paused.

Birth mom? Gen had hoped for an abandoned baby, a child without a mother.

"Gen?" It was Maggie. "Are you there?"

Her breath caught in her throat. "Yes," she finally managed.

"You don't have to decide right now. Talk to Jeff. But we need to keep the pair together."

"Okay. Thanks," Gen said. "We'll get back to you tomorrow."

"Give it a few days if you need to."

Jeff's smile grew with each word as Gen relayed what Maggie had said. They stood in the kitchen and leaned against the counter. "There are no guarantees when it comes to children." Jeff reached over for Gen's hand. "Birth or adopted, newborn or older."

"But you didn't take the attachment disorders class." Gen had gone into Portland for it on a Saturday in January while Jeff fixed a broken irrigation line. *What will Sharon and Don say? And Dad?* She thought of Nhat all those years ago. He had been two. *Why did Maggie even call about an older child? We said we wanted a baby. Or twin babies. Not a four-year-old.*

"I'm going to call Mom," Jeff said.

"No," Gen said. "Wait, please wait. Wait until we decide."

She knew he had decided. She followed him through the kitchen door into the dining room. He walked around the table and headed to the bathroom to take a shower. She turned up the heat and went into their bedroom to change into a pair of sweats.

They were quiet during dinner. Gen had heated up a jar of spaghetti sauce. She had cooked the pasta too long and burned the broiled garlic bread.

Jeff smiled. Gen grimaced.

"Please don't," he said as he finished his salad.

She raised her eyebrows.

"This is good news, this referral." Jeff twirled spaghetti onto his fork.

"It puts us in a bad spot," she said.

"I thought you said you wanted God to pick the child." He took a bite.

"I wanted God to pick the baby. Or babies."

Jeff swallowed. "I think he's made his choice."

"So you've already decided?"

"He's decided," Jeff said.

"And we say yes? Just like that?" A dull ache spread behind her eyes.

"What is it, Genni?"

She took a deep breath. "It's Binh. But not just what issues he might have. I think it's more than that." She paused. *Do I even know, exactly?* She felt so sad. "He's lost his mother. I know what that's like."

Jeff nodded. "And?"

"But his mother is still alive. He knows that. Will he feel like we've taken him from her?"

"He knows she took him to the orphanage."

"But he still might feel like we've stolen him away from her. How horrible to lose your mom and know she's still alive but never be able to get back to her." She wanted to crawl into their bed, pull the covers over her head, and sob.

Jeff took another piece of garlic bread. "So you think it would be better to leave him at the orphanage?"

Gen went to bed early and feigned sleep as sorrow surged through her. Sorrow for the loss of her mother, still, after all these years. Sorrow for Binh and his mother, for their loss of each other. *God, why can't any of this be easy? Why does it have to be so hard?*

Gen called Jeff during the five minutes she had between recess duty and read-aloud. "I told Mom about the children," he said. "I know you didn't want me to, but I couldn't help it."

"What did she say?" She knew he would call Sharon; she was surprised he'd waited as long as he had. She envied him that he had a mother to call.

"She thinks it's great. She said they'll have each other besides having us. She said she can't wait to have two grandkids."

Gen parked the Subaru station wagon in the driveway and hurried into the house. The lights were on, and the house was warm. She dashed down the hall to the office and found Jeff at the computer.

"Look, Genni." His smile was bigger and brighter than she had ever seen it. "Maggie e-mailed the pictures."

Gen stood, mesmerized by the baby on the screen.

"This is Mai," Jeff said softly. He sat tall and looked intently at Gen, then back at the monitor. Dark, straight hair topped the newborn's sweet round face; she held her eyes half open, as if she'd just decided to take a nap or maybe wake up. She wore a white T-shirt and lay on an olive green mat.

"Isn't she beautiful?" Jeff asked. Gen's chest constricted.

"And this," Jeff said, clicking the mouse to close Mai's file and open the next, "is Binh." The screen filled with the photo of a boy with short raggedy hair and the dark eyes of a deer caught in bright headlights. His mouth hung half open on his thin, gaunt face. Doors deep inside Gen flew open. In an instant the ache in her heart turned into a longing, a fierce, desperate longing. It was more than the desire to be a mom. It was a longing to be Binh and Mai's mom. She wanted to reach inside the monitor and pull them out, pull them home.

"He needs us," Jeff said. "Maybe even more than Mai does." Gen closed her eyes. She could still see Binh. *Anyone would take the baby.* "I called Maggie today," Jeff said. "She said the birth mom…" *Birth mom. Those words.* "…took the children to the orphanage last week. Maggie said that there's no identifiable father. She said the mom can't afford to feed the children, to take care of them." Jeff spun around in the office chair. He reached out his arms and pulled Gen onto his lap. "I really think this is what we're supposed to do," he said. "I really think God wants these children to be ours."

Tears welled in Gen's eyes. She nodded. "When did Maggie say we would travel?"

"The first of April."

A sob rose up in Gen. *In just six weeks! Mai would still be a little baby. Binh wouldn't have to be in the orphanage much longer.*

Jeff squeezed her. "It's finally going to happen," he said. "We're finally going to be parents."

Gen's chest constricted again. A tear slid down her face. She peered into Jeff's brown eyes. He wiped her tear.

"Aren't you happy?" he asked.

She nodded. She wanted the children. She wanted the baby. She wanted the boy. How could photos make her so certain?

"Binh is a little guy," Jeff said. "Only twenty-eight pounds and thirty-six inches."

Gen stood and estimated three feet to be several inches below her hip. She thought of the kindergarten kids at school. Binh was much, much smaller.

"Want me to call Maggie? To give her the okay?"

"No, I will." Gen ran the back of her hand under her eyes, wiping away the next tear.

"And then call your dad," Jeff said.

Gen nodded, but she wouldn't. Not yet. She'd wait a few more days. She could only handle so much at a time.

A week later the teachers at school gave Gen a shower. That night she and Jeff sat on the floor of the children's room and pulled sleepers and T-shirts and shorts and shoes and bibs out of the gift bags. Two matching blue Winnie-the-Pooh sleepers for next winter. Nike sandals for Binh. A daisy-print sundress for Mai.

The pieces of the crib leaned against the wall. They would shop for a toddler's bed and dressers Saturday morning. They planned to paint the walls yellow on Saturday afternoon.

"Do you think they'll want to share a room?" Gen asked.

Jeff nodded. "They're used to being with lots of kids."

"Do you think they'll like this room?"

Jeff wrinkled his nose. "Of course they'll like this room. And this house. And the orchards. And The Dalles. And Oregon. And us."

Gen placed the books on the white bookcase and then refolded the clothes and slowly bundled them back in the bags.

"Shouldn't we wash these?" Jeff said. How many times had she told him that clothes needed to be washed before they were worn?

"Not yet," she said. "I'll do it later." Washing them now felt presumptuous. Waiting felt superstitious. Still, she would wait.

Jeff stood and stretched his arms and back. "Your dad called. He's coming Saturday to help us paint. Why didn't you tell him about the referrals?"

"Should you be up on that ladder?" Gen asked her father.

"I'm fine," he answered, looking down. Bright yellow paint peppered his white hair. "Are we doing the ceiling today too?"

"You're not," Gen answered. He climbed down, taking the rungs carefully, one at a time, brush in hand.

"Why didn't you call to tell me about the referrals sooner? It's the boy, isn't it?" Her father's gray eyes pierced her.

And you telling us not to adopt from Vietnam. Why couldn't he get over Vietnam? Still, here he was helping them. "No," she said. "I just wanted to wait until we knew more."

Gen focused on painting the trim around a window while her father filled his paint tray and then climbed back up the ladder.

A few weeks after the caseworker visited last summer, a copy of the home study came in the mail. Gen had smiled as she read it. It sounded too good. It sounded as if they would be the best parents ever. "Gen is a petite, vibrant young woman who loves children and has plenty of energy to be a mom. Jeff is a responsible man respected by his entire family and those who work for him. He can easily provide for a child. Their extended family, grandparents in particular, are thrilled that Gen and Jeff want to adopt from Vietnam." The last line made Gen smile. *Oh well,* she had thought. *Never mind if the details aren't accurate.* What Gen treasured most in the home study was the explanation about the adopted child and his or her inheritance. "Any child adopted by Jefferson and Genevieve Taylor shall share equally with all other children in the family inheritance left by the couple." She imagined someone in Vietnam reading the report. It made her shiver. It made her think about being adopted into God's family, about sharing an eternal inheritance.

"Your aunt wants to give you one of those baby showers. At our church," her father said, looking down from the ladder.

"Aunt Marie?" Gen asked.

Her father nodded and dipped the roller into the pan.

Why would Aunt Marie want to give me a shower? With the church ladies? The ones who refer to Mom as "Marshall's young wife," even now after all these years? The ones who make me feel as if Mom died on purpose? Those ladies? And why does Aunt Marie want to organize it? She doesn't even want us to adopt, let alone from Vietnam.

"Aunt Marie will give you a call. She's hoping to put it on in a week or two." Her dad didn't say anything more about the adoptions as he painted his grandchildren's room.

When Jeff set up the crib, Gen took photos of the room. "Let me take your picture," she said to her father. "We're going to send photos to Vietnam, to the children."

He shook his head and started down the stairs to wash out the paint roller.

Exasperated, Gen let out a sigh. "One minute he's supportive," she said to Jeff, "the next he's aloof. I wish he would make up his mind."

"Give him time," he said. "He'll come around."

Aunt Marie scheduled the shower for early March. Gen arrived ahead of time and sat in the church parking lot. She didn't want to go in and watch her aunt scurry around, criticizing the centerpieces and complaining about the cake. Gen wore black pants and a lavender blouse. Now she wondered if she should have worn a dress or at least a skirt.

She had spent the day in Portland shopping for a pair of cargo pants with zip-off legs for Jeff and a cotton skirt and a Lycra blend shirt for herself. She imagined being at the orphanage, wearing the blue skirt, holding Mai, kneeling down to say hello to Binh. She'd been practicing from the phrase book. *Chao em.* "Hello, little one."

She stayed up late the night before, visiting Web sites about Vietnam. After reading an article about a possible moratorium on adoptions, she linked to an INS site and read through guidelines for adoptive parents. The list defined an orphan as a child with only one identifiable parent. From there she went to the CIA Vietnam page. The average purchasing power of a Vietnamese citizen was twenty-one hundred dollars U.S., and thirty-seven percent of the people lived below the poverty line. Back to Google and she typed in "Vietnam tourism." She found a site on Vung Tau. The town had served as a seaside resort for the French. Today throngs of people from Ho Chi Minh City traveled to the city on weekends and enjoyed the white, sandy beaches and seafood.

The next site was about a clinic that Vietnam vets had built. From there she went to "Vietnam death trip" and "fallen friends." Then on to stories about Vietnam. A Vietnamese refugee who escaped as a child after the war wrote, "I fear I will forever be without a homeland." Gen logged off the Internet. *Is that how my children will feel? That they will always be without a homeland?*

She and Jeff would fly into Ho Chi Minh City. Then they would travel to Vung Tau in the adoption agency's van. Maggie would travel with them. Gen had an e-mail from Robyn two weeks ago that said they had received a referral for a five-month-old girl and would travel in April also.

Dime-sized drops of rain began to pelt the windshield. She grabbed her purse and dashed into the church.

An hour later she sat in the fellowship hall surrounded by gifts—blankets, booties, bonnets, and books. She smiled around the circle of ladies. "Thank you," she said. She was touched by their generosity, by Aunt Marie's gesture of goodwill.

"You know what will happen now, Genevieve," Aunt Marie said as she handed her a piece of German chocolate cake. Gen took the plate and shook her head. "You'll get pregnant! You'll be a modern-day Sarah."

Gen tried to smile. Had Aunt Marie forgotten Gen's story? And besides, Sarah hadn't adopted first; she'd made other arrangements. Gen took a bite of cake. "Aunt Marie, this is your best cake ever."

Aunt Marie beamed. "Has your church in The Dalles thrown a shower for you yet?"

Gen shook her head. "The teachers at school have." She didn't want Aunt Marie to get started about their church in The Dalles. She was always asking questions, trying to determine how involved they were. She and Jeff were too old for the young marrieds' class, and they were the only people without children in the other adult class. So instead of attending a class, they taught the third and fourth graders. They avoided special-event Sundays like Mother's Day when the oldest mom and the woman with the most children were honored. For twenty-six years, Mother's Day had been the hardest day of the year for Gen.

People at church had stopped asking years ago when they planned to start a family. So far, they hadn't told many people there that they planned to adopt. Gen was waiting for the right time.

Aunt Marie sat down next to Gen. "Did you like your shower?" she asked.

"It was wonderful," Gen answered. "Thank you."

❧

As Gen climbed into the station wagon after loading the gifts in the back, her cell phone rang. *Jeff. He's calling to ask about the shower.* She pulled the phone out of her purse.

It was Jeff, but he didn't ask about the shower. "Robyn just called asking for you," he said. "You need to call her right back."

"Why?" Gen asked, alarmed.

"They lost their referral. The investigation turned up a birth dad."

"What?"

"If two birth parents are identified, the United States INS won't allow the adoption," Jeff explained.

"They can't adopt their baby?"

"No."

"What's going to happen?" Gen gripped the steering wheel with her left hand.

"They'll get another referral. Maggie's working on it. But Robyn's devastated."

Gen scribbled Robyn's number on the back of a receipt, asked Jeff to stay up until she got home, and told him good-bye.

She sat for a moment and then dialed the number. Robyn answered. "I'm sorry," Gen said. "So sorry."

Robyn began to cry. "It feels just like the last time," she sobbed.

"The last time?" Gen asked.

"We had a failed domestic adoption a year ago. I saw her born, held her, even dressed her. And then the birth mom changed her mind. It feels just like that all over again. I didn't think anything like this would happen with international adoption."

"I'm so sorry," Gen said.

"I knew you'd understand," Robyn said.

"What will happen to the baby?" Gen shivered.

"Maggie said that she hoped the mother will take her home so she doesn't have to stay in the orphanage. She said Mercy for Children is trying to start a sponsorship program to help mothers keep their children."

"What's next?" Gen glanced into the rearview mirror of her car, out into the empty parking lot.

"Maggie said she'd call me tomorrow," Robyn said. "There may be another referral in the works. We won't travel with you though."

Gen listened for a few more minutes and then told Robyn she'd call her the next day. Her hand shook as she pushed the End button. *Birth father.* She hadn't thought about a birth father. Did Mai and Binh have the same birth father? Or different fathers? What if one turned up? What if they both turned up?

*L*an handed the Australian tourist a bag of green oranges. She bowed as she said in English, "Thank you. Have a good day." The man smiled. She was selling fruit in the market again and, along with Truc's cigarettes and souvenirs, on the beaches. Mrs. Le hadn't said anything about Lan taking Binh to the orphanage, but word had gotten around.

The man who worked for the adoption people came to a stop on his scooter in front of the fruit stand. "My ride is here," Lan said to Mrs. Le. The man nodded as Lan climbed on for the ride to the Justice Department. He wore a clean white shirt and shoes, not flip-flops, smelled of soap and aftershave, and carried a cell phone on his belt and a book bag slung over his shoulder. He drove quickly, weaving in and out of the traffic. Lan's braid bounced against her back as they rode over the rough street.

The adoption worker walked into the office and spoke in a quiet voice with the official while Lan sat on the second floor landing with her head down. A mouse ran into the corner and disappeared in the shadows. In a few minutes the adoption worker came out, sat beside her, and dialed a number on his phone.

She closed her eyes and listened as he spoke in English. After a while the official, still sitting at his desk, called out Lan's name. She walked into his office. Uneven stacks of paper lined the walls, and sunlight wafted through foggy windowpanes. The ceiling bulb was off, a sign the electricity was down. Another citywide blackout, most likely. The official wore a pale green shirt and slightly darker pants. A cigarette burned in the ashtray on his desk. Lines creased his aged face. He appeared to be in his midfifties, maybe even sixty. Old for a Vietnamese man.

"You've come to relinquish your child," he said.

"Children," Lan corrected. A horn honked on the street below.

The official wrote the date on a document. At the top Lan read: *The Socialist Republic of Vietnam. Independence-Liberty-Happiness.* The official squinted at Lan in the dim light. Her blouse stuck to her sweaty skin. She bowed her head, looking down at her rough hands resting in her lap.

"Do you write?" the official said. "Or would you like me to write the statement?"

"You, please." It had been so long since she had written.

"Why do you seek to relinquish your children?"

"I cannot provide for them." She tucked a loose strand of hair that had fallen from her braid behind her ear. "I cannot give them enough food. I will not be able to pay for them to go to school."

The official glanced up at her. "There is no cost for elementary school."

Lan took a breath. "I cannot afford to buy clothes for my children to wear to school. I cannot afford the books. I wish to give my children to the people of Vietnam, to the orphanage."

"Do you realize," he said, putting down his pen, "that they could be adopted by a person from another country? From France, Sweden, England, Germany, or even the United States?" He picked up his cigarette and slowly inhaled. Tires screeched on the street below. Two men shouted at each other.

"Yes," she whispered. No one in Vietnam adopted children. No one she had ever heard of, anyway. Maybe an uncle would take a nephew, but no stranger in Vietnam would want her children. In Vietnam it was all about who your father was. Her children had no father.

He blew the smoke toward Lan as he rested the cigarette on the edge of the ashtray. "Answer me properly."

"Yes, I realize they could be adopted by a person from another country," she said softly. Her stomach began to hurt.

"Do you have a husband?"

"I did have a husband. He and I had a child, my older daughter, together."

"And where is your husband now?" The man tapped his fingertips on the desk.

She bowed her head deeply and shook her head. "I do not know."

"And how about the two younger children? Did you have a husband when you had them?"

She shook her head.

"And yet you had children?" The official's stern gaze pierced her.

Lan nodded.

"Answer me properly," he demanded.

"I had these two children outside of marriage. I did a shameful thing. They have no father to care for them." Her voice quivered.

"Who are their fathers?"

She shook her head a third time. "I do not know." Her face grew hot.

He looked at her harshly, then finished writing and spun the paper around. She struggled to read what he had written.

"Sign it," he said. "I'm in a hurry."

She read the words "donate my children." *Donate.* As if she had children to spare. *That isn't it,* she wanted to scream. *I don't have children to spare. I cannot spare these children.* Her eyes stung, and her hand shook as she signed her name.

The adoption worker held her elbow as they walked down the stairs. Still she stumbled on the bottom step. When they reached the sidewalk, the bright light momentarily blinded her. The man pulled out his sunglasses and climbed on his scooter. Lan settled behind him.

He started the bike. "I'm going to the orphanage to deliver a book of photos I just received and to take photos to send to the United States," he said over the motor, patting the bag slung over his shoulder. "I will check on your children."

"Take me with you," Lan said.

"I shouldn't."

"Please take me with you," she begged.

"We'll only stay a few minutes," the adoption worker said.

Lan walked into the baby room. The orphanage worker handed her Mai. She kissed the sleeping baby's forehead and handed her back to the woman.

"Where is Binh?" Lan asked the adoption worker, stepping back onto the second-floor veranda to look out over the dirt soccer field below.

"Mama!" She turned, and there he was, racing across the tiles. He threw himself at her. She stumbled backward, caught herself against the rail, and stooped to wrap her arms around him.

He tilted his face toward hers. "Where is Hang?"

"At school."

"Have you come to take me home?" He clung to her.

"No. Just to visit."

Binh began to cry.

"You must stay here, little one," Lan said.

He let go of her and stood tall. "I never see Little Sister, and there's not much food here, either."

"Soon you will have plenty to eat. And you will see your sister. Wait and see."

"Take me home. I miss Grandmother. And Hang. And you."

The adoption worker walked up behind Binh. "Little boy," he said, "she can't take you home." He opened a small book of photographs. "Look, here is a family for you to live with in America."

Lan studied the photo. A tall American man with brown curly hair and a big smile stood with his arm around a woman with short, dark hair. They stood in front of a gigantic white house. On the next page was a picture of a room with yellow walls and two little beds, one with a fence around it. Next, the couple stood in a grove of white flowering trees, a white mountain rising behind them. *Snow.* She'd heard of snow but had never seen it. The nuns told her about snow, about mountains in France that touched the sky. *White as snow,* they'd say. *Clean as snow. As high as the mountains. As close to heaven as the mountaintops.*

"These are the people who want to adopt your children. They want both of them. Most people want babies, but they want Binh, too."

Binh pushed against the album, knocking it to the veranda floor. It slid along the tile, bounced through the railing, and fell to the dirt courtyard below. Lan grabbed Binh's hand, ashamed to have him act this way. The orphanage people would think she hadn't taught him to behave. "Take me home!" he wailed.

Lan let go of his hand and turned away from him.

"Mama! What are you doing?" he sobbed. "Don't leave me." He dove to the floor and slid across the smooth tile and then grabbed Lan's ankle.

"This wasn't a good idea," the adoption worker said. "I shouldn't have brought you here."

"Binh, Binh." Lan turned and bent down. "You need to be a big boy. Big boys don't act this way. Be brave." Binh sobbed. Lan reached for him. He threw his head against her shoulder, banging his forehead against her collarbone.

Lan turned toward the adoption worker. "I can't leave him." She began to cry.

"Why not?"

"I can't do this to my child."

"But he'll have a wonderful life in America. He'll go to school, have plenty of food, have all that he needs."

The orphanage director, Mrs. Ho, came out of her office.

"She wants to take her son," the adoption worker said.

Mrs. Ho shook her head. "You can't."

Stubbornness welled inside of Lan. *He's still my son.* "I take either Binh or the baby girl. Which would you prefer?"

Lan and Binh walked the ten kilometers home. She carried him the last third of the way, feeling faint. The sweat, tears, and dirt from his face stained her shirt. He wound his legs around her waist. The sun had set, but still the heat under her hat stole her breath, settled in her throat, pounded against her chest. Pain shot through her feet and back with each step.

Binh sobbed the entire way. It wasn't until he saw Hang and crawled onto her lap that he quieted.

"You brought Binh back?" Mother crouched in front of the family altar.

"I couldn't leave him. He cried and cried," Lan said.

"You brought him back for good?"

Lan nodded.

"You shouldn't have gone to visit."

Binh began to cry again.

"You could have sent him to heaven and instead you brought him back to hell? Don't be selfish, Lan." Mother shook her head.

The couple looks kind; the house is huge. Mai will have lots of books and will live among the trees. Lan shifted her eyes from Mother to her two children.

Mother's voice softened. "Now, now. How is the baby?"

"Better. She's getting fat."

"Binh looks better too. In another month or two he would have been a chubby boy. Do you love Binh less than the baby? Is that why you brought him back?"

Lan sighed. She'd lost a day of work. And now she had another mouth to feed.

*G*en stood at the dining room table and placed the passports in the gray accordion file along with copies of their home study and tax forms. She lined up the Deet mosquito repellant, malaria medication, antibiotics, lice shampoo, and diaper-rash ointment along the edge of the table.

She fingered the velvet jewelry box that held a locket with Mai and Binh's photos. She hoped the birth mother would like it. She stacked the books she planned to take—*Goodnight Moon, Where the Wild Things Are, Noah's Ark, Baby Moses,* and *Brown Bear, Brown Bear, What Do You See?* Next she opened the Playmobile set of a family—a dad, mom, child, and baby with a blue car, roof rack, and bicycles—and put the pieces in a Ziploc bag with a pink zipper. She carefully placed the books and toys in a red backpack and added a small notebook of unlined paper, crayons, a toothbrush and toothpaste, a box of animal crackers, and another Ziploc bag filled with pouches of fruit snacks.

The two car seats sat against the wall. Binh's was a high-back booster seat with a cup holder; Mai's was an infant seat. A double jogger stroller waited next to the car seats. They were told it could handle the gravel roads around their house. Maggie had said that a stroller couldn't handle the uneven streets and crumbling sidewalks of Vietnam; instead a front pack for the baby would work best. Jeff could carry Binh.

Gen filled the backpack with diapers, baby toys, a teething ring, a pacifier, and two bottles. Maggie had said not to take formula; they would buy whatever Mai had been fed in the orphanage in Vietnam.

Gen headed upstairs to the children's room. *The children.* The words sang to her. She repeated them over and over in her head several times a day. She took the hamper from the corner and carried it to the dresser. She opened the top drawer and took out Osh-Kosh baby T-shirts and Old Navy little boy

59

underwear. Snipping the tags off with the little scissors, she dropped each item of clothing into the hamper—shorts and shirts, little dresses, socks, sun hats, bibs, and two bath towels with sewn-in hoods. *The children. The children's room. The children's clothes.* She pulled four flannel blankets and a stack of spit rags from the shelf above the changing table. How many years had she dreamed of draping a spit rag over her shoulder for her own baby? Her heart swelled. She'd been waiting her entire life for this. They would travel next week. That's what Maggie had said. It was time to wash the clothes.

They were meeting her dad, Sharon, Don, Jake, and Aunt Marie at the Columbia Gorge Hotel for Jeff's birthday dinner. Gen had left school at three thirty to get some things done at home first. For a decade she had watched other teachers rush out to pick up their kids from day care or rush a child to music lessons or basketball practice. Now she was rushing home to wash baby clothes and pack books and toys.

Maggie had said she would call in a day or two with the exact travel date, and she would fax the itinerary as soon as possible. It was really going to happen. Gen threw the last of Binh's shorts into the basket. *Binh.* They'd decided to call him by his Vietnamese name. They'd also give him the American name Samuel, "asked of God." Samuel Binh Taylor. Mai's first name would be Olivia. Olivia Mai Taylor. Olivia meant "olive branch, peace." Gen chose it in memory of her mother. They hadn't decided on whether they would call her Olivia or Mai. They wanted to wait to see if it would be confusing for Binh if they called her Olivia.

Gen picked up the laundry hamper and headed to the landing. In a few weeks Binh would be running up and down the stairs. In a year Mai would follow her brother. Mai was nearly two months now. Gen ached to travel. She didn't want her children to spend any more time in the orphanage than they had to.

She backed through the swinging kitchen door and headed to the washer on the mud porch. She opened the lid and pulled the colored shorts and shirts and big boy underwear and bright sundresses out of the basket and tossed them in the washer, added the soap, and spun the dial.

The phone rang. She hoped it wasn't Jake saying he would be late. He'd been in Japan on business.

Gen picked up the phone with a cheery hello. It wasn't Jake. It was Maggie.

"Hello, Gen," she said. "I need you to sit down, okay?"

Gen hated it when people said that. She leaned against the counter.

"Are you sitting?"

"Yes," Gen lied.

"Is Jeff home yet?"

"Not yet. Soon." *What is Maggie getting at?*

"Bad news. Binh's not at the orphanage. One of our Vietnamese adoption workers called. I waited a few days to phone you, hoping the birth mom would take Binh back, but she hasn't."

"What?" *Take Binh back? What is Maggie talking about?*

"The birth mom went to the orphanage last week. She took Binh home. She's decided not to relinquish him."

Decided not to relinquish him? Can she do that? "I thought it was a done deal." Never in her wildest fears had Gen imagined the birth mom changing her mind. That was what American birth moms did.

"Gen," Maggie said with a hint of irritation in her voice, "it's not a done deal until you get that final approval from the United States Consulate after you've gone through all the Vietnamese procedures and the U.S. INS." Maggie's voice grew softer. "I'm sorry. Sometimes these things happen."

"You said you'd never had a Vietnamese birth mom change her mind."

Maggie paused. "You're right. I did say that. And I haven't, until now. You have to think that these things happen for a reason." *What reason?* Gen wanted to scream. "At least he's with his mom," Maggie added.

Gen thought of the little girl that Robyn and Sean had planned to adopt. The last word on her was that the mom couldn't take her back, that she would stay at the orphanage.

"Can Binh's birth mom provide for him? You said she was destitute."

"The adoption worker says that she loves him very much."

"But can she take care of him?" Gen felt a flood of resentment.

"That's for her to decide."

"What about Mai?"

"She's at the orphanage. The adoption worker said the birth mother has no intention of taking Mai back."

"How can we know for sure?"

"Mai is a newborn. Binh is four years old. It's harder to give up a child that you've lived with."

Gen turned from the counter and leaned her back against the doorframe. She slid to the floor.

"Gen." Maggie's voice surged with concern. "Are you okay?"

No. No, I'm not okay. He was my child. She thought of Robyn. She'd thought she had understood when Robyn and Sean lost their referral. Now she really understood.

"Gen?"

"I'm okay."

"I know you're not okay, not really. It will take time. When you're ready, we could look for another child if you'd like."

"Can we still travel next week?"

"No, you'll have to wait. Or travel twice."

Gen's head began to pound. They couldn't afford to travel twice. "If we wait, Mai will be older." *What if she gets sick while we wait? What if she gets tuberculosis or even polio?* They couldn't wait.

"Talk to Jeff," Maggie said. Had Maggie waited to call until late in the afternoon, thinking Jeff would be home? "Call me back tomorrow. If I haven't heard from you by the time office hours are over, I'll call you."

Gen stood at the window and gazed out over the orchards. *Why, God? Why did you let this happen?* Why, when they hadn't thought of adopting an older child in the first place? Why, when she'd fallen in love with Binh's startled face?

Jeff's pickup pulled into the driveway. She left the window and walked slowly into the kitchen, squeezing through the swinging door, not wanting to push it wide open. The washer with the load of children's clothes began to spin. She opened the door to Jeff. "Maggie called," she said.

He smiled.

Gen shook her head. "It's not good." Her words tumbled out over each other as she relayed the news.

"Maybe Binh's birth mom will change her mind," Jeff said.

There were times when Jeff's optimism sustained Gen, but not this time. "I can't think that way."

He took her hand, and they sank, side by side, to the kitchen floor. Gen rested her head against Jeff's flannel shirt. She began to cry. He put his arm around her shoulder.

"At least we still have Mai."

"I feel so empty without Binh."

"I know." Jeff ran his fingers through her hair.

Gen thought of the birth mom and felt a flicker of compassion. If Gen felt this way about losing Binh, whom she'd never met, how did the birth mom feel about giving up Mai, whom she had birthed? "This adoption thing is so hard," Gen said. Her head pounded harder. "Why does it have to be so hard? Why after infertility do we have to go through all this? It's too hard."

"Don't think of them as one ordeal. Try to separate them, okay? Infertility is all about loss. Adoption is about loss and gain."

"Right now it feels as though they're both all about loss."

Jeff peered into Gen's face.

"Why do we have to want this so badly?" Gen said.

Jeff shook his head. "Maybe because God really wants us to be parents."

On the freeway, headed toward the Columbia Gorge Hotel, Gen said she didn't want to tell their families about the birth mom taking Binh back.

"We have to," Jeff said. "They'll know something is wrong."

"I don't want to talk about it. They'll have questions we don't have answers to."

Jeff shook his head.

"What?"

"They'll feel bad for us, that's all. Your dad will pray for us. If we don't tell them tonight, it'll be harder to tell them tomorrow."

Would her father chalk it up to the country, that only bad things come from Vietnam? Would Aunt Marie think that they had "asked for it" in agreeing to take an older child? "You're right; we should tell them," she relented. "But please don't let the conversation center on Binh all evening. It's too hard."

Gen sat and stared at the whitecaps on the Columbia River through the restaurant window. Her father and Aunt Marie studied their menus. Storm clouds scudded over the rim rocks across the Gorge. The young pine trees clung to the cliffs outside the window and bent in the shapes of bows, ready to fire their arrows. A kaleidoscope of windsurfer sails turned in unison—first north, then south—riding the waves. Gen folded her arms, trying to ward off the chill.

Sharon asked Jake about his latest girlfriend. "I'm going to pop the question," Jake said.

Sharon clapped her hands. "When?"

Jake laughed. "Give me a few months. Probably this summer."

Sharon shook her head and turned to Gen. "Janet called last night. They've been trying to get pregnant for months. I had no idea. She's starting to feel a little frantic." Janet had finished her doctorate last spring and was teaching at the University of Houston.

"That's too bad," Gen said. "Have they gone to the doctor?"

"She has an appointment next week."

"Tell her to relax," Jeff said.

The conversation shifted back to Jake and then on to Japan and other Asian cultures. Jake asked what airline Jeff and Gen would fly to Vietnam and what cities they would visit. Jeff hadn't said anything about Binh yet. Jake asked if they would land in Hanoi or Saigon.

"At Tan Son Nhut Airport in Saigon," Jeff said.

Gen shot a glance at her father. He seemed unfazed. They would land where her mother had died. On most days she purposely kept herself from thinking about it. She looked back out onto the whitecaps of the river. A windsurfer dipped his sail into the water and fell off his board. Gen watched him struggle to climb back on.

Jeff reached for her hand. "Your turn," he whispered. Sharon stared at her. The waitress stood, pen poised to take the order.

"The trout," Gen said. "I'll take the trout." She always ordered the trout.

"What's wrong?" Sharon asked.

Jeff glanced at Gen, and she gave him a small nod. "We're not going to be able to adopt Binh." Jeff's voice cracked as he said it.

Sharon's hand flew to her mouth. "What happened?"

"The birth mom took him home."

"Oh, no," Sharon said.

Aunt Marie dropped her menu on the table. Dad lowered his slowly.

"What about the baby?" Don asked.

"She's still at the orphanage." Jeff's voice grew stronger.

"What about all the things you have for Binh?" Sharon asked. "What will you do with those?"

"We could still take them with us," Gen said as she looked at Jeff. He nodded. Gen stroked a short strand of hair behind her ear. "We'll take all his stuff. The toys and clothes. The books." Gen smiled a little. That felt a bit better, to think of Binh with his things. They'd leave his photo in the locket for the birth mother too. That way she'd have photos of both her children.

"Maybe it's for the best," Aunt Marie said.

Jeff shook his head. Gen pulled another strand of hair behind her ear. Here it came.

"You know, Gen, you wondered if you should take an older child," her aunt continued.

"Marie," Dad said.

Sharon stared at her. Don shifted in his chair.

Aunt Marie flung her napkin open in her lap. "It has to be for the best. Better for this to happen now than when you're over there. And taking an older child is full of risks."

Gen took a deep breath and let it out. She knew Aunt Marie had tamed her response because they were with Jeff's family. Otherwise, she probably would have said it wasn't too late to back out of adopting Mai, that it was time for Gen to learn to be content, and that losing Binh's referral was confirmation of Gen and Jeff's foolishness. She frowned at her aunt and then softened, thinking of the shower, of Aunt Marie's good intentions. "At first I wondered what issues he might have too," Gen said, "but after I saw his picture, none of that mattered. I just wanted to be his mom."

Sharon reached across the table and squeezed Gen's hand. "Honey, we know. We're so sorry."

"I'm just trying to look on the bright side." Aunt Marie took a sip of water.

Gen blinked quickly. *There is no bright side. Except for Binh's birth mom. And Binh.* It was all such an emotional tangle.

"Will you request another child?" Sharon's gaze was gentle.

"No. We'd have to wait to travel. We don't want Mai to be in the orphanage any longer than necessary."

"One little girl is all it takes," Aunt Marie said, smiling around the table, her eyes falling on Gen.

One child is a blessing, a miracle. God, I don't want to be ungrateful. But Gen's heart ached for Binh.

"Jeff. Gen." Her father cleared his throat. Gen turned her head toward her dad. "I'm sorry. Sincerely sorry for your loss."

*L*an stood on the roadway, out of breath. Hang played with a stick and a shell in the dirt yard. "Hang, get your brother."

She had kept Hang home from school again to watch Binh. He'd been out of sorts since she had brought him home from the orphanage, clinging to her one minute and then wandering off the next. Yesterday he had darted into the street in front of a scooter. The driver had swerved, skidded up on the sidewalk, and almost hit two women walking near the beach. Lan was afraid to have Mother watch him, afraid she wouldn't be able to control him. She couldn't take Binh to the market where Mrs. Le would see him.

The midafternoon sun beat against Lan's shoulders. She had stopped by the shack to take the children to the beach so Hang could help carry the baskets filled with lychee nuts and coconut drinks. She hoped the beach would be crowded with tourists who had money in their pockets.

Binh ran up to her and shook his head from side to side. He grinned. His hair covered his eyebrows. He held up his arms and flexed his muscles. "I'm strong!" he shouted. "Let me carry the baskets."

"In a few years," Lan said to him, her irritation growing. "Come with me. Hurry, we need to get to the beach while the tourists are still hungry."

Binh fell to his knees in the road and rolled onto his back. "What are you doing?" Lan asked. He smiled. "Get up," she said.

"I want to watch the sky."

"Come on," Lan said.

Hang grabbed her brother under his arms and pulled him to his feet. Binh squirmed away from her and ran down the street. At the beach Binh ran into the water over and over. Hang finally threw up her hands, exasperated. "Mama!" she called out. "I can't control him!"

"Let's go," Lan said quietly. Binh ran away from them into the waves. Lan hurried after him, soaking her pants. On the way home they stopped by the market to pay Mrs. Le. Lan told Hang to wait with Binh a block away. As she hurried away from the market, after bowing quickly to Mrs. Le, she heard Binh yelling. "I want grapes!" Hang held the younger child by the arm; Binh pulled and pulled, trying to escape his sister. Lan began to run, her stomach aching; she hoped Mrs. Le's ears and eyes were as bad as they seemed.

Lan spooned the rice into the plastic bowls and then dipped the spoon into the container of bean curd and spread a little over the top of the rice. Mother had picked morning glory leaves from the field at the end of the road. Binh shook his head at the cooked green leaves. Hang held out her bowl. Lan put the greens in each child's bowl and then took Binh's from him. She filled the spoon and moved it toward her son's mouth.

"No, no," he said. "Chopsticks."

"Let Mama do it," Lan said. She mixed the rice and greens and bean curd. He opened his mouth, and she filled it with food. Hang squatted beside her mother and held her bowl close to her mouth. She shoveled the food in quickly with her chopsticks. Binh opened his mouth like a baby bird. Lan fed him spoonful after spoonful. Every third or fourth turn she took a bite. The food settled her stomach.

"Eat, Mother," Lan said.

Her mother lay in the hammock with her eyes closed. "I'm too tired to eat."

"Here, Hang." Lan handed her the third bowl. "Take this to your grandmother."

During the night Binh cried out in his sleep. "Mama," he sobbed, "don't leave!" Lan reached over and found him in the dark, off the mat and out from under the mosquito net. She pulled him to her, tucking his thin body under the protection of her arm. Later he cried out again, this time in pain.

"Binh, Binh, go back to sleep. Let all of us sleep." Lan stroked his arm.

"He's been whimpering half the night," Mother said.

Lan felt Binh's forehead. It was hot. She would take him to the doctor in the evening, to the one who saw patients in her home after ten hours at the hospital. The government paid her little for her work; she made up for it by seeing patients after hours.

During the day Lan left Binh with Mother while she hurried from tourist spot to tourist spot selling lychee nuts and souvenirs. She caught herself watching for the couple from the photos, the tall man with curly hair and the woman with caring eyes.

"Fifty-thousand dong," the doctor said.

"I only have thirty thousand," Lan said. She shifted Binh on her hip and pulled the money out of the bag she carried around her neck.

"Then you owe me the rest before I treat your son again." The doctor took the wad of currency from Lan. "Give him the pills morning and night for three days. His ears and throat are infected. And his lungs don't sound good. Has anyone told you that he has asthma?"

"You're the only doctor who has seen him."

"Bring him to me if his wheezing gets bad. More little ones have asthma now. It's the pollution."

Lan bowed to the doctor and turned to leave the shop. Hang followed her into the humid night. Binh whimpered and reached for Hang. Relieved, Lan slid her son into the arms of his sister. A block later Binh reached for Lan. They still had a kilometer to walk. They turned off the sidewalk onto the dirt road, and soon a scooter slowed beside them. "Hello, Lan." It was Cuong. A pretty young girl, maybe seventeen or eighteen, with a short, stylish haircut rode behind him.

Lan nodded. Binh yanked on her single braid as she carried him.

"How are you?" Cuong asked.

"We are well." She wanted to ask when he had come back, whether he had work for her. She didn't want to tell him about Mai, about the baby.

"I wanted to say hello. I'm in town for a few days. Then I'll return to Ho Chi Minh City. Business is good there." When Lan did not answer, he revved the engine and sped off. He didn't work in the sugar refinery, Lan was sure. He'd been in the city all this time making lots of money.

Selfish and stubborn, Mother would say if she knew Lan hadn't responded to Cuong. Surely she could have gotten something from him, perhaps money or black-market goods. Lan transferred Binh to her other hip. His head bounced against her shoulder.

Hang went to school the next day while Binh stayed with Mother and Lan sold cigarettes along the beach. It was Friday, and crowds of people from Ho Chi Minh City had arrived by bus for a long weekend. Again Lan looked for the American couple but didn't see them. When she arrived home, Binh sat at the doorway to the hut with a bottle of Coca-Cola in his hands and a smile on his face. "Grandmother bought Coca," he said impishly. A plastic container of half-eaten orange rice sat beside him.

"Where is Hang?" Lan peered behind him through the doorway.

"Playing down the road with her school friends."

"Mother," Lan called out, adjusting her eyes to the dim interior of the hut. Where had Mother gotten the money?

Lan walked toward the form in the hammock. "Mother." She reached over and shook her mother's shoulder. She didn't stir. "Mother!" Lan's heart quickened. "Mother!"

"Let me sleep." Mother's raspy voice startled Lan, and she pushed against her mother's body. The hammock swung back and forth.

"I thought you were dead." Lan's heart raced.

"Not yet."

"Where did you get the money for Coca-Cola?" Lan asked.

"Cuong stopped by."

"You took his money?"

"Of course." Mother sat up.

"Don't take it again. I don't want him coming by." She missed him, missed being with a man, missed his money, but his money meant his company and then another baby. She didn't want any more babies. She couldn't give another one away. Let him spend his time with the teenage girl.

Mother coughed.

"Why didn't you buy medicine with the money?" Lan pushed the hammock again, this time gently.

"Look at Binh. He's so happy. And it's keeping him quiet so I can sleep." Mother pulled the thin, faded red blanket over her head.

"Mama." Binh took her hand, the Coca-Cola bottle tightly clutched in his other hand. "I feel better."

"Good, Binh." She felt his forehead.

"My ears don't hurt. All better." He smiled his impish grin.

Lan bent down and picked up her son and held him tightly. "Oh, Binh, what are we going to do?"

"Let's eat dinner." He smiled and then laughed as if he'd told the best joke ever.

"I love you, little one." Lan squeezed her son and then slid him down her torso to the floor. She remembered how she used to play with Hang. She would tickle her and chase her around the yard. They would play hide-and-seek in the shack after the sun had set, before bedtime. That was when she felt young and still hopeful that Chinh would send for her, hopeful that life would soon get better. "Let's go find some morning glories to go with the rice," Lan said to her son.

Binh shook his head. "No, no. I'll drink Coca-Cola and eat the sweet orange rice."

"No, no." Irritation filled Lan's voice. "You'll eat what Mama tells you."

*G*en sat at her desk and looked around her classroom, at the alphabet above the chalkboard, the bulletin board with I Love to Read in neon green letters, and the colorful flock of origami cranes suspended from the ceiling. The sweaty smell of the students hung in the air, and the janitor's broom made a swishing noise over the linoleum in the hall.

She glanced back down at the last week of April in her lesson-plan book. Maggie had phoned early that morning to say they would fly out in two days and be gone for just over two weeks.

Although Gen would take off the rest of the year and half of next year, she planned to bring Mai in for the children to see the last week of school. She smiled as she thought of their excitement. The pain of losing Binh was starting to ease. Throughout the day, she thought of him with his mother. What four-year-old child would choose enough food and an education over his mother?

Tomorrow she planned to read a book about international adoption to her students and show them photos from Vietnam. She knew they'd especially like the photo of the little boy riding a water buffalo.

She heard a rapping on the window and peered through the glass. It was Jeff.

"Your cell phone was off," he said as Gen swung open the outside door. He pulled her to him. He wore his brown corduroy jacket with the fuzzy collar. Gen smelled the orchard on his neck. "Maggie called."

Maggie called. She hated those words. She studied Jeff's face. He cleared his throat. "We can't travel this week. It may be a few weeks."

"What happened now?"

"The Vietnamese national paper ran a series of articles, and the last one was just published. The Vung Tau People's Committee wants to suspend adoptions until they can do an investigation."

Gen's eyes filled with tears. *Not another setback.*

"It's going to be okay." Jeff squeezed Gen's shoulder.

"First Binh and now this."

"Maggie said this sort of thing happens frequently. She said that adoptions in the whole country should be shut down and reorganized like China's into a national program instead of each province having its own rules."

"Not shut down! Not now."

"Not now. But sometime."

"How long does she think it will be?"

"Two weeks." Jeff said. *Mai will be in the orphanage for two more weeks. We'll be without our baby. She'll be without her mama and daddy.* "Maggie said that she would e-mail us a new photo of Mai tomorrow," Jeff added.

Gen barely listened. Mai was already more than two months old. She would be over three months by the time they got there. *God, why can't we travel now? I don't want our baby to grow up in an orphanage. I want her to grow up with us.*

"We need to pray we'll travel soon," Jeff said. "We'll be up against harvest if this goes on much longer."

Gen opened the back door to the house. She slid her backpack over her shoulder and down to the floor as she headed into the office. She had to see if the photo had come by e-mail. Gen clicked on AOL; there was an e-mail from Maggie. With a double click, words filled the screen. Gen ignored the message and opened the attachment. Her heart swelled. There was her sweet baby. She'd grown so much. Her brown eyes were wide open, her eyebrows raised, her full lips parted slightly as if contemplating a smile. Her little nose barely existed. Gen's hand went to her own large nose. She chuckled. *Oh, baby. If nothing else, you'll know you were adopted because of that sweet little nose.* Mai lay on an orange woven mat, and she wore a white T-shirt. There were a few red marks on her chin.

Gen hit Print and closed the attachment. The message popped back up on the screen.

Dear Gen and Jeff,

I talked to Vietnam today. I have more information about what's going on. A series of articles in which the author seems to have distorted the information has caused concern among Vietnamese and American officials. There's talk of a moratorium on adoptions by August. This will not affect you in any way. However, we are not having families travel at this time. We plan to have you travel in two weeks. I was assured by my contact in Vietnam that all of Mai's paperwork is complete. Call me or e-mail me back if you have any questions. I'll let you know as soon as I know anything more definite. Keep your chins up.

Maggie

"The Vietnamese adoption chat rooms are buzzing about the articles," Robyn said over the phone. "I'll forward them to you." Gen was sure Robyn spent hours each day on the Internet, finding out everything she could about Vietnam and adoptions.

Gen read the articles to Jeff before they went to sleep. The writer talked of foreigners "hunting" babies and offering money to mothers before their babies were born. He said that foreigners adopted Vietnamese children as tax breaks and because they were lonely. He wrote that babies were put in feeding centers to fatten them up before foreigners would take them. He spoke of avoiding "the separation of blood relations." He also claimed that a Vietnamese official said that twenty percent of the adopted children don't integrate into a foreign living situation. "No one cares about how these children live abroad," he wrote.

A rebuttal by a U.S. official in Vietnam followed. He wrote that the Vietnamese official clarified that he had said, "Eighty percent of adoptions go smoothly" not that "twenty percent of children don't integrate," but the U.S. official admitted that baby buying did exist in Vietnam.

"What have we gotten into?" Gen dropped the stack of papers to the floor on her side of the bed.

Jeff shook his head.

"What do we do?"

"Trust God that he will work this out," he said.

In the night Gen woke with the image of Mai floating in her head, the near smile, the shock of dark hair, the tiny nose. *I want to trust you, Lord,* Gen prayed. *Show me how to trust.*

Gen didn't realize she wasn't singing until the song was over and Jeff closed the hymnbook. The congregation sat.

"What's on your heart today?" the pastor boomed from the pulpit. Gen glanced up, startled. Was he talking to her? She smiled, realizing that it was the introduction to his sermon.

He read the scripture: " 'You have been given fullness in Christ, who is the head over every power and authority.' Colossians 2:10." Over every power and authority? Even officials in foreign countries?

Her mind wandered again to the articles and the investigation, Mai in the orphanage, Binh and his mother. She thought of her own mother and her love for the people of Vietnam, of Kim and the nameless girl in Vietnam she'd prayed for all those years ago. The girl would be in her thirties now.

A half hour later she realized the pastor was reading prayer requests. That meant the service was almost over. "We have time for sharing," the pastor said.

Jeff stood. "I'd like to ask you to pray for our daughter, Mai, who is in an orphanage in Vietnam. Gen and I are adopting her. We thought we would be there today, but our travel has been delayed. Please pray that God would keep our baby safe, that we would travel soon, and that God would use us during our time in Vietnam."

Jeff sat down. Gen took his hand. Several people prayed.

"What can we do to help, besides pray?" The man sitting behind Gen put his hand on her shoulder after the last song ended. His daughter was in their Sunday school class.

"We'd like to do something," his wife said. "Do you need anything for the baby?"

"No, we have what we need," Gen answered.

"How about for the other children in the orphanage?" the woman asked. "The church members could donate things for you to take over."

Gen looked at Jeff. She thought of Robyn and Sean's first referral who would grow up in the orphanage. "I think that's a great idea," Gen said. "We'll ask our adoption contact, just to make sure."

"Sure," Maggie responded. "Clothes, shoes, art supplies, soccer balls. Medical supplies. Money. Any of that would be appreciated." By the end of the week there were boxes at their church, her father's church in Portland, and the school. Gen stood in the hall outside her classroom. The children and teachers had brought coloring books, crayons, sandals, shorts, pajamas, T-shirts, and Matchbox cars. It was Friday afternoon. She was anxious to get home and see if Maggie had left an e-mail or a voice mail.

Her cell phone began to ring. Maybe it was Maggie saying they would travel by the end of the week. It was Jeff. "Maggie called. It's gotten worse. The Justice Department of Vung Tau has called for a police investigation. All adoptions are on hold until it's finished."

*L*an carried her baskets along the sidewalk, swinging her yoke to fit through the crowd. It was near sunset, and she had bean curd and a squash to go with rice for dinner. She turned at the Justice Department and headed east; across the street a small black car pulled to a stop. A man climbed out and faced her for a second. *Jet black hair. Square face. Around forty-five. Older Brother?*

He turned toward the driver. Lan froze, willing the man to turn toward her again. He did. He wore a light green shirt, black trousers, and polished shoes. The man closed the car door and headed toward the outside stairwell of the Justice Department. Lan watched his dark head bob up a few steps and then disappear.

She crossed the street and waited by a street barber on the sidewalk; she toyed with the idea of climbing the stairs to the Justice Department but decided against it. *Maybe it isn't Older Brother.* The day darkened. Mother and the children would be hungry, impatient for their dinner. She stood and lifted her yoke onto her shoulders. It wasn't Older Brother. She couldn't trust her eyes—or her memory. Footsteps started down the stairs; a man's head appeared in the shadows and then his face.

"Quan?" she said.

The man stopped and tilted his head.

Lan pushed her hat back from her face.

"Little Sister?" he said.

"Yes, I'm Lan." Her heart raced as she said it.

"How are you?" he said.

She bowed, swinging the baskets, forcing the yoke onto the base of her neck. There was a long silence. "Are you down from Hanoi on business?" Lan stood straight again.

"I've been working here," he said. "For a few weeks. I've been transferred to the Justice Department of Vung Tau." He clasped his hands behind his back.

"Have you been well?" Lan tipped her head to the side and peered at Older Brother from under the brim of her hat.

"Yes, yes. And you? Did you recover from the land-mine incident?"

"Yes. Thank you for your help all those years ago." *How long ago had it been? Twenty years?*

"How is Mother? Is she still alive?"

Lan nodded. "She is sick but living."

"Good, good," Quan said. "Have her call on me here sometime."

Lan watched him go. Her face burned. Sweat trickled from the base of her skull, under her braid, down her back. *The state is more important than family, play, religion, and traditions.* Lan remembered those words from school all those years. *More important than family.* She would not tell Mother that she had seen Quan. It would only make her hope that he would help.

"You had a male visitor," the neighbor said the next evening when Lan returned home.

She raised her eyebrows. *Not Cuong.* "Where is Mother?" she asked.

"She took the little one and left with the man."

Lan quickly put her baskets in the shack and headed down the road, her knees shaking as she walked. *Where is Binh? Where is Mother?* She heard Hang and a friend laughing.

"Daughter," she called out. "Where is Binh? Where is your grandmother?"

Hang shook her head. "They were gone when I got back from school."

Lan headed back toward her home. A black car came toward her. *Older Brother.* She shielded her eyes against the setting sun. The car stopped, and the door opened. Binh ran toward her, and Lan scooped him up. His breath smelled of fish sauce. Mother slowly crawled out of the backseat.

"Where have you been?" Lan demanded.

"With me," Quan said as he unfolded his body from the car. "Why didn't you tell Mother you saw me last night?"

Mother smiled across the table at Lan. A waitress stood behind her. Lan listened as Older Brother ordered for all of them, pots of seafood and vegetables. Lan had walked by the restaurant many times, but she had never dreamed of eating in it. Older Brother ordered tea for the grownups and watermelon drinks for the children.

"How is school?" Older Brother asked Hang.

"Good, Uncle," she said. Lan knew her daughter was pleased to have suddenly acquired an uncle, a real uncle.

"How about you?" Older Brother asked Binh. "When do you start school?"

Binh tapped his chopsticks on the table, beating out a rhythm.

Lan took the sticks from her son. "Answer the question, Binh." *Why was Older Brother so distant last night and now so friendly?*

"Next year!" Binh exclaimed. Lan felt her stomach tighten. How could she afford to send him?

"Good," Quan said.

He wants something. Older Brother is after something. What could it be? The waitress brought a stack of bowls and spoons and a warmer full of rice. The boiling pots of seafood, simmering with vegetables, followed.

"Eat," Mother whispered to Lan. "Eat all you can." *Eat to make up for the last twenty-five years?* It would take the rest of her life.

Two days later Lan worked the fruit stall at the market. Her eyes grew heavy as she sat in the shade of the canopy that covered the stall. Business was light. Most people were home napping.

"Mother said I would find you here." Lan's eyes crept open. Older Brother stood in front of her, holding a large brown envelope in his hand. "I came across your name in the files at the Justice Department. Could I ask you some questions?"

He knows he can ask me whatever he wants. Lan sat up straight and slipped her feet back into her flip-flops. She nodded, preparing herself to give him safe answers, answers that wouldn't bring harm to her or Mother or her children.

"I was surprised to see that you relinquished a child for adoption."

Lan nodded again.

"Why?"

"I can't raise another child. I wouldn't be able to give her enough to eat. To send her to school." *I spend most of my money on medicine for Mother, with no help from anyone, especially not you.*

"You've had three children now without the benefit of marriage?" He posed it as a question.

"I was married," Lan said.

Older Brother raised his eyebrows. "What happened?"

"He—" Lan paused. A fly flew under the brim of her hat. She brushed it away.

"Go on."

"Disappeared," she said.

"When?"

"Years ago." So many years ago. She was old now, so far from being the twenty-year-old girl in love with her husband.

"Before the last two children?"

Lan nodded. An older boy ran by the fruit stand, kicking a rock.

"Who asked you to give up your baby?"

"No one." Lan took a deep breath. Dare she tell him she gave up Binh, too, only to take him back? "I took her to the orphanage."

"How much money did they pay you?" Older Brother tucked the brown envelope under his arm and clasped his hands behind his back.

Lan felt confused. "For the baby?"

He nodded.

"Nothing." *Why is he asking these questions?*

"Then why did you take Binh back? Did they refuse to give you money for him? Since Americans want babies, not four-year-old little boys." The intensity of Older Brother's voice startled Lan.

"No. No, that wasn't it at all." *Of course he knew she'd originally given up Binh, too. He'd seen the paperwork.* "I took Binh back because he was so home-sick. Because he begged me to take him home."

"Have you been able to feed him since you brought him home from the orphanage?" Quan asked.

"Barely." She glanced up at Older Brother and then down at the ground. After dinner the other night she had been thinking about him nonstop. Perhaps he would help them now. Pay for Hang's schooling. Bring a big bag of rice to the shack now and then. Buy medicine for Mother, maybe even take Mother to his home. Maybe he would take all of them.

"So you really didn't need to take him to the orphanage after all?" Older Brother stood tall and towered over Lan.

She didn't answer. He had no idea what it was like to worry every day if there would be enough money to buy food, to count the days since they'd had more to eat with their rice than morning glory, sweet potato leaves, and smelly fish. Sweat trickled down her back. She shifted in the plastic chair.

"Be honest with me, Lan. Who paid you for the children? Who decided not to pay you for Binh?"

Lan shook her head and looked at Older Brother. "No one paid me for my children."

He raised his eyebrows at her in a mocking expression. "It was because Binh is older, wasn't it? Because they only want babies."

She laughed, quietly at first and then louder. She thought of the couple in the picture, the husband and wife who wanted Binh, too. The old man selling baskets across the street stared at her. Abruptly she stopped laughing. "Look at me. Do I look like anyone has paid me any money? Did you ask Mother how much rice we have in the house? Did you ask her how long it's been since she's had medicine?" She brushed at her shirt and pants. "Do you see the holes in my clothes?"

He glanced off in the distance and then focused back on Lan. He bowed slightly and said with determination, "We'll talk more, soon."

Blowing rain continued through the night. Lightning flashed and thunder clapped all around the shack, and thick air filled the tiny home. Mother coughed in her hammock. Binh began to wheeze and cry out in his sleep. Lan pulled him to her, sat up, and lifted him onto her lap. The wheezing continued. She dragged him out from under the mosquito net and stood with him in her arms.

"Mama," he called out. He clung to her. She swayed back and forth and clucked her tongue to soothe him. She walked to the door and eased it open. The rain had stopped. She stepped into the yard and gazed up at the sky, where the stars twinkled behind thin clouds.

Binh, with his eyes still closed, began to cluck his tongue too. Lan held him tightly. The dawn would soon arrive. The loudspeaker crackled to life with patriotic music.

J eff and Gen sat in the Dragonfish Café, a Pan-Asian restaurant in downtown Portland, on Mother's Day Eve.

"How are your noodles?" Jeff asked Gen.

"Good." She put her fork down and sipped her tea.

Three weeks ago she'd looked forward to Mother's Day for the first time in all these years. Tonight she dreaded it, worse than ever before. No mother to give a gift to, no baby to make her a mom.

She took another bite of her dinner and thought about Maggie's daily e-mails that usually started with "I talked to Vietnam today." The image of Maggie standing with a cutout S-shaped map of Vietnam held to her ear popped into Gen's head each time.

This morning's e-mail said again that there were political problems between government officials in Vietnam concerning adoption. She assured them it had nothing to do with their case. However, the couple from Ohio had backed out because of the problems. Robyn and Sean still waited for a referral, so Gen and Jeff would be the only adoptive parents traveling from their group, which was uncommon with Mercy for Children. Maggie added that Mai was healthy, waiting for them in the orphanage.

Gen twirled noodles around her fork. "Maggie said if we can't travel next week, she will travel to Vung Tau and see if she can talk to someone at the Justice Department."

Jeff nodded. "I read the e-mail."

"Do you think it's worse than Maggie is letting on?" So far she had believed Maggie, believed that twists and turns were to be expected in international adoptions.

"I don't know." Jeff took a bite of his red curry.

She put down her fork. "Maggie's daughter is expecting a baby at the end of June. At least that's what Robyn told me."

"End of June?" he asked.

She nodded.

"You didn't tell me that. I wish it were the middle of June. She would have more motivation to get us back home in time for harvest."

"It's a travesty." Gen sat up straight. "Mai shouldn't have to be in the orphanage this long. Not when she has parents who will take care of her."

Jeff nodded.

"What if it doesn't work out?"

"It will work out." He raised his cup of tea. "Happy Mother's Day."

Monday after school Gen stopped by the grocery store. They needed milk and bread. *If I stock up on everything, we'll travel this week.* She imagined the produce turning into slime, the milk curdling, the bread molding. She smiled as she chose three cucumbers, red-leaf lettuce, on-the-vine tomatoes, a big bunch of bananas, grapes, and three lemons. She picked out whole-wheat bread, bagels, cream cheese, and salsa, and put hamburger, chicken, and steaks into the cart.

She gazed out across the Columbia as she drove toward home. To the east, The Dalles Dam spread across the river between two bends; the gray water flowed effortlessly toward the Pacific.

Cherry harvest would start the week after school ended. The cherries were coming on. Every day they listened to the weather report and watched the clouds, anticipating rain. As Jeff explained it all those years ago, the water on the inside of the cherry and the water on the outside try to get together. Too much rain would cause the cherries to split. They hired a helicopter pilot to blow the water off the trees when it stormed.

Jeff had been working from sunup to sundown to get everything done—

spraying, repairing ladders, fixing sprinklers, getting the cabins ready for the workers, and mowing between the rows of trees. The plan was to get as much done as possible before they left, and then Don would keep things going while they were gone. If they traveled soon, they would be back for harvest. Gen wouldn't drive the truck this summer. Sharon had half-jokingly volunteered to watch Mai so Gen could. Gen politely declined.

Gen pulled into the driveway, grabbed her backpack and the two gallons of milk from the back, and headed into the house. She left the rest of the groceries while she turned on the computer. She opened up AOL and clicked on the message from Maggie.

> I talked with Vietnam today. I cannot confirm a date for you to
> travel. A newly assigned official to the Justice Department is conduct-
> ing an independent investigation in Vung Tau. We must wait for the
> police report to be completed before the Justice Department will
> schedule a Giving and Receiving Ceremony. I'll get back to you as
> soon as I know anything.

Gen quickly wrote back: "But the police report was already completed!" And hit Send. She hurried out to the car and carried the rest of the groceries into the kitchen and then checked her e-mail again.

Maggie's reply was waiting when she returned.

> It was completed. The official ordered that it be redone. It appears to be
> a formality. There's no indication anything is wrong with Mai's case. I'm
> going to fly out tomorrow and be in Vung Tau by Thursday. I have an
> appointment to meet with the official. Then I'll go to the orphanage
> and take photos of Mai and e-mail them to you. Try not to worry.

Gen logged off the Internet. *Try not to worry.* She put the groceries away and then changed into jeans and a T-shirt, slipped on her work boots and gloves, and headed up the hill through the trees to help Jeff.

*T*he early morning sun hurried the day as Lan walked quickly to the market, feeling stronger than she had in a year. Binh had slept well the night before. Hang would go to school today. Mother was up to watching Binh; she was happier, she walked with a little bounce, she didn't sleep as long in the afternoons, and she had extra money in her pocket, most likely from Older Brother.

Lan turned one block before the Justice Department and headed west. On the edge of the market, a car pulled to a stop behind her. She quickened her steps.

"Sister!" She turned. Older Brother climbed out of the car and hurried toward her. "I have a favor to ask." He took her elbow, turning her toward him. "I want to see your daughter."

"She's at the orphanage." He knew that.

He shook his head. "I don't want to see her in the orphanage. I want to see her at your home."

"Why?"

"Shouldn't I be able to see my own niece before she goes to America?"

"The orphanage director won't let me take her." She pulled away from him, releasing her arm from his hand.

"Of course she will. I've already sent a request saying that your mother is old and very sick and wants to see her grandbaby one more time. I wrote that you have no intention of keeping the baby."

Lan stared at him. He had no idea what he was asking. ›

"I'll send a driver for you tomorrow, Saturday, first thing in the morning. I'll come to your house at noon to see the little girl. I'll pay for lunch for all of us."

Lan walked slowly to the fruit stand. All of us. What if he did invite all of them to live with him? What if he paid for Hang and Binh to go to school? What if tomorrow he said they would all live as a family—Older Brother, Mother, Lan, the children, even Mai?

The dream simmered all day, like a pot of broth ready for the noodles. She thought of the couple in the photo. *There are other Vietnam babies. There are lots at the orphanage. They will get a baby, a different baby.*

On the way home, she walked by the Justice Department. Maybe she would see Older Brother. Maybe a glimpse of his face would reveal his intentions. A motorcycle pulled into the garage on the first floor of the building. In the shadows, Lan saw a woman climb off and then a Vietnamese man. As they walked out of the garage onto the sidewalk before turning up the stairs, Lan saw it was the man who worked for the adoption agency and a white woman with long gray hair.

Lan held Mai tightly to her as the motorbike driver sped through the streets. She had expected Older Brother to send a car. Instead he had sent a scooter. Lan breathed deeply, taking in the smell of exhaust, the hot asphalt, the sewage, all mixed with the sweet scent of her baby.

"That'll be ten thousand dong," the driver said as he pulled in front of the shack. Binh came running out, followed by Hang and then Mother.

Lan climbed off the scooter confused. "My brother arranged this. Didn't he pay you?" Hang snatched Mai from Lan's arms.

The driver shook his head.

"There must be a mistake."

"No mistake. Just money. Ten thousand dong."

Mother shrugged, pulled the money from her pouch, and handed it to the driver.

"Have you forgiven Older Brother?" Lan ran her hand down her braid.

"What for?" Mother said. "Not paying the driver?"

Lan shook her head. *What for?* For standing by while the Viet Cong shot Father. For kicking them off the land. For ignoring them all these years.

"I'm an old woman; it was so long ago. He's still my son, my only son."

Could Lan forgive him? Perhaps if he helped them, if he had even a glimmer of hope to give her.

Older Brother arrived an hour late. He brought rice, two catfish, bamboo shoots, a yellow watermelon, and sugar cane drinks in plastic bags with straws for the children. "I thought it would be better to eat here," he said. "Easier with the baby." He held Mai awkwardly while Lan cooked the rice and fried the catfish. The baby began to fuss; he held her straight in front of him and assessed her from head to toe. "What do they feed her in the orphanage?"

Lan took out the baby bottle the worker had given her and the plastic bag of powdered mix. Binh pulled the straw from his mouth and grabbed at the bottle. "No, no," Lan said. "It's for the baby."

Mai let out a wail. Older Brother handed her back to Lan.

"Sit, sit," Mother said to Quan. First he filled a bowl of food and then sat beside her. "Tell me about your house," she said.

"House?" He laughed. "Apartment. A small apartment meant for one. It's smaller than your shack…but nicer."

"We don't mind being crowded," Mother said.

"What do you mean?" he said.

"In your apartment." Mother smiled, showing the gaps in her teeth.

"Oh, no," he said. "I have too much work to do, and I may not be here long. Besides, my first obligation is to the Republic of Vietnam."

Lan waited for him to say more. He stood and walked to the stove and spooned more fish and rice into his bowl. The light went out of Mother's eyes.

Lan worked the nipple of the bottle into Mai's mouth and stared into the baby's inky eyes. *I was as big a fool as Mother.* She wanted to curl up with the baby and sleep; she wanted to forget Older Brother and his laughter, Mother and her disappointment.

When Older Brother stood to leave, Lan asked if he could give her a ride to the orphanage to take the baby back. "I have a meeting in fifteen minutes. The driver will come for you."

"We don't have money to pay the driver," Mother said.

Older Brother dug into his pocket and pulled out five thousand dong and handed it to Lan. "I have more questions for you, Little Sister," he said. "I will find you in the market this week."

After he left, Lan sent Hang to ask Truc for a ride to the orphanage. She'd heard her motorbike fifteen minutes before. She must have stopped by her house to pick up more souvenirs to sell. Lan mixed the white powder in the bottle with water from the spigot; the baby quickly drained the milk again. Lan filled the bottle with just water and this time added a little bit of sugar for the ride back to the orphanage.

"Why aren't you working today?" Truc asked Lan.

"I will as soon as I get the baby back to the orphanage." Lan thought of all the tourists on the beach. Mai felt heavy in her arms. Yesterday Lan dreamed of keeping all her children, all of them living together with Older Brother. Now she was back to dreaming of a better life for her daughter.

*G*en woke at six Sunday morning. Jeff's side of the bed was empty. He'd said the night before that he planned to get four hours of work in before church. Gen padded down the hall to the study and turned on the computer and then logged on to e-mail. Up popped a message from Maggie.

Dear Gen and Jeff,

Good news!

I met with the official at the Vung Tau Justice Department. He was very nice. He said the investigations are nearly complete and that I should have you travel. Tickets are being reserved for Thursday, May 24. Call the travel agency tomorrow.

That's the good news. Don't think I have bad news—because I don't—but when I went to the orphanage Mai wasn't there, so I don't have a photo for you. The orphanage director told me that her family wanted to see her one last time. Mai's birth mother came and took her for the day, on Saturday. The orphanage director assured me that Mai's mother is destitute and has no intention of keeping the baby. Please do not worry.

I will meet you at Tan Son Nhut Airport in Ho Chi Minh City next Saturday. E-mail is hard to come by in Vung Tau, so you won't hear from me again (unless Mai's birth mom does change her mind).

Gen sat and stared at the computer screen. Then she gazed at the photos taped to the wall—the latest one of Mai with her dark hair sticking up and her half smile, the newborn photo with nearly closed eyes, the photo of Binh with his startled expression.

She wanted to beg God for Mai. She stood and focused on the baby girl. *If I were her birth mother, I would do everything possible to keep her. She changed her mind about Binh. What's to keep her from changing her mind about Mai?*

Gen sank back down into her chair. *Dear God, only you know what's best for Mai. Please let it be us.* She read the e-mail again, lingering on "Tan Son Nhut Airport" and "Unless Mai's birth mom does change her mind." What if Dad was right? What if only heartache came from Vietnam?

Gen's head began to ache, a dull sensation between her eyes. She went into the kitchen for water, Advil, and then a Diet Coke. She opened the back door and gazed out at the orchard. A robin hurried along the freshly mowed grass between the trees, searching for food for her babies, babies that were hidden safely in a tree. Gen didn't want to wait until Thursday to travel. She had waited long enough. She wanted to go now.

She closed the door and hurried up the stairs to Mai's room. Their suitcases were on the bed, on Binh's bed that he would never use. They had left it up for Mai, for when she was older.

Gen stepped to the closet and ran her fingers along the little dresses. Mai was more than three months old; she would be nearly four months by the time they brought her home. She would be smiling and laughing, grasping objects, but still small enough to fit in the front pack. Gen pulled several three-to-six-month-size dresses from the closet and then opened Mai's suitcase and pulled out the newborn-size clothes. How big would her daughter be?

On the floor by the bed were the suitcase and the backpack for Binh and the two large duffel bags of clothes and school supplies for the orphanage. Gen grabbed the duffel bags and dragged them down the stairs. Then, two by two, she carried all their bags down, including the folder with copies of their papers.

When Jeff came in to shower for church, the suitcases were piled in the living room.

"We had an e-mail from Maggie," Gen explained. "We travel on Thursday at the latest. I decided to get everything ready. Now I can help you prepare for harvest."

"We travel on Thursday? Really?" He gave her a broad smile.

Gen nodded. She would wait until they were driving to church to tell him about the birth mom taking Mai for the day. Gen wanted to be sitting down when she told him.

$\mathcal{L}$ an hurried through the doorway of the shack. She made out a small shape in the hammock. Binh. Where was Mother? She heard footsteps in the yard and turned, ready to scold Mother for leaving Binh alone again.

"Tran Thuy Lan?" It was a man wearing a khaki uniform.

"Yes?" Lan answered, alarmed.

"Tran Van Quan commands that you and your son report to the Justice Department." He turned abruptly and left.

What did Older Brother want now? She lifted Binh from the hammock. "Where's Grandmother?" she whispered. Binh whimpered. Lan clucked her tongue. "There, there," she said.

She hurried along the sidewalk, dragging Binh by his sticky hand. Sweat beaded around her brow under her hat. He wiggled away from her and slumped to the ground, scooting up against the concrete wall of a bicycle shop. "I'm tired," he whined. "I want to go home. I want to sleep."

"Uncle wants to see us."

"Why can't he come to us?" Binh put his head in the crook of his arm.

Why couldn't Quan stop by the shack? She was growing tired of his demands. Her stomach hurt. She grabbed Binh by his arm, jerked him to his feet, and then lifted him into her arms. He began to whimper again. He was too heavy to carry; her lower back ached. His head knocked against her hat, sending it off her head to her back. The ribbon tightened around her neck.

"My ear hurts." Binh pushed his head against Lan's cheek.

She squeezed him in frustration. Not his ear again. She didn't have the extra money for the doctor. Lan hurried up the stairs to the Justice Department, through the open door, and then stopped as she entered the dark landing, unable to see. "Grandmother." Binh slid from Lan's arms.

"Mother?" Lan's eyes adjusted. "Why are you here? Why did you leave Binh alone?"

"Lan, look who is here! Older Sister!" Mother smiled, showing her broken teeth, and grabbed the hand of the woman next to her.

Binh climbed onto the wooden chair and stood. The woman sitting beside Mother rose to her feet.

Lan took a step forward.

"Yes. It's me. Cam My."

Older Sister hugged Lan close. Lan felt her sister's soft flesh, her plump arms, her full breasts. Lan pulled away, taking in Cam My's short auburn hair, her round face, her light skin; the eye shadow, the color on her lips, the scent of good perfume; the Western skirt, and the sleeveless top.

"Older Sister has been in America," Mother said, "all these years."

"No, no." Older Sister shook her head. "Since the late seventies. But hush; we must not talk about it now."

"Why are you here at the Justice Department?" Lan peered at Cam My and then down at her own dirty blouse and dry, dark skin. Her single braid weighed against her back.

"Brother brought me here. He's investigating me." Older Sister laughed nervously.

"Why?" Lan stood with her arm around Cam My's waist.

"Adoptions. I facilitated adoptions in the North. But he seems to think that I've been working down here, too."

The three women turned toward the sound of footsteps. Older Brother stood in the doorway. "Come in," he said and then cleared his throat. "All of you."

Three chairs faced his desk. The women sat, and Lan pulled Binh onto her lap. He reached toward the desk, aiming to grab the pen that stood in a holder. Lan pulled him back. It was the same office Lan had sat in more than two months before when she had relinquished the children, but now light made its way through the windows, and the stacks of papers were gone.

"It's time for honest answers," Older Brother said. "I am ashamed to be investigating my own sisters. I need answers so I can write my report. A couple from America is traveling to adopt Mai from the orphanage, and I need to finish the investigation. I believe Lan accepted money for her daughter, and, Cam My, I think you're involved."

Lan bowed her head. What was Older Brother talking about? She glanced furtively from Older Sister to Older Brother.

"You're speculating. I would never pay a mother for her baby." Older Sister held her head high.

"No? But you've worked with the Americans who are arranging Mai's adoption." Older Brother sat tall behind the desk.

"I did, but I haven't associated with them since last year, and then it was in the North, not here in Vung Tau." Older Sister crossed her legs.

"Why do you no longer work with them?" Quan's eyes bored through Older Sister.

"They no longer take babies from the North."

"Why?"

Older Sister shrugged her shoulders. "Did you ask them?"

How could Cam My be so flippant with Older Brother? Didn't she care that he was a government official?

"I did. I asked Mrs. Benson, Mrs. Maggie Benson. She said they were uncertain of the facilitator's qualifications. The facilitator. That would be you."

"We had a misunderstanding," Cam My answered. Binh reached out to grab the pen from the desktop again. Lan jerked him back.

"You paid a birth mother for her baby," Quan said.

"I would never buy a baby. I told you that."

"No one paid you for your own baby?" Older Brother asked. Mother put her hand to her mouth; Lan pulled Binh closer. Why was Quan bringing Chi into the conversation?

Cam My paused and then asked sharply, "My own baby?"

Older Brother nodded.

Cam My shook her head. "For Chi?" She took a cigarette from her leather purse. "Of course not. You're as bad as the Americans, remembering the past like it was yesterday. Chi left Vietnam nearly thirty years ago."

"And you haven't regretted giving her up?"

Older Sister lit her cigarette and looked at Lan, then at Mother, and finally at Binh. She put the cigarette to her lips, inhaled, and then glared at Older Brother. He pushed an ashtray toward her. "What kind of life would she have had here?" Cam My's perfectly manicured nails caught the light as she flicked ashes from her cigarette. Her hand shook slightly.

Older Brother turned toward Lan. "Did Older Sister pay you for Mai?" Binh buried his head against his mother's chest. Lan closed her eyes and pulled Binh tightly against her midriff, against the spot in her stomach that began to burn.

"Quan." Cam My leaned forward, waving her cigarette toward him. She said his name with force, the way she had when they were children. "Lan and I haven't seen each other in twenty-six years. I already told you that."

How can Cam My be so brave?

"I don't believe you." Older Brother leaned back in his chair.

"Believe me. I had no idea where they were. I went back to the rubber plantation, but they were gone. No one knew where they went. I searched in Saigon—Ho Chi Minh City—but no one knew of them. You have…" Older Sister paused, as if she searched for the right word. "…reunited us; your suspicions have brought us together, and for that I'm very thankful." She bowed her head.

Older Brother scowled at Lan. "I'll ask you one more time. Did Cam My pay you for Mai?"

"No." Lan's voice quivered as she said the single word, her head bowed deeply.

"Let's go eat," Older Sister said, waving for a taxi. "Maggie Benson told me about a barbecue place here in Vung Tau." A taxi stopped, and the women

and Binh climbed in the back. Older Sister sat in the middle. Mother took
her hand and held it tightly. Lan pulled Binh onto her lap.

The taxi driver turned south. "Wait," Lan said. "Turn back. We need to
go to our place to get Hang."

"Hang?"

"My oldest child."

"How many children do you have?"

"The two." Lan hesitated. "And the baby girl. And you? How many children do you have?"

"Just Chi." She inhaled and then exhaled slowly, flicking ashes out the
window. "Is this the first time you've given up a child?"

Lan nodded. "I took Binh to the orphanage too." Her son tilted his face
toward hers. "A couple from America wanted to adopt him—the same ones
who are coming for Mai—but I took him home."

Older Sister licked the tip of her index finger and shook her head. "He
would have had a good life in America. Plenty to eat. School. College."

"That's what I told her," Mother said. "A woman has to put her children
before herself. Didn't I do that for you, Lan?"

"You never took me to an orphanage."

Mother shrugged her shoulders. "You were all I had. Everyone else was
gone. I needed someone to take care of me when I was old. Besides, no one
would have adopted you; you were too old."

"You wouldn't have gone to America anyway," Older Sister said. "Maybe
France. After the war Americans couldn't adopt from Vietnam, not until the
early nineties."

Lan directed the taxi driver down the dirt road toward the shack. "I was
married to Hang's father. He left before he knew I was pregnant."

"By boat?" Cam My asked.

Lan nodded.

"Did he make it?"

"I never heard from him." Lan held Binh close.

"I'm sorry. So many died," Cam My said. "Only three on my boat survived. At first I wished I hadn't. I hope it was quick for him."

Lan felt the pain spread from her stomach to her chest. She took a big breath and then smiled as Hang ran toward the car, waving and grinning, her braids flying. Cam My laughed. Lan rolled down her window. "Get in," she said. "I have someone for you to meet."

"Our luck has changed," Mother whispered across the restaurant table to Lan. "First Quan shows up and now Cam My. Life will finally get better."

Lan nodded, a little dizzy from the thought of both Older Sister and Older Brother showing up within weeks of each other. Surely she could take care of Hang and Binh now. Older Sister would help support them. She thought again of the baby, but the little one felt farther away now, felt as if she had already started her journey to America. Lan shook her head. Her stomach hurt.

Older Sister ordered for all of them—pork and french fries, salt-and-pepper shrimp and Coca-Colas. She lit a cigarette and blew the smoke toward Hang. "Don't ever smoke," she said to her. "It's very bad for you. In America the children are told not to smoke." Hang stared at her newfound aunt with big, admiring eyes.

At the next table, a group of young people in their twenties toasted each other with Tiger beers, shouting, "Yo!" in unison. Lan thought of Cuong. She glanced down at her sweat-stained blouse, then at Older Sister in her pretty clothes, then back at the young people. There was a cake with white frosting on the table.

"What are they doing?" Lan asked.

"Celebrating a birthday."

Binh pulled at his ear. Lan ignored him, hoping it was just sore and not infected again.

"Everyone in America celebrates birthdays," Older Sister said.

"I want a birthday!" Binh knelt on his chair. She wasn't sure of the exact date Binh was born. It was after the midautumn festival—that's what she told the orphanage director. The director said they would choose a birthday for him.

"Why did you take your daughter to the orphanage?" Older Sister asked.

"I can't provide for another child." She was weary of her answer. It stabbed at her, reminded her of her failure.

"I wish I could help, but I think I'm going to get kicked out of Vietnam. Then I won't have a job." Older Sister pulled an ashtray from the center of the table and flicked ashes onto the clear glass bottom.

"Why?"

"I gave a birth mom money, actually a few birth moms in the North. Mind you, I didn't pay them for their babies, not like Older Brother thinks, but I gave them money to make things easier after they took their babies to the orphanages. They were so sad, so lost. I remember what that's like. Brother interviewed one of the birth moms. She was nervous, confused. She said I gave her money for the baby. I have the Vietnamese after me, well, mainly Brother, and now the American INS."

"What will happen?" Lan asked.

The young people at the next table toasted again, yelling, "Yo!"

Older Sister shrugged. "I'll go back to California. Maybe I'll find a job translating in social services again. Although the need isn't as great now."

"The U.S. will let you go back?" Lan rested her hand on Binh's shoulder to stop him from rocking back and forth on his knees.

"They have to. I'm a citizen," Cam My answered.

"Send us money when you go back." Mother's eyes filled with tears.

Older Sister patted her hand. "I will...when I can, when I find another job. If my legal bills aren't too high." She put the cigarette back to her lips and mumbled, "If I don't end up in prison."

The waitress brought five Coca-Colas to the table. Lan pulled Binh onto her lap and held the glass for him. She didn't want him to spill it and draw attention.

"Have you seen Chi?" Lan positioned the straw in Binh's mouth. He stared at the young men and women at the next table.

Older Sister took a drink of her Coca-Cola and then began to light another cigarette. "I've e-mailed her a few times and talked on the phone twice. Her American name is Cheryl." Cam My inhaled and then exhaled slowly. "One of the American women I work with helped me track her down. She was adopted by a family in Colorado." Lan raised her eyebrows. "It's in the U.S. It's a state close to the middle of the country."

"Go on," Mother said, as if she'd heard of Colorado before.

"She graduated from college. She lives in Chicago; it's a big city in America. She married a white man and designs programs."

"What does she do?" Mother squinted at Cam My.

"Computer work."

Mother nodded her head. "That's good. Maybe she will send us money."

"No." Cam My wrinkled her nose. "She's American. She wouldn't understand."

"How did you leave Vietnam?" Lan trailed her fingers along Binh's neck, playing with his hair. The waitress slapped a stack of napkins on the table.

"I left from here, just south of Vung Tau, on a fishing boat in 1978." Older Sister's hand shook a little as she rested it by the ashtray. "I ended up in a refugee camp in Indonesia for two years before going to America. Because I could speak English, I got a job as a translator for social services. Learning English from my American boyfriend paid off."

Lan thought about Chinh. Hang had been born in 1989. That meant Chinh had left in 1988, long after Older Sister had fled the country. "Are you married?" she asked Older Sister.

"Twice. Divorced twice."

"Did you search for your American boyfriend?"

She nodded. "But I was too late." She took another drag from her cigarette, tilted her head, and blew the smoke toward the open-beam ceiling, and then looked from Mother to Lan. "He died in a car accident two years after he returned home."

Lan thought of the big American with hair the color of sand. Life was hard even in America.

Older Sister put out her cigarette. "Where's our food? I'm starving."

Hang squinted at her and laughed, then filled her cheeks with air and moved her head from side to side. Lan shook her head at her daughter and slid Binh onto Hang's lap. Hang was right—Older Sister looked far from starving. Life in America had been good to her. A waitress served the group celebrating the birthday. Although the other patrons were far better off than Mother, Hang, Binh, and Lan, none of them appeared to be as wealthy as Older Sister.

Mother clapped her hands. "I want all of my children together before Cam My goes back to America. And my grandchildren. Sunday we should all have a dinner to make up for lost time."

"Even Older Brother?" Cam My fingered her gold earring.

"Of course. He is my son, my long-lost son. Even the baby," Mother said. "I will see her one last time before she goes to America to start her happy life."

Lan shook her head.

"Yes, Lan. Do it for me." Mother patted her bun at the back of her neck.

"I can't take her back to the orphanage again."

"I'll help you," Older Sister said. "I'll go with you to the orphanage, both to get her and then to take her back. I'd like to see her."

Rain began to pour outside the open door of the restaurant. The waitress bringing in the barbecued pork from outside rushed toward them, her long hair wet, her white shirt splattered with rain. She placed a platter of pork on the table, followed by a platter of shrimp. A second waitress brought french fries. The smell of the food made Lan's mouth water. As the waitresses hurried around the table, Binh jumped from Hang's lap and scurried over to where the young people celebrated. Lan caught sight of him and then gasped as he poked his finger through the white frosting into the cake. She stood quickly, pushing her plastic chair back on the concrete. "Binh!" she called out. "Stop it!"

A young woman who sat next to the cake grabbed Binh's wrist and scolded him. The man sitting next to her laughed. Binh smiled. The young woman let go, and Lan snatched Binh by the arm and then pulled him back to the table as she apologized. Binh climbed back in his chair and grabbed a handful of french fries.

"I see that one gives you trouble," Cam My said and then smiled. "I like his spirit."

Lan pulled her chair to the table and glanced at Binh. She had left marks on his arm. She took a long drink of Coca-Cola. Her stomach hurt just above her belly button. She pressed her thumb against the spot.

"Look what we've become." Older Sister glanced down at her plate as she cut her pork with a knife and fork, then up at Lan. "Older Brother, the investigator. Me, the baby buyer, and you, the uneducated, unwed mother."

Part 3

May 25–June 28, 2001

*And we know that all things work together for good
to those who love God, to those who are the called
according to His purpose.*

ROMANS 8:28

The airplane soared over the lush landscape topped with wisps of clouds; a river cut through the greenery; a hill jutted through the canopy of trees that gave way to villages, then to large buildings all jumbled together. The crowded plane buzzed with Vietnamese conversations. Gen imagined the stories of the passengers, the people who escaped and were now returning to see their homeland and their families.

"How do you feel?" Jeff took her hand.

"Like I'm nine." *As if it had all just happened—the war, Mom's death, losing Nhat.* She turned from the window to face Jeff.

"You're brave to come here," he said. They were just minutes away from Tan Son Nhut Airport, where her mother had died.

The plane began to descend. A sea of rooftops gave way to a runway lined by decrepit hangars, concrete half circles, and old helicopters. Ramshackle homes backed up against a fence just a few feet from the runway. Gen braced herself for the jolt of the landing. Jeff squeezed her hand as she searched the terrain outside the window. *Where did my mother die?* The plane taxied around an old hangar; a new building and a bus came into view.

A blanket of hot, steamy air smothered them as they stepped off the plane, walked down the metal stairway onto the burning tarmac, and boarded the crowded bus. Gen held on to Jeff to keep from bumping into the travelers crammed against them.

They made their way through the check-in, answering the officials' terse questions, and then descended the stairs to the concrete floor of the dingy terminal. Jeff swung each of their bags off the conveyor belt and loaded them onto a cart. After customs they headed out the door and into the throng of people crowded around the exit.

"What if Maggie isn't here?"

"Then we'll take a taxi to the hotel," Jeff said. He looked like a giant in the crowd. All around, Vietnamese nationals searched for their loved ones coming home from America. The travelers carried boxes containing televisions, microwaves, rice cookers, and fans.

"Need a taxi?" shouted dozens of drivers outside the terminal.

Gen shook her head. "There she is!"

Maggie waved at them. She wore silk pants and a blouse; her gray hair was knotted on top of her head.

"Isn't this great?" Jeff shot Gen a smile as they followed Maggie through the tunnel of people. It *was* great. The crowd, the energy, the adventure, and the baby ahead of them.

The adoption agency van was air-conditioned. "This is Bao," Maggie said, nodding at the driver. "He works for the agency as a driver, interpreter, and now as a facilitator."

Gen watched Maggie fan herself as they pulled away from the airport. "It's been unbearably hot," she said. "It's cooler in Vung Tau, but there are more mosquitoes." Bao pulled into traffic. A man on a scooter buzzed by, then another carrying a woman and two children. The woman wore a floppy cotton hat and tattered, long-sleeved gloves.

Gen reached into her backpack for a roll of mints. She dug past her bathroom bag, journal, pen, and extra set of clothes. She felt along the very bottom and found the mints, along with a small package. She pulled it out. Who had put it in her bag? Jeff shook his head. She read the tag taped to the purple wrapping paper. "To Gen; Love, Dad. May you find what you are searching for in Vietnam." He had carried her backpack at the Portland airport on their way to the gate. He must have slipped it in without her seeing. She felt the package. *The figurine of the old man,* she guessed. *Dad's giving it back to me.* She felt a rush of relief.

"Who's it from?" Jeff asked.

"Dad." She peeled back the paper. It wasn't the old man with the white beard and cane; it was the Vietnamese girl in the red tunic and pants holding the wooden doll. She gasped.

"What's wrong?" Jeff asked.

"I haven't seen this since long before we got married." Gen ran her finger over the figurine's chipped nose, along the carved braids, and then over the faded red tunic and pants. "Dad must have had her all these years." Why had he decided to return her now?

The van came to a sudden stop; Gen wrapped her fingers around the carving, hiding the figurine in her hand. A river of scooters flowed around them, the drivers weaving in and out of traffic. A load of bananas was strapped to one, a keg of beer to another. Three girls wearing white ao dais, conical hats, and long gloves crowded on another.

Buildings made of wood sagged next to sturdy new structures painted in pastel colors. Beggars walked beside men in suits. A white building came into view. "What's that?" Gen turned her head, taking in the cross perched atop a boxy steeple.

"A disco," Maggie answered.

The van inched along. "There's the U.S. Consulate." Maggie pointed to a new, sprawling stucco building with green trim and an American flag. "That will be your last stop before going home."

"I predict that two weeks is all it takes," Jeff said to Gen. "We'll be home for harvest in plenty of time."

Gen smiled at her optimistic husband. If they didn't need to get back for harvest, she would choose to stay longer. She slipped the carving back into her bag. A taxi driver honked at a scooter ahead of them and swerved onto the sidewalk as he turned the corner. A woman on a bicycle stopped to avoid being hit. A cyclo driver pedaled across the street, causing Bao to brake abruptly. Gen grabbed the armrest. There were no seat belts in the van.

"That's Notre Dame Cathedral," Maggie said. "It's a smaller replica of the one in Paris. Our hotel is just a few blocks from here." A bride wearing a Western gown posed in front of the red bricks of the cathedral. An entourage of attendants, her groom, and a professional photographer stood on the sidewalk. On the corner an amputee dressed in ragged pants and no shirt leaned on one crutch and held out his hat to those passing by.

The van crept around a corner as a wave of scooters sped by and then pulled to a stop. The pale yellow People's Committee Building towered majestically over the plaza in front of the hotel. A garden of orange, red, and yellow zinnias surrounded a statue of Ho Chi Minh holding a child on his lap. Gen stepped out of the van into the heart of Saigon. The red-tiled roofs of the buildings scraped the brilliant blue sky. The blaring horns and blistering heat swept over her, welcomed her, and enticed her as she and Jeff headed up the stairs and through the open doors to the lobby of their hotel.

"Try to get a good night's sleep," Maggie said as they waited to register. "We'll leave for Vung Tau tomorrow in the early afternoon and go straight to the orphanage to see Mai." The marble floor reflected the light from the giant chandelier; a waist-high vase filled with tropical flowers stood in the center of the lobby. The woman behind the counter wore a burgundy ao dai. The hotel was more elegant than Gen had expected.

"I need your passports," Maggie said.

"Why?" Jeff asked.

"The hotel keeps them on file while you're here. Government regulations. It's how they keep track of foreigners."

"But I didn't think we should give anyone our passports, ever." Jeff ran his hand through his curls.

"You have to in Vietnam. It's the way things work," she said.

Gen smiled nervously as Jeff handed Maggie both their passports.

Gen and Jeff stood on the corner by the hotel. The buzz and honks of the four lanes of motorbikes and cars reverberated around them. "You buy gum?" a girl who looked five shouted, pulling on Jeff's arm. He pulled out two five-thousand-dong notes and handed them to her.

Gen hoped someone was watching the little girl. She spotted a woman sitting on the plaza in front of the statue of Ho Chi Minh make eye contact with the child. Relieved, Gen smiled and took Jeff's arm. "Honey, if you keep giving away your money, you won't be a millionaire for very long." They'd just exchanged a hundred U.S. dollars for a million and a half Vietnamese dong.

"It was around sixty cents," Jeff said. The traffic slowed, and he stepped out into the street. "Stay with me," he said to Gen. A surge of scooters and cars headed toward them. "Don't slow down." The motorbikes buzzed around them like a raging river around a log drifting downstream. Exhilarated, they reached the other side.

"Madame, monsieur, buy postcards!" a girl yelled. "Fans! Books!" She stood on the corner. "How about stamps?" The girl opened her book. "Are you from America?"

"Yes," he answered.

"Why are you here?"

"To adopt a baby."

The girl smiled.

"Where did you learn English?" Gen asked.

"Some in school, but I quit when I was ten. Mostly I learn from Americans. I want to go to USA."

"What about your family?"

"They don't want me to go. I support them. You buy postcards? stamps? books?"

"Postcards," she said. "I'll take ten postcards."

"Fifteen thousand dong." The girl quickly folded the three notes from Jeff and stuffed them in a money belt around her waist. "You find me, okay? Buy from me, okay?"

"We're going to Vung Tau tomorrow," Jeff said.

"Oh, Vung Tau. The beach. I've always wanted to go to Vung Tau. It's like heaven. Okay, you buy from me when you get back."

A scooter buzzed past with a cage full of croaking toads strapped to the back. A group of men sat on the sidewalk in small plastic chairs, smoking and drinking tea. A man pedaling a cyclo pulled onto the sidewalk beside them. "Need a ride?" he called out.

"No, thank you," Jeff said.

"So many people speak English. And they seem to like us. I expected them to resent Americans," Gen said, as a woman selling white blossoms stopped in front of them.

"Lotus flower," she said. "You buy?"

Jeff took out his wad of money, peeled off a note, and handed it to the woman as she handed him a single bloom. The woman swung her yoke back over her shoulders and hurried on with her buckets of flowers.

Jeff handed Gen the lotus flower. "Thank you," he said, bending down and kissing her on top of her head, "for wanting to adopt from Vietnam." The smell of exhaust from the sea of motorbikes and cars, mixed with cigarette smoke, whiffs of sewage, and a dash of incense, swirled through the sweltering air around them.

After dinner, full from spring rolls and lemongrass chicken that Gen had eaten with a fork, they headed back toward the hotel. The tropical sun had set an hour before, and now the cars and motorbikes had their headlights on, adding to the carnival atmosphere of the street. Throngs of people gathered on the plaza in front of the hotel. Children rode tricycles and bicycles. The entire crowd seemed to be waltzing to the music of an ice cream cart that an old man pushed through the square.

Gen and Jeff ducked into the store kitty-cornered from the plaza to buy water for the trip to Vung Tau. Light from the overhead fluorescent bulbs bounced off the linoleum floor. Umbrellas, rain slickers, shoes, clothes, food, and snacks lined the shelves. An American man with dark, thinning hair stood with a little Vietnamese boy by his side, shopping for camera film. "Chao em," Gen said to the boy, estimating that he was near Binh's size. He smiled. "Hello," she said to the man.

"Bryce Gordon." He extended his hand. "And this is Daniel."

"I'm Gen Taylor. This is my husband, Jeff." She bent down to the little boy. "Hi, Daniel." He smiled, showing brown teeth, and hugged his father's leg. Gen looked up at Bryce. "He's wonderful. How old?"

"Nearly three."

"How long have you been here?" Jeff asked.

"Four months."

"What?" Gen felt herself falter. *Four months!*

"We have twenty left to go."

Daniel continued to hug Bryce's leg as his father spoke. Bryce and his wife had traveled to North Vietnam in February to take Daniel home. Their adoption agency had assured them that all the investigations and paperwork were done. It turned out that the investigation hadn't been completed and the paperwork was delayed.

Each day they were told they would have the documents "tomorrow" or "the next day." They trusted that the details had been taken care of and that the delay was routine, but after five weeks in Hanoi and no straight answers on why the adoption was delayed, they traveled to Ho Chi Minh City, hoping to iron things out with the help of the United States INS. When they met with the INS, they found out that their facilitator was under investigation by both Vietnamese and American officials. Bryce's wife, Sue, an attorney, needed to return home to Atlanta. They decided that Bryce would stay and finish up the paperwork.

"After I'd been in Vietnam nine weeks, they told me that the birth mother had been paid. It might make sense for a birth mom to be paid for a baby, if a facilitator was really crooked, but not for a two-year-old. Most people don't want two-year-olds. We didn't. We wanted a baby, until we saw Daniel's photo, and we knew he was the child for us. After the final investigation we were told we couldn't adopt him."

"Why?" Gen was horrified by the story.

"Because the birth mom had been paid. We had a choice. Take Daniel back to the orphanage and have him live there the rest of his childhood to be turned out on the streets at sixteen, or I could live here in Vietnam with him for two years."

"I don't get it," Jeff said.

"The United States INS will recognize a child as yours if you live in the child's native country for two years *with* the child," Bryce explained.

"What about your wife?" Gen was dumbfounded. They planned to live apart for two years? She couldn't imagine it.

"She'll come over when she can. In fact, she should be here in two weeks."

"What do you do?" Gen asked.

"I'm a writer. Theoretically, I can work from here, over the Internet. I have a laptop. Daniel and I spend quite a bit of time in Internet cafés."

"Where are you staying?" Jeff asked.

"I found an apartment a few blocks from here that costs much less than a hotel."

Gen shook her head. "Unbelievable. It must be so hard to be away from your wife. To not be together as a family."

Bryce smiled a little and shook his head. "What else could we do? What would you do?"

What would we do? Gen glanced at Jeff and then back at Bryce and Daniel.

"What a great little kid," Gen said, avoiding the question. *What would we do?*

A torrential rain poured as Gen and Jeff hurried from the store. They dashed across the street, each swinging a five-liter jug of water. Gen held her white lotus blossom close to her body, trying to protect it from the pelting rain. In seconds they were soaked and standing under the awning of the hotel with dozens of other people, some sitting on their scooters and bicycles to wait out the storm, others holding baskets of fruit and flowers. "Would you like to buy a rose?" a little girl asked Jeff, holding a red rose out to him. She wore a frilly Western dress and scuffed white sandals. Scabs covered her legs. Jeff dug in his pocket, gave the girl the money, and then handed the rose to Gen, bending down to kiss her on the head again. Gen smiled and wagged her finger at him.

"Don't do that teacher thing." Jeff laughed.

"Stop buying things," she said. "We're going to run out of money."

A man on crutches extended his hat toward them. Jeff gave him a few notes, and then they dashed through the doors of the hotel, leaving behind the humid mix of exhaust and rain. The storm continued as they stood on their balcony, watching the motorbikes circle the plaza. The drivers hunched forward with colored rain slickers draped over their headlights. Red, blue, yellow, and green lights paraded by, casting reflections on the wet pavement. Jeff put his arm around Gen's shoulder.

"I'm so happy," he said. Gen couldn't speak. She thought of the figurine in the bottom of her backpack. She thought of Mai. A baby from Vietnam. Life felt balanced. She thought of her mother. *How could she stand to be away from Nhat for an entire year, from the time she first held him until the time she traveled back to bring him home? How did she feel when she held him again?* The closer they got to Mai, the more she understood Mom. Gen gripped the rail in front of her. *And then Mom put Nhat on the plane alone, hoping to get her friend Kim to the United States.* That Gen couldn't understand.

Gen leaned forward, extending her hand to the night, to the rain, to Saigon, to Vietnam.

Gen woke thinking about Bryce and Daniel. *What would we do?* A stream of light peeked between the yellow drapes. The bedside clock read 5:15. She heard voices in the street and then a bouncing ball. She opened the balcony door and stepped out. Below, a group of barefoot boys around twelve years old played soccer in the street as the sun rose. They used the back of a parked bus as a goal. Across the street a man thrust his arms and legs in martial arts kicks and punches.

"This is the day that I meet my daughter," she whispered into the muggy dawn.

Chapter 32

I saw Older Brother's apartment yesterday," Cam My said to Lan. "It's very nice. TV, stereo, video player, microwave. Small, but nice." They sat outside the doctor's house on plastic chairs.

Binh clung to Lan's neck and whimpered. "I should have brought him yesterday. I hoped it would pass. Now Mother will be disappointed if we don't get Mai and get back to the house." It was Sunday morning, the busiest selling time of the week. Lan had planned to work in the morning and then go get Mai. Now she would miss a whole day.

"It will be all right," Cam My said.

"Why do you think he gets ear infections all the time?" Lan shifted Binh to her arms and rocked him gently like a baby.

Cam My shrugged. "In the U.S. they'd put tubes in his ears. He wouldn't be able to go swimming, but his ears would get better."

"Tubes?"

"It helps the fluid drain and keeps it from getting infected."

Binh sat up and rubbed his eyes and then his ears. He peered into Lan's face and thrust his head against her shoulder. Having Older Sister along calmed Lan. People listened to Cam My. She got things done; she took charge and didn't seem afraid of anything. All the neighbors, including Truc, who was the most successful of Lan's friends, were in awe of Older Sister. Even Mother took notice when Older Sister scolded her for napping instead of watching Binh. "Lan works hard to support you," she had said to Mother. "The least you can do is take good care of her son." When Lan explained that she still owed the doctor money, Cam My said that she would take care of it. Lan's stomach hadn't bothered her in two days.

"What time does Older Brother plan to come today?" Cam My asked.

"In the early afternoon," Lan said.

Three hours later the doctor saw Binh. "He needs stronger medicine," she said. "More expensive medicine."

"What about tubes?" Lan shifted Binh to her other hip. "Can you put tubes in his ears?"

The doctor laughed. "Who have you been talking to?"

Lan nodded at Older Sister.

"Are you from America?" The doctor picked up a penlight.

Cam My nodded.

"You should take him to America, then, and have tubes put in his ears," she said, her voice thick with sarcasm. She examined Binh's mouth and throat. "His throat is infected too. And his teeth are worse. He's going to get abscesses soon." She counted nine pills from a jar and slid them into a small bottle. "Give him three a day—morning, noon, and night—under his tongue until they dissolve. That will be a hundred thousand dong, plus the twenty thousand dong you already owe."

Lan patted Binh's back and shifted her eyes to the concrete floor. Cam My quickly pulled the money out of her purse. "One hundred twenty thousand dong, just under nine dollars U.S.," she said. "You would have to pay ten times that in the U.S. for a doctor's visit and medicine." Lan raised her head and nodded, smiling slightly at her sister as she swallowed the uneasiness that had pooled in the back of her throat.

Cam My called Quan and told him to meet them at the shack mid-afternoon. Then she hailed a taxi, and they headed toward the orphanage for Mai. Binh curled up in Lan's lap and fell asleep. Older Sister reached out and stroked his hair, pushing it from his sweaty forehead, and then she took Lan's hand and held it for just a moment. "Would you reconsider sending him to America? He would get the medical and dental care he needs. He could have permanent hearing loss if these infections continue, and his teeth really are awful. He would also get an education. Almost all Americans who adopt send their kids to college or at least offer that to their children. And if not, he could work and pay for it on his own."

The taxi driver turned onto the main street. A truck honked. A scooter swerved in front of them. "When I took him to the orphanage with the baby, he cried and cried. He was miserable." Lan braced herself, her foot pushed against the floor.

"Most of them are miserable at the orphanage. But they do fine when they're adopted."

"Older Brother thinks it's wrong to give up a child."

"He's never cared for a child, has he? He doesn't know what it's like to scrounge for food and medicine, to know your child will never be educated, to lose hope." Cam My pulled her cigarettes from her bag.

"I'm hoping he will help me with Hang and Binh."

"Don't hold your breath. He'll go back to Hanoi soon. If he was going to help you, he would have by now. You've been here all along. He, unlike me, knew where to find you. He doesn't mean to be cruel. He just doesn't comprehend your life." Older Sister paused. "How ironic that now that I've found you, I may not be able to come back to Vietnam."

They rode in silence. Older Sister lit a cigarette and rolled her window down a crack. Lan longed for her to stay. How much easier life would be if Older Sister were with them, especially if she had her American money.

When they arrived at the orphanage, Lan touched Cam My's arm. "Can you go up and get her while I stay with Binh? I have a permission note from Brother, signed Tran Van Quan. Don't tell them he's our brother, though. I don't want them to know."

Older Sister flicked her cigarette out the window, climbed out of the taxi, and headed up the stairs of the orphanage. Lan stroked Binh's hair. She didn't want him to wake up and see where they were.

Cam My held Mai as they drove away. The baby smiled up at her. "She's beautiful." Older Sister turned toward Lan. "Do you ever think of how things would have been if there hadn't been the war? If we hadn't all left the rubber plantation?"

Lan nodded. *All the time.*

"Older Brother would be the foreman," Cam My said. "Father would be an old man."

"Second Brother would be married and have children." Lan stroked Binh's cheek.

"Chi would have children by now. I'd be a grandmother." Cam My touched the tip of Mai's tiny nose with her finger.

"And I would have a husband, and all my children would be with me." Lan took a deep breath.

Older Sister shook her head at Lan. "Let's not think about it. It hurts too badly." She looked back down at Mai and smiled. The baby began to cry. Cam My put her over her shoulder and patted her back. "They said she's had a little bit of diarrhea. And that she needs to get plenty to drink."

Lan nodded.

"I'm sorry it's hard to see her."

Lan nodded again. "Mother and Older Brother don't understand. It eats me up. When I don't see her, I try not to think about her, or I think about how good her life is going to be. But when I see her, then I think about everything I'm going to miss."

"I know," Older Sister said. She rested her head against Lan's shoulder. "I'm sorry."

Lan turned her head toward the window. She didn't want to cry. Binh stirred on her lap. She put her hands under his armpits and lifted him up so his head rested on her breast and his legs on either side of her hips.

"What are the Americans like who adopt Vietnam babies?" Lan leaned down to touch her cheek to the top of Binh's head.

"They're good people. Every once in a while a couple thinks mostly of themselves, but even then they want what's best for the child. Many of them can't have kids of their own, but some of them can. They both love and hate Vietnam. They like the food, the people, the landscape, and the shopping. They hate the paperwork and the heat. I think some of them choose Vietnam to make them feel better about the war. Many pick Vietnam because the children adapt so well, others because at the time they decided to adopt it was an easy country to adopt from. It's getting harder and harder now, though."

She told Lan about a moratorium that was planned to put an end to Vietnamese adoptions until a countrywide system could be established. She was certain Older Brother was involved in the politics behind the moratorium. "It's actually a good thing," she said. "Just too bad for the kids waiting in the orphanages while the government officials hash things out."

The taxi driver headed down the dirt road to the shack. "If you change your mind about Binh, you should do it soon." Older Sister shifted Mai off her shoulder. The baby slept. "Otherwise, you'd have to wait for several months, maybe even years, and there would be no guarantee that he would go to the same family as Mai."

⤙⤚

Older Brother opened the taxi door for Lan. "I only have a short time," he said. "I need to get back to the Justice Department for a meeting."

They all gathered in the yard. Mother squatted and gazed with longing into the face of Older Brother and then Older Sister. Lan waited for Mother to look at her, but she didn't. She glanced at Hang, then at Binh sleeping on a mat in front of the door, then at Mai in Cam My's arms.

"My family," Mother said, clasping her hands. "All together for this afternoon."

"Let's get a picture," Cam My said. She handed the baby to Lan and then pulled a camera out of her bag. "Everyone go sit by Binh."

"Lan, hand Mai back to Cam My. You take the photo," Mother said.

"We'll take turns," Cam My said. "Or better yet, Hang, go ask one of your neighbors."

"Go get Truc," Lan said. She was probably home since it was the hottest part of the day.

Lan woke Binh and pulled him into her arms. Cam My held the baby.

Older Brother stood in the middle with Mother beside him. Hang came back into the yard with Truc and stood beside her mother. Lan's stomach began to churn as Truc clicked the camera.

After speaking with Mother for a few minutes, Older Brother announced that his car would arrive any minute and that he should say his good-byes.

"And we should head back to the orphanage," Cam My said, handing Mai to Mother. "But first I have to use the latrine."

The pit toilet with the tarp strung around it embarrassed Lan. She handed Binh to Hang, ran water from the spigot in the yard into the bottle, then poured in the formula and shook the bottle. Lan gave Binh his medicine and said she would be back after dark. The sun was already setting. "Hang, watch your brother. You be responsible for him."

Older Sister told her brother good-bye. "I won't see you anytime soon, but I do hope I'll see you again." She laughed as she patted his shoulder. Lan marveled at Cam My's boldness. Would Older Brother be offended?

He frowned. "Official business and family ties make for complicated interactions." He caught Cam My's gaze. "Yes?" he asked in English.

"Yes," she said and then spoke in Vietnamese again. "I am happy to have seen you, although I follow what you are saying. I wish it had been only because we're family." She tucked her short hair behind her ear.

Mai began to fuss, and Lan took the baby from Mother.

"Take care of Mother and Lan, please. And her children. Binh needs more medical care. Hang needs a future." Older Sister bowed her head to Brother.

"I'll do what I can," he said. He called out to Lan, "I'll be in touch."

The two sisters walked slowly toward the dirt road. Cam My lit a cigarette. Lan carried the woven bag with the bottle slung over her shoulder and jostled the baby.

"The Americans who are coming for Mai arrive this evening. That's what the orphanage worker told me." Cam My inhaled the cigarette.

"They're taking her this evening?" Lan wanted to curl up with her baby and hold her through one more night.

Older Sister pulled the cigarette away from her face, flicking the ashes toward the ditch. "No, they won't let them take her this soon. They'll have to visit a few times, go by the Justice Department. Do all of that. If they get to Vung Tau early enough, the orphanage director thought they might stop by to see her."

Lan held Mai close. The baby began to cry.

"I hope we arrive while the Americans are there," Cam My said. "Maggie Benson is with them. She's the American I used to work with in the North." They reached the main street, and Cam My signaled a taxi. "We were friends. At least I thought we were, but now she won't answer my e-mails."

Lan held Mai as the driver sped through the streets of Vung Tau toward the orphanage, stroking her cheek against her daughter's fine hair. *Grow up to be a good person. Study hard. Don't forget me.*

Chapter 33

*M*ai is not here," the director said to Maggie in halting English. "Her family took her for the day." The director switched to Vietnamese, and Bao translated. He explained that the aunt had come with a note from an inspector at the Justice Department. The grandmother wanted to see Mai one more time. The inspector approved the request; there was nothing the director could do.

"The director says that the aunt asked about you specifically," Bao translated to Maggie. "She wondered what time you were expected. She said she would bring the baby back then."

"What did the woman look like?"

After more Vietnamese words back and forth, Bao said to Maggie, "She's Vietnamese-American. Short hair, nice clothes, midforties."

Maggie hesitated for a moment. "What time did the director say she expected us?"

The translator and the director spoke back and forth again. The translator's voice rose and then fell in Vietnamese. Then he spoke to Maggie in English. "She told the aunt you would be here around 5:00 p.m."

Maggie shook her head. "I told her 4:00 p.m."

Bao shrugged his shoulders. "That's what I told her. She said, 'No. You said 5:00 p.m.'"

Maggie bowed toward the director. Jeff and Gen walked to the veranda railing. In the yard below, children played. Three boys kicked a rock between them. A little girl chased a blue butterfly.

Jeff put his arm on the small of Gen's back. His curls had tightened in the humidity, and his eyes shone bright. She leaned against him.

A group of children drew in the dirt with sticks.

"Sorry," Maggie said, moving toward the railing. "I would have called ahead if I'd had any idea what was going on."

"What can we do?" Jeff asked.

"I'll call this evening. We'll come back tomorrow."

"Can't we wait?" Gen grasped the metal railing.

Maggie shook her head. "We would make the director nervous. We don't want to do that."

"Can we give them the supplies for the orphanage now?" Gen swallowed hard, suddenly aware of how thirsty she was. "Those boys would be so happy to see the soccer balls."

"Let's wait," Maggie said. "I think the director is annoyed with these interruptions."

"What did the director say about Mai's aunt?" Gen let go of the railing and wiped her sweaty hand on her skirt.

"Mai's aunt may have worked as an adoption facilitator in the North. If so, I'm acquainted with her."

"How bizarre," Gen said.

"My sentiments exactly." Maggie put her arm around Gen's shoulders, pressing Gen's cotton blouse against her sweaty skin. "Don't worry. These things work out. You'll see."

Jeff nodded. They walked down the stairs. One of the girls in the yard dropped her stick and hurried toward them, her short hair bobbing as she ran.

"Chao em," Gen said.

"Hello," the girl said in perfect English.

Gen smiled in surprise. "What is your name?"

"Hue."

"How old are you?"

Hue quickly held up one hand, flashing her fingers twice. Ten? She couldn't be ten.

"Five?" Gen asked. The girl was as short as the smallest kids at school, and skinny. Her arms were hardly bigger than the stick she had been playing with.

"No!" Hue held up both hands. "I'm ten." She reached for Gen's hand. "You come for a baby?"

Gen nodded.

"You take me, too?" Hue grinned at Gen with hopeful eyes.

"Hue isn't adoptable," Maggie said. "Both of her parents are alive. They can't afford to raise her, so she stays here."

"So you take me?" Hue was oblivious to Maggie's words.

"I can't," Gen said slowly. "You have parents, both a mother and father," Gen said. *I wish I could take you, too.* She scanned the dirt yard. *I wish I could take all of you.* She swallowed around the lump in her throat and thought of her mother. *So this was how she felt. This was why she wanted to save the children of Vietnam.*

Maggie directed Jeff and Gen back to the van.

The vehicle lurched as it bumped back out of the yard, past a faded rainbow of thin garments that hung on a clothesline. Gen's head began to ache. She closed her eyes, willing the headache to go away.

"It'll be okay," Maggie said. "These things work out. You'll see."

Hadn't Maggie just said that while they were on the veranda? Was Maggie nervous? Did she think it might not work out?

⚬

"Good-bye, little one," Lan whispered into her daughter's ear as she patted her back. They turned onto the red clay road and passed shrimp ponds, a group of shacks, rice fields, and peasants hurrying home for something to eat before bed, before sleep, before it was time to start all over again. A van, headed the opposite way, passed them.

"I bet that's Maggie," Cam My said. "Stop the taxi!" Cam My opened her door and stepped out into the middle of the road waving her arms. When the van didn't pull over, she ran after it, stirring up the dust around her sandals and skirt. She returned short of breath. "They didn't see me," she said in quick gasps as she climbed back into the car.

The van lurched again. Gen glanced over her shoulder at the orphanage. A red taxi had stopped in the middle of the dirt road. One door stood open. "Who's in that car?"

Maggie turned and squinted. "Probably someone who sees us as an easy target. Wants to get some money out of us."

"What if it's Mai's birth mother?" Gen strained to see through the dust-covered back window.

"It's not. She wouldn't be able to afford a taxi."

"How would she get Mai back to the orphanage?"

"By scooter, maybe a bike or a cyclo." Maggie glanced at Bao and then straight ahead.

The taxi faded from sight, and the van turned the corner back onto the main road. As Gen dug in her backpack for a water bottle, her hand brushed against the figurine of the little girl.

An hour later Gen sat in a tub of cold water. The hotel wasn't as luxurious as the one in Saigon, but it was more than adequate. It was clean and roomy with a small balcony over an empty parking lot. The air conditioning worked but not the hot water. The inside of her head felt like a stormy ocean that surged against the backs of her eyes, and nausea crept up her throat.

"Are you almost ready?" Jeff opened the door a crack. Maggie wanted to take them to a barbecue place for dinner.

"I don't think I'm going to make it. I think I'm going to be sick." Gen couldn't stop the headache. It was the stress, the jet lag, the heat, and the chaos of traveling from Ho Chi Minh City. *Be honest*. It was Mai. What if Mai's birth mom didn't return her to the orphanage? What if she did change her mind? What if there was a problem with the aunt?

God, Gen prayed, *would you bring us this far and not allow us to adopt Mai?*

"Is it turning into a migraine?" Jeff stood in the middle of the white-tile bathroom.

"I think so." She'd had a few migraines over the years, not frequent, but often enough to make her fear one now. She rose.

He held out a towel. "You're cold." He wrapped it around her.

"There wasn't any hot water."

Jeff reached above the toilet and flipped a switch. "This is the water heater," he said. "I'll tell Maggie we're going to stay here."

"What will you do for dinner?"

"I'll go down to the hotel restaurant. I'll get you some soup."

Gen nodded.

She lay on the hard bed with a towel over her eyes. Would God bring them to Vietnam only to have the adoption fail? Look what he had allowed with her mother. With Nhat. *No, God,* she prayed. *Please let us take Mai home.*

She considered how happy they were the night before, standing on the balcony of the hotel in Saigon. She had felt a perfect harmony as the scooters and cars buzzed by, as the rain fell and the ice cream music waltzed through the night.

Now she wanted to trust Jeff's optimism and Maggie's experience. Was she too afraid to trust God? Her throat thickened as she scrambled off the bed and hurried into the bathroom, retching into the toilet. She rinsed her mouth and stumbled back to bed. She should have asked Jeff to stay with her. Lights started to dance; she closed her eyes. The lights continued. She pulled the towel back over her head. "God, I trust you," she whispered. "I do. It's just that I'm so afraid, afraid of what you might allow."

Later she heard Jeff's and Maggie's voices at the door, and then, later still, she was conscious of Jeff's sitting at the table eating. When he came to bed, he reached for her hand.

❧

Gen stepped onto the balcony overlooking the parking lot. The South China Sea sparkled in the distance, and closer in, early morning sunlight streamed through the palm trees. Workers bustled around a half-constructed building. Bamboo scaffolding lined the structure, and poles, barely bigger than sticks, supported the beams.

"How are you?" Jeff called through the open door.

"Fine." Her stomach still felt upset, but the headache was gone.

"Want to go for a walk before breakfast? Maggie said she'd meet us at seven thirty in the restaurant. We have two hours."

A half hour later they strolled along the beach. Children ran in the waves, fishermen strung nets along the sand, small black boats and blue and red vessels bobbed in the ocean. A woman walked by with baskets of bananas secured to a yoke that she carried over her neck. Her arms were covered with long sleeves; a conical hat protected her head.

"Last night I read in the guidebook about Vung Tau," Jeff said. "It said that lots of the boat people escaped from here."

Gen thought of junior high and high school, of Hoa and her other Vietnamese classmates. Had some of them escaped their homeland from here? Had they bobbed in tiny boats on the South China Sea until a ship rescued them or they made it to Thailand? Why hadn't she asked more questions? Where had they lived in Vietnam? In a city? In one of the tiny villages between Saigon and Vung Tau? On one of the rice farms?

A woman unloaded a small stove, a pot, a stack of plastic bowls, and three kindergarten-sized plastic chairs from her baskets. Gen tugged on Jeff's arm and slowed so she could watch. The woman put the pot on the burner, lit the flame, and then set the three chairs off to the side.

"It'll be a while," Jeff said. "The pot has to heat." They picked up their pace.

"What did Maggie say last night?" A small bird scurried in front of Gen.

"She was worried about you."

"What else was she worried about? Did she say anything about Mai's aunt?" Gen stepped over a small stream of water that steadily cut a channel through the sand to the ocean.

"Are you sure you're feeling okay? I don't want you to worry more and get another migraine."

Gen picked up a perfect shell with scalloped edges. She handed it to Jeff. "Just tell me what she said."

"It's not that she said a lot—she seemed a little evasive, actually—just that Mai's aunt is probably the same woman Maggie used to work with who was involved in adoptions in the North." Jeff slipped the shell into his pocket. "If she is, then both the U.S. INS and the Vietnamese are investigating her."

"Did you ask if she's the same facilitator involved in Daniel's adoption?"

Jeff nodded. "Maggie just shrugged her shoulders."

Gen stopped. "Did she say anything else?"

Jeff reached for Gen's hand. "That Mercy for Children can't afford to work with a facilitator who is under the least bit of suspicion. It's too dangerous for the children and the adoptive families. They stopped working with this woman at the first hint of a problem."

"Does she think that Mai's aunt is corrupt?"

"She wouldn't say," Jeff said.

"Is she worried that the aunt had something to do with Mai's adoption?"

"She said she wasn't. She said that Bao handled all the paperwork on Mai and that the investigations, both of them, came out fine." Jeff stopped walking.

Gen turned toward him. "What do you think?"

"I think the sooner we can get Mai and get out of here the better, but I'm not worried." He squeezed her hand.

They turned and headed back toward the hotel. The woman with the portable soup restaurant had two customers sitting in the tiny chairs, slurping broth and noodles with spoons and chopsticks.

"It must be pho," Gen said. "Mom used to talk about eating it for breakfast."

"Amazing, isn't it?" Jeff said. "It's seven o'clock in the morning, and all of this is going on. All of this hard work to make a little bit of money, to keep things going for another day."

"I think of Mai's birth mother every time I see these women, especially the younger ones. I keep searching for Binh." Gen scanned the beach, looking north and then south. "They could be here on the beach right now."

✤

Maggie stood as they walked into the restaurant through the open french doors. "Good news!" she said as they approached the table. "I just talked to the orphanage director. Mai's birth mother brought her back last night. We can go see her after breakfast. I also talked with Bao. He said we have an appointment at the Justice Department for the Giving and Receiving Ceremony at one o'clock."

"That's great!" Jeff put his arm around Gen. "We really should be able to get home in two weeks. We're off to a great start."

"Lord willing," Maggie said. She turned toward Gen. "Are you feeling better?"

"Much, thank you." Gen asked the waiter, who spoke near-perfect English, for an omelet; Jeff ordered a bowl of pho. "Next time I'll just get it on the beach," he joked.

"Make sure it's boiling and all the meat and greens have been dunked under the hot liquid," Maggie warned. They would need to boil the water for Mai's bottles. Maggie said the hotel would have a hot water pot they could use.

Gen tore in half the small loaf of french bread that came with her omelet. "So what's the deal with Mai's aunt? Do you think she could be the facilitator for the little boy we met in Saigon?" Gen glanced at Jeff and then back at Maggie. "His name is Daniel. His dad's name is Bryce Gordon."

"She could be." Maggie took a sip of french coffee. "I know that she's been investigated regarding a couple of different adoptions. Thankfully, none of them were through us." Maggie lifted her cup again.

"What do you think Mai's aunt is doing here?" Gen pretended to concentrate on buttering her bread, giving Maggie time for another drink of coffee.

"I don't know." She put the cup back on the saucer. "She's probably just visiting her sister and mother. I hope that's all."

"Will you try to see her?" Gen asked.

"No. We settled everything between us last winter in the North. Besides it wouldn't be wise for me to have contact with her right now."

"What's her name?" Gen asked.

"Gen, some things are better left unknown. What if the United States INS finds out she's here and starts asking me questions and then you? How much information do you want to have?"

They walked along the veranda of the orphanage to the baby room. "She's sleeping," Bao said to Gen, "but her caregiver said you can see her."

Gen carried the backpack filled with diapers, clothes, toys, and bottles; Jeff carried the camera in one hand and the video camera in the other. They passed a room with the windows opened, an office, probably where the director worked. They passed a half-open door; three sets of bunk beds with a foot-wide walkway between them filled the room.

A door opened at the end of the veranda. A woman smiled at them. "That is her caregiver, Lien," Bao said. He stepped back and let them enter the room first. A row of hammocks hung from the ceiling. Two babies slept in some; in others, just one. Lien pointed to the last hammock. Mai slept alone. She wore a yellow cotton onesie. Her dark hair stuck straight up.

Gen knelt; the knotted twine framed her daughter's face. Mai stirred, stretched an arm, and opened one eye. She made an O shape with her mouth and opened her other eye. Jeff clicked the camera. The caregiver spoke in Vietnamese to Bao. "She says you can pick her up. She's napped long enough," Bao translated.

Gen stood and put the backpack against the wall. Her eyes met Jeff's as she lifted their daughter from the hammock and pulled her close. She felt the soft skin of her legs, the way her bottom fit into the crook of her arm. Gen trembled slightly and smiled. She held the baby to her face and breathed deeply. She smelled of sour milk and urine, not powder and baby shampoo. But still, she smelled wonderful. Jeff clicked the camera again. Gen sat in a wooden chair against the wall, cradling Mai in her arms, gazing into her big eyes. Mai made the O shape with her mouth again and relaxed it into a hint of a smile before her lips went straight. She glanced expectantly at Gen and then was startled as Jeff took another photo. Gen couldn't breathe deeply enough. She wanted to pull it all in—her baby, Jeff's smiling face, the happiness that filled the room.

Maggie came into the room with the director. "Oh, these are my favorite moments." She clasped her hands together. "Jeff, give me the camera. Stand beside Gen and Mai."

Gen patted Mai's bottom; the T-shirt hung loosely, and there was no padding.

"No, they don't use diapers in the orphanage." Maggie laughed as she took a photo. "Most children in Vietnam never experience a diaper."

"What do they use?"

"Thin cloths. Moss in the country. Rags if they're available. By the time a child can walk, they usually run around naked in the yard. It makes for fast potty training."

Jeff pulled a chair next to Gen. She handed Mai to him. The baby turned her mouth down.

"She hasn't been around men much, if at all," Maggie said. "Let alone tall men with curly hair."

Jeff bounced his leg. Mai smiled a bit and then began to cry. Gen reached for her. "There, there," she said. Mai stopped crying and gazed into Gen's face.

"She already recognizes your voice." Maggie snapped another photo. "The three of you are beautiful."

Gen snuggled the baby against her shoulder and patted her back. Jeff folded his arms around both of them. He whispered into Gen's ear, "Are you happy?"

"So happy. How about you?"

"I never imagined it would be this wonderful."

Maggie snapped another photo. "These will always be your happy-baby photos. There's nothing like this moment."

Jeff's smile filled the room. Gen imagined it filling the orphanage, spreading through the city of Vung Tau, along the coastline, through the entire country of Vietnam. Could Jeff's parents and her dad, seventy-five hundred miles away, feel his smile? She thought again of the carved figurine in her backpack. She felt the way she had all those years ago before her mother left for Vietnam the last time. She felt optimistic, remembered by God, chosen. Part of a family.

An hour later Jeff, Gen, and Maggie sat on the landing of the Justice Department, waiting for the Giving and Receiving Ceremony. "Not everyone understands that this isn't really a ceremony," Maggie said. "It's really a formality to sign the papers. There is no giving or receiving. Not now. I hope you can take Mai in a couple of days. It depends on how quickly we get the two documents we need. You'll sign the first one today. Then the Vietnamese officials will complete it along with the Decision on Adoption. Mr. Tran seems eager to get this done."

"Tran. That's Mai's last name," Jeff said.

"It's a very common family name, one of the most common next to Nguyen. There aren't as many last names in Vietnam as in most other countries."

Gen thought about the words *giving* and *receiving*. She had thought that this was a ceremony. That they would "give" their commitment to care for Mai. That they would "receive" the blessing of the Vietnamese government to do so. Gen folded her arms against her chest. She longed for Mai.

"Mr. and Mrs. Taylor," a voice called out from the doorway. A light shone behind the figure, and Gen had a hard time distinguishing his face. "Please come into my office." His English was good. Gen and Jeff stood. Maggie remained seated.

"Aren't you coming with us?" Jeff asked.

Maggie shook her head. "You're on your own. Sorry. In fact, I'm going to catch a taxi to an Internet café. Bao will be back in half an hour to take you to the hotel."

Jeff and Gen sat in the wooden chairs on the other side of Mr. Tran's desk. He stood facing them with his hands behind his back. He was quite tall, with black hair and a solid, square face. He wore a perfectly pressed green uniform. Gen's shoulders tensed.

Mr. Tran sat in a wooden chair and cleared his throat. "What makes you think you will be a good mother to Mai, Mrs. Taylor?"

"Because I love Mai." The words flew from her mouth.

"How can you love a baby you do not know?" the official asked, picking up his pen.

"I've loved her since the minute I saw her photo."

He tapped the end of his pen on the desktop. "You can love someone from a photo?"

"Yes," she answered.

"And you, Mr. Taylor"—Mr. Tran glared at Jeff with intense eyes—"can you, too, love a baby girl from a photo?"

"Yes." He smiled gently at Mr. Tran.

"And did you love Binh when you saw his photo?"

Gen's head began to hurt. Why was he asking about Binh?

"Yes," Jeff said calmly, "we did."

"And you?" Mr. Tran turned his head toward Gen.

She nodded. What was he getting at?

"Were you asked to pay for the baby and for Binh?" Mr. Tran leaned forward.

"What do you mean?" Gen sat up straight and held her shoulders back.

"Answer the question."

"Of course not." Gen felt a wave of panic. "We've paid the adoption fees and our travel fees, but no one has asked us to pay for Mai or for Binh." Was he going to deny the adoption? She clenched her hands in her lap.

"I'm afraid you were asked to buy them both but didn't want Binh badly enough to pay the additional money."

"No!" Gen hardly recognized her own voice. Her head began to pound. She wanted to flee the Justice Department and rush back to the orphanage; she wanted Mai in her arms. She wanted to beg the director to let them take their daughter. *Please, God.* She struggled to breathe in the thick air. Sweat trickled down the small of her back.

"We did want Binh, but the birth mother made the decision not to relinquish him," Jeff said calmly. "We did *not* pay money for Mai."

Mr. Tran drilled them with his eyes. Finally he spoke, looking at Jeff. "What do you do for a living?"

"I'm a cherry grower. We own an orchard in Oregon."

"Cherries. Really? Did you know 'Mai' means cherry blossom?" Mr. Tran glanced from Jeff to Gen.

Jeff's eyes questioned Gen. She shook her head. Why hadn't she looked up the meaning? Cherry blossom—Mai was meant to be theirs.

"Are there cherry trees here, in Vietnam?" Jeff asked.

"In the North. Of course, it is too hot here in the South."

Jeff nodded in agreement.

"Do you live among the trees?" Mr. Tran's eyes softened.

"Our house is on the property."

"Do you own the land?"

"Yes," Jeff said.

"Do you earn a sufficient amount of money?"

"Yes."

Mr. Tran opened a desk drawer and pulled out a file. "I've struggled with this case, but I'm going to go ahead and get the paperwork started. Either everyone is lying, or no one is. Rarely do so many people agree. I'm afraid I've reached a dead end, and I must leave for Ho Chi Minh City tomorrow for a week of meetings." He turned the papers toward them. "This is where you sign." His dark eyes softened. Was he smiling? Gen wasn't sure. She un-clenched her hands. At least he wasn't frowning or drilling them with those black eyes. "I have all the paperwork here. The documents for Binh, too. To show your good faith, that you truly were willing to adopt Binh, would you sign these, too?"

"Even though the birth mother changed her mind? Even though there's no chance that Binh will be our son?" Gen asked, the pitch of her voice ris-ing. She could feel red blotches forming around her collar.

Jeff put his hand on Gen's leg. Her head began to pound. She folded her hands in her lap. It was a test; Mr. Tran was testing them. What did it mat-ter if they signed the papers? She picked up the pen and read the words trans-lated from Vietnamese into both French and English. *Socialist Republic of Vietnam. Independence-Freedom-Happiness. For delivering and receiving adopted children between Vietnamese citizen and foreigner.* It listed her name and birth date and the same information for Jeff.

"Sign here," Mr. Tran said. *Representative of the receiving party,* she read. She signed the document. "And here," he said. She signed again, on Binh's document, and passed the pen to Jeff.

"Let's go up to the Giant Jesus this afternoon," Jeff said as Bao pulled up to the hotel. Gen had been silent since they'd left the Justice Department. Jeff and Bao had talked about the traffic, the vendors, the shrubs shaped into dragons.

"It'll be hot," Gen said.

"Do you feel up to it?"

She nodded; she was determined not to get another migraine.

They took a taxi from the hotel to the landmark, a statue like the one in Rio. They started up the steps. Lush vegetation lined the stone walkways and stairs. The back of Gen's neck burned.

She fell into step with Jeff. "What were you feeling when we were in Mr. Tran's office?"

"That we needed to get through it. That it was a formality."

Gen concentrated on each step. "I felt totally helpless." She increased her speed.

Jeff took two extra long steps and caught up with her. "Did you think he had decided to deny the adoption?"

"No. Well, maybe. I was aware that if he decided not to let us sign, I had no idea what to do next. And all those accusations about us paying for Mai and not wanting to pay for Binh made me wonder how we could prove to him that we hadn't paid. What would make him believe us if he had already made up his mind?"

"It's okay, though," Jeff said. "We signed the papers. He's approving the adoption."

"Do you think it was a test? That he wanted to know how sincere we were?" Gen lifted her head. The nearly hundred-foot-high statue of Jesus loomed above them. His eyes, set back in his rectangular face, gazed down at them.

"I don't know," Jeff said. "He seemed like a nice enough man, like he was just doing his job."

"Why does God let these things happen? Why can't it be easy?" Gen tripped on the next stair, catching herself before she fell.

Jeff put out his hand to steady her. "He wants us to trust him. This is how we learn. We're going to have to trust him with Mai for the rest of our lives. We had better start trusting now."

They kept walking. Sweat soaked through Jeff's T-shirt. His hair curled tightly around his baseball hat. Gen fell behind him a few steps. She had trusted God to take care of her mother, and look what had happened.

At the feet of Jesus was a garden of containers filled with roses. Red lettering covered several of the white pots. "Look," Gen said. "Portland, Oregon, USA." Vietnamese words preceded the Portland inscription. "Do you think they were donated by people back home?"

"Maybe from the Vietnamese church close to your dad's," Jeff answered. "Maybe they send money to take care of the gardens."

They walked around to the back of the hollow statue and started up the narrow stairs. "You'll never fit," a woman said to Jeff in perfect English. She laughed as they passed her on the stairwell. They popped back into the daylight through the small opening on top of one arm. Before them spread all of Vung Tau—the tall buildings, the red rooftops, the shacks, the ocean and inlets, the hilltops to the east, the rice fields, the shrimp ponds.

Sadness hung heavy as Gen took in the panoramic view; this was where Mai had been born. Someday it would be as foreign to her as it was to Gen. Had Mom ever come to Vung Tau? Perhaps for a vacation? Maybe with her friend Kim? Maybe not. She ached for her mother, longed to know her stories, longed for her advice.

"Let's go over to the other arm and see what the view is like from there." Jeff caught her hand. They crawled back into the stairwell and made their way through the narrow opening to the other side. A woman gazed out at the South China Sea. Beside her, on the enclosed shelf, a little boy slept.

I think Hang has the flu," Lan said to Older Sister. "She's vomited four times today." Lan handed her oldest child a cup of water. Mother stirred in the hammock in the corner.

Hang sat up. "It hurts worse," she said to her mother. "My stomach really hurts."

Older Sister stepped back. "It's probably a bug. She'll be better soon. I swear, half the time I'm sick as a dog by the time I leave Vietnam. I'm always picking up something here."

Lan headed back to the yard and knelt by the stove to stir the chicken broth. Hang hadn't had anything to eat all day, only a little water. Binh picked up a small limb that had fallen into the yard from the neighbor's catalpa tree. "Put the stick down," Lan said, taking the lid off the pot.

"I'd better go," Older Sister said. "I'll stop by tomorrow morning before I head to Saigon. I may be there a week or two. If I can, I'll come back before I leave for the U.S."

Lan hugged Cam My. "Let Mother sleep. I'll tell her you'll be by tomorrow."

Older Sister turned and headed toward the road.

"Mama!" Hang called out. Lan turned and hurried to her.

"It hurts here." She pointed to her abdomen. Lan felt her forehead. It was hot, very hot, as hot as any of her children had ever been.

"Hush," she said. "Try to rest." She stroked her daughter's hair, guiding it away from her sweaty forehead.

"It really hurts," she said. It wasn't like Hang to exaggerate.

Lan felt her daughter's belly. "Here?" she asked. Hang nodded, unresponsive as Lan pushed inward. When she stopped pushing and removed her hand, Hang let out a cry.

Lan stood. "Mother, could you wake up?"

Binh poked his head in the door, waving the stick.

"Put the stick down, Binh." Lan turned back toward the hammock. "Mother! I need your help."

"What is it?"

"Hang is sick. Her stomach hurts. She's running a fever."

Mother rolled over and slowly eased her legs off the hammock. She shuffled over to the mat and squatted down on the other side of Hang. "Might be what one of the Nguyen girls had. Do you remember? Back at our old place. Appendicitis. They said if her father hadn't gotten her to the hospital she would have died."

Lan felt Hang's forehead again.

"You'd better take her to the hospital. Just in case," Mother said, crouching by the altar.

"I'll see if Truc is home, if I can borrow her scooter." Why hadn't she asked Older Sister to wait? Binh swung at the empty water bucket in the yard and missed. Lan bent, intending to take the boiling pot of broth off the flame. When Binh swung at the water bucket again, the stick flew from his hand and hit the pot, knocking it off the stove. The broth flooded onto Lan's right hand and splashed onto her legs and then her foot as she fell backward.

"Binh!" she yelled, using her left hand to push herself to her knees, away from the steaming soup that covered the powdery dirt. "Binh! Why did you do that?" Her rage grew as the pain seared through her. Her legs felt warm, but they didn't burn like her hand and foot. She rose to her feet and staggered to the spigot. She turned the handle and thrust her hand under the cold water.

"I'm sorry," Binh whimpered, standing beside her.

"Go get Grandmother!" Lan yelled. "Go!" *First Hang, now this!*

"Spread your hand out." Mother hurried through the doorway. "Don't let your fingers stick together."

"Go get some ice," Lan begged her Mother. "Please hurry. Take Binh with you." The skin on her fingers and hand looked like melted plastic. She put her foot under the faucet. Nausea swept over her. She felt faint. She thrust her hand back under the water.

"Mama!" It was Hang.

"Just a minute," she called out. "I'll get you to the hospital as soon as I can." The ice would help or at least make the pain tolerable. Her foot hurt, but she could stand it. It was her hand that made the world spin.

"Mama."

She turned toward the doorway. Hang half stood, bent over like an old woman. She staggered out into the yard. Lan heard a scooter. She turned off the spigot and hurried to the road. "Truc," she called out, waving her good hand at her friend. "Can you take us to the hospital?"

Truc stopped and gasped at the sight of Lan's hand. "What happened?"

"Not me. It's Hang. I think she has appendicitis."

"Come on," Truc said.

"Hang," Lan called. The world started to spin again. Lan sat down. "I need ice."

"Come on!" Truc called out to Hang, who sat against the shack. "Let's get you to the hospital. We'll get ice down at the corner."

Lan sat with her hand in the bag of melting ice; the water dripped on her leg. Hang lay on two chairs. The doctor walked into the room. "Where's the girl with the possible appendicitis?"

"Over here," Lan said.

"Follow me."

Lan helped Hang off the chairs with her left hand. The doctor walked ahead of them. They made their way into a small room with a metal table. The doctor felt Hang's stomach and then pressed. Hang gasped as the doctor let go. "A classic sign," he said. "I'll order a blood test and let the surgeon know."

He turned to Lan. "Let me see your hand." She pulled it from the bag of ice. The doctor examined each finger and turned it over. "You have second degree burns. Don't pop the blisters when they form, or they will become infected. Keep it clean."

"Thank you." Lan bowed her head. "I can't pay until morning. My sister will come then." She hoped Older Sister would come to the hospital. Surely Mother would send her to help in the morning. She thought of Mother coming back with the ice and finding them gone. At least Mother had taken Binh with her. Now she regretted being so angry with him. Still, if he hadn't disobeyed her, she wouldn't be injured.

The nurse drew Hang's blood. "Could I have more ice?" Lan held up the bag of water. The nurse returned twenty minutes later with a paper cup of ice. Lan poured the warm water down the drain in the corner of the room and dumped the ice into the bag. She held it against her hand; still, the heat seeped deeper and deeper into her fingers and hand until it felt as if it reached her bones.

Hang dozed on the table, moaning every couple of minutes. Lan kissed her forehead. *My angel.* Finally another doctor came into the room. "I'm the surgeon," he said. "It is appendicitis and quite advanced, I'm afraid. We need to operate immediately."

❦

Lan stood at the open window. *Car c'est à toi qu'appartiennent le règne, la puissance et la gloire, pour les siècles des siècles. For thine is the kingdom, the power and the glory for ever and ever,* she prayed into the dark night. *Please don't let her die.* She couldn't bear life without Hang.

The nuns had told her that God would never give her more than she could bear. She'd borne enough. Chinh had told her that God would never leave her. She hadn't felt God for years.

Her hand throbbed, her toes and feet, too. She pulled up her left pant leg; red blotches covered her skin, matching the anguish inside her soul. The ice in the bag had melted again. She was thirsty. She drank the warm water, spilling some of it on her shirt, and then sat on the metal chair, leaned her head back, and closed her eyes. What would make life bearable? To have Hang be well. To have Binh behave. To have Older Sister stay in Vietnam. To not have to worry about money. What would make her happy? To keep Mai. To have Quan act like a brother. To have Chinh come back and take care of her. She squeezed her eyes tight. What would Chinh think of her? She took a deep breath. *What did it matter what he might think?* He'd left her to fend for herself. She'd done the best she could, shameful as it was.

Why was she thinking about Chinh, anyway? Older Sister was right. He was dead. All these years he'd been dead. He would never come back. It was her dream in times of trouble, extreme trouble. *Be strong, Lan,* she said to herself. *Take care of Mother and your children. Do what you have to do.* Her stomach hurt as if a sore oozed deep inside. She hadn't eaten in nearly a day.

What would bring her peace? She walked to the window. A sliver of the moon drifted among the stars.

❧

Lan opened her eyes as the surgeon walked toward her. "She's out of the operating room. We caught it just in time, before it ruptured, but it was septic. The lining of her abdomen is infected, and she needs to be on antibiotics."

Relief flooded Lan. "May I see her?"

The surgeon nodded. Lan followed him down the hall to the recovery room. Hang lay on a gurney with her eyes closed.

A nurse sat down, her gaze falling on Lan's hand. "You'd better watch out," she said. "You may get an infection in here."

Lan hid her hand behind her back. "How is Hang?"

"She'll be fine. It will take her two or three weeks to get back to normal, but she will. Twelve is a good age to have an appendix out."

Hang opened her eyes and then closed them again. Lan reached out and stroked her daughter's forehead, then ran her fingers through Hang's tangled hair. Her heart hurt. Her love for Hang filled the room, pushed against the cracked walls, pounded against the door. *Notre Père, merci.* She felt a sliver of peace in her soul.

"Lan." Older Sister rushed into the room. "How is she?"

Lan raised her head. She had pushed her chair against the end of the gurney and used it as a pillow. "The doctor and nurse both said she will be okay. They said it will take a couple of weeks but that she'll soon be back to normal." She needed to ask about the money. She glanced at Hang, who slept peacefully.

"Thank goodness," Cam My said. She searched the room. "Where's Binh?"

Lan sat up straight. "He's with Mother."

"Mother said he was with you."

"I told Mother to take him with her to get ice."

"She said he stayed with you and then went to the hospital when you took Hang." Cam My ran her fingers through her hair, leaving her hand on top of her head.

"No!" Lan jumped to her feet. Her stomach lurched, and then the pain settled back into the usual spot. Her hand was red and swollen, topped by ugly masses of mangled, blistered skin. Pain shot through her foot and toes.

"Your hand is horrible," Older Sister said.

"Never mind about my hand. Binh is supposed to be with Mother."

"He's not." Older Sister clutched her black leather purse against her abdomen.

Lan took two steps and vomited into the plastic wastebasket by the door. She raised her head and then quickly lowered it. She vomited again. She wiped her mouth. *This is more than I can bear.* "I've got to go find him. Do you have money for a taxi?"

Older Sister dug in her purse. "Did anyone examine your hand?"

Lan nodded.

"I need to go to Saigon today." Older Sister handed her a few bills. "I have to meet with the American INS tomorrow."

Lan nodded. "I'll be back as soon as I can." She hurried out the door, realizing she hadn't asked Sister to pay the doctor's fee. The nurse would bring it up with Cam My. Surely she had the money.

Had Binh run off on purpose? Had she scared him with her anger? He must be hiding at Truc's; that was surely where he had gone.

⚲

He hadn't gone to Truc's or to any of the other neighbors. Mother sat down in the yard as Lan leaned against the shack.

"Think like Binh," Lan said. "Where would you go?"

"The orphanage," Mother said.

"He would never go to the orphanage."

"The Justice Department." Mother's eyes searched Lan's face.

Lan shook her head.

"The market?"

"Maybe." Yes, he'd gone there before on his own. She limped toward the street, calling over her shoulder, "Stay here in case he comes back."

Where had he slept last night? Had he found anything to eat? She reached the fruit stall and called out to Mrs. Le, "Have you seen Binh?" Lan gasped for breath.

"I thought he was at the orphanage."

Lan shook her head.

"Lan, you look horrible."

"I need to find Binh." She turned and headed toward the Justice Department. She would ask Older Brother for help. She would beg him. She should have asked Mrs. Le for a handful of grapes, for anything to eat. It was too late now, and she didn't have the energy to turn back. She could feel the heat of the sun on her hand. The plastic of her flip-flop rubbed against the burns on her foot.

She turned the corner toward the Justice Building, glancing from one side of the street to the other, scanning the shops and doorways. A small figure caught her attention under the window of the bookstore. She quickened her step, forgetting her pain. It was Binh. She began to run.

He was asleep with his head resting on his folded hands. Dried tears streaked his dirty face. A red burn marked his leg. She hadn't realized the soup had splattered his leg too. She bent down and scooped him up. A businessman walked around them. Binh opened his eyes. "Mama?" he said and wrapped his arms around her neck. He smelled of urine; she pulled him to her.

"I paid the doctor," Older Sister said.

Lan nodded. "Thank you."

"I have to go." She pressed a wad of currency into Lan's hand. "Get something to eat. Buy Hang's medicine. I'd give you more, but I'm almost out of money. I'll be staying in downtown Saigon. The INS wants to keep tabs on me."

Lan began to cry. What would she have done these last two weeks without Older Sister?

Cam My glanced at Binh, who sat in the chair staring at Hang, and then looked at Lan. "Come out in the hall a minute."

Lan followed her out.

"Little Sister, please hear me. Consider taking Binh back to the orphanage before it's too late. If he were six or seven, able to go to school, I'd say keep him with you. But he's four and full of energy. Mother is no help to you, not the way she was when Hang was young. If Hang were sixteen or seventeen, I'd say keep Binh. Hang could work, and you could care for Binh. But Hang is twelve. Lan, you can't keep this up. You can't take care of Mother and Binh. Do it for Binh. Think of the life he can have in America. What will he have here?"

The hall began to spin. Lan reached out with her good hand, pressing it against the wall.

"And now you're injured and sick. Did you know there was blood in your vomit this morning? The nurse pointed it out when she emptied the trash. You probably have a bleeding ulcer. Hang needs you, and you need to get her raised, not kill yourself trying to do everything. If I could help you, I would. You know that. But I'm in trouble."

Lan slid down the wall to the linoleum floor.

"I'm sorry," Older Sister said. Tears filled her eyes.

She's right. This is more than I can handle. Cam My sat beside her and put her arm around Lan. After a minute she took a cigarette from her purse and lit it. Binh walked out of Hang's room and climbed onto Lan's lap.

*G*en held the bottle of Pedialyte. Bao stood between her and the caregiver. "Please tell Lien that I think this will help Mai. She may be getting dehydrated from the diarrhea." The box of diapers Gen brought the day before were still unopened. "And using the diapers will help keep Mai's bottom clean and lower the chances of infecting the other babies."

Boa translated. Lien shook her head. Gen glanced down at Mai in the hammock and then at Lien. The orphanage worker nodded, and Gen pulled Mai into her arms.

"Gen, Jeff." Maggie came through the door. "How would you like to take Mai with you today?"

"Are you joking?" Gen positioned Mai on her shoulder.

"No. The director said we can take her. The paperwork is supposed to be processed tomorrow."

Jeff walked behind Gen and gently high-fived Mai's flailing hand. The baby hiccuped.

"What a relief," Gen said. "I can give her Pedialyte and put a diaper on her."

"We should give the director the clothes and supplies you brought now," Maggie said.

"Can you go get the bags?" Gen asked Jeff. "And the gift bag for the caregiver?" She had brought American cosmetics to show their appreciation.

Minutes later Jeff presented the clothes, school supplies, medical supplies, and soccer balls to the director. A crowd of children gathered, their hands behind their backs, and stared at the donations. If only the people back home who gave the clothes and supplies could see how much it meant to the kids in the orphanage.

Lien came out of the nursery and put out her hands to Mai. Gen passed her the baby, and Lien said a few words in Vietnamese and kissed the little one's forehead. *"Cam on,"* Gen said. "Thank you for taking care of Mai." Lien nodded and handed the baby back. Gen and Jeff hurried down the stairs with their daughter, trailed by the orphans who followed them out to the van. They would never forget these children.

Gen bumped Mai's head against the doorframe of the van as she crawled in. "Oops," she said, suddenly feeling inadequate. She had felt so competent in the orphanage nursery, showing off the Pedialyte and diapers. As they drove away, Gen quickly put a diaper on Mai. "I'm so glad we brought the things for the kids."

"If they get them," Maggie said.

"What?"

Maggie shook her head. "I'm tired. Sometimes we see the kids with the things that we bring to them. Sometimes we don't. They might get one of the balls. The others will probably be sold. One might go to the director's own children, along with a portion of the clothes and school supplies. You never know."

Gen shook her head. *Was nothing certain here? Not even good deeds?* She patted Mai's back—there were no car seats in Vietnam, no seat belts, no safety measures. The driver stopped at a store for formula and more diapers. Gen had left the big box at the orphanage, hoping Lien would decide to use them. After they left the store, Gen spotted a billboard in a field that read "Vietnam. A Destination for the New Millennium." Underneath was a lean-to shack made of discarded boards and a blue tarp. Two boys and a little girl played in the dirt. *Do they have enough to eat? Do they go to school? Are they healthy?*

Gen hugged Mai and then kissed her baby's head. She breathed deeply, taking in Mai's musty smell. Gen ran her finger behind Mai's ears and felt a crusty mess. The baby shampoo, soap, powder, and diaper rash ointment waited back at the hotel. Gen would wash every centimeter of her baby.

"We finally reached the birth mother," Maggie said at dinner over the racket of Mai's crying. Gen continued to pat her daughter's back as she raised her eyebrows. She didn't know that Maggie had been trying to reach her.

"You need to meet with her before we go back to Saigon." Maggie took a sip of coffee.

Gen nodded and thought about the locket. She hadn't forgotten about the meeting, not entirely.

"I'll take Mai," Jeff said, reaching for the baby as the waitress brought their food.

"No, you eat first."

The waitress put Gen's beef satay and rice in front of her, then clapped her hands at Mai and reached for the baby. Gen glanced at Maggie.

"It's okay," Maggie said. "The staff does this all the time."

"How old?" the waitress asked in English as she bounced Mai.

"Four months," Gen said.

"She's so lucky," the young woman said.

"No, we're lucky," Jeff said.

The waitress smiled and clucked her tongue. Mai stopped crying. The waitress walked around the dining room with her, clucking and bouncing. Gen began to eat. A minute later Mai was completely quiet; soon she was asleep in the waitress's arms.

Gen put down her fork. "Okay, I admit it. I'm no good as a Vietnamese mom."

Jeff laughed and wiggled his chopsticks. "Well if you're no good, then I'm a dismal failure."

Maggie smiled. "It's like magic, that clucking. You'll both have to take lessons. Back to the birth mom. We've been trying since Monday to contact Mai's birth family. Bao talked to the grandmother a few times, but she wasn't any help. Bao went over again today, and finally the birth mom was there."

"Where has she been?"

"The hospital. Mai's sister had an appendectomy."

"Sister?!"

"Yes, she has an older sister."

"She has a sister older than Binh?" Jeff asked.

Maggie nodded.

"How old?"

"I don't know, exactly," Maggie answered. "Maybe around ten."

"Does she have any other siblings?" Gen asked. Suddenly Gen saw the birth mom as older—late twenties, maybe even thirty.

"I don't think so."

"Is the older sister all right?" Jeff placed his chopsticks across his plate.

Maggie nodded. "Bao seemed to think so. He also said that the mom, Lan, had a nasty burn on her hand and that she was limping."

Gen stared at Maggie, at a loss for words. After a moment she said, "Do you think she needs some help? Could Bao take her some money?"

"Of course not. That could be construed as paying for Mai," Maggie said as Jeff put his arm around Gen. "Anyway," Maggie continued, "we have set up a time to see her—tomorrow morning at eleven."

"Will we take Mai?" Gen turned her head. The waitress stood with the baby at the kitchen door.

"No. We'll have one of the hotel maids stay with her."

"You're kidding."

"No. We've done this before when we've gotten the child before the visit with the birth mom."

The waitress brought Mai back to the table. With one hand she pulled out a chair and then pushed another toward it, seat to seat. She deftly laid Mai down on her stomach. Gen stared at her daughter; she wanted to pick her up. "She's probably grieving." Maggie patted the baby's leg.

Gen knew what Maggie was talking about. Babies grieved for the women who cared for them in the orphanage, just as they grieved for their mothers after they were taken to the orphanage. But Gen didn't want to talk about it. She felt helpless. What could they do but get through it?

"What do you hear from your daughter? The one who is due any day?" Gen pulled a piece of beef off the skewer.

"How did you know my daughter is pregnant?" Maggie cocked her head to the side.

"Robyn told me."

Maggie laughed. "I haven't heard from Jennifer in several days. She's due in two weeks. I did hear from Robyn today, though. In fact I hear from Robyn nearly every day."

Gen smiled. "What's the status on their referral?"

"I sent it to her yesterday. It's a baby boy from the Ho Chi Minh City orphanage. He's been abandoned. There shouldn't be any complications. He's healthy and just three weeks old. They'll travel next month."

Gen and Jeff sat at the back table of the small bakery with Maggie. The suitcase and backpack for Binh rested against Gen's chair. "Bao said this is close to her house, within walking distance," Maggie explained.

Bao waited at the door. Gen felt unsettled. She hated leaving Mai; she wished they'd brought her with them. She felt powerless in all this. And she dreaded the thought of meeting the birth mom. Bao had picked up the completed documents from the Justice Department that morning and brought them to the hotel. Lan's birth date was listed as 1967. She was only a year younger than Gen. It made Gen feel even sadder. She wasn't a teenager with a future still ahead of her. Mai's birth mom was a grown woman, thirty-four years old and desperate.

She read the list of questions on the notepad in front of her for Bao to translate. *What do you do for a living? What do you want us to tell Mai? How was Mai's birth? Are there any family illnesses we should know about? What do you want to know about us?* Maggie had said not to ask anything about Mai's birth father, explaining that such a question would embarrass the mother.

Gen heard the door creak. Bao directed a tiny woman wearing a pale blue blouse and pants and a single braid down her back to their table. She held a conical hat in one hand. Jeff craned his neck. "Binh is out on the sidewalk," he whispered, "with a girl."

Gen sat up straight and craned her neck; all she could see was the display of french bread in front of the window.

Maggie stood. Gen and Jeff did too. The birth mother came to just above Gen's shoulder. Maggie bowed. Relief swept over Gen. Yes, bow. She knew to bow; she'd learned that in the adoption classes. But she suddenly wanted to shake the birth mother's hand or, worse, hug her. As she lifted her head, Gen saw the birth mom's right hand, covered with blisters. Gen glanced down at the scar on her own hand where she had burned herself in grade school. Then she looked up into the birth mom's face, into the frightened image of Binh from the photo, into Mai's full lips.

"This is Tran Thuy Lan," Bao said, "Mai's birth mother."

Gen bowed again. Bao said something in Vietnamese and then, "Jeff and Gen Taylor." Gen bowed a third time. How badly did Lan's hand hurt?

Maggie sat in the chair at the end of the table. Bao and Lan sat in the chairs across from Jeff and Gen. "Ask if she wants some coffee and a roll," Maggie said to Bao. He translated. Lan peered at Gen with a questioning look and then answered Bao. "She will if we do too," Bao translated. Maggie stood and headed to the counter.

Sweat beaded around Lan's brow. The silk of her blouse was frayed across both shoulders. Her dark eyes watered a little as she stared at Gen. Gen smiled. Lan smiled back. Gen felt self-conscious. Suddenly Gen was aware of the jade cross around her neck. Why hadn't she tucked it into her shirt? Would Lan be uncomfortable with Christians raising her baby? Lan smiled again. Gen remembered the locket and the gold chain. She pulled the box from her pocket and handed it across the table. "Bao, would you tell Lan this is for her. I left the photo of Binh in the locket because I thought she would like it. I didn't know at the time that she had a child older than Binh."

Lan opened the box, then the locket, and nodded. "Cam on." She put it in her lap.

"You're welcome," Gen said.

Maggie and the counter girl brought five cups of coffee. A waitress followed with a plate of cream puffs and éclairs. "How is her daughter?" Jeff asked Bao. "The one who had the appendectomy."

Bao translated. Lan bowed her head as he spoke and nodded to Jeff and Gen, then spoke to Bao. "She is much better, she says. She thanks you for asking," Bao said slowly.

"How is Binh?" Jeff wrapped his hands around his coffee cup.

"He is fine too," Bao translated.

Gen remembered the things they brought for Binh and lifted the child's suitcase and backpack and handed them to Lan. "These are for Binh. Clothes, books, and some toys." She wished they'd known sooner about the older daughter.

Lan quickly took the small suitcase and backpack from Gen. She put the suitcase on the floor behind her but kept the backpack in her lap and unzipped it. She pulled out the books, the notebook, the box of twenty-four crayons, and the toy set of the family and the car and put each item on the table. Next came the toothbrush and toothpaste, then the one set of clothes Gen had packed all those months ago. Lan unfolded the shorts, the Old Navy T-shirt, and the red underwear. She smiled at Gen. Next she pulled out the box of animal crackers and the Ziploc bag filled with pouches of fruit snacks. Lan bowed her head slightly, then carefully returned all the items to the backpack.

Flustered, Gen read her list of questions again while Bao and Lan spoke. "She says thank you for the things for Binh," Bao translated.

Lan took a sip of her coffee. Gen picked up a cream puff, hoping Lan would take one too. Lan took another sip of coffee. Gen put the pastry down on a napkin.

"Ask her what she would like us to tell Mai," Gen blurted out. Her head began to hurt. She hoped the caffeine from the coffee would help. It was strong and bitter. She wanted to add sugar and cream but didn't see any on the table.

Bao ended up asking all of Gen's questions and translating the answers back into English. He said that Lan wanted them to tell Mai that she loved her very much and that she wanted a better life for her than she would have in Vietnam.

"Lan would like you to tell Mai that she cannot provide for her," Bao translated. "Tell her that her mother wouldn't be able to send her to school or be sure she would have enough to eat." Bao translated that Lan sold snacks and souvenirs for a living, that she wanted Mai to know that her sister, brother, and grandmother also loved her very much, and that she had an uncle and an aunt.

Gen shot a look at Maggie at the mention of an aunt. Maggie took another sip of coffee. Gen touched the cream puff on the napkin and then drew her hand away. She couldn't take a bite.

Bao continued. "Lan said that Mai's birth was easy and that she doesn't know of any family illnesses."

No one spoke for a moment. Gen glanced from Jeff to Bao. "Please ask Lan what she would like to know about us."

Lan wanted to know what Jeff did for a living. Jeff responded that he grew cherries. Lan seemed puzzled as she listened to Bao. "Tell her that we own the land," Jeff added. Lan smiled and nodded as Bao translated.

"Please tell her that I'm a teacher, but I will take time off from work to be with Mai," Gen said.

Lan smiled again as Bao spoke in Vietnamese.

"Ask if we can take a photo of her with Gen and Jeff," Maggie said to Bao.

Bao spoke in Vietnamese. Lan nodded and put the jewelry box on the table. They all stood and moved toward the back wall. Gen felt as if she were floating in a bad dream. How could Lan stand it? How could she bear to give up her child? As much as Gen had wanted Binh, she was relieved that he would stay with Lan. It seemed fair. If she had to give up her baby, at least she could keep her only son.

"Everyone smile," Maggie said as she pointed the camera.

Gen's hand brushed against Lan's good hand. Gen felt fingers wrap around her palm. Tears filled her eyes. She squeezed Lan's hand. Lan began to cry.

"Smile one more time," Maggie said. Bao translated. Lan attempted a smile through her tears. "One more picture," Maggie said as she clicked the camera again.

Gen took a deep breath. Lan let go of her hand and sat back down at the table, lifting Binh's backpack onto her lap.

The bakery door opened, and a customer walked in. A horn honked outside, then a car skidded, followed by the sound of a crash. "Binh!" a voice shouted. "Binh!"

Lan said something in Vietnamese, jumped to her feet, and grabbed the locket box. The backpack fell to the floor, and she stumbled over the suitcase behind her chair. Bao headed to the door.

Jeff took four giant steps and slipped through the door before Bao. Lan and Gen rushed after the men. The girl pointed across the street at Binh and yelled. The driver of a small Toyota shouted at the boy. The child began to run. The car's front tires rested on the sidewalk. A metal cart lay on its side in the middle of the pavement. Baskets and an assortment of vegetables rolled in the street. A man pulled on the cart, trying to right it. Jeff raced across the street, followed by Lan. Binh hurried around the corner and disappeared from sight. Jeff and Lan rushed after him. Bao and Maggie helped the man right his cart. The girl, with one hand held against her stomach, bent to pick up the vegetables.

Gen stooped to help her. "Chao em," she said.

The girl dipped her head. Her long hair hung loosely over her shoulders.

"My name is Gen." She pointed to herself with an eggplant.

"My name is Hang," the girl answered, one syllable at a time in English. "How are you?" She gathered bamboo shoots off the pavement.

"Fine, thank you," Gen answered, smiled, and turned her head. Jeff walked around the corner, looking like a giant carrying Binh in his arms. Lan walked beside them, her eyes on her son. Was she scolding him? It seemed that way. Traffic began to inch around the stopped car. The owner of the cart waved his hand at the driver, yelled something, and pointed at the dent in his cart. The driver shook his head and pointed at Binh. The boy rode solemnly in Jeff's arms, ignoring his mother, ignoring the men yelling at each other.

Jeff stopped in front of the group. "Now what?" he said to Maggie.

"Someone has to pay for the damage," Maggie said.

"The man who owns the cart wants the driver to pay," Bao explained. "The driver says it was Binh's fault, that his family should pay."

"Was it Binh's fault?" Jeff frowned.

"It seems he ran out into the street in front of the driver," Bao said. "The car swerved and went up on the sidewalk and knocked the cart over."

"How much does he want?"

Bao asked the man and then turned again to Jeff. "He says it will cost eight hundred thousand dong for a new cart."

"But he doesn't need a new cart. He just needs to get this one fixed," Jeff said.

Gen and Hang finished filling the baskets with the bamboo shoots, eggplants, cucumbers, cabbages, and mushrooms. Bao spoke with the man again. The man's voice rose. Lan said something as she slipped the jewelry box into the small pouch that she wore around her neck.

"What did the man say?" Jeff asked Bao.

"That you can afford to buy him a new cart."

"Tell him I want to pay to fix this one."

The man said something in an angry voice. Jeff shifted Binh to his other arm and reached into his pants pocket and pulled out two twenty-dollar bills. He handed them to the man.

Gen and Hang put the baskets on the sidewalk.

The owner of the cart said something to Bao. Hang shook her head. "He says his vegetables are bruised. He needs money for those," Bao translated. Lan said something to the man and then looked up at Jeff.

The owner of the Toyota climbed into his car, started the motor, and stared straight ahead with a blank expression as he inched his vehicle past the group of people. Jeff reached in his pocket and took out another twenty-dollar bill. Lan grabbed Gen's hand and said something in Vietnamese again.

"She says he's taking advantage of you because you're Americans. She says he's a crook," Bao said to Jeff and Gen.

The owner of the cart snatched the bill out of Jeff's hand, righted the cart, and then put the baskets of vegetables in place. Lan scolded him. He began to push the cart.

"It's okay," Gen said to Lan and then turned to Bao. "Tell her it's okay. Please tell her we want to help. We're just glad that Binh is all right." Gen reached out and touched Binh's bare toe. He pulled it away and put his head on Jeff's shoulder. He had a scar on his ankle and a fresh burn on his calf.

"Well," Maggie said, "I've never had this happen before."

Jeff handed Binh to Lan. She winced as he slid over her hand onto her hip. "Thank you," she said in English, first to Jeff and then again to Gen. Tears welled in Gen's eyes again. She wanted to hold on to Lan, to say, *No, thank you. Thank you for Mai. We will tell her about you and her sister and brother.* She wanted to hold on and say, *I'm sorry. I'm sorry you have to give her up. I'm sorry that your life is so hard.* Gen stood on the sidewalk of Vung Tau, and for just a minute she hated the world.

"Ma," Binh said. "Ma" with a hard *a* sound as in *apple.* "Ma," he said again and then something more in Vietnamese. Gen could see that his front teeth were brown. Lan patted his bottom in a reassuring, "it's okay" sort of pat.

Lan turned toward Gen and spoke quickly.

"She asks that you teach Mai to be a good person," Bao translated.

Gen nodded. She didn't want to leave, didn't want to walk away from Lan and Binh and Hang. Or maybe she did. Maybe she wanted to run fast and far. To forget this pain that pulsed through her head. And her pain, her little bit of sympathy toward Lan, minimized what this mother of three must feel. *How can Lan bear it?*

"Good-bye," Lan said, again in English. She nodded to Hang. She bowed to Jeff and then to Gen, dipping Binh with the movement of her body. Jeff put his arm around Gen as they watched the trio walk down the street. Lan limped as she walked, Hang held her side, and Binh watched from over his mother's shoulder. Gen began to cry. Jeff wrapped both his arms around her. "This has been the hardest day of my life," she whispered.

"Mine, too," he said.

"I feel like a baby buyer. Even worse, I feel like we're stealing Mai from Lan."

"She took Mai to the orphanage," Jeff said.

"I know."

"Feel sad for Lan," he said, holding her closer. "Cry for Lan and Hang and Binh, but don't feel as though we've done anything wrong. We're doing everything right."

Lan and her children turned the corner. "They forgot the suitcase and the backpack," Gen said. She could see the bags through the bakery window, past the french bread, near the table where the waitress was righting the chairs. She hurried inside to grab them. "Maybe we can catch Lan."

Maggie shook her head. "Take Binh's things back to the hotel. Bao can deliver them later."

Gen could hear Mai's cries as she bounded up the stairs of the hotel. The maid stood in the doorway of their room and held the baby toward Gen as she rushed down the hall. "There, there, sweetheart," Gen cooed as she took her daughter. The maid smiled and pointed at the half-empty bottle and then at the garbage pail with three dirty diapers. Gen nodded, "Cam on," she told the maid.

Jeff put Binh's bags down, pulled out several bills, and paid the young woman. She bowed.

"Shh, shh," Gen said to Mai. The baby hiccuped and started to settle. Gen walked around the room. They shouldn't have left her behind. Jeff fell onto the hard mattress with a thud. Mai closed her eyes, and Gen eased her way onto the bed, patting Mai's back as she rested her head against the pillow.

"That was exhausting," Jeff said.

"How did it feel to hold Binh?" Gen smiled at him.

"Good."

Gen wished she could have held Binh. "Wasn't it incredible to meet Lan—and Binh and Hang? I'm embarrassed that I felt threatened by the birth mom, felt that she had so much control over our future. But meeting her changed all that. Now she's Lan, not just the birth mom." Gen continued to pat Mai's back.

"I think God wants us to pray for Binh. If we had just heard about him or even seen him, we might not be as compelled to pray for him." Jeff rolled on his side and ran his finger down Mai's leg. "I talked to Maggie about sending Lan money after we get home. I asked her about it that night you had the migraine."

"What did she say?"

"That there aren't any guarantees about getting the money to Lan, but that they would do their best. It should work if Bao is out here on business. Otherwise, it would be difficult. Maggie said it's best for Bao to buy things for the birth families, not just give them money. An adoptive family bought one birth mom a water buffalo. Another paid for a concrete floor."

"How much do you think we should send?"

"I don't know. A hundred dollars would go a long way. A hundred dollars a few times a year could make a big difference for them." Jeff stretched out his long legs, sending his feet over the end of the bed. "How long do you think Mai will nap?"

Gen turned her head toward the baby's peaceful face. "Maybe an hour. Maybe five minutes."

Jeff yawned. "Just think, in a week we'll be home, ready to start harvest," he said. "Everyone will want to see Mai. Mom and Dad will probably be camped out at our house. Your dad, too." He winked. "Even Aunt Marie."

Gen sighed. "I can't wait for her baby advice. 'Get that baby on a schedule. Don't pick her up when she cries. Wean her off the bottle, or her teeth will rot.'"

"Speaking of," Jeff said. "Did you notice Binh's teeth?"

Gen nodded. "Dental care is definitely one of the many things they need."

Jeff yawned again. "As far as baby-raising advice, I think we should follow our intuition. Aunt Marie and your dad are so logical, so focused on doing the right thing. I think they raised you to be that way, but it's not really you."

Was Lan intuitive? Was that why she took Binh back from the orphanage? What would Lan need? Money to send the children to school? Childcare for Binh? What was Lan's house like? Did she have a dirt floor? "Did Maggie say what they might need?" she asked Jeff. He didn't answer. "Jeff?" She turned her head. He was asleep. The air conditioning stopped. Another citywide blackout. The drapes shielded the room from the hot sun. Mai's little body pressed against Gen; the baby's breathing calmed her. She took in the scent of Mai's clean head. She rubbed her nose against the baby's fine hair and hugged her daughter gently.

Lan stood in the doorway of the shack and realized that she had forgotten the books, clothes, and toys for Binh. Hang collapsed on the sleeping mat. Lan stepped back into the yard, sat down, and examined her hand. The blisters oozed yellow pus. Binh sat beside her.

"I'm hungry," he said.

Irritated, she turned away from him and wiped the yellow ooze with the end of her blouse.

"I'm hungry," he said again.

"We're all hungry," she answered.

"I had enough food in the orphanage."

The orphanage. Everyone thought she should take him to the orphanage. She thought about Mr. and Mrs. Taylor. She rose and walked into the shack, took the box from her pouch, and put it on the back of the altar, behind Second Brother's photo. Hopefully Mother wouldn't notice it. She pulled her sleeve down over her hand. She shouldn't have taken Hang and Binh with her to meet them. Hang had begged to go to catch a glimpse of the Americans who had come for Mai. Lan had been afraid to leave Binh with Mother. *Notre Père, I know what I must do.*

*T*he sound slowly pried Gen awake. First she was aware of Mai on her chest, then Jeff beside her, then someone knocking at the door.

"Who is it?" Jeff mumbled.

"I don't know. Probably Maggie. Go answer it, okay?"

Jeff stumbled through the dark room and pulled open the door.

"I've got good news!" Maggie hurried inside. "The orphanage director called. Binh is there. Lan wants you to adopt him, too."

Gen struggled to sit up without waking Mai. The room spun.

"What?" Jeff asked.

"I don't want Lan to have to give him up." Gen leaned against the headboard.

"But she took him back to the orphanage," Jeff said, sitting on the edge of the bed.

Gen positioned Mai across her lap. "What if Lan changes her mind again?"

"The director says that she is serious. She wants you to raise him." Maggie stood at the end of the bed.

"Could we sponsor him? Give her the money for food for him, for dental care?" *What am I asking?*

"Genni," Jeff said. "What's wrong?"

"I feel sick. For Lan." The baby breathed quietly, the side of her face against Gen's leg.

"There's no guarantee that we could get the money to her or that she would use it on him," Maggie said. "Other things would take priority. And there's no guarantee that after a few years you would keep giving."

A pained expression crossed Jeff's face.

"You need to make your decision based on what's best for Binh and on what is best for you as a family. That's what we want for all of you," Maggie said, looking from Jeff to Gen. She continued, "Lan has essentially chosen you. I've never had this happen before. She's entrusting Binh to you."

"Do you think knowing we want Binh made her decide to give him up?" Gen asked. Her eyes had adjusted to the dark room. Maggie's shoulders drooped with exhaustion.

"She took him to the orphanage the first time, long before she knew about you." Maggie sat on the end of the bed and turned her head toward them. "I think I understand what you're getting at," she said. "Do you wonder if you're making her life worse in the long run?"

Gen nodded. The back of her knees sweated against the bedspread. Mai's body heat soaked her shirt. When would the air conditioning come back on?

"It's the same issue the agency deals with all the time, except ours is on a larger scale. Does facilitating adoption in Vietnam perpetuate adoption?" Maggie stroked Mai's arm. "You have to remember that the government of Vietnam asked us ten years ago to find families for the children they couldn't provide for. That's exactly what Lan is asking of you."

Beads of sweat formed on Gen's upper lip.

Maggie continued. "She's seeking a personal solution for Mai and now for Binh. That's what we do for each child too. Our first preference is for the child to stay with the mother. Our second is for the child to be adopted by a Vietnamese family, which hardly ever happens. Our third preference is international adoption."

"It feels like exploitation," Gen said. "It's the haves and the have nots. We can have these children simply because we have more money."

"I know," Maggie said. "It's one of the great inequities in this world. That's why we work with the Vietnamese government to support children in general. Our goal is to eliminate adoption."

Gen glanced at Jeff.

"I'm serious," Maggie said. "I love my job, but I'd prefer not to be needed here."

Mai began to fuss. Gen lifted the baby and gently patted her back, tapping out a rhythm.

"For Lan, the only way she can keep her oldest child healthy and provide for her mother is to relinquish Mai and Binh. Often mothers will keep an older child and take the younger ones to the orphanage. Usually it's an older boy that they choose to keep. You have to understand that the culture is different, the expectations are different."

"I won't feel guilty if we take Binh," Jeff said. "I already feel responsible for him. And responsible for Lan and Hang and even the grandmother."

Gen thought about the nameless Vietnamese girl she had prayed for all those years. She shivered.

"Vietnam is a wonderful place," Maggie said, "and I can tell that Lan truly loves her children. But that doesn't mean Binh will get what he needs here."

"I hope our love can equal Lan's and our lifelong support will make the difference for Mai and Binh." Jeff searched Gen's eyes.

She took a deep breath. *Can my love equal Lan's? Will Binh's love for us ever equal his love for Lan?* They were all silent for a moment.

"Think about your mom, Genni," Jeff whispered. "That's why we're here, isn't it? Because of her love for the people of Vietnam?"

Gen stopped patting Mai's back. *Is this what Lan wants? Is this what God wants?*

"What would your mom do?" Jeff asked in a quiet voice. Gen focused on the baby's thin legs. She didn't want to talk about her mother in front of Maggie.

"Is this about your sadness, Gen? Your grief for Lan? And for Binh?" Maggie asked, ignoring Jeff's question.

Gen nodded. "I think so."

"You will be sad your entire life that Mai and Binh had to leave Lan. And you will be thankful your entire life that they came to you. It will be the paradox of your life."

Gen tried to swallow the tearless lump in her throat. "Is this what you want?" she asked Jeff.

"More than anything."

"Okay," Gen said. "Let's go see our son."

Lan sat beside Binh on the veranda of the orphanage as the director walked toward them. "I talked with Mrs. Benson. She said she would speak with Mr. and Mrs. Taylor immediately and call me back."

Binh hadn't cried when they arrived. Now he poked at an ant crawling across the bench. Lan fingered the hair at the base of his neck with her good hand. She hadn't told him he was going to be adopted, just that he would stay at the orphanage and the couple from America, the big man who'd carried him and the woman with the kind eyes, would come to visit him. She hoped they would come, hoped they would adopt him. She put her head back against the railing and closed her eyes. The shade of the building barely made the heat tolerable.

A phone rang; Lan opened her eyes. Binh had curled up on the bench and was breathing slowly, as if he was asleep. The director's voice floated onto the veranda, but the words disappeared in the sweltering heat. Time stopped for a moment. *I hope Binh and Mai will be together. Mother, Hang, and I will have each other. It's the best I can do for all of us.*

"Lan." The director walked toward them. "Mr. and Mrs. Taylor have agreed to take Binh, too. They'll come to the orphanage today to visit him and then take him tomorrow."

Binh sat up, stood, and then walked to the railing of the veranda.

"Here." The director handed Lan a tube of ointment. "The Americans donated medical supplies to the orphanage. Put the antibiotic on your hand. It will keep it from getting infected."

"Thank you." Lan took the medicine; she would use it later. "It's for the best," she said to Binh. She stood and faced the yard; children kicked a soccer ball in the dirt below. "You'll have enough food. You'll go to school. You'll have everything you need. A mother and a father. You will be with Little Sister. The two of you will grow up together." She was silent for a moment. "Binh," she continued, "I love you. I'm doing this because I love you."

He looked at her and then back at the yard. A four-year-old couldn't understand such a horrible love. She stood and bent to hug him. He held his body straight.

"Good-bye," she said. "Be good." Grief flowed alongside the rivulet of peace as she turned and headed toward the stairs and then glanced back one more time. "Be good," she said again. "Don't forget me." Pieces of Lan's heart broke off.

Binh nodded but did not cry.

꩜

Lan sat in the yard outside the shack and gently rubbed the ointment over her burn. A few of the blisters had popped, leaving shrunken skin dangling over bright red patches on her fingers and hand. Some of the sores oozed pus. She wrapped the gauze around her hand and then rose to light the charcoal stove. Older Sister had given them a bag of rice before she left. At least they had that for dinner.

Hang would be furious with her for giving up Binh again. Maybe not today or even for a few days, but when she felt better, she would be angry. And with good reason. She hadn't even given Hang the chance to say good-bye.

She lifted the little door at the bottom of the stove and scraped out the burnt charcoal with a stick. She took one of the three remaining charcoal bricks from the bag and dropped it into the stove, then struck a match and lit it in a quick motion. It was so quiet without Binh. Quiet without him, chaotic with him. He needed more than she could give.

Mother stood in the doorway. "What is there to eat?" she asked, stretching her arm over her head.

"Rice," Lan said.

"Did you work today?"

Lan shook her head. Mother frowned.

"How is Hang?" Lan made out the curve of her daughter's body in the dim light of the open door.

"She's been asleep all afternoon. Where is Binh?"

"I took him to the orphanage." Lan began to cry.

"Now, now," Mother said. "It's for the best. Now he will have a future."

Lan pulled the tail of her shirt to her face and wiped her tears. "I know. Still, it's hard."

"It will get easier."

Lan filled the pot with water from the spigot and put it on the stove. She wished she had some vegetables and beef for Hang. The girl needed more nourishment. She heard a rustling in the shack; Hang stood in the doorway.

"How are you?" Lan lit the stove.

"Better." Her pale face was gaunt. Her shoulders hunched forward.

"Are you in pain?" There were only two pills left from the hospital. If the pain became intolerable, Lan would need to go to the pharmacy tomorrow.

"A little."

"Are you hungry?"

She shook her head. "Where is Binh?"

Lan stared at the stove. "At the orphanage."

"Mama. Why?" Hang sounded as if she'd been kicked in the stomach. "Why did you take him again? I told you I would take care of him. I'll quit school. Let me work."

Hang was twelve, almost a woman. No, she was still a child. She had to stay in school. For what, Lan didn't know. Maybe Older Brother would find Hang a job. Maybe Older Brother would find her a place in the university. "I'm sorry," she said, rising to comfort Hang, but her daughter waved her away and walked back into the shack.

*H*e's been sitting here since his mother left." Bao translated the director's words to Gen and Jeff as they walked up the stairs of the orphanage. Gen carried Mai. Jeff carried Binh's backpack and suitcase that Lan had left in the bakery. They turned on the veranda landing, and there was Binh on the bench, staring at the floor.

"Chao em," Jeff said, bending down. "I have something for you." Jeff unzipped the backpack and sat beside him.

Maggie took a photo. Gen kissed the top of Mai's head. Bao said something in Vietnamese. Binh peered into the backpack as Jeff tugged out the books, and then he smiled a little as Jeff opened *Brown Bear, Brown Bear* and began reading the words. After Jeff finished the last page, Binh pulled the backpack onto his lap and reached in, taking out the box of animal crackers. Jeff opened the cardboard and wrapper and handed one to Binh. He smelled the cracker, then licked it and made a face. Jeff opened a fruit-snack pouch and handed a purple tiger to Binh. He smelled it, licked it, smiled, put the animal cracker back in the box and the fruit snack in his mouth. Then he pulled *Goodnight Moon* from the stack and dropped it on Jeff's leg.

Jeff grabbed the book before it fell to the floor and pulled Binh onto his lap. The boy tried to turn the pages in a bunch. Jeff took his hand and showed him how to turn the pages one at a time as Binh rested his head against Jeff's chest. Gen sat down beside them on the bench, and Binh reached out and touched Mai's hand. Gen closed her eyes and felt the baby's breath against her neck, her husband's leg pressed against her own, and her little boy's body just inches away. She listened as Jeff read the book. She breathed in the dust from the yard and listened to the yells of the children playing soccer below.

"The director says we need to go," Maggie said. "It's time to feed the children."

Jeff stood, holding Binh in his arms. "Can you tell him we'll be back tomorrow?" Jeff asked Bao. Binh slid from Jeff's arms to the floor, put the books in the backpack, and zipped it while Bao spoke to him. Then he pulled the pack over his shoulders, picked up the suitcase, and headed to the staircase. Bao called out to him. Binh responded and then kept walking. Jeff hurried after him and took the suitcase in one hand and Binh's hand in the other. They waited for the others on the first floor veranda.

"He wants to go with you now," Bao said, glancing at Gen and then the orphanage director. The director shook her head, took Binh's hand, and spoke to Bao.

"She says tomorrow," he translated. "Tomorrow morning. She'll recheck his paperwork tonight and make sure all that is needed is Mr. Tran's signature, plus your signatures, which we'll do on Monday."

"We already signed for Binh," Gen said.

"What?" Maggie asked.

"At the giving and receiving ceremony. Mr. Tran made us sign for Binh to show that we were sincere in wanting him. He thought we had paid for Mai but didn't want Binh because he was older. Somehow having us sign for Binh made him less suspicious."

Maggie shook her head. "And you didn't tell me?"

"You had already left. It was bizarre, but we didn't think it meant anything," Gen said. *God, you were looking ahead, weren't you? Taking care of us. And I was so angry with Mr. Tran.*

"I wonder what he's up to." Maggie tapped her foot on the tile floor. "Whatever it is, it should work to our advantage. I'll have Bao call the Justice Department right now and double-check. We should be able to leave for Ho Chi Minh City on Sunday."

❧

"Boa talked to Mr. Tran's assistant late this afternoon and confirmed that you signed for Binh," Maggie said at dinner. "We should be on schedule."

"What happens after we get to Ho Chi Minh City?" Jeff asked.

"We'll take the children to the U.S. INS on Tuesday after we get Binh's papers."

Mai began to fuss. Gen stood with the baby. The evening breeze flowed through the open french doors. The waitress headed toward their table, her arms outstretched. Gen shook her head. "No, thank you," she said to the waitress. "I'll hold her."

"And then how long will it take?" Jeff asked, shooting a quick glance at Gen.

He's counting the days until harvest starts.

"I'm hoping we can all fly home by the end of the week." Maggie's eyes sparkled.

"Wow," Jeff said.

Wow is right. Amazing. They'd come for one child; they'd go home with two.

"Can we try to e-mail from here?" Jeff pushed his plate to the middle of the table.

"The e-mail from the hotel is impossible," Maggie said. "But we can go to an Internet café after dinner."

"I want to tell Mom and Dad and your dad about Binh," Jeff said to Gen. She nodded.

The Internet café was the front room of a family's home. Six computers sat on plywood tables. The mother directed Gen and Jeff to the first computer. Gen logged on to their Hotmail account and checked their in-box while Jeff held the baby. There were six messages from Sharon and one from her dad. Sharon's messages were full of information about what Don had been doing in the orchards. Gen answered the last one. Halfway through her reply the computer crashed. After rebooting, she checked her father's note; the message was four lines:

> I met a Vietnamese pastor last night. He works at a church
> in Southeast Portland. He wants you to visit a pastor in
> Saigon named Trung Duy Ho Tam. I'm praying for you.
> Let me know if there's anything you need.
>
> Love, Dad

"Do you think we'll have time to find this man?" Jeff said as he bounced Mai.

"How can we find him? There are nine million people in the city. I think we need more information about him."

Gen quickly e-mailed her father back, suggesting he get a phone number or an address of the man, and then she composed a group e-mail to all their parents.

> E-mail in Vung Tau is hard to come by. We'll e-mail more as soon as
> we get to Ho Chi Minh City on Sunday. We have good news and will
> share details later. We will be coming home with two children! Mai
> and Binh. We're the luckiest parents in the world!
>
> Love, Gen and Jeff

Binh stood at the bottom of the stairs with his backpack on and his suitcase at his side. He smiled as Jeff and Gen climbed out of the van. *"Ba!"* he called out to Jeff. It was early evening. They'd waited all day for the call from the director. Finally, as they were having an early dinner in the hotel restaurant, the phone call came.

"He called me Ba," Jeff said to Gen and handed her Mai. He hurried to the little boy.

Gen walked over to Jeff and Binh and knelt beside her son, balancing Mai against her shoulder. "Chao em," she said.

He ignored her, took Jeff's hand, and said something in Vietnamese.

Bao laughed. "He said it's time to go. He wants to leave the orphanage now."

Back at the hotel Gen ran bathwater for Binh while Jeff sang, "Splish splash, I was taking a bath...thinkin' everything was all right..." as he helped Binh undress. Gen smiled. How many years had Jeff wanted to sing that song to a child? Binh started to crawl into the tub. "No," Gen said. "It's hot. How do you say hot in Vietnamese?" she said to Jeff frantically.

"No, no," Jeff said to Binh.

"Nong!" Gen said, remembering from all those months ago when she'd memorized Vietnamese safety words. "It's nong! It's hot!"

Binh looked up, puzzled. Gen bent down and felt the water. He did the same. Gen turned the hot water down. He felt the tap water and then turned the hot water off and shook his head. He climbed into the tub and bent his head under the faucet. Gen felt the water. "It's ice cold," she said.

"He's probably never bathed in warm water," Jeff said. Mai began to cry, and Jeff walked to her crib and picked her up. Gen squeezed baby soap onto Binh's hair; his hands flew to his scalp and began to scrub. "Come look at this!" Gen said to Jeff. They both stared as Binh washed his hair and then bent under the faucet and quickly rinsed it. "Here, let me take Mai so you can wash him." Gen thought Binh might feel more comfortable with Jeff.

Jeff grabbed a washcloth and squirted liquid baby soap onto it.

"Scrub behind his ears and all around his neck, okay? Then let's get him dressed and go for a quick walk on the beach before bedtime." She walked back into the bedroom and changed Mai's diaper. In a few minutes Jeff came out carrying Binh, wrapped in a towel. "Look, Ba," Gen said, "you've got a boy."

Jeff laughed. Binh smiled. "Look, Ma," Jeff said, nodding toward Mai, "you've got a baby."

"We've got a family," Gen said. She hoped Binh would continue to call Jeff "ba," but she hoped he would call her "mama." He already had a Vietnamese ma.

*T*he sun set as Lan walked into the yard. She'd sold cigarettes and souvenirs all day on the beach. She had searched for Truc, hoping for more goods to sell, thinking she could work into the evening, but she hadn't found her. Regardless, she had made enough money for dinner and for Hang's medicine, which she carried in her basket. The beach had been packed with tourists from the city and from China and Japan. Lan had seen a few Americans on the beach but not the Taylors and Binh and Mai.

She swung her yoke and baskets over her neck and onto the ground, stretching her back and then her arms and her red, raw hand. She heard a car on the road and turned her head. It was a black car. *Older Brother.* She walked toward the road. He climbed out and slammed the door. She bowed to him. Why had he come? She was too tired to talk with him tonight.

"Hello, Little Sister," he said. "How are you?"

"As well as can be expected." She swung her yoke back onto her shoulders.

"May I sit with you?"

Lan turned and walked back into the yard. Older Brother followed. "I've just come from Ho Chi Minh City. I saw Older Sister there, and she told me of your troubles. How is Hang?"

"She's resting." Had he come to help?

"Is she recovering?" Quan held his head high, his back straight.

"Yes," Lan said. She swung the baskets back to the ground and leaned against the house.

"I've been thinking about you and your children. I would like to help. Hang is too old. She must stay with you, but Sister said she encouraged you to take Binh back to the orphanage, to put him up for adoption." Older Brother clasped his hands behind his back.

Lan nodded. She didn't want to tell him that she had.

"Don't take him to the orphanage. I am going to adopt Binh."

Lan slid down the wall of the shack and put her head in her hands. *Adopt Binh?*

"I am growing old with no children. I thought about this all the way from the city. It's what's best for all of us. I will have a son; Binh will have a father. He'll go to the best school in Hanoi." Older Brother stood over Lan.

"Who would care for him?" Lan asked, staring up at Quan.

"I would."

"Who would care for him while you work? While you travel?"

"I'll hire someone to help." Older Brother's voice rose.

A mother *and* a father. That was what she wanted for Binh. The pain in her stomach flared. He would take Binh to Hanoi. *What is best for Binh?*

She knew what was best for Binh. Today she had longed to see him, but she hadn't worried about him once. "I already took him to the orphanage. The American couple, the ones who are adopting Mai, are adopting him, too." Lan stood. "It's what is best for him."

"What does Mother think of this?"

"She supports me."

"What about Hang?" Quan asked.

Lan bowed her head. "She is still a child. She does not understand these things."

"Now I understand." Hang stood in the doorway. "You told me that you took Binh to the orphanage. Not that he was to be adopted. He's going to America? With Little Sister?"

Mother came out of the shack, moving past Hang like a solemn shadow in the early night. "Lan, what's for dinner?" Her gray hair hung loose around her face.

Irritated, Lan struggled to her feet and turned toward Mother. *Can't she think of anything besides food?*

"We have a guest." Lan leaned against the shack. Hang turned away.

"It's me, Mother. Quan." Older Brother bowed slightly.

"What are you doing here?" Mother squinted in the dim light.

"I came to talk to Lan. I'd like to adopt Binh."

"Good. You should. He's at the orphanage. Go get him." Mother ran her fingers through her hair.

"No," Lan said.

"What?" Mother asked.

"It's been decided. The American couple will adopt him. I want him to go to America."

"When he can stay with family? Blood is blood, Lan. Don't be stubborn," Mother said.

"Blood is blood? How can you trust Older Brother so easily?" Lan folded her arms.

"He's my son. What did you buy for dinner?" Mother pulled her hair into a single strand and began to twist it.

"Cabbage and bean curd. He watched Father be executed. How can you forgive him so easily?" She shouldn't be talking so boldly in front of Quan.

"I'm tired of bean curd. He saved your life."

"My life?" Lan put her good hand on her hip.

"At the hospital. When the land mine exploded. You were all that I had left. He got the doctor to care for you that evening, not two days later," Mother said, securing her hair in a bun.

"And then he left us, just like that." Lan wanted to stamp her foot. "All those years he left us to fend for ourselves."

Mother shrugged. "He wants to help you now. He's helped me. These last few months have been much better. Don't be so angry."

"That doesn't mean going to Hanoi would be best for Binh." Her hand throbbed; her stomach churned.

"Hanoi would be closer than America," Hang said, standing in the doorway again. Lan could barely see her face in the dark. "Maybe we would get to see him."

Lan faced Older Brother. "Would we get to see him?"

"Maybe," he said, clasping his hands behind his back. "I probably won't travel to Vung Tau for my job, just to Ho Chi Minh City. I'll have to see how busy I am. Maybe you could travel to the north."

Mother clapped her hands.

"How would we have the money to travel? If I had the money to travel, I wouldn't be giving up my children." Lan kicked at the dirt.

Older Brother shrugged. "You'll never see Binh again if you send him to America."

"I want to see Binh again," Hang said, walking toward Lan.

Surely they would see Binh and Mai someday—perhaps when they were grown. Lan shook her head and put her hand around Hang's waist. "It's for the best, Hang. Someday you will understand. It's what a mother does for her children. She gives them the best she can." She had to go with her feelings; they were all she had.

"Have you forgotten?" Older Brother asked. "It's not up to you to decide what is best. Right now, I'm the one person in all of Vietnam who can decide what's best for Binh."

$\mathscr{A}$ fter chasing Binh on the beach, Gen and Jeff washed their feet in the footbath outside the hotel and returned to their room. Binh pulled on his Nike shoes, opened the compact refrigerator door, peered inside, and took out a container of yogurt and a box of juice. Gen opened the two. Binh smelled the yogurt and took a tiny taste with a plastic spoon. He raised his eyebrows and took another bite and then ate spoonful after spoonful until it was gone. He drank the juice in three slurps.

Jeff tried to take Binh's new Nikes off, but the boy began to cry. "Just leave them on," Gen said, shrugging. "Maybe when he sees that we don't sleep in our shoes, he'll take them off." Jeff worked Binh's shorts off over his shoes and then pulled his pajamas on over them too.

Gen handed Mai to Jeff, then pulled out Binh's toothbrush and led him into the bathroom. Binh wouldn't open his mouth. Gen got out her own toothbrush and brushed her teeth. Binh kept his mouth clenched. When she tickled his lips with the brush, he began to cry.

Jeff said to wait, that maybe they could get Bao to explain it to him tomorrow. Jeff read Binh a story, and then Binh pulled all his clothes, books, and toys out of his bags and arranged them in piles on his bed. Jeff and Gen watched, amused. Binh was oblivious to them. He dumped the car and family out of the Ziploc bag onto his mattress and then zipped the pink pull on the bag back and forth, back and forth, ignoring the toys. He giggled each time. Jeff tried to get Binh to put his head on his pillow and close his eyes.

Binh threw the pillow onto the floor and picked up *Goodnight Moon* and handed it to Jeff. Jeff read him the book, then went into the bathroom to brush his teeth. Binh grabbed the book, hustled over to the refrigerator, pulled out a container of yogurt, hurried around Jeff and Gen's bed, and climbed up on Jeff's side. He threw Jeff's pillow on the floor, spread his body out straight on top of the blanket with the toes of his shoes pointed straight up, squeezed his eyes shut, and began to make the clucking sound that the waitress had made to Mai, with the book and yogurt still in his hands.

The baby, who had been fussing in Gen's arms, grew quiet. Gen moved from the window, where she'd been bouncing Mai, to the bed, but when she sat on it, Binh stopped clucking, and Mai started crying. The little boy opened one eye and peeked quickly at Gen, then squeezed both eyes shut again. Maggie had explained that children slept with their parents in Vietnam and that Binh might not want to sleep alone.

Jeff watched from the bathroom door and chuckled.

"It's going to be a fun night." Gen handed Mai to Jeff and went into the bathroom to make Mai's bottle. Binh began to cluck again.

Gen woke as the first rays of light made their way through the patio door drapes. A gecko crawled along the wall and then scurried behind the framed ink drawing of a woman in an ao dai walking along a village path. Mai stirred in the crib beside the bed. Jeff slept on his side, facing Gen; she craned her neck to see Binh. He was sprawled sideways on the bed with his shoes in his father's back. Jeff couldn't have gotten much sleep between Mai crying at two o'clock in the morning and Binh thrashing around all night. Jeff opened one eye and looked at Gen. He smiled. "Are you happy?"

Gen nodded. She was so happy and so in love with Jeff, and now with the children.

"I'm exhausted," he said. "I never knew sleeping could be such hard work."

"Trying to sleep isn't the same as sleeping."

"He loves me," Jeff said. "Just like that, he loves me. Isn't it freaky how much he trusts me? It's both reassuring and scary. What if I weren't trustworthy?"

"I wish he loved and trusted me," Gen said.

"He will. He didn't have a dad. It makes sense he'd warm to me first. He did have a mom. That has to make it more complicated."

Gen nodded. She hoped she could win him over before long. "Isn't it ironic that we went to our first adoption meeting when Lan was pregnant with Binh?" Gen propped her head on her hand. "What if we had gotten our act together then? Maybe we would have had him from the beginning. And then come back for Mai."

"But Lan didn't give him up then."

"But maybe she would have," Gen said, "if we'd been ready."

"It doesn't matter. We have him now. And Mai. And Lan had that time with him. It was what was meant to be."

"Where's the yogurt? And the book?" Gen patted the bed around Jeff.

"On the floor. I tossed them during the night. He had them wedged in my back too."

By the time they'd made it to the dining room for breakfast, Maggie was done eating. She sat facing the window toward the ocean, drinking her coffee. She turned and laughed as Gen and Jeff approached. "It looks like two kids is a different story than one," she said, pulling out a chair for Gen. The waitress hurried over with a booster seat for Binh. Eyes bright, he sat on his throne and scanned the room. He reached down and pulled out a fruit snack pouch from the waistband of his shorts and handed it to Jeff to open.

"Did you give him that?" Gen said, suppressing a laugh.

"No."

"He'll do that," Maggie said. "Hoard food. He might want you to leave a plate of food on the table once you get home. He needs to know it's available. He'll get over it."

Attachment issues. Bonding issues. Grieving issues. *Food issues.* Gen added the last item to her mental list. "What shall we order for Binh?"

"The waitress can ask him what he wants." Jeff smiled at the boy.

Ten minutes later the waitress came out with a bowl of beef noodle soup and a Coke. Gen was horrified. Maggie began to laugh. "Oops," Jeff said, reaching for the glass.

"Just let him have it," Maggie said. "He's not going to understand if you take it away. One more Coke isn't going to make those teeth any worse."

Binh smiled down at his food and then up at Jeff, a dazzling, full-face grin. "He has your smile," Gen said and then laughed.

The waitress whispered something to Binh. He nodded.

Gen cocked her head. "What do you think the waitress said to him?"

"Probably how lucky he is," Maggie said. "People will tell him that over and over."

"But we won't know for sure *what* they're saying." Gen didn't like the idea of that.

Binh sucked the fizzy liquid up through the straw and then dunked the beef in his bowl under the steaming broth. He picked up his chopsticks and deftly maneuvered the noodles into his mouth. Gen stared at his hand, at the fluidity of his motions as he maneuvered the chopsticks from the bowl to his mouth, over and over.

He seemed so familiar and yet so foreign to Gen, all at the same time.

"How does he like the things you brought him?" Maggie ran her finger along the rim of her cup.

"He loves the books but doesn't seem to know what to do with the toys." Gen took a bite of her omelet.

"That's because he's never had any toys to play with. Give him a stick, and he'll know what to do with that."

"He likes his shoes," Jeff said.

Gen began to laugh. "He wouldn't take them off at bedtime." She laughed harder as she thought about Binh in bed with his tennis shoes, kicking Jeff's back.

Jeff began to laugh too. They were tired. Exhausted. Gen's eyes watered. She glanced from her omelet to Mai's head. She'd dropped egg into her baby's hair. That was funny too. The waitress walked over with her hands out and took Mai. Gen laughed harder. Binh smiled as he continued moving his chopsticks from his bowl to his mouth. He slurped the last of his noodles, picked out the last piece of meat, then lifted the bowl to his mouth and drank the broth.

"Let's pack up this morning," Maggie said. "We'll have lunch at the Bamboo Restaurant on the way out of town."

Sadness swept over Gen as she watched Binh consume a crab at the restaurant. They sat at an outside table next to the seawall. Below, the waves of the South China Sea crashed against the rocks. This had been his home. Binh cracked the back of the crustacean and quickly scraped his teeth along the inside shell. He pulled the meat from the legs and then scooped out the pinkish matter and plopped it into his mouth. In just a few minutes, the crab was eaten clean, and he started on a second.

"He's a pro," Jeff said as he rubbed Mai's back. She slept on the chair beside him.

Binh obviously had a taste for seafood. He stood on his chair and reached for the clams steaming on the propane burner. "Hey, big guy," Jeff said, taking Binh's arm and guiding it back. "I'll get that for you." Bao said something in Vietnamese to Binh. The boy sat back on his chair and waited for Jeff.

"You're going to have to keep a close eye on this one," Maggie said. "Especially in Ho Chi Minh City."

Gen thought of the traffic. She would have to look up the Vietnamese word for *stop* again. Binh picked up his chopsticks and began eating his clams and rice. Gen put down her fork and picked up her chopsticks. Binh barely held his; they seemed to flow in his hand. His head, not his hand, seemed to guide them. Gen loosened her grip and emulated Binh's motion, willing the chopsticks to travel from her plate to her mouth. They arrived with the rice still balanced on them. She'd been trying too hard all these years. Maybe using chopsticks was like trusting; it was better to believe they would arrive.

She smiled at Jeff and nodded at her chopsticks.

"Good job," he said.

"Binh's teaching me," she said. The little boy kept eating, his chopsticks flying from his plate to his mouth.

The waiter brought the bill and handed it to Maggie. "How much?" Jeff asked.

"Ten dollars for the four of us. Nothing for Binh, even though he ate the most." Maggie stared at Binh as he ran his finger around his plate and then licked it.

"I'm going to miss these prices," Jeff said, handing Maggie the money.

As Bao drove through the streets of Vung Tau to the main highway, rain began to fall. The pavement steamed as the water hit the hot asphalt. Gen held Mai in the middle seat; Binh leaned his head against Jeff in the backseat.

"How are you doing?" Maggie asked as she glanced back at Gen. "Do you want me to hold Mai for a while?"

Gen shook her head as she patted her baby's back. "I feel sad to be leaving Vung Tau. This was their home."

Maggie nodded. "It's hard. But think of the life they'll have with you and Jeff."

"I know." Gen peered out the window and then back at Maggie. "But do you think they'll resent us for taking them away from their homeland?"

"They'll go through their issues, no doubt. All kids, all people, no matter their origins, have their own story, their own heartaches. You can't protect any child from that." Maggie smiled. "Life happens." Gen thought of her own sad story, of her mother. Maggie continued, "Yes, they'll have different issues than the kids they grow up around. And sometimes they'll have to deal with race and culture, all of that."

"How have your adopted kids done?" Gen asked.

Maggie shrugged. "They've gone through some hard times. They've both come back to Vietnam, and that helped. Seeing what their lives would have been like if they had grown up in the orphanage was a good thing for them."

"What did you do to help them?"

"Language classes. Cultural camp. Counseling for one of them." Maggie pulled a water bottle from her bag and unfastened the lid.

"How old are they now?" Gen placed her hand against the side of Mai's head.

"They were two and three when they came home to us. They're twenty-eight and twenty-nine now," Maggie answered, holding the bottle in one hand and the lid in the other.

"Early 1970s then?" Gen asked.

"It was 1974 to be exact." She took a sip of water.

"I didn't realize they were that old. I thought they were teenagers." Gen paused. "Were you over here then?"

"I was here for a week, just long enough to get my girls." She took another drink.

"How old are your other kids?" Gen shifted Mai to her shoulder.

"I have two boys who are twenty-two and twenty-four. It wasn't until my first son was born that I realized how much I missed by not having my girls when they were babies."

"So your daughter who is having the baby is Vietnamese?"

"Yes," Maggie answered, putting her water bottle back into her bag. "It's her first baby. I was with her older sister, Michelle, when she gave birth to her first baby last year. I want to be there for Jennifer, too."

"You gave them American names?" Gen asked.

Maggie nodded. "We kept their Vietnamese names as middle names."

"Did they resent you for giving them American names?"

Maggie shook her head. "No, but most kids resent their parents for something at some point." She smiled.

"Do you ever think they would have been better off with their own people? In their own country?" Bao slammed on the brakes for a truck that pulled out in front of them. Gen held on tightly to Mai; Binh slept as Jeff held him steady.

Maggie waited to answer until Bao changed lanes. "It's very rare for a Vietnamese family to adopt, even to adopt their own kin. What kind of life would my girls have had? It was so chaotic at the end of the war. They might have been thrown out of the orphanage and become street children. At best, they would have been thrown out at age sixteen after having been cared for by a parade of people. What would they have done? Prostitution would have been the most profitable."

Bao turned the windshield wipers up to high. The road was barely visible through the sheet of water covering the glass. Gen sighed. "I keep thinking that the money we'll pay each month for Binh's preschool would support Lan, her mother, and all three of her kids."

"And then some," Maggie said.

"You're not helping." Gen smiled weakly.

"There's no guarantee they'd get the money or that they'd use it for Binh or for Mai," Maggie said. "I know it's hard, but consider the serendipity of all this. Lan can't keep Mai, waffles about keeping Binh, meets you and Jeff, and wants you to parent both her children. It was meant to be."

The words soothed Gen. "Why do you keep coming back?" She held her cheek against the top of Mai's head.

"Vietnam gets in your blood." Maggie shifted in her seat and turned toward Gen again. "When you get back home, you'll see. You'll dream about Vietnam. You'll ache for it. You'll long for the tastes, for the smells, for the people."

A man sped by on a motorbike, hunched under a sheet of clear plastic. Chickens huddled together in a crate on the back of his bike. Three women rode bicycles along the edge of the road, their hats little protection from the rain.

Gen glanced back at Jeff again. His head was tilted against the back of the seat, and Binh was sprawled out, half on his father's lap. She turned back toward Maggie. She opened her mouth and then stopped.

"What is it?" Maggie frowned.

"That's exactly what my mother said about Vietnam. That it gets into your blood."

"When was your mother here?"

"During the early '60s and then again in '74 and '75."

"Really? Why?"

"First to work in a leprosarium, then to help in an orphanage, then to adopt a little boy."

"You have a Vietnamese brother! Why didn't you tell me?"

"I *almost* had a Vietnamese-American brother. It didn't work out."

"What happened?" Maggie asked.

It was always hard to tell the story. "My mom died in the Operation Babylift crash."

"Oh, no." Maggie turned in the seat and leaned toward Gen. "What about the boy? Did he die too?"

Gen shook her head. "He had flown out the day before. He ended up going to another family."

Maggie was silent for a moment. "Gen, you have an understanding of Binh's grief. You can truly empathize with what he'll go through. But the difference is that he'll have you."

And Jeff, Gen thought. *That's really the difference.*

Maggie paused a moment and then asked, "What was your mother's name?"

"Sally Hauer."

Maggie shook her head. "I didn't know her. We lived in Maryland when all that happened. It was horrible. My husband was stationed at the Pentagon at the time."

"Your husband was in the military?" Gen couldn't hide the surprise in her voice.

"That's why we adopted from Vietnam. He'd done two army tours here in the '60s."

Bao slowed the van and then pumped the brakes. "There's a wreck ahead," he said as the vehicle stopped. The rain drummed on the roof and cascaded down the windows. Ahead two trucks had collided and blocked the road. A sea of motorbikes gathered around the van. The drivers wore plastic ponchos—green, red, yellow, and blue—that draped over the lights of their bikes, casting the colors onto the wet pavement. Horns honked. A group of men gathered around the trucks.

"I'm going to go help push," Bao said, opening his door. Rain pelted into the van.

Mai stirred; Gen's arms ached from holding the baby. "How far are we from the city?"

"At least an hour, longer if the traffic stays bad," Maggie said.

They were at a junction with a store. A woman held a baby in a hammock under a tarp on the side of the building, seemingly oblivious to the nearby chaos. Gen longed to take life slowly and enjoy her children, to play with them, to love them deeply.

A trail of motorbikes rode through the parking lot in front of the store, bypassing the wreck, and then back onto the highway.

"What's going on?" Jeff called from the backseat.

"There's a wreck. Bao went to help move the trucks," Gen said, turning as Jeff eased Binh's head off his lap.

"I'll go too." He opened the van door and slid out into the rain.

Binh woke as Jeff slammed the door against the storm. "Ba?" The boy stood on the seat and watched as Jeff ran toward the trucks. "Ba!" Binh screamed.

"It's okay," Gen said. "Ba will be right back."

Binh crumpled onto the seat and began to cry.

"I'll take Mai," Maggie said.

Gen handed her the baby and climbed into the backseat. She tried to lift Binh onto her lap. He pulled away from her, curled his body into the corner, and kept crying. "Binh," she said, "it's okay. Ba will be right back." She stroked his back, but his muscles tensed even more.

Binh began to sob. Gen looked out the rain-streaked windshield. She could barely make out the trucks ahead. She couldn't see Jeff at all. *Hurry. We need you.* He had only been gone a few minutes when Binh tucked his head into the crook of his elbow and began to scream.

*L*an sat on the beach and pulled her finger through the blistering sand. It was crazy to be here on a Monday at noon. It was nearly deserted. The few tourists who hadn't returned to the city were back at their hotels having lunch. Then they would nap before returning to the beach in the late afternoon. She gazed out at the waves.

Hang had hardly talked to her since Older Brother had left two nights before. Mother acted as if nothing had happened. What would Older Brother do? Would he take Binh? She'd been tempted to go by the orphanage to see if her son was still there. *Her son.* He would always be her son.

She stood and walked toward the waves. The hot sun scorched her back; the sand burned her feet through the bottoms of her flip-flops. She reached the water, watched it lap against her feet. She missed Binh, she missed Older Sister, and her empty arms still ached for the baby.

Years ago on their family holiday to Vung Tau, she had played on this beach, raced through the waves, soaked in the heat of the sand and the sun and the laughter of her siblings. Now she was a middle-aged woman who couldn't care for her children. No. She *was* caring for her children. She was giving them the best life possible.

"Lan!"

She turned toward the road. The glare of the sun blinded her for a moment.

"Lan!" It sounded like Older Brother. Why couldn't he leave her alone? "I have Hang and Mother in the car. I'm taking all of you to Ho Chi Minh City."

She shuffled toward the figure.

"We need to leave right away. Binh is already there." Older Brother held a large envelope in his hands. "We need to sign some papers. But first I want to get the old ones from the Americans."

Lan shook her head and stretched out her stride. "I told you I didn't want you to adopt Binh."

He clasped his hands behind his back. "Come to the city. We'll see Binh. He's staying at the same hotel as Older Sister. We'll stay there too—my treat. It will be our last reunion before Cam My returns to America."

Lan stopped in front of Older Brother and tipped her hat back on her head. "I already signed the papers. I don't want to sign new ones."

"Come with us," he said, his voice softer. He put his arm around Lan.

Lan tensed at Older Brother's touch. "I don't think Hang is strong enough to travel."

"She'll be fine. The ride will be easy, and then she can rest at the hotel. She'll be better off there than here."

"What about Mother?" Lan took a step backward.

"She's pleased. We'll drive by the rubber plantation on the way," Quan said.

Lan wanted to insist again that she wouldn't sign new papers, but she also wanted to go to Saigon. She wanted to see Older Sister again. And Binh. But it would make it harder for him. And for Hang.

"Mama." Hang stood at the top of the dune just below the street. "Are you coming?" She heard pleading in her voice. She wanted to go. And Mother, too. She couldn't let them go without her. Older Brother might turn Hang further against her; he might even try to take Hang away from her to help with Binh.

"Hang and Mother already have their things. They packed for you, too," Quan said.

She wriggled away from Older Brother's arm and hurried up the dune toward her daughter.

Quan sat up front beside the driver. Lan sat in the middle of the backseat between Hang and Mother, and both rested their heads on her shoulders as they slept. "The rubber plantation is coming up," Older Brother said without turning his head. He'd been going through a stack of papers.

"Mother, wake up. We're almost to our old place." Lan said. She had nearly said, "We're almost home." *Home.* The shack didn't feel like home the way the plantation had, the way the land had. Mother stirred, sat up straight, and gazed through the window.

"I miss the land," she said, reaching for Lan's hand.

"It wasn't ours," Older Brother said.

"It was ours," Mother answered.

"No. The French wouldn't let the Vietnamese own rubber plantations."

"But the land belonged to your father's family."

"The French confiscated it. They just let us manage it." Quan looked over his shoulder at Mother.

"It belonged to us during the war," she said.

"No. It belonged to the government of the South," Older Brother said.

"And now?" Mother grasped Lan's arm. "Who does it belong to now?"

"The people of Vietnam, to all of us." Older Brother smiled.

"And that's supposed to be better? At least when it didn't belong to us, we were able to live on it." Mother glared out the window.

The rows of trees whizzed by. "Slow down!" Mother cried out. The driver questioned Older Brother. He nodded. The car passed by the trees, the forlorn house. Chickens pecked in the dirt in front of it, and a small child squatted by the door. *Home.* The trees were tall and healthy. Lan thought of the workers cutting the trees, of the sap that bled through the bark. Caoutchouc—wood that weeps. Still the trees stayed alive, grew stronger, created more sap to be turned into more rubber. Lan gently touched her burned hand. Hang's head slid from her shoulder. Mother began to cry. Older Brother concentrated on his paperwork.

Light bounced off the glass chandelier hanging in the center of the hotel lobby; underneath it a bouquet of flowers stood taller than Binh. Older Brother talked in a low voice with a woman in a burgundy ao dai. A group of middle-aged American men came through the lobby. Hang sat in a chair and watched tropical fish swim in a large tank. Mother had dried her tears on Lan's shoulder by the time they'd reached the outskirts of the city. She had been like a child as they drove through the crowded streets, pointing at the shops and restaurants, exclaiming about the tall buildings, the cathedral, and the Reunification Palace.

She smiled a wide, nearly toothless grin and grabbed Lan's hand as they stood in the lobby. "See what Quan can do for us?" she said. "Maybe he'll take us to a fine restaurant for dinner."

Lan looked down at their wrinkled clothes. She wondered if Older Brother would be too embarrassed to take his family out in public. Lan heard a baby cry. An American woman walked into the lobby, but it wasn't the American woman Lan was looking for, and the baby wasn't Mai.

Older Brother thanked the woman in the burgundy ao dai and said, "This way to our rooms." He picked up his suitcase and nodded at Lan and Mother and then at Hang. Carrying their small bags made from woven mats, they followed him through a doorway at the far end of the lobby and down a long hallway. To their left, tropical plants and roses filled a brick courtyard.

"You must not leave your room without me," Older Brother said. "You don't have proper documentation to be in the city. Do you understand?" Mother and Lan nodded.

"I'm hungry," Hang said.

"You must take me seriously, Hang. Do you understand?" Older Brother placed his hand on the girl's shoulder for just a moment.

"Yes, Uncle." Hang bowed her head.

"What will we do for dinner?" Mother asked, taking Older Brother's hand.

He pulled away. "I'll have food sent to your room."

"Is Older Sister still here?" Lan asked.

"Yes. The investigation into her work continues. Perhaps I'll meet with her in the morning."

He stopped and unlocked a door. "Here is your room," he said. Lan peered into darkness.

"Where is your room?" Mother surveyed the dark hall.

"On the fifth floor. I'll check on you in the morning."

Lan, Mother, and Hang tiptoed through the doorway. Gold-colored drapes let a beam of light through the window. The room held a large bed, a desk, a TV, and a rocking chair. Lan moved toward the window and pulled the cord. Outside in an alley a man in a cook's uniform smoked a cigarette. At least ten bicycles leaned against the wall of the hotel. Two women wearing blue dresses disappeared through a door. Mother put her basket on the bed and then carefully sat down on the yellow comforter. Hang turned on the TV. Two people hit a small ball back and forth across green grass. Hang changed the channel. A beautiful woman sang in Chinese. Hang sat on the edge of the bed and smiled.

Mother stood and picked up the small basket of mangoes on the desk. Two cups and a pot of hot water and tea bags sat on a tray. Mother smiled broadly as she took it all in. "There's a bathroom!" Lan followed her through the door with Hang right behind them.

"What is that?" Hang wrinkled her nose.

"Une toilette!" Lan said.

"What are you saying?" Hang ran her hand through her hair.

"It's the latrine. You sit on it. Do not stand on it; it may break."

"And a bathtub!" Mother turned on the water. "How do I make it stay?"

Lan pushed down on the metal plug, which made the round post on the faucet pop up. "Like this," she said, pleased with herself.

Mother took a bath while Lan made tea. Then Mother cut up the mangoes while Lan took a bath. Hang fell asleep on the end of the bed watching the Chinese singer.

Lan stepped out of the bathroom. "Is our dinner here yet?" She felt relaxed, at ease, for the first time in years. For a few moments she'd forgotten to worry.

"No." Mother popped a piece of mango into her mouth.

An hour later a woman arrived with three bowls on a tray. Lan had never imagined such luxury.

A rapping on the door woke her. How long had they slept? Hang was curled at the end of the bed. Mother had moved to the floor sometime during the night.

Lan opened the door cautiously. Perhaps it was Older Brother. Would he chastise them for sleeping late?

"Let me in!" It was Cam My. Lan swung the door open. Older Sister switched on the light. "It's so hot in here. Why isn't your air on?" She walked to the console beside the bed and turned a knob. The air conditioner above the window began to sputter.

"Wake up!" Older Sister said to Hang, shaking her shoulder. "Where is Mother?"

"On the floor." Lan nodded to the other side of the bed.

"She has a bed and she sleeps on the floor?"

"It was too soft for my old bones," Mother said, sitting up.

"You've missed breakfast." Cam My wore a brown skirt and an orange top.

"Breakfast?" Lan glanced toward the door.

"It's part of staying here. You get breakfast in the morning up in the restaurant. I assume that's how Older Brother arranged things. Maybe not, though. Where is he?"

"Fifth floor."

Older Sister rolled her eyes. "In a much nicer room than this. I wonder if he had to beg to get the worst room in the entire hotel for you."

"The worst? This is wonderful!" Mother said.

Older Sister smiled. "You're right. It is wonderful." She turned to Hang and then to Lan. "Why didn't you tell me that you took Binh to the orphanage?"

"How could I tell you?" Lan touched Cam My's arm.

"I never would have said anything to Older Brother about his adopting Binh if I'd known."

Lan folded her arms across her chest. "You've really made a mess of things."

"I gathered that from what Older Brother told me on the phone this morning." Cam My sat on the edge of the bed. "Don't be angry with me."

Lan held the heel of her good hand to her forehead. "Why does he want to adopt Binh?"

Hang stood, walked into the bathroom, and closed the door.

"He seems to think he's missing out by not having a child to raise." Cam My crossed her legs.

"Did you tell him that?"

"I only meant to help you, Little Sister. And you should consider it. Binh would be in Vietnam."

"I've had few choices in my life," Lan said, standing tall. "If I'm going to give up my child, I would at least like to decide who will raise him."

Older Sister pulled a cigarette from her bag and lit it. "Let's get going. We'll get won ton soup at the market across the street."

"Older Brother told us not to leave our room," Lan said.

"Why?" Cam My reached for the ashtray on the bedside table.

"We don't have the right papers."

"Oh, bother. No one's going to check your papers. Older Brother just wants to keep you under his thumb." Older Sister put the cigarette to her mouth and inhaled.

"I thought you were low on money."

"I am. But I can still buy you each a fifty-cent bowl of soup."

After the soup, Older Sister said she needed to check her e-mail at a nearby Internet café and asked if they wanted to go with her.

"We should get back to our room." Lan stood from the table. "Older Brother is probably looking for us."

"What would it hurt to be out a little longer?" Mother tugged on Lan's hand.

"It's just two blocks away. We'll walk by many fine shops."

Mother's eyes lit up as she pushed her chair back.

"Mother, what do shops matter when you can't afford to buy anything?" Lan took a step toward the market exit.

"It's fun to look."

"I'd like to go back to the hotel and watch TV," Hang said.

"But you'll find the Internet café fascinating," Older Sister said. "I'll show you how to use a computer."

Hang shrugged. "I'd rather watch TV."

"Wait until you see how the computer works. All the kids in America have their own computers."

Mother peered into each window as they walked along Dong Khoi Street, past shops filled with silk garments, shoes, purses, lacquerware, and carvings. Cam My took Lan's arm. "I saw them at breakfast this morning." She began to laugh. "Binh was his usual bouncy self. He fell off his chair trying to reach his orange juice. You can tell that the man and woman love Mai and Binh very much."

"How was the baby?" Lan's heart skipped a beat.

"She slept through breakfast. The woman held her."

"Did Binh recognize you?" Lan gently swerved to avoid bumping into a man dressed in a black suit and shiny shoes.

"I don't think so." Cam My let go of Lan's arm as they crossed the street. Lan held Mother's elbow.

"Can you talk to Mr. and Mrs. Taylor tomorrow at breakfast? Find out more about them?" Lan followed Cam My as she stepped up onto the sidewalk. She steadied Mother as she took the step.

"But then Binh will recognize me."

"But the man and woman will never know."

"Unless Binh says something to the waiter, something like, 'That's my aunt. Why is she here?'" Cam My tripped on the broken concrete but caught herself before she fell.

"What are the chances of that?"

Older Sister pulled a pack of cigarettes from her purse and lit one. "Binh very likely may see you in the hotel or on the street."

"I'll try to stay away from him." Still, she hoped to catch a glimpse of him from a distance.

They walked into the Internet café, then up the stairs to a room filled with computers. Cam My pulled up a chair so that Hang could sit beside her. Mother and Lan sat behind them in a booth. The young man who sat at the desk rose and handed Older Sister an ashtray. Lan felt self-conscious. She didn't deserve to be in the city. She bit her lip. They should be back at the hotel. What if Older Brother was angry?

J eff and Gen sat in the office of the United States INS on the top
floor of the Saigon Centre Building. Binh stood at the window, facing the city.

The officer, Mr. Davis, spoke to Binh in Vietnamese. The boy answered.

"He says he's four," Mr. Davis said. The man wore his blond hair short.

Gen nodded. "That's right."

The officer spoke to Binh again. The boy hurried over to Jeff, climbed
onto his lap, and then answered.

"He says his mother took him to the orphanage twice. He said they never
had enough food, that he was always hungry." Mr. Davis shuffled papers on
his desk. "He's smart. And he looks like he's a lot of fun."

Jeff nodded.

The officer stood and held out his hands for Mai. Gen handed him the
baby. "Is she healthy?" he asked.

"Very," Gen answered.

"Any reason to believe that they're not siblings?"

Gen and Jeff said, "No," in unison.

"Did you meet the birth mom?"

Together, they said, "Yes."

Mr. Davis looked comfortable holding the baby. "Any reason to believe
she is mentally unstable?"

They shook their heads.

"Coerced into relinquishing her children?" He bounced Mai gently.

They shook their heads again, and the officer handed Mai back to Gen.
The phone rang, and Mr. Davis pushed a button. "Mr. Tran on line three.
He says it's urgent," said a woman's voice with a Vietnamese accent.

"Excuse me," the officer said to Gen and Jeff. "I'll be right back." He retreated through the door to the receptionist area.

"Mr. Tran!" Gen whispered to Jeff.

"There are lots of Mr. Trans in Saigon. Remember, Maggie said it's a very common name."

Binh sat perfectly still on Jeff's lap. They all sat like statues, except for Mai who pulled on Gen's blouse. "It's going to be okay," Jeff whispered as the officer returned to the room.

Mr. Davis took out a rubber stamp and an inkpad from his desk drawer. Gen exhaled. Jeff reached over and squeezed her hand.

"I'm going to approve the baby's paperwork," he said. "But I'm going to hold on to Binh's and make a few phone calls." He shifted his eyes from Gen to Jeff. "We investigate these randomly. I'll call in an hour or two and let you know if I plan to do a full investigation. It could be that you'll be able to pick up the papers this afternoon, or you might not know for several days."

Gen sat at one of the hotel's computers and waited. The machine had already crashed twice. She wanted to e-mail her father and ask him to pray. Her account popped back up on the screen. She had two messages. She opened the first one. "It's from your sister," she said to Jeff. He held Binh and Mai in his arms as he read over Gen's shoulder. Janet congratulated them on Binh and then wrote that she was pregnant. Gen nearly laughed at life's irony. She smiled at the thought of having a niece or nephew; Binh and Mai would have a cousin. An intense desire to take her children home swept over her. *Please let Binh's paperwork be approved today.*

Jeff finished reading the message. "That's great!" he said, jostling Mai. "I'm so happy for them."

The second e-mail was from her dad. He'd sent the phone number of the Vietnamese man that he wanted them to contact. She printed the e-mail. She couldn't imagine calling the man now, not today, not until they knew more about the investigation into Binh's adoption. She replied to her father, said they would try to call, and asked him to pray.

"Do you want to call this guy?" Gen asked Jeff as they walked to the elevator. A week ago she was thrilled to be in Vietnam. Now she longed to board the plane with Jeff and the children. *With the children.* She thought of her mother on the fateful flight with the orphans. She thought of her father. Did he think about that every day?

"It would mean a lot to your dad if we contacted this pastor," Jeff said.

Gen nodded. "Let's wait until tomorrow."

They walked into their room; Jeff sat down on their bed and began playing with Binh's toys, fitting the family into the car. Binh zipped the Ziploc bag one way and then the other. Every few minutes he would run his little hand through Jeff's curls and laugh.

Gen changed Mai's diaper on the other bed and then fixed a bottle. "Let's not wait around," she said. "Let's go get lunch."

She carried Mai in the front pack, and Jeff held Binh's hand as they walked into the hall. The phone rang just as Jeff closed the door. He fumbled for his key. "I'd better get it. It might be the INS."

She waited in the hall with Mai. Binh followed Jeff. "It was the INS," Jeff said, relocking the door. "They're going to do the long investigation into Binh's case."

"Oh, no." Gen's heart fell.

"It will be okay."

"Stop saying that." She turned and walked down the hall. She wanted to trust Jeff on this, but she couldn't. He had no way of knowing how it would all work out; neither of them had any control over the INS or the investigation. *Why is it so hard to trust God? Why do I have to remind myself that he is in control?*

They stepped onto the elevator. "Push the One button," Jeff said to Binh. The boy smiled and poked at the button. "Push it hard." He poked it again, the button lit up, and the elevator began to descend. Binh grabbed Jeff's leg and squealed in delight.

Jeff smiled at Binh and then at Gen. "Remember, Mr. Davis said that it was routine, that they choose the cases randomly."

"I don't believe it." She stroked the top of Mai's head.

"We can ask Maggie when she gets back from her meeting," he said.

"So we'll go ahead, take Mai to the doctor, get her passport and visa, and then do it all over again with Binh?"

"I think we should."

"But why, if you know it will all work out?" She met his gaze.

"Genni, don't. This isn't my fault. I'm just trying to move ahead, to figure this out."

The elevator doors opened. Jeff scooped Binh into his arms, and they all walked into the lobby. Binh waved to the doorman as he swung the glass doors wide. "Bye-bye!" Binh said in English. "Bye-bye!"

They crossed the street and headed to the French café on the corner. "Did he say how long the investigation would take?"

"Two or three days," Jeff answered.

"So we can still get out by Friday?"

"It might be Monday or even Tuesday." They stopped for the rushing sea of traffic.

"What about harvest?"

"I'll e-mail Dad again and see how things are going, see when he thinks we need to start."

"You could go ahead," Gen said. The cars and scooters slowed, and they stepped off the curb.

"And leave you with the kids?"

Gen nodded.

Jeff shook his head. "I don't want to do that. I want us all to go home together." The driver of a scooter honked and swerved around them. They hurried to the sidewalk.

"But if we had to, we could do that."

"It would be so hard for you. And Maggie wouldn't be here to help you.

No one would." Jeff opened the door to the café. "Dad can start harvest without me."

"Let's wait and see," Gen said as they settled into a booth.

Binh chatted away with the waiter. "He wants pumpkin soup," the waiter said in broken English. "And a Coke."

Gen shook her head. "No, no. Bring him the soup and milk, not Coke."

A woman slid into the booth behind them and lit a cigarette. Binh stood on the seat and stared at the woman. She turned and spoke to Binh in Vietnamese. He shook his head and climbed onto Jeff's lap.

"Your son is very cute," the woman said in English. "And the baby is beautiful."

"Thank you," Gen said.

The woman put out her cigarette.

"You must be adopting."

Gen nodded. Jeff shifted in the seat so he could see the woman.

"Where do you live?" she asked.

"In Oregon. About an hour east of Portland."

The woman nodded. "I've been to Oregon, to Portland a few times."

"Where do you live?" Jeff asked.

"Southern California."

"Where are you from originally?" Gen asked.

"Here. I grew up about an hour out of the city. I left in 1978."

"Is this your first trip back?" Gen asked.

The woman shook her head. "No, I've been back several times."

"To visit family?" Gen asked.

The woman nodded. "My mother, sister, and brother still live here."

Binh pushed his face against Jeff's chest.

"Your little boy seems to really love his daddy," the woman said.

Gen nodded. "I wish he was as fond of me. I hope that will come in time."

"I'm sure it will."

"Would you join us?" Gen asked.

"I'd love to." The woman collected her black leather purse and water glass and slid into the booth beside Gen and Mai. "May I hold the baby?"

Gen pulled Mai out of the front pack and handed her to the woman. Binh turned his head away from Jeff's chest and said something in Vietnamese.

"What did he say?" Jeff asked.

"That it's his baby, and I can't have her." The woman laughed as she moved Mai to her shoulder. Mai began to fuss. The woman clucked several times; the baby quieted.

"We're Jeff and Genevieve Taylor, and these are our children, Binh and Mai," Jeff said.

"Pleased to meet you. How old is the baby?"

"Four months. What do you do in California?" Gen asked.

"I work as a translator for social workers mostly."

"How long will you be in Vietnam?"

"I'm not sure," the woman said.

"Where are you staying?" Gen asked, aware that the woman hadn't said her name.

"At the hotel across the square."

"So are we," Jeff said.

"Really?" the woman patted Mai's back. "Tell me about yourselves."

"I'm a cherry grower," Jeff said. "We own an orchard that has been in my family for over a hundred years. And Gen is a teacher."

"What grade?"

"Third."

"Good. Do you have other children?" the woman asked.

Gen shook her head. "These are our first."

"Where did you get them?"

"An orphanage in Vung Tau." Gen unwrapped a straw and put it in her water.

"A boy and a girl. Birth siblings. How lucky you are."

"How did you know they're siblings?" Gen asked. Why did she feel uneasy?

"They look like siblings. Are they?"

"You're right. They're birth siblings," Jeff said.

The waitress brought Binh's soup. He crawled off Jeff's lap and began slurping the liquid with his spoon. The woman said something to him in Vietnamese and then, "Ouch!"

"What's wrong?" Gen asked.

"Nothing. The boy bumped me, that's all."

"Did he kick you?" Jeff asked.

"Oh, no!"

"Look, Gen," Jeff stared through the window. "It's the man that we met that first night, before we went to Vung Tau. Bryce. And that must be his wife." A woman held the little boy's hand. Bryce motioned to Jeff.

"I'll be right back," Jeff said.

"What did you say your name is?" Gen asked the woman.

She handed the baby back to Gen and grabbed her purse. "I need to get going," she said.

"What about your lunch?"

"I'm suddenly not feeling well. I'm going back to my room to rest."

"Ba!" Binh called out, dropping his soupspoon onto the table.

"He'll be right back," Gen said. Mai began to cry. The woman said something in Vietnamese to Binh as she slid out of the booth.

"I hope we'll see you in the hotel. Maybe at breakfast," Gen said.

"I hope so too." A quick expression of pain passed over the woman's face. She headed to the side door.

How odd. Gen watched Jeff, Bryce, and the American woman as they spoke. After a moment, they turned to look at Gen and the children. The man gestured beyond them.

"Ba!" Binh banged on the window.

"No, no," Gen said.

Jeff swung through the door, followed by Bryce and his family.

"Hi!" Gen said, over Mai's crying. She needed to stand up with the baby. Jeff needed to sit down with Binh.

"This is Bryce's wife, Sue. That's the woman who botched their adoption," Jeff said.

"What?"

"Cammy Johnson. She's the facilitator who botched Daniel's adoption," Bryce said.

"No." Gen stood.

Bryce and Sue nodded.

"That means she's Binh and Mai's aunt." Jeff's deep voice was filled with distress. Binh stood on the seat and reached for his father. Gen sat back down and slid, with the baby, over to the window.

"You've got to be kidding." Sue fell into the booth beside Gen. "What a nightmare."

Gen walked around the marble border of the hotel lobby, bouncing Mai. Jeff stood at the counter, checking their messages. Perhaps the INS officer had called to say that he had changed his mind. Binh clung to Jeff's leg. Gen's gaze drifted down the hall at the far corner of the lobby. Toward the end, five figures walked away from her. One was Cammy Johnson. One was an old woman. One, from the back, appeared to be a Vietnamese official. The other two looked like Lan and Hang. "Jeff!" Gen called out.

He turned toward her.

"Come here, quick."

Jeff thanked the woman at the desk and walked toward Gen, holding a yellow piece of paper in his hand. He scooped up Binh.

"Come with me," Gen said and then glanced at Binh. No, they couldn't take off down the hall, not with him. She stopped.

"What is it?" Jeff asked.

"I think I saw Lan with Cammy." She pointed down the hall.

"Are you sure?"

"Yes. Wait here with Binh and Mai. I'll go see." Without waiting for an answer, Gen handed him the baby and started down the hall, walking quickly, then running, her sandals slapping against the tiles. She couldn't see the group of five; they'd turned the corner. She reached the end of the hall and peered to the right. The hallway sloped downward.

She looked to the left toward two elevators. The hotel was huge; it covered an entire block. Which way had they gone? She'd never find them if they had gone up the elevator. She looked to the right. Why were they here? Had Lan changed her mind again? Had Binh's investigation already started? Had the INS official brought Lan to Ho Chi Minh City to question her? No, they had only met Mr. Davis this morning. There was no way he would have brought Lan to the city before he saw Mai's and Binh's paperwork.

What if the Vietnamese man was Mr. Tran? Gen took a few steps down the hallway. She heard the sound of a door closing but had no idea which one. What would she say to Lan? To Cammy? She stood in the middle of the hall.

It was too much. Gen turned and walked slowly back to the lobby. Jeff sat in a chair by the fishtank; he held both children in his lap and the piece of yellow paper in his hand.

"It's a telegram." Jeff said.

"Who sends telegrams anymore?"

"My brother."

"What's wrong?" Gen asked.

"My dad had a heart attack."

I got through to the INS officer during the Taylors' interview," Older Brother said. He sat in the rocking chair. Hang watched a funny game called rugby on the TV. Big, burly white men attacked each other while a ball flew over their heads. "The officer decided to call for an investigation after I told him what was going on."

"What did you tell him?" Cam My asked.

Lan stood by the window, watching three men park their bikes in the alley.

"That you're Lan's sister. That I think Mai's adoption is legitimate but that I'm uneasy about Binh's." Older Brother's voice sounded flat.

A small bird landed on a bicycle seat. Lan held her good hand at the base of her throat. She hoped Mrs. Taylor wasn't frightened. She turned back toward Older Sister and Older Brother.

Cam My pulled a cigarette from her pack and lit it. "You shouldn't treat Lan this way. She's had enough heartache in her life."

"You're the one who said I should adopt Binh." Quan rocked the chair back and forth.

"I said Binh needed to be adopted." Cam My said.

Lan turned toward her siblings. They both stared at her.

Hang turned up the volume on the TV.

Mother poured tea for Older Brother and Cam My. Quan stopped rocking and took a sip.

"You should spend some time with Binh before you decide," Older Sister said to Older Brother. "Actually, you should spy on Binh with his new father. It would probably change your mind."

"Why?" Older Brother asked.

"Binh sticks to him like glue. He won't let him out of his sight. The man carries Binh everywhere."

Hang turned the volume on the TV louder.

"Can't you control your daughter?" Older Brother stared at Lan, then handed his empty cup to Mother.

Lan stood and took the remote from Hang's hand. "How does this work?" she asked.

Hang grabbed the remote back and turned down the volume.

"I can't ask the Americans to let me spend time with Binh," Older Brother said to Cam My. "I don't want them to know that I'm Lan's brother or that I want to adopt him."

"Then go and watch Binh. Spy. Go to breakfast tomorrow morning. See what a busy boy he is. See whether you think you could be his father, if you could handle him."

"Of course I could be his father. I'd teach him to behave." Older Brother started rocking again.

"Like Father taught you?" Lan asked. "With whippings?"

"That's the way to raise a son," Older Brother said, and then he nodded at Hang. "It's the way to raise a daughter, too."

Minutes later Older Brother left.

❧

Cam My smashed her cigarette in the ashtray on the desk. Hang slept on the end of the bed. Mother slept on the floor.

"Come up to my room," Older Sister said.

Lan shook her head. "I shouldn't." She felt like a hostage. She wanted to go back to Vung Tau, back to the shack, back to selling cigarettes and souvenirs on the beach. Lan's stomach hurt; the knot burned deeper. She wanted one last glimpse of Binh before she left.

"Come on," Older Sister said. "I'm going to check out of here tomorrow or the next day and find a cheaper hotel. I can't afford to stay here any longer. I have some food in my room. We'll have more tea."

Lan followed Cam My to the elevators in the back of the hotel and up to the third floor. They walked along a balcony surrounding the courtyard. "When do you think you'll return to the United States?" Lan asked as they entered Older Sister's room. Besides two twin beds, Older Sister had a sitting area with a small settee and a refrigerator.

"Now that Older Brother has implicated me in Binh's case, who knows? Maybe in another week." Older Sister plopped down on a bed. "I need to tell you," she said, "that the Taylors know who I am."

"What do you mean?"

"I sat with them at lunch. A couple walked by with their little boy. I'd arranged their son's adoption."

"I don't understand," Lan said, sitting beside Older Sister.

"That adoption has already been investigated. The family is furious with me, and now it seems they know the Taylors. I'm sure they told them that I facilitated their adoption. If Maggie Benson told the Taylors the facilitator who is in trouble—that would be me—is your sister, they would put it all together. They'll know I had lunch with them on purpose and that Binh and Mai are my nephew and niece."

"Did Binh speak to you at lunch?"

"He said he likes his ba, all the food he gets, and the gifts they brought." Cam My lit a cigarette.

Lan smiled as she thought about the backpack and the suitcase.

"He asked about you." Older Sister sat on the other bed, opposite Lan, and flicked her cigarette in the full ashtray beside the bed.

"What did he ask?" Lan ran her hand along the smooth, satin bedspread.

"If you and Hang could come live with his ba and him here at the hotel," Cam My said.

Lan tried to smile. *A child's fantasy.* "What did he say about his new mother?" Lan's voice quivered as she spoke.

"Nothing. He got upset when his ba left the restaurant to talk with the other family on the sidewalk."

Lan closed her eyes. "What do I do about Older Brother?"

"I don't think there's anything you can do."

"What do you mean?" Lan opened her eyes.

"I think he can do whatever he wants. He's just trying to save face by calling for an investigation and redoing the paperwork." Cam My stood and walked to the window overlooking the courtyard.

A knock on the door startled Lan.

"It's probably my laundry," Older Sister said. She went to open the door. "Oh, it's you."

"Is Lan here?" Older Brother's words shot through the room.

"Yes."

Lan stood and walked toward the door.

"I told you to stay in your room." Older Brother's harsh words stung Lan. She looked at the floor.

"I wanted to take you and Hang to an amusement park," Older Brother continued, his voice softened.

"No," Older Sister said, sarcasm filling her voice. "Do you really think they should have some fun in the big city?"

Lan peered into Older Brother's face.

"Go tell Hang to get ready. I'll meet the two of you in your room in fifteen minutes. First, I must talk to Older Sister about her future."

Older Brother moved aside, and Lan went out the door.

"Wait," Older Sister said, reaching for Lan's hand. "I'll come see you later this afternoon. Tell Mother that I'll see her then."

"Ma!"

Lan turned instinctively. It was Binh. He was on the opposite balcony.

"Ma!"

Lan froze. Mr. and Mrs. Taylor were with him. The woman held Mai. Binh began to climb the railing. "Binh! Stop!" Lan shouted.

The man quickly pulled Binh from the railing and held him in his arms.

"Ma!" Binh yelled again.

"Quick," Older Sister said. "Get back in the room."

"t *is* Lan," Gen said, as she grabbed the rail of the balcony with one hand and held Mai with the other. "And she's with her sister. And the man—he looks like Mr. Tran from the Justice Department in Vung Tau. It probably *is* the same Mr. Tran who called INS this morning."

"Ma!" Binh yelled again and then began to cry. He clung to Jeff's neck as if he were drowning.

"It can't be Mr. Tran." Jeff turned Binh's face toward his shoulder.

"Earlier you told me it couldn't be Lan." Gen ran past Jeff.

"Where are you going?" he called out.

"To Maggie's room. I hope she has some answers."

"I need to call Jake." Jeff had left a message on his brother's cell phone saying he would call every half hour until he got through. They had decided to walk around the hotel while they waited, hoping to get Binh ready to nap.

"Go. Call Jake."

Binh began to sob. Mai's lip curled. Gen stopped. "Don't cry, sweetheart," she whispered. Mai was upset by Binh's crying. They were all upset.

"We need to talk about what to do once I find out how bad things are back home." Jeff patted Binh's back.

"We need to talk to Maggie and find out how bad things are here. You call home. I'll go talk to Maggie." Adrenaline rushed through her.

"Genni." Jeff stopped patting Binh's back and touched her arm.

She stopped. Jeff's dad had just had a heart attack. The cherries had to be harvested. Binh's birth mother and aunt and the officer from the Vung Tau Justice Department were all staying at their hotel. The INS had called for an investigation. Multiple catastrophes hung over their heads. She met her husband's gaze. "Okay," she said. "Let's call home. Then talk to Maggie. We can discuss with her a plan to get through all this…and about Mai and Binh's birth family all showing up in Saigon with Mr. Tran."

"We don't know if it is Mr. Tran." Jeff shifted Binh to his other hip. The boy hiccuped and strengthened his grip around Jeff's neck.

"Jeff, it's Mr. Tran." She grabbed his free hand and squeezed it.

Gen gave Mai her bottle while Jeff made the call. Binh sat on the bed beside Jeff, zipping the pull on the Ziploc bag back and forth. It was unbelievable that Don had had a heart attack.

There was no answer at the house. Jeff dialed Jake's number.

"Jake?" Jeff asked. Gen listened to Jeff's side of the conversation. "At Emanuel? Ninety percent blocked?" Gen ached for Don and Sharon.

She thought about the adoption paperwork. Fortunately, they had put her name first on all the documents. She would be the one who needed to stay. She was listed as the primary parent, as if there were such a thing. How would Binh do with Jeff gone? She thought of the few minutes in the last four days when she'd had both children without Jeff. The short time in the van with Maggie and the few minutes in the restaurant with Cammy. Both times Binh had panicked until Jeff returned. She glanced down at Mai sucking on her bottle and concentrated on the motion of her daughter's mouth.

"It's bad," Jeff said as he hung up the phone. "They flew him by helicopter to Portland. He needs surgery. Jake said the harvest should start this weekend. He said José hasn't shown up yet, and Mom and Dad haven't heard from him. Jake said he will take time off work, even cancel his next trip to Japan, to take charge of the harvest."

"That's nice of him," Gen said.

"But unrealistic. He hasn't helped with the harvest in fifteen years."

"What do we do?" Gen asked.

"What do you think we should do?"

Gen pulled the empty bottle from Mai's mouth and put it on the floor. She lifted the baby to her shoulder. There was only one thing they could do. Jeff had to go home. She had to stay.

"Genni?" Jeff leaned toward her.

"Let's talk to Maggie."

Maggie came to the door wearing a silk robe, her gray hair pulled back in a ponytail. "I was napping," she said with a yawn. "I tried to call your room earlier. I'm flying out tomorrow. My daughter sent a frantic e-mail—she wants me home as soon as possible."

"Can we come in?" Gen's heart beat faster.

"What's wrong?" Maggie patted Binh's leg. "Our little guy looks sad."

"Everything is wrong." Gen blurted out the details.

Maggie took a deep breath when Gen finished. "That's pretty routine."

"Routine! What's routine? The heart attack! A birth family showing up! Mr. Tran being here!"

"The investigation. Come on." Maggie turned on the light. Gen and Jeff followed her into the room. "Sit down," Maggie said, motioning to the rattan chairs around the table. "Okay, I'm sleepy. Don't jump on me, Gen. The investigation is routine. None of the rest of it is. I've honestly never had any of the rest happen before."

"We think it might be Mr. Tran," Jeff said, glancing at Gen.

"I'm certain it's Mr. Tran." Gen tried to calm her voice. Jeff, in his eternal optimism, couldn't let go of the hope that it wasn't.

"Let's start with the INS." Maggie pulled the sash of her robe tighter.

"I wish you had been at the meeting," Gen said.

"I couldn't be there. I had the meeting at the orphanage here in Ho Chi Minh City. And I couldn't have gone in with you anyway; they don't allow it."

"The investigator got a phone call in the middle of the meeting from a Mr. Tran. It seemed as if it was about our case. About Binh," Gen said.

"Why do you think it's the same Mr. Tran?" Maggie shook her head slightly.

"Because we saw him here in the hotel with Lan and Cammy," Gen said.

Maggie sighed. "I don't know what to say. I can't believe it's Mr. Tran. That's too coincidental."

Gen had read that the antimalaria medicine could cause paranoia. Was she having paranoid hallucinations? Is that what Maggie thought?

"The phone call might not have been about your case. There could be a million Mr. Trans in this city alone. Investigations are usually random and always routine. You should be fine. All the paperwork is in order. Let's talk about Jeff's father." Maggie turned to Jeff.

"It's not just my father. It's the cherry harvest. Our income depends on the next three weeks. I can't risk harvest being unsuccessful because I'm not there. And it's not just us it affects; it's my parents and everyone who works for us."

"We're thinking about Jeff's going back." There, she'd said it.

"And you'll stay alone with the kids?" Maggie's voice softened.

Gen nodded.

"Could someone fly over to help you? It would be really good for you to have someone else with you. It's hard to take care of little ones here alone. I know you'll be fine in the U.S., but everything is harder here." Maggie gazed at Gen intently.

Gen shook her head. She couldn't think of anyone who could help her.

"I'm sorry I have to go back," Maggie said. Her eyes glistened for just a moment. Was pragmatic Maggie getting emotional?

Gen nodded. She wanted to cry.

"Now, let's talk about Binh and Mai's birth mom. Where did you see her?"

"Across the courtyard. We were on the balcony on the third floor looking down at the plants when Binh yelled, 'Ma!' There she was on the opposite balcony with her sister," Jeff said.

"With Cammy?" Maggie crossed her arms.

"And listen to this. Cammy had lunch with us, or almost did. She must have followed us to the restaurant and then sat by us. She struck up a conversation, and we invited her to join us."

"But then we saw the Gordons out the window. They motioned for me to come out and told me who she was. By the time I got back to the table Cammy was gone," Jeff explained, shifting in his chair. Binh continued to cling to his neck.

Maggie shook her head. "I purposely didn't tell you any details about Cammy's case. Cam My is her Vietnamese name. I didn't want you to know if the INS officer asked you. Now you know."

"Why would Mr. Tran, Cammy, and Lan all be together?"

"I don't know, Gen."

"Maybe he's investigating Binh's case." Gen gazed at her son, at his skinny little arms and legs wrapped around Jeff. He hiccuped, and his whole body shook. Gen's heart jumped.

"That's unlikely," Maggie said. "He already signed the paperwork."

"What advice do you have for us?" Jeff asked.

"It sounds like you need to go home." Maggie smiled at Jeff. "Mai's case should be done by Thursday. You can try to get your ticket changed and take her with you."

Gen shook her head. She had already thought through that option, and she couldn't bear letting Mai go without her.

"It will be difficult for you to care for both children by yourself," Maggie said gently. "Especially with Binh so active."

"There's no one at home to take care of Mai," Gen said.

"I could find someone." Jeff peered down at Binh as he wiped his nose across Jeff's shirt.

"No. I want Mai to stay with me." The baby's eyelids fluttered as she drifted off to sleep.

"You could both go home and then come back for Binh, after the investigation," Maggie said. "Bao can take him back to the orphanage."

"No!" Gen shot Jeff a panicked look.

"We can't leave Binh here. It's going to be hard enough on him for me to leave," Jeff said. Gen thought of Mom's putting Nhat on the plane, of Mom's staying behind and then flying out the next day. The children had to stay with her.

"So Jeff goes and Gen stays. You two have already decided what you're going to do. What do you need me for?"

"To tell us it will work," Gen said.

"I can't tell you that, Gen. I hope with all my heart that you get out of here with both your children, and I honestly think you will, but I can't promise that." Maggie stood.

Gen swallowed hard. Tears pricked her eyes. She knew Maggie was right. Even though it wasn't the answer she wanted, she was thankful for her honesty.

"We'd better walk over to the Korean Air office to see if I can get out of here tomorrow." Jeff stood, lifting Binh to his shoulder.

Gen nodded. She didn't have the energy to speak.

"Want to do dinner tonight?" Maggie pulled the fastener from her hair. "There's a great Cambodian restaurant down the street. Really good food."

Gen glanced at Jeff. He turned to Maggie and said, "We were going to go out with Bryce, Sue, and Daniel. What if we all go out together?"

"Okay by me," Maggie said, shaking her hair loose.

Gen slumped back in the chair. Mai's little body sweated against her chest. She could feel the weave of the rattan against her back. She felt too exhausted to move.

What would her mother tell her now if she were here? *Trust God. Remember, things work out.* That's probably what Jeff would say too if she gave him the chance. Gen didn't want to hear it. If there was one thing she was sure of, it was that she didn't always like how God worked things out.

Maggie sat beside Gen. Her silk robe gaped around her collarbone, showing wrinkles and age spots. Maggie stroked Mai's back and then took Gen's hand. Her touch comforted Gen. Suddenly she wanted the older woman to hug her, to take her and the baby in her arms, and Jeff and Binh, to tell them everything would be all right.

*L*an and Hang smiled at each other as they walked through the gate of the park. Hang laughed and started to run ahead, as if she'd forgotten her stitches. She stopped and Lan caught up with her. A water fountain bubbled; a stream flowed between two lush lawns; a noise rushed above their heads. Hang pointed upward. Lan was startled. A train sped by on a track high above them.

"Come this way," Older Brother said. They followed.

It was so peaceful, even with the crowds of people. There were no cars, no scooters, no bikes. Hang stopped at a vendor selling sweet popcorn; Older Brother bought a bag. Lan's tooth hurt as she chewed it.

They followed Older Brother into a bonsai garden. "This is one of my favorite places in the city," he said.

"How did you find it?" Lan ran her fingertips along a ceramic pot that held a perfectly pruned miniature tree.

"It's in all the travel books," Older Brother said gruffly. His voice softened. "An old friend brought me here."

Lan raised her eyebrows. "A woman friend?"

Older Brother nodded.

"Where is she now?"

"France. She's studying there for two years."

Hang walked toward the exit from the bonsai garden.

"Come back," Lan called out.

"It's okay. I know she wants to see the other sights. This garden is for old men like me. Let's go ride the monorail."

Hang grinned the way she used to. Lan clutched the rail in front of her as the train took off, her fists white. "It's all right, Mama." Hang laughed. She sat on the inside, where she would have the best view. Lan sat in the middle. Below, families sauntered along the paths. Grandfathers stood along the river, fishing.

"I can't believe there's a place like this in the city," Lan said. "It's so beautiful, so peaceful."

"Let's live here," Hang said. "We could go back and rescue Binh and Mai and eat the spilled popcorn all over the ground and catch fish from the river."

Lan laughed. She felt happy for the first time in months.

"I wanted to bring you here today because I'm sending you back to Vung Tau tomorrow," Older Brother said. The train sped by two huge yellow concrete dragons facing each other next to a fountain. A bride, dressed in a Western gown, posed for a photographer.

"Tomorrow?" Lan leaned toward her daughter.

"It was foolish of me to bring you at all. I thought that maybe the INS would want to interview you. But I can see now that bringing you here was a mistake. I nearly revealed myself as your brother when I talked with the officer this morning. You need to be back in Vung Tau in case they want to speak with you. It will seem suspicious if you're gone."

"What do you expect me to tell the officer?"

"That Cam My is your sister," Older Brother said.

"What else?"

"I don't expect you to lie. Telling the truth will raise enough suspicion."

"Why do you want Binh?" Lan asked.

"I'm getting old. I'm forty-five. I have no family of my own. The only woman I ever wanted to marry now lives in another country."

"Do you want to care for Binh?"

"I'd like to raise him. He's a boy who needs direction. Binh needs a strong hand." Lan glanced away from Quan, out over the park. Below, a father carried a small boy on his shoulders.

"And you don't think the Americans would do that?" She grasped the rail.

"Little Sister, if he leaves Vietnam, he will no longer be Vietnamese. He will lose his language, his culture. He will forget you and Hang. The Americans won't allow him to return, not even to visit."

"I think they will. I think they care about Binh, about us," Lan said.

Older Brother shook his head. "They only care about themselves."

"And who do you care about?" Her knuckles grew white against the rail.

Older Brother turned toward the wooden fence that surrounded the grounds.

After the monorail ride, before they left the park, Lan rested on a concrete bench and stared at the two dragons. Hang sat on her lap, nearly covering Lan's small body with her own. Lan pulled her daughter to her, smelled the fresh scent of the hotel shampoo in her hair, then wrapped her arms tightly around her oldest child. Hang relaxed against her; their bodies melted into one. Older Brother stood a few feet away; he turned his head, embarrassed.

They rode back to the hotel in silence. Lan kept her face straight. She would tell Older Sister good-bye, not knowing when she would see her again or if she'd ever see her again. They would return to Vung Tau.

"I'm being transferred to Hanoi next week," Older Brother said.

Good. "You were in Vung Tau such a short time."

The time in the water park with Hang had been worth the trip to Saigon. For a few moments Lan had stopped aching for Mai and Binh. For a few moments she had felt carefree, almost young again, not like the old woman she was quickly becoming with her decaying teeth, scarred hand, and bad stomach.

When they arrived at the hotel, Older Brother instructed them to go straight to their rooms. He had a meeting across town. As the taxi pulled away, Lan saw Older Sister and Mother standing in front of the glass door in the lobby. Hang took a few steps down the sidewalk. Was she following her uncle's taxi? "Hang," Lan called to her. "Aunt Cam My is here to greet us."

Hang kept walking, hunched over a little, her hand against her side. Lan gazed beyond her, to the corner. The Taylors were walking away from them with Binh and Mai. "Hang!" Binh called out over the man's shoulder.

"Come back!" Lan yelled.

"Ma!" Binh screamed.

"Oh, no." Older Sister stood beside Lan. Hang started jogging. "Come on," Cam My said. "We'd better get her." The couple turned the corner, followed by Hang. Older Sister reached them first, just as Hang grabbed hold of Binh's foot.

He screamed, "Ma!" again and reached for Hang.

"We're so sorry," Older Sister said, gasping for breath. Lan understood Cam My's simple English words.

Binh began to howl. The man tried to hold on to him, but Binh flung himself at Hang. Lan realized that she shouldn't have followed Hang; Older Sister should have taken care of the situation.

"Don't scream," Older Sister said to Binh. "We can't be with you on the street if you're going to scream." Binh stopped and reached for Lan. "Take him," Older Sister instructed quickly and then, turning to the Taylors, said something else in English that Lan didn't understand. They nodded.

"What's going on?" Mother asked, out of breath, as she squinted at the Americans.

"We'll go into the café," Cam My explained. "We can't stand here on the street. Everyone is staring at us." Lan looked up, away from her children. It was true. A crowd had gathered. "Come on," Cam My said to Mother. She said something else to the Taylors in English, pointed at Mother, and then said, "They say they're pleased to meet you, Mother."

Mother bowed. They ducked through the door into a café. Mr. Taylor pulled out a chair for Lan and then for his wife; Mother sat at the head of the table and smiled widely. Binh turned and looked at each person and then hiccuped. Mai reached for the American woman's hair, then pulled on the woman's lower lip. Lan's heart squeezed. Would the woman love the children as much as she did? She pulled on the waistband of Binh's red shorts. He wore a pair of underwear underneath. He'd never had underwear before. His shoes were brand-new. So was the red-and-orange-striped shirt he wore. He looked good in orange. He looked good, period. His skin seemed lighter. Already he was heavier. The sores on his face had cleared up.

Older Sister extended her hand to Mr. Taylor and then to Mrs. Taylor. "Cam My Johnson," she said. Lan realized that her sister was introducing herself to the Taylors properly. She then apologized to the Taylors again, at least Lan assumed that's what she was saying. The baby reached for Mrs. Taylor's jade cross. Lan wondered if she had bought the necklace in Vietnam, maybe down at the Ben Thanh Market. Lan wanted to see the market. She remembered Cuong talking about it, but they were going home in the morning, so she would not see it.

The waitress came. Mrs. Taylor talked to Older Sister, then to the waitress. The waitress left, then returned with Coca-Colas for everyone. Binh smiled and slid off Lan's lap and into his own chair.

Older Sister and Mrs. Taylor talked some more, and then Older Sister said to Lan, "Is there anything you want to know?"

"Ask them if Binh seems happy with them."

Older Sister sighed. "What are they going to answer, Lan? That he doesn't? I told you that he is. I've seen him."

Embarrassed, Lan paused for a moment and then said, "Ask them when they're going back."

"You know they don't know that. It depends on how badly Brother messes them up." Older Sister pulled her cigarettes from her purse, stopped, and then put them back and dropped her purse to the floor.

Lan felt flustered, annoyed with Older Sister, yet relieved that she was with them, a bridge to the Americans.

Mrs. Taylor said something more. Lan raised her head, and Older Sister turned to her and said, "Mrs. Taylor says that her husband's father had a heart attack and that Mr. Taylor will return tomorrow. She said she'll wait until the children's paperwork is completed."

Lan pulled Binh back onto her lap and then against her chest.

"They haven't been able to tell Binh yet," Cam My added.

"Do you understand what your aunt said?" Lan spoke quietly into Binh's ear. He nodded. "You must be a very good boy for Mrs. Taylor, and then you'll see your ba soon."

He glanced at Mr. Taylor, then Mrs. Taylor. He climbed from Lan's lap onto his chair and took a drink of Coke.

Nobody spoke for a moment.

Mr. Taylor asked Cam My a question.

"He wants to know how you're doing," Older Sister translated to Hang.

Mai began to fuss. Mrs. Taylor pulled a bottle out of her bag and tilted the baby back. Lan's breasts began to tingle. She wanted to hold Mai close, to feed her.

"Tell him I'm fine," Hang said.

"What do you think of them?" Lan asked Hang. Was Hang jealous? Did she wish she was going to the United States?

"They seem nice." Hang took a drink of her Coca-Cola. "Binh and Mai are lucky."

The tingle in Lan's breasts turned into the hurt in her stomach. Older Sister and the Taylors talked some more.

"Mrs. Taylor wants to know if we were with Mr. Tran earlier today," Cam My said.

"Tell her yes. That he's here from Vung Tau to investigate Binh's adoption." Lan paused. "Should you tell her he's our brother?"

"No." Cam My turned her head and spoke to the couple again. Mr. Taylor leaned forward. Mrs. Taylor said something to her husband, and they talked back and forth quietly.

"They're worried about the investigation," Cam My said to Lan. She paused. "And they want to know if you need anything," Older Sister added.

Lan shook her head.

"Lan, Lan," Mother clucked. "Of course you need something; you need lots of things."

Cam My ignored Mother. "Like the necklace Mrs. Taylor is wearing. She thinks you like it."

Lan blushed and shook her head again.

"Well, they think we're in a bad spot," Cam My continued. "If they take Binh from you now, he'll cry and cry. They wondered if we want to walk down to the market with them. They have a few gifts to buy before Mr. Taylor leaves tomorrow."

"What would Older Brother think?" Lan took a sip of Coke.

Older Sister shrugged. "He'll be gone for a while."

Lan carried Binh the first block, but at the intersection Mr. Taylor reached for him. He shook his head. "Let your ba carry you," Lan said, "or you'll have to walk." Binh went to his father. Lan followed behind. "Binh, you be a good boy," she said. "We're going to the market, and I'll be with you. Then you will fall asleep, and your ba will carry you back to the hotel. Soon you will go to America. You think about me, and I'll think about you. Someday we will see each other again."

Binh turned his head away from her. She fell back beside Mrs. Taylor. A beggar held out his hat. A woman holding a baby chattered away at Mr. Taylor in English. Mrs. Taylor seemed embarrassed. Lan reached, with her good hand, for Mrs. Taylor's hand.

"American women don't hold hands," Cam My said quietly.

"She doesn't seem to mind," Lan said, glancing at Mrs. Taylor and then down at Mai, asleep in the funny pack. "What did the woman with the baby say?"

"That she would sell them her little boy for a hundred dollars," Cam My translated.

Lan held her burned hand in front of her. The blisters had popped. The skin was healing. She would have scars on the back of her hand and fingers. Lan kept walking, still holding Mrs. Taylor's hand.

Lan gasped as they walked through the entrance of the Ben Thanh Market. Stalls of goods spread out under the huge ceiling as far as she could see. She'd spent most of her life around markets, but never had she seen anything so big. Streams of people flowed through. The market ladies called out to each other, gossiping, borrowing fingernail polish, and buying snacks from each other.

They strolled through the market, looking at the goods, the spices, the tea, and the coffee. Live crabs crawled over each other in baskets; fish swam back and forth in tubs; tiger prawns floated in glass tanks; chickens, ducks, and geese clucked and quacked in cages. The smell of blood and feathers rose from the butcher blocks. The Taylors stopped to watch.

"There are no markets like this in the U.S.," Cam My said to Lan.

They passed buckets of flowers—lotus, lilies, roses, and zinnias. Then baskets heaped with fruit—orange star fruit, guava blushed with pink, and dark red lychees. Mother squeezed a mango and then tossed it back in the basket, shaking her head. The smell of the fruit permeated the air, taking away the smell of blood and flesh. Lan knew the good smell wouldn't last. By the end of the day, the ripening fruit would rot.

They passed shoes, clothes, linens, stoneware, and china. Mother stopped and pointed at a green teapot. Mr. Taylor quickly bought it, paying full price.

"Fool," Mother said and smiled. Lan knew it was a story she would tell over and over back home.

"You're welcome," Mr. Taylor said. Lan understood his English and smiled. "Thank you," she said in English. "For my mother's—" She couldn't remember the word for gift.

He smiled a full, warm smile.

The market was packed with goods. She had never imagined so much food, so many things to buy.

It turned out that the gifts the Taylors wanted to buy were for Lan, Hang, and Mother. Mrs. Taylor found a jade cross on a gold chain. She took the one from around her neck, which was higher quality jade, and put it on Lan. Mrs. Taylor spoke in English to Older Sister.

"She says that this one was her mother's," Cam My said.

Lan felt puzzled.

"She wants you to have it."

"No, I can't." Lan placed her burned hand at the base of her neck.

"No, take it. She wouldn't give it to you if she didn't want you to have it."

They bought two jade bracelets, one for Mother and one for Hang. Then they stopped at an ao dai stall.

"For you and Hang," Cam My translated.

Lan shook her head.

"Yes, yes." Mrs. Taylor said, pulling a white ao dai from the rack for Hang. Lan chose a blue green one, the color of the South China Sea.

Mai began to fuss, and Mrs. Taylor pulled her from the funny pack.

"Tell them we should get back to the hotel," Lan said. Older Sister spoke. Mrs. Taylor held the baby with one hand, then reached out and took Lan's good hand and squeezed it. Mrs. Taylor handed her the baby. For a moment Lan didn't want to hold her daughter, but then she changed her mind. She smelled the baby's sweet, clean hair, ran her hand along her head, then pulled up her dress and felt her diaper underneath the cotton pants. Little lace socks covered her feet.

"Where's Binh?" Hang asked.

Lan searched the crowd and immediately spotted tall Mr. Taylor carrying a sleeping Binh down the aisle. She sighed and handed the baby back to Mrs. Taylor. As Mr. Taylor approached, she reached out and squeezed Binh's leg. The man, perfectly balancing Binh, knelt on the concrete floor of the market. Lan kissed her sleeping son gently on the lips. He stirred and then settled. "Good-bye," she whispered. "Be a good boy. I will remember you, and you will remember me, and someday we will see each other again." Lan swallowed hard. She would not cry, not again. Her heart broke in two and then came back together, mostly.

*I*t *is* the same Mr. Tran," Gen said as she walked beside Maggie to the restaurant for a late dinner. The sun had long since set. It seemed like days, not just a few hours, since they had poured out their worries to Maggie. Now they had even more to tell her. Gen treasured the time with Lan and her family, the time in the café and market—except for the talk about Mr. Tran and the investigation.

"How do you know?" Maggie asked.

"Cam My told us. I mean Cammy."

In an anxious rush, as they hurried down the sidewalk, Gen explained to Maggie what had happened.

"Cammy says that he's investigating Binh's case again," Jeff added.

"But that's ridiculous. He already signed the papers." Maggie's voice grew louder over the sound of the traffic.

Jeff shrugged his shoulders. "Cammy said Mr. Tran reopened the investigation." Jeff scooped up Binh as they crossed the street. "Gen was right; I was wrong."

"So you're not paranoid after all." Maggie patted Gen's back. "I'm sorry."

Gen didn't care that she was right. "I wish that's what it was. Just paranoia instead of this ordeal."

The conversation continued as they sat around the table with the Gordons. When they got to the part about going to the market, Jeff began to list the things they gave Lan, Hang, and the grandmother, who reminded Gen of a dried-apple doll, worn out from life.

"You gave them all that?" Bryce asked as the waitress put a dish of banana flower salad on the table.

"Yes," Gen answered. She took a spoonful of fish soup. The food was delicious; she was surprised that she could enjoy it.

"Don't you think that could be construed as payment?" Bryce turned to Maggie.

She shook her head. "I don't think so. People give birth mothers gifts all the time. Like the lockets with the photos."

The conversation turned to Bryce's work. He planned to pitch a series of articles to the *New York Times* on international adoption. Gen scooped salad onto Binh's plate and then onto her own.

"Sue, when will you come back again?" Jeff pushed his soup bowl aside.

"Every other month or so," Sue said, stroking the back of Daniel's head.

Binh picked the chicken out of his salad with his chopsticks. Gen put down her fork and picked up her chopsticks. She concentrated on not holding them too tightly as she plunged them into her salad.

Daniel plucked a piece of chicken off Binh's plate. Binh moved closer to Jeff. Mai began to fuss on the bench next to Gen, and the Cambodian woman who managed the restaurant walked over and picked up the baby.

Jeff put his arm around Binh and then turned toward Maggie. "What time do you leave tomorrow?"

"Not until late afternoon."

"Will you check in with Gen before you go?" Jeff passed the soup tureen to Maggie.

She nodded. "I'll tell you good-bye tonight, though. I'll also call Bao and have him make some phone calls. See if he can figure out what's going on with the Justice Department."

"I hope you'll be on your way too in a few days," Bryce said to Gen. "If not, give us a call. We can commiserate."

"Thank you," Jeff and Gen said at the same time. Then they laughed, a little too loudly. What would they do if the U.S. government wouldn't allow Binh's adoption?

"I think it's our phone," Gen said as they neared their door. "Maybe it's Jake with news about your dad."

Jeff struggled with the key, slipping Binh to the floor. He held the door open wide, and Gen hurried in to answer it.

"Genni?" It was her father's voice. "I have a ticket. I'm coming to Vietnam to help you."

"Who is it?" Jeff asked.

Dad, Gen mouthed. "I don't want you to do that," Gen said into the phone. "It's such a hard trip. I'd worry about you." *And about your landing at Tan Son Nhut Airport, and about your heart, and about how Vietnam might make you feel.*

"Genni," Jeff said, "your father wants to come?"

She nodded.

"I'll be fine," her father said.

"Let him come," Jeff said. "I've been praying that he would decide to come help you."

"Genni, I said I'll be fine," her father repeated.

"Hold on, Dad. I'm going to let you and Jeff talk."

Jeff winked at her and took the phone. "Hi, Dad." He listened for a moment. "You or Aunt Marie, huh?" Jeff gave her another wink. She shook her head.

"I think it's a great idea. Let me ask Genni again." Jeff put his hand over the receiver. "Don't you think it's a great idea?"

"No."

"He has a passport," Jeff said. "And a ticket."

"But he had a panic attack when he was supposed to go to Kazakhstan, and this is Vietnam. I don't want anything to happen to him." Binh walked toward Gen. "Remember my mother? My dad's breakdown?" Gen sat on the bed, and Binh sat beside her.

"How many years ago? Twenty-six?" Jeff smiled.

"Twenty-five since the breakdown but just a year since the panic attack."

"I think he's over that. I think this would be good for him. I think it

would be good for you. I think," Jeff said, looking at Binh, "it might pre-
serve our son's life. I think it would be really good for him to have his grandfather here."

Her father would never follow through with it. He might plan to come,
but he would change his mind. "What about his visa?"

"Good question." Jeff put the phone back up to his ear.

"Did you get a visa?" he said and then listened. He put his hand over the
receiver again and turned to Gen. "He's applied for an emergency visa that
will come by Federal Express tomorrow afternoon. He has a ticket for Wednesday, and he'll arrive Friday."

What was Dad thinking? It was a long trip, but the time change made it
sound unbearable. Binh reached into his backpack and retrieved the toy car
and then ran it along the bed.

"Dad wants to talk to you." Jeff handed Gen the phone as she passed
Mai to him.

"Have you had a chance to call Tam?" Dad sounded hesitant.

"Who?"

"The man I e-mailed you about, twice," Dad said.

The e-mail. It seemed as if it had been a year ago. Was the second e-mail
just this morning? "No. I didn't get to that yet."

"Wait. Don't phone him. I'll call when I get to Saigon." His voice grew
stronger with each word. "Your mother would want me to. See you in two
days—or is it three? I get so confused with these time changes."

"Dad," she said, holding a hand across her brow. "I'm afraid to have you
come here. I'll be okay with Binh and Mai. I can manage."

"Nonsense," Dad said firmly. "I want to come. Your mother would want
me to. It's settled."

"Dad—"

"I've been on the phone long enough. I have no idea how much this will
cost," he said. "I'll see you Friday, Vietnam time."

"Dad!"

"Bye, Genni." She heard the click of the phone and held the receiver away from her ear for a moment. *Your mother would want me to.* That was so unlike Dad to say that out loud.

"Why the sudden change in his attitude?" she asked Jeff, still holding the receiver in midair. It wasn't a good idea for him to come to Vietnam; she was sure of it.

"I don't think it's sudden. I think it's been coming ever since we decided to adopt from Vietnam."

She put the phone in its cradle and then reached into her backpack to retrieve the carving of the girl. In all the commotion of the last week, she'd forgotten about the place-card holder. She sat on the bed and held it in her open hand, "Binh, look," she said. He snatched the figurine and sat on the bed beside her, smiling as he examined the girl, her braids, her chipped nose, her faded clothes, and her doll.

Rain poured throughout the night. Gen could hear the water in the gutters, a raging river that ran off the hotel roof. She climbed out of bed at 4:45 and stepped onto the balcony. Scooter drivers hurried off to work in the stormy predawn light. She felt as if the rain came from inside her, mixed with her grief, doubts, and fears; it filled the skies and then flowed over, rushing, pounding, drumming—beating out a rhythm too sad to bear.

Lan kissed Binh good-bye on the lips. Gen remembered such a kiss. It had been from her mother twenty-six years ago. A woman wearing a conical hat pushed a rusty bike across the street. "God," Gen said out loud, "I will stay here with Binh if you give me back my mother." Gen frowned. Why was she trying to bargain with God? It was true; all these years a part of her felt her mother was alive in Vietnam, that she had chosen to stay, to live. That she had given up Gen and Dad and even Nhat for this country she loved. And now Gen understood why she loved it so much. Gen studied the woman below. Who knew? Maybe her mother was living incognito in Vietnam, had been all these years, and Gen would find her.

"Okay, God? Is it a deal?" She was losing her mind.

The old woman reached the other side, threw up her head to the rain, and smiled. Her hat bounced against her back, suspended by a ribbon. Her bike began to fall; the woman steadied it.

"She has nothing," Gen said out loud, "and yet she seems content. I've had every opportunity, and I still can't let go."

The rain slowed as the day dawned. Had God decided to smile again, to laugh, to stop his warm tears? Steam rose from the pavement. *Trust me with the details now so you'll learn to trust me with your children throughout their lives.*

She had no choice but to trust God; there was no one else to trust. *I will trust you with my children,* she prayed.

Through the mist, Gen saw the woman lean her bike against the wall and take something out of her pocket. She put it to her mouth and began to chew. *Trust me about your mother.* Gen wrapped her hands around the railing of the balcony. God could have intervened, could have saved her mother. He didn't.

She tightened her grip. "I don't know why you allowed it, but I will trust you about Mama. And I will trust you with Daddy. But help, help me to truly trust." She grasped the rail tighter.

"I heard voices." Jeff stood in the doorway. "Who are you talking to?"

"God." Gen let go of the railing.

"Did he answer?"

"Yes," Gen said.

"Come back to bed," Jeff said, "before the children wake."

The children. They were the two most beautiful words in the world.

"Would you pray first?" Gen asked. Neither one of them had any control over whether she would leave Vietnam with one child or two. *I've wanted to trust humans when God has wanted me to trust him. And not because my trust will control the outcome, but by trusting I'll be faithful, by trusting I'll be changed.*

They stood on the balcony and held hands as Jeff whispered his prayer into the dawning day and the woman across the street ate her breakfast.

❧

"I want to go to the airport with you," Gen said, gently swinging Mai in her front pack and holding Binh's hand as they stood on the bottom step of the hotel.

"It's not a good idea," Jeff said. "You would end up chasing Binh all over. What if you lost him?"

"It's hard to think about your flying out alone."

"Do you think your being at the airport will make any difference? It won't make you worry any less, and then you'd just have Binh to worry about too."

Gen knew he was right. "Give your dad a kiss. Tell him he's in my prayers," she said. "Give your mom a hug. Tell Jake hello and Janet, too, when she arrives."

Jeff swung his travel bag into the trunk of the taxi. Binh lifted up his hands to his father. Jeff swung him up and hugged him. "Ba has to go bye-bye," he said. "I'll see you in a few days. You help Mama with our baby. Okay?"

Binh pushed out his lower lip.

"This could be ugly," Jeff said over the boy's head.

How much can one little guy take? Gen patted Binh's leg.

Jeff, with Binh still in his arms, hugged Gen and Mai. Gen's heart thrashed against her chest as if it had wings. It felt as if Mai and the front pack were keeping it from flying out, keeping it from going with Jeff. "You're strong. You'll be okay," he said. "This will all work out."

Jeff slipped Binh to the sidewalk and bent to hug him. Binh began to cry. Gen took his hand. Binh jerked it away. "No," Jeff said, gently pulling Binh to Gen. "Take Mama's hand."

"You'd better go," Gen said.

Binh began to scream. Gen lifted him into her arms, holding him on her hip. He began to kick Mai's foot. "No," Gen said.

Jeff's taxi pulled away. A motorbike took its place. Binh wailed. Cammy climbed off the motorbike. "Can I help?" she asked. As Gen turned toward her, she caught sight of Mr. Tran across the street standing with his hands behind his back by the statue of Ho Chi Minh. Was he spying on them? Well, not spying. He certainly wasn't concealed. Was it a trap? Here was Cammy, wanting to help. There was Mr. Tran. Gen glanced around for someone who could be from the INS.

Jeff, she wanted to scream. She wanted to run and flag down his taxi. *It doesn't matter that your father had a heart attack. It doesn't matter that we might not make any money this year. Come back!*

Binh began kicking again.

"Here, let me take him." Cammy reached out; Binh fell into her arms.

"Is that Mr. Tran by the statue?" Gen shaded her eyes.

Cammy paused. "Ignore him."

When they reached Gen's room, she asked Cammy to come in. Cammy attempted to put Binh down, but he clung to her.

"Sit on the bed with him," Gen said, pulling off the front pack and putting Mai in her crib for her morning nap. Binh continued to cry, soaking Cammy's shirt. Gen sat beside them on the bed and patted Binh's back. After several minutes he stopped crying, crawled off Cammy, grabbed the figurine of the girl off the bedside table, and clambered onto Gen's lap, planting his head against her breast. He began to suck his thumb.

"Well," Gen whispered. "He hasn't done this before—sucked his thumb or wanted anything to do with me."

"He's wild, this one," Cammy said.

"Where's Lan?"

"She, Mother, and Hang returned to Vung Tau this morning by bus."

Gen closed her eyes, imagining Lan traveling home. "How is she doing?" Gen whispered.

"She's okay."

"I feel so sad for her." Gen made eye contact with Cammy for a brief moment.

"She feels happy that you will raise her children," Cammy said.

"Why?"

"She likes you. She feels good about you. It was very nice of you to give her your mother's necklace."

"I could tell she liked it," Gen said.

"She likes the cross."

"Why?"

"She believed what the nuns said, more than I did or our brother, anyway."

"The nuns?" Gen asked.

"In school." Cammy paused and then continued, "She really wants you to have both Mai and Binh. She doesn't want Binh to stay in Vietnam."

"How can she feel that way?"

"She wants what's best for him."

"Wouldn't that be to stay with her?" Gen said softly. What was she saying? She didn't want Binh to stay in Vietnam. She wanted Binh. Jeff wanted Binh.

Cammy shook her head. "I don't see any way that Lan can keep Binh. And you and your husband are so gentle with him. He needs a father." Cammy stood and walked to the window. "Our brothers were beaten when they were young. It's how boys are raised here. She worried Binh would be beaten if she took a man into her home, if he…were raised by someone else, here."

"Does she feel she can provide for Hang?" Gen peered down at Binh. His eyes closed, fluttered open, and then closed again.

"She loves all her children." Cammy paused. "It's different here. So hard for Americans to understand. It's a patriarchal society. It's all about who your father is. Hang is her oldest and the daughter of her husband—"

"Husband? No one said anything about a husband."

"He's gone. Long gone. Before Hang was born, even. But Lan loved him. And she always intended to keep Hang. When Binh was born, she would have taken him to the orphanage if he'd been a girl. But then, this last year, off and on, she realized she couldn't provide for Binh. And of course not for Mai." Cammy took a deep breath.

They were silent for a moment. Gen gently stroked Binh's back. "Why don't the Vietnamese people hate Americans? Everyone has been so kind to us. No one seems to have held a grudge." There were so many questions Gen wanted to ask Cammy.

Cammy folded her hands. "The American war was just one of many wars over many centuries for my people—that's one reason. The Chinese. The Japanese. The French. The Cambodians. Another is that the population here is so young that most of the people were born after the war. And the Vietnamese are pragmatic. For the most part, they don't carry grudges. They're opportunistic; they want to move on; they want to make money. Americans can help."

Binh stirred. Maggie had said not to ask about Mai and Binh's birth dad. She wouldn't. She would go to the next topic that consumed her thoughts. "Why is Mr. Tran investigating Binh's adoption?"

"Do you mind if I smoke?" Cammy stood and began digging in her leather purse.

Gen considered it for a moment. She didn't want the children to breathe the cigarette smoke, but she wanted Cammy to keep talking. "Go ahead."

Cammy lit up and inhaled and then blew it out slowly. She inhaled a second time. "Mr. Tran wants to adopt Binh."

Gen felt as if she were falling. Her heart, that a moment ago wanted to fly after Jeff, turned to lead. "What?"

Cammy nodded. "He got it in his head that he wants a son; he wants Binh."

"Why?" Gen could hardly get the word out. "Why Binh?" She'd never imagined this, not even in her worst fit of worry.

Cammy inhaled again. "I shouldn't be talking to you." She took the ashtray off the bedside table and put it on the yellow bedspread and sat down beside it. "Oh, well. It probably doesn't matter now. I'm toast. Binh's adoption is too."

Gen's head pounded. "Why?"

"Mr. Tran is Binh's uncle."

"Binh's uncle?" She couldn't comprehend the two words together.

"He's my brother. Lan's brother. He's told the INS that I'm Lan's sister, and that's why they're investigating. He's already drawn up the paperwork to adopt Binh."

Gen gasped and tightened her hold on the little boy in her arms. *God! Why?* Cammy reached out her hand and touched Gen's back.

"But he has the same last name as Lan. Why doesn't she go by her husband's name?"

"Vietnamese women keep their family name," Cammy explained.

Gen stared at her baby asleep in the crib. "Does he want Mai, too?"

"No. Just Binh."

⚓

"There are such things as failed adoptions," Maggie said. They stood in the lobby. Gen held Mai in her arms. Binh stood with his nose pressed against the tropical fishtank and breathed against the glass.

Maggie sighed. "Does he want Mai, too?"

"No," Gen answered.

"What a spot we're in." Maggie glanced at Binh. "I don't think the children should be separated. I hope the Vietnamese government will agree. Otherwise, it does look better that Binh go to a Vietnamese family."

"Mr. Tran is not a family."

"Gen," Maggie said and reached out to touch her arm.

Gen sighed. "What are my options? If the INS says no, can I stay here for two years like Bryce is doing?"

Maggie shook her head. "If Mr. Tran wants the boy, I don't see that there's anything you can do. Our INS won't help you."

"So it would be me against him?"

"Gen, there is no 'you' in this. I'm sorry. I'm shocked that Mr. Tran is Lan's brother. And Cammy's." Maggie bent down and said something to Binh in Vietnamese and then, in English, "Good-bye, little one." Binh smiled and then went back to pressing his nose against the fishtank. "Be thankful for Mai, for the child you have. Don't forget her four o'clock doctor's appointment today. Then you'll get her passport tomorrow. After you visit the consulate, you can fly out with her Friday afternoon."

Gen felt the hair on the back of her neck rise. "I can't leave Binh." The words flew out of her mouth. Was she growing claws? Had hair just covered her body? She didn't mean to do the mama-bear thing.

"I hope you don't have to," Maggie said. "But it doesn't look good. I wish I didn't have to go; I wish I could stay with you. I feel so torn, but I've been here too long already. I have to get back; I'm risking not getting there in time as it is. Bao will take care of you. Ask him what he's heard from Vung Tau when you see him this afternoon." Maggie bent down and picked up her carry-on luggage.

Binh ran around to the other side of the fishtank. Gen followed him with her eyes.

"I really am sorry, Gen. I had no idea any of this was in the works. I wouldn't have pursued Binh's adoption if I'd known. Honestly," Maggie said. "I'll touch base with you every day. Call me if there's an emergency."

Gen wanted to laugh—or cry. *Emergency?* It was the longest emergency of her life.

❧

She poured hot water into a cup of instant soup and set it on the table. Binh watched her. "Nong," Gen said. "Hot."

"Hot," Binh said solemnly.

Gen handed him his crayons and notebook, then picked up the phone. Sharon would be at the hospital. Jeff was in the air. Her father was probably in Los Angeles waiting for his flight.

She could hardly breathe, knowing that Mr. Tran was Binh's uncle and not being able to talk with Jeff about it. *Aunt Marie.* She would call Aunt Marie.

Her aunt answered the phone.

"Genevieve, is that you?" she cried out.

"Yes."

"I've been so worried. I wanted to come. I didn't want your father to, but he insisted." Aunt Marie's words tumbled into Gen's ear.

"Listen, Aunt Marie. I need your help. Would you call your church and ask them to pray? And then call our church in The Dalles and ask them to pray too? There are problems with Binh's paperwork. Big problems. Ask people to pray that I will trust God. Ask them to pray for what's best for Binh."

"Oh, honey, I have been praying for you *and* for the children. And now for Marshall, too. Everyone I know is praying. I'll call your church right now."

Gen felt shaky as she hung up the phone and sat down in the rocking chair. Binh had drawn a page full of yellow suns.

"Good work," she said to him. A week ago he had never held a crayon. Now he was a pro. "Come here," Gen said. Binh walked toward her, and she lifted him onto her lap. "Let's write your name. B-I-N-H. Binh."

He took the red crayon and copied the B. Pleased with himself, he climbed off Gen's lap and peered into Mai's crib. "Night, night," he said. "Binh's baby, night, night."

Gen nodded. "Do you want your soup?" She pointed toward the table.

Binh shook his head and then took Mai's half-full bottle from the corner of the crib and walked over to Gen's lap. "Baby," he said, pointing at himself. Gen pulled him onto her lap and cradled his head. She took the bottle from him and positioned it in his mouth. He closed his eyes and began to suck.

Baby. My babies. She felt the words in her breast and then deep inside, next to that place that hurt for Lan. Binh was with her, at least for now. *God I trust you with him.*

Every night she had sung to Mai at bedtime but not to Binh. He'd only let Jeff put him to bed. Jeff sang him Beatles' songs, usually "Yellow Submarine," which was a hoot considering the yellow comforter, yellow drapes, and gold carpet in the room. She would try another song; she began quietly. "I've got a home in glory land that outshines the sun, I've got a home in glory land that outshines the sun, I've got a home in glory land that outshines the sun, look away beyond the blue." And then louder, "Do Lord, oh do, Lord, oh do remember me. Do Lord, oh do, Lord, oh do remember me. Do Lord, oh do, Lord, oh do remember me, look away beyond the blue."

L an squatted in the yard next to the charcoal stove. She had sold fruit all day and made enough money to buy medicine for Mother and fried rice and fish for dinner. Mother had gone down the street for an iced coffee, which meant she still had money from Older Brother. Hang, exhausted after her first day back at school, slept in the shack. Lan was tired too. The trip to Ho Chi Minh City had left her weary. She fingered the cross around her neck; perhaps she would ask Hang to read Chinh's Bible to her.

Tomorrow, if she had any extra money, she would ask the pharmacist for medicine for her stomach. Perhaps she would even go to the doctor, and if her tooth kept hurting, she would go to the dentist and have it pulled. Soon she would be eating only rice and soup like Mother. Where had her life gone?

She stood to fill the kettle with water but stopped when she saw movement in the shadows toward the road. Perhaps a neighbor child had come to play with Hang or even with Binh. She hated telling the neighbors he was gone.

"Hello," she said.

There was no answer.

"Who's there?" A neighbor's bike had been stolen two weeks before. Was a burglar hiding in the shadows?

A figure moved away from her, toward the road; it looked like Older Brother.

"Quan?" she called out. Why was he lurking near her house?

The figure stopped. "Yes," he said, "it's me."

"What are you doing?" Lan took a step toward the road.

"I don't know."

"Where's your car?" she asked.

"I walked from the main road. I thought that seeing you might help me make up my mind." He moved toward her.

"About?"

"Binh." He stopped in front of her.

"I thought you had already made up your mind." She was tired of his games.

"I had, but now I'm not sure." His hands hung at his side.

Lan turned back toward the stove. What had made him uncertain when he had been so sure? She lifted the kettle from the stove and took a step toward the spigot.

Older Brother took the kettle from her. "How is your hand?" he asked, holding the kettle under the water.

"Better."

He placed the kettle on the stove. "I leave tomorrow for Hanoi."

Lan nodded. She had wondered when he would go.

"The investigation won't be complete until next week. I would need to come back down to get Binh."

"And?"

He was silent.

"What is it?" For a second she felt compassion toward her brother. She remembered their father whipping him all those years ago and how she used to cry for both of her brothers when they were disciplined. They had learned not to shed a tear.

"I watched the American man with Binh. Binh seemed secure and happy with him. Yesterday when Mr. Taylor left, Binh cried and cried." Older Brother stroked his clean-shaven chin.

Tell me more, she wanted to say, to beg.

Older Brother continued. "I stood in the square and watched. It appeared that he hated to go, hated to leave his wife and the children. Then Sister came and helped Mrs. Taylor."

Lan ducked her head and lit the stove with the quick strike of a match. She could imagine it—the steps up to the hotel, the statue of Ho Chi Minh on the plaza, Older Sister taking Binh.

"I thought I wanted to be Binh's father," he said, "but now I'm not sure."

"Why don't you find a wife?" Lan extinguished the match with the flick of her wrist. "Write to the woman in France. Maybe she will come home and have your children."

"But you don't want me to be a father to your child," Quan said.

Lan bowed her head. *No. I know what is best for my son.*

Mother came from the street into the yard, carrying a plastic cup.

"Quan," she said, squinting in the darkness, "you're here!" Older Brother stood and hugged her. "Do you have another trip planned for us?" Mother asked.

He shook his head. "I leave for Hanoi tomorrow. I just came to say good-bye."

"But you'll be back to get Binh? Will they bring him here or to the orphanage?" Mother glanced from Older Brother to Lan and back again.

"I'm going to stop the investigation. I'll call tomorrow and talk with the U.S. INS officer. He's in Vung Tau now. I know he talked with the orphanage director today. I'll ask that he stop the U.S. investigation, too."

"No," Mother said. "Don't do that. You should have Binh."

"No," he answered. "I've decided I shouldn't. I've decided that Lan is right."

"So it's settled?" Lan said. "Mr. and Mrs. Taylor will have Binh? Mrs. Taylor will be able to take him to America?"

Quan clasped his hands behind his back. "That's up to the United States government. If they deny the adoption, the Taylors can't adopt Binh unless one of them lives with him in Vietnam for two years."

Why? Why did he intervene? Lan turned toward the stove. Hot tears stabbed her eyes. She didn't want Binh to grow up in the orphanage, but if the Taylors couldn't adopt him, and she took him back home, they would be in the same bad spot—not enough food, not enough money for medicine, no way to keep him safe unless Hang quit school.

"Good-bye," Older Brother said.

Lan nodded but did not turn toward him.

Mother followed him out to the road. A few minutes later she returned.

"You're foolish," she said. "He was our hope. If he had Binh, we would stay connected to him. Now he'll have no reason to keep helping us."

"Who knows?" Lan said. Nothing seemed certain.

Mother took a long drink of her coffee, sucking it through her straw.

Lan longed for a cup of hot tea, for a long night's sleep. *Notre Père, please take care of Binh. Please allow the Taylors to adopt my son.*

"Tran Thuy Lan," a voice with a heavy American accent called out. She turned her head, balancing her baskets on her back, stopping at the entrance of the market. The midday sun beat down on her. A white man wearing a business shirt and black pants stood staring at her. "Tran Thuy Lan?" he asked. Sweat beaded on his face around his hairline, dripping into his short blond hair.

"Yes," she answered.

"United States INS. I'm Mr. Davis." He held out a piece of identification that she couldn't read. "May I ask you some questions?" His Vietnamese was good for an American.

She nodded.

"Is there a café nearby where we could sit?"

"There's a bakery a block away," Lan said.

He paid for two coffees and carried them to the table while Lan placed her yoke and baskets against the wall.

"I'm investigating the adoption of your son, Binh."

Lan struggled to hide the fear that knotted her stomach and pushed against her chest.

"I need honest answers from you. Not what you think I want to hear, but honest answers about what really happened," Mr. Davis said.

Lan nodded.

"Are you acquainted with Cammy Johnson, also known as Tran Cam My?"

Lan nodded. "Yes, she is my sister."

"Did she talk you into relinquishing your son for adoption?" Mr. Davis asked.

"She advised me to give up Binh," Lan answered.

The officer took out a small notebook. "Why?"

"She didn't think I could take care of him, give him what he needed."

"Did she pay you to relinquish Binh?" Mr. Davis opened the notebook.

"No."

"Did the Taylors pay you for Binh?"

"No." Her stomach hurt.

"There's been some speculation that the Taylors decided they didn't want Binh at first, but when they actually saw him here in Vung Tau, they changed their minds. Is that how you see it?" asked Mr. Davis.

"No. I'm the one who changed my mind. I took him to the orphanage and then took him back home. But then I realized I couldn't keep him, couldn't give him enough food, an education—all the things he needs. And once I met the Taylors, I saw they would be good parents. I wanted them to raise him."

Mr. Davis wrote in the notebook and then looked at Lan. "And no one paid you?"

"No. I promise you that no one paid me." She pulled the jade cross out from the neckline of her shirt. "I swear on this cross that no one paid me. Please let the Taylors raise my son."

The officer scribbled more notes and then asked, "Is there anything else you need to tell me?"

Lan hesitated. If she didn't tell him that Mr. Tran was her brother and he found out, would he think she had lied about Older Sister? If she did tell him, would it prolong the investigation?

"Is there anything else you need to tell me?" he asked again.

She nodded. *Notre Père qui es aux cieux. Our Father who art in heaven,* she prayed silently and then began to talk.

Chapter 47

*B*ao rode in the taxi with Gen and the children from the Vietnamese Consulate to the hotel.

"Thank you." Gen wriggled out of the backseat, holding Mai with one arm and dragging the backpack with the other. The sights and sounds of Vietnam that had enticed her when they first arrived exhausted her today. The rush of the traffic and the constant honking had her on edge. She feared losing Binh in the crowds swarming the square. Even the colors seemed too bright, too bold.

"Come on, Binh," she said. He sat against the far door, staring out the window. Was he looking for Jeff?

Bao said something in Vietnamese. Binh quickly scurried out of the car and took Gen's hand. She hurried up the stairs and through the open door with the children. Bao followed. Standing in the middle of the lobby, looking up at the chandelier was Dad. *He made it.* Dad was in Vietnam. Relief swept through her as she rushed toward him.

His eyes fell on her. "There you are!" he said, striding toward her, his arms outstretched. "With the children!" He gave her a long hug, kissed Mai's forehead, and then dropped to one knee in front of Binh.

"This is my father," Gen said to Bao. "Would you tell Binh?"

Bao spoke in Vietnamese. Binh smiled, quickly touched his grandfather's white hair, laughed, and then hugged him.

"Wow," Gen said, glancing from her father and Binh to Bao. "That was unexpected."

"I've got to go," Bao said. "I'll call you if I hear anything about Binh's case."

"Thank you," Gen said.

"Let's see if I can pick you up." Her dad stood and lifted Binh. "Light as a feather."

"Be careful, Dad."

He gave her a little scowl.

"You must be tired," Gen said.

"Stop treating me like an old man."

"You are an old man." She laughed, relieved that he had arrived. "Where's your luggage?"

"On that rack." He pointed toward the counter.

They headed up to the room. At least it had two queen beds, and they wouldn't have to move.

"What's the game plan?" Gen's father quickly surveyed the room and then walked to the window with Binh still in his arms. No comments about Saigon or Tan Son Nhut Airport. None of that.

"Game plan?"

"As far as the adoptions."

"Mai's is almost done. I'll get her Vietnamese passport this afternoon and then go to the U.S. Consulate tomorrow morning. She passed her physical with flying colors." She lowered the baby into the crib.

"Any word on Binh's investigation?" Her father pointed out a truck on the street below to the boy. Binh nodded.

"No. But listen to this. It turns out that Mr. Tran, the government official, is the children's uncle."

Her father put Binh down in the rocking chair. "Does that matter?" he asked.

Gen nodded. "He wants to adopt Binh."

Her father shook his head. "What will happen?"

"We don't know." She sat down on her bed with Mai.

"Then we wait," he said matter-of-factly.

"You can have that bed," Gen said, pointing to the queen closest to the bathroom. "They're going to bring in a rollaway for Binh, but he'll probably try to sleep with you." He had been sleeping in the same bed as Gen, on Jeff's side. "Do you want to have lunch or try to get some sleep?"

"I want to call Tam, the pastor I told you about."

"Why do you want to see him?" Gen asked.

"Aren't you interested in finding out about the church here?"

She was, or would be if she weren't overwhelmed with taking care of the children and hoping they would be able to leave for home. "Sure."

"I used to help support missionaries here in Vietnam. Remember?"

"Twenty-six years ago."

"If I can help support the church here again, I'd like to."

Binh crawled up on his grandfather's bed with a stack of books and began arranging them.

"But I thought Vietnam made you sad," Gen said.

"It did make me sad," he smiled slightly. "It will probably always make me sad. But I'm not as sad now as I was all those years ago. Your adopting from here, the possibility of talking with someone who is active in the church here—all that makes me happy. It would make your mother happy." He paused for a moment and then continued. "I felt like my heart had been gutted after your mother died. I felt that way for years. I don't feel that way anymore."

Binh began sliding his books off the bed, one by one, like objects off a cliff.

"No, no," Gen said. He stopped, picked up all the books, shoved them into his backpack, and then started jumping on the bed.

A knock on the door interrupted them. It was the bellboy with the luggage. As Gen tipped him, Binh unzipped the largest bag.

"No," Gen said, turning from the door toward her son.

"It's okay." Dad pulled up a chair close to Binh.

The boy pulled out a plastic bag and dumped its contents onto the floor and quickly unwrapped a small wad of paper towels. Out fell the little boy on the water buffalo.

"Dad!" Gen stood with her hands on her hips.

Binh squealed, grabbed the little girl off the table, and rushed back to the pile on the floor. Frantically he unwrapped the others—the father holding a scythe, the mother with a baby strapped to her back, the grandmother with the basket of mangoes, the grandfather with the cane—and arranged them in a row on the bed.

Gen crossed her arms.

"I hope you don't mind," her father said. "I went to your house. I thought they needed to be reunited." He began to laugh.

"Was that before or after you slipped the little girl into my bag?"

"After! The day before I left I finally found them above your kitchen sink," he said and slapped his knee. "I wanted them to accompany me to Vietnam. I wanted my grandson to have them."

Binh lined up the figurines, nodded to his grandfather, pointed to the old man with the white hair and cane, and began to laugh. He threw back his head. Gen's father began to laugh again too, this time at Binh.

Gen chuckled at the two of them. They were tired. They were all tired. Except for Mai. She rolled over in the crib toward them, lifted her head, and cooed.

　　　　　　　　　　　　　　　　◈

Steep steps led to the narrow church wedged between two taller buildings that were far from the hotel in an area the taxi driver did not know. "Pastor Tam said that this congregation has doubled in size over the last two years." Gen's father had reached the pastor on the phone the day before. He took Binh's hand as they started up the stairs.

Gen shifted Mai to one arm and checked her watch as they walked through the open door. They were five minutes late. It was obviously a government-approved church. The pastor in Portland had told her father that the government approved a limited number of churches. Gen estimated that four hundred people sat in the auditorium.

A young man and woman in the back row rose from their chairs and motioned to Gen and her dad, offering their chairs. Gen shook her head and smiled. The woman and man nodded in unison and made their way to the aisle. Gen and her father took the chairs, holding the children on their laps.

Mai slept in Gen's arms. Binh played with the figurine of the little boy on the water buffalo and sat surprisingly still. Gen gently nudged her dad when his eyes began to close. Several of the worshipers stared at them from time to time. During the singing, Gen recognized many of the melodies. Binh fell asleep for the last half hour of the service, sprawled across his grandfather's lap.

As the notes of the last song ended, the pastor slipped down the side aisle to greet them. "Marshall Hauer?"

"Yes." Gen's father stood, hoisted Binh high into his arms, and guided the boy's head onto his shoulder.

"I'm Pastor Tam. I'm pleased that you came."

Gen gathered the diaper bag and spit rag. The young man and woman who had given up their chairs approached. The woman held out her arms for Mai and took her. Binh stirred, and the young man began to talk to him over his grandfather's shoulder.

"You adopt?" the woman asked.

"Yes."

"Lucky girl and boy," she said.

"No, no," Gen said. "I'm the lucky one."

"That your husband?" she asked.

"No! My father. My husband had to return to the U.S."

"You, no babies?"

Gen shook her head. "But it's okay. Now I have these babies." *At least this baby. Hopefully I will have both these babies.*

The woman clucked at Mai. Gen tried to listen to her father and Pastor Tam's conversation. "In the country some people walk an entire day to get to church," Tam explained.

Her father said something, but she missed it. An older woman circled around them and then headed down to the front of the sanctuary. Gold and jade bracelets jangled on her thin wrists as she walked by.

"Discouraged? No! The contrary. My people are resilient. Their faith is alive and strong. They trust God for everything—well, nearly everything. That is our prayer. To depend on him," Pastor Tam said.

Mai began to fuss and reached out her arms to Gen.

"She likes you," the young woman said.

"She loves me," Gen said, taking the baby. "Your English is so good. Where did you learn it?"

"School. I study English. I practice whenever I can."

"Is that your husband?" Gen asked, nodding at the man talking to Binh.

The young woman giggled. "Boyfriend. We're both studying at the university."

Dad asked about persecution.

Pastor Tam seemed uncomfortable for a moment and said softly, "Yes. Many have suffered."

The older woman with the bracelets walked toward them again and then stopped. She wore Western pants, a tailored blouse, and high heels. *She probably wants to talk to Pastor Tam.* Gen smiled at her. A middle-aged man approached the woman and struck up a conversation.

"Did you know any missionaries here during the war?" Gen's father's voice sounded serious.

Pastor Tam shook his head. "I came to know Christ twenty years ago in an underground church here in the city."

Gen lifted Mai to her shoulder. Binh wiggled out of his grandfather's arms and tugged on the diaper bag hanging on Gen's shoulder.

"I'd like to stay in touch," her father said.

Pastor Tam pulled a card out of his shirt pocket and handed it to her dad, who tucked it inside his wallet. The pastor bowed slightly. Binh tugged on the diaper bag again, and Mai began to fuss.

Pastor Tam said good-bye and then turned toward the older woman with the bracelets and the man talking with her.

Gen's father lifted Binh into his arms and started toward the door; Gen followed and then stopped. The woman waved her hand, her bracelets jangling as they fell toward her elbow.

"Mr. Hauer," Pastor Tam called out, "this sister knew missionaries here years ago."

Gen glanced ahead at her father. Had he heard? He turned, his body framed in the doorway, his face lost in the light of the noon sun.

"Mr. Hauer?" The older woman moved toward them. "Marshall Hauer?"

"Yes," he said, stepping back into the church with a befuddled look on his face.

How did this woman know Dad's name? Her father walked past Gen, and she followed.

The woman moved toward them quickly. "I'm Kim Long."

"Pleased to meet you," he said, shifting Binh to his left arm and extending his hand to the woman.

Bow, Dad. Wait. Kim? Could it be?

"Mom's friend Kim?" Gen stammered.

"Yes."

The three adults stood for a moment in a silent circle, the children between them. Time stopped, then lurched forward as Kim let go of Dad's hand and reached for Gen's. "You look so much like your mother. I kept staring during the service and then afterward. I was afraid I was hallucinating."

The small woman wrapped her arms around Gen and Mai. Gen hadn't even dreamed to ask God for this. All those years she had prayed for Kim. She began to cry. Now God had given her this. She felt Mom's love, God's love, Kim's love. She pulled away and wiped her tears on Mai's flannel spit rag. She smiled at Kim and saw that she was crying too. She offered her the cloth. They both laughed. Kim took it and dabbed at her tears. The young woman and man took Binh and Mai. Pastor Tam pulled several chairs together, and they sat down.

"I worked with Mr. Hauer's wife, Sally, in a leprosarium in the early sixties," Kim said to the pastor.

Gen reached for her father's hand. He sat perfectly still.

"Sister Kim is one of our most faithful," Pastor Tam said. "She tirelessly serves the orphans, widows, and poor."

"It's because of Sally. After she died, I decided to stay in Vietnam to do what I could for my people. Mr. Hauer, did you get my letters?"

Dad shook his head.

"I wrote to let you know that I prayed for you and Genni and Nhat every day." Kim folded her hands together, and the bracelets chimed against each other on her wrists. "And I wanted you to have as many details as you could about the accident."

"Details?" Gen asked.

"I was waiting for a flight out. I was there right after the crash. I'm a nurse."

Gen nodded.

"You remember that." Kim took a deep breath. "I helped care for the wounded. I came across your mother's body after it was pulled from the wreck. She still held a baby in her arms. They both died. It's unbelievable that she held on to that little one through the crash."

Gen squeezed her father's hand and reached out and put her other hand on Kim's arm.

"How is Nhat?" Kim asked.

"He went to another family." He stared at the floor.

"I'm so sorry," Kim said.

Gen tried to smile. *Oh, Dad. We were so brokenhearted about Mom, so sad about Nhat, but we had no idea what we lost when you let him go.* She couldn't bear to lose Binh. *Oh, God, I'll do whatever it takes, whatever you want me to do, but I trust you with him.*

"For years I felt it was my fault that Sally died." Kim folded her hands in her lap.

Gen shook her head.

"No," her father said, "of course it wasn't."

"I know that," Kim said. "Still it was hard to accept."

"But you continued on. You were faithful." Gen's voice faltered. "You trusted God."

"So did you," Kim answered. "And now you've come to give these children a future." Kim glanced behind her at Binh and Mai and then turned back. "Sally's death will always be a catastrophe, yet we can see the good that God has worked in spite of such a tragedy."

And we know that all things work together for good to those who love God.
That was the verse Gen had resented all these years. Yet she could see the
good that God was working. Kim was right; the good didn't obliterate the
loss of her mom. It simply meant that God was greater than the tragedy, than
the loss of a mother.

What now? She didn't want to leave Kim. Gen asked about her work.
Kim talked about her job in a pediatric unit and her trips to orphanages and
clinics throughout Vietnam. She often assisted American doctors, many veterans, who returned for short stays to do surgeries on children with cleft
palates and other disabilities. She had never married but had several nieces
and nephews who lived nearby.

Binh ran toward them and pulled a pouch of fruit snacks from the diaper bag. He offered one to each of the adults.

"Cam on," Kim said to Binh. He smiled and patted her hand.

Gen told Kim about Jeff and the cherry orchard, about her work as a
teacher. Her father spoke about his church. He relaxed as he talked. "I never
dreamed I would travel to Vietnam."

"I'm glad you are here." Kim paused for a moment and added, "Is there
anything I can do for you?"

Gen thought for a moment. "Do you ever go to Vung Tau?"

"No, but I could."

"If I wired you money, could you take it to Mai and Binh's birth mom?
And then let us know how she's doing? Tell her I think about her every day.
Each time I take a photo of the children I think of her. Every time I look into
their faces, I see her face."

Kim took a card from her purse. "Wire it to this address." She pointed to
the card. "This is my e-mail. Send me the woman's name and where she lives."

"There's one more thing you can do for me, for us." Gen took Kim's
card. "Binh's adoption is being investigated. We don't know for sure if he'll
be ours. Would you pray for us?"

Kim squeezed Gen's hand. Her eyes sparkled. "It is my privilege to pray
for you and your children."

Mai began to fuss. The young woman handed her back to Gen again. Binh followed and patted the baby's head.

"I remember your mother told me that she named you Genevieve because the name meant peace," Kim said.

Gen and Dad shared a smile.

"Did you know that 'Binh' means peace?"

"Really?" Gen said. Why hadn't she looked it up or asked someone what "Binh" meant? Especially after having found out that "Mai" meant cherry blossom.

"Yes," Kim said, "peace. Finally we have found peace."

That afternoon as they crossed the street to go to lunch, Gen took to heart that the drivers of the cars and motorbikes weren't after her and her family, that they weren't really trying to run them down. They were simply getting from point A to point B. And, besides, they were the same kind people who helped her with the children in the shops and restaurants. She held up her head and walked quickly, taking in the sounds of the horns and engines, thankful they weren't racing through a downpour.

Her father began to laugh as they reached the other side. Binh held his grandfather's hand and parroted the laughter, throwing back his head.

"Dad, what is it?"

"I was thinking that adoption is like crossing the street in Vietnam. You have to push forward, merge, and trust that you'll get to the other side even when seemingly random and very large objects are speeding toward you."

Gen nodded. Adoption *was* like that. So was life. Her life had merged with Lan's and now with Kim's. Soon, Lan and Kim would meet too. She smiled and turned her head toward the blue, blue sky. *Work good in Lan's life,* she prayed. *Bring her hope. Bring her peace.*

The phone rang as Gen locked the door behind her. They were headed to the hotel restaurant for breakfast and then to the market so her dad could do some shopping. She quickly unlocked the door and hurried back in, juggling her umbrella. It had been raining since sunrise.

Maybe it was Jeff. She had talked with him once since he had arrived home; she had told him about Mr. Tran being the children's uncle and wanting to adopt Binh. Somehow Jeff remained optimistic and unflappable. She both longed and hated to hear him say, "Everything will work out." He told her that José and Marta had arrived, that harvest was under way, that his father would be released from the hospital soon, and that Janet had flown in from Texas.

Now Gen longed to tell him about yesterday's meeting with Kim. "Hello!" she said into the receiver, a little out of breath.

"This is Mr. Davis with the United States INS. May I speak with Mr. or Mrs. Taylor?" the voice said.

"This is Mrs. Taylor." She braced herself, wishing Jeff was with her.

"I wanted to inform you that I have completed the investigation into the adoption of Tran Van Binh." He paused.

"And?"

"It's been approved."

Approved? Gen wanted to hug the man through the phone. "Thank you," she said. "Thank you!"

"It's been a most remarkable case," the inspector said. "I was afraid it wasn't going to come out in your favor. I had my doubts, even after Mr. Tran...removed himself from the case. But I found no evidence of any ill motives or wrongdoing."

"Thank you," Gen said again, counting off the days. She would call Bao, have him set up the appointment for the physical, hopefully for the afternoon, and then they would apply for the passport the next day and go to the U.S. Consulate on Wednesday morning. They could fly out by Thursday.

She said good-bye to Mr. Davis and hung up. For a second she thought of the Gordons. She would call before they left; she would e-mail them once they were home; she would keep them in her prayers. She would call Kim, too, and share the good news.

Gen picked up the receiver again and began dialing Jeff's cell number. She didn't care how much the call would cost.

L an stood on the sweltering beach, her head turned toward the sky. High above, a jet headed north, flying far away. *Que ta volonté soit faite, sur la terre comme au ciel. Thy will be done,* she prayed, *on earth as it is in heaven.* She shifted her eyes down. In the distance, Hang walked slowly through the waves. Mother had rented a chair and sat back on the beach, ready to nap.

A man approached Hang. He wore tan trousers and a white, short-sleeved shirt. Lan strained against the bright sun as she watched Hang laugh and walk toward him. The man laughed too. *Older Brother.* It had been so many years since she had seen him out of uniform. Why wasn't he in Hanoi? He walked toward her.

"Why are you still here?" she called out, trying to keep her voice even. "I thought you were in Hanoi." She searched his face for a sign. Did he know she'd told the United States INS officer that he was her brother?

"I was delayed. I ended up going back to Ho Chi Minh City to clear up some business."

"Hang, go check on your grandmother." Lan motioned her head toward Mother. Hang glanced at her uncle and then walked away.

"How are you?" Quan raised his dark brows.

"Sad." She paused. "I told INS that I am your sister." The words shook as they fell from her mouth.

"I know," Older Brother said. "I tried to find Mr. Davis here in Vung Tau after the last time I saw you. When I couldn't find him, I went back to the city." Older Brother chuckled. "Mr. Davis returned that afternoon, and I talked with him then. I told him that I had wanted to adopt Binh but then changed my mind."

"Thank you," Lan said.

"I saw Sister, too."

"How is she?" Lan asked.

"Discouraged. She leaves tomorrow. Actually, she's being deported."

Lan swallowed hard. She didn't want to cry in front of Brother. That was the last thing she wanted. It was just that she'd lost so much at once, again; it felt like the end of the war, like when Chinh had left.

"Did you see Binh and Mai?"

"No. The staff at the hotel told me that Mrs. Taylor's father came to help her with the children. They said that they are all well."

Binh and Mai had grandfathers. She liked that. "What else did you find out from the staff?"

"That Mrs. Taylor is relieved the investigation is over, and she'll soon be going home with the children."

Lan turned and started to walk back toward Mother. *Merci, Père,* she prayed. Still, sadness overcame her.

"Lan, I'm sorry," Older Brother said.

"Sorry?" To say one was sorry was to lose face. She bowed her head. Why would Older Brother say he was sorry?

He stopped walking. "Do you remember when we were children, when we came here?"

Lan nodded.

"We were so happy then. I think that's why Mother chose to move to Vung Tau after the war. Because of that one week. Remember Second Brother? Remember how much he loved the ocean, how he always smiled? Even Father was happy that week. And you. I remember you wearing a little pair of sunglasses and filling a pink bucket with water and sand."

Lan nodded again.

"That's why I'm sorry. I'm sorry for the way life turned out, for all of us. I'm sorry you could never have the family you deserved. I'm sorry this has all been so hard." He stood with his hands at his side.

"It's not your fault." Had she forgiven him? He had been so young, so idealistic, so unaware of how his neglect affected their lives.

He faced the ocean. "Some of it is my fault. I shouldn't have turned my back on you and Mother after you were in the hospital. I didn't protect you. I could have cared for you. Your life would have been different."

"You didn't know. You were young." She reached for him with her scarred hand. They stood quietly. "Take us out to dinner before you leave," Lan finally said. "It would mean so much to Mother for us to be together for one last meal."

They walked around a fishing net spread across the sand, waiting to be mended. Mother waved as they approached. Hang gazed past her mother and uncle; Lan followed Hang's gaze out to the jade-colored ocean.

"I'll help with Mother," Quan said softly. "I'll send money for her medicine and cash for her to spend."

Mother stood. Older Brother bowed his head.

Lan longed to lose herself in the roar of the warm water behind her, in the crashing waves, in the salty smell of the sea. Instead she took Hang's hand and headed up the sand dune to Older Brother's waiting car.

Gen and her father locked eyes over Binh as their plane took off from Tan Son Nhut Airport. She had never felt so close to her dad. She knew they both held on to her mother for just a moment. *Good-bye. Thank you.* The sprawl of Saigon turned into emerald green rice fields that met the baby blue sky. Then in no time the landscape fell away as drifts of clouds covered the plane like a soft blanket.

Binh kept Gen awake from Saigon to Seoul and then from Seoul to Los Angeles, thrashing around in the seat beside her. He pulled on his ear several times in his sleep and whimpered. Gen had planned to take him to the doctor in a day or two; now she would call as soon as they arrived home. Mai slept in the bassinet in front of Gen. She kissed the children as they landed in L.A. Thanks to the new adoption laws, all it took for them to become U.S. citizens was to land on U.S. soil. They would just need to file the paperwork to make it all official. Joy and sadness welled up inside her—the loss of their country, the loss of Lan, the gain of security. The paradox of adoption.

Her father took care of both children on the last leg to Portland, insisting that she sleep.

"We're about to land." He gently touched her shoulder from across the aisle. She opened one eye. He held Mai in his arms. Binh slept on the seat beside his grandfather.

"Thanks," she said, sitting up straight. She could see Mount Hood through the window for half a second as the plane began to descend.

A half hour later she pulled the carry-on bag from overhead, slung the backpack over her shoulder, and then took Mai. "Go first," Gen said to her father as he lifted his grandson into his arms. She couldn't wait for Binh to see Jeff. She followed her son and her father off the plane, up the warm Jetway, and through the open door. Binh lifted his head from his grandfather's shoulder.

"Ba!" There was Jeff holding out his strong arms. Binh flew into them, followed by Gen and the baby. They were home. They were safe.

"Thank you," Jeff said to his father-in-law over Gen's head. Sharon, Jake, Janet, and Aunt Marie all gathered around the family.

Gen began to cry. Jeff pulled her face to his. They were finally home.

Acknowledgments

First, my thanks and love to my husband, Peter, for his undying optimism toward my writing and toward life. Second, a tribute to our brave daughter Lily Thao. Although this is not her story, her adoption inspired this novel. She continues to fill our hearts each day, just as she did the moment we first saw her photo. She and her siblings, Kaleb, Taylor, and Hana, are our greatest joy.

A special thanks to my sister-in-law Abby Khanh Gould for providing insights into her homeland, to my brothers-in-law Quy and Thoa Gould for being the amazing young men that they are, and to cousins-in-law Ben and Connor Peterson for leading the way in the six Vietnamese adoptions in our extended family. Thanks also to my parents-in-law, Tami and Rod Gould, for their example in adopting and to my parents, Bruce and Leora Egger, for their example in supporting orphans.

I'm grateful to Vickie Hollingsworth, Kate Commerford, Dee Lee Gibson, and Birgit Lee for sharing their adoption stories and to Nicky Losse of Children's Hope International for reading the manuscript in its early stage. A very special thanks to Nancy, Tracey, and Jack Truitt for countless memories during our travels in Vietnam and for priceless stories since, which now include Maddox. I also want to acknowledge the other families in our travel group and their wonderful children.

Thanks to Anaïs Theron for her support while I wrote, to Rod Richards for his quick research skills, to Dorothy Heins for introducing me to her dear parents, David and Barbara Pink, and to the Pinks for the tour of their cherry orchard. A very special thanks to Diane Noble for her sage editing advice.

Most important, I want to honor God the Father, who designed adoption and uses it to create families for his purpose. The paradox of adoption is truly the good that he works from heartbreaking loss.

For more information on international adoption, contact Children's Hope International at 1-888-899-2349 or visit www.childrenshope.com. Please also visit www.lesliegould.com. I would love to hear your adoption stories and comments.